Dragon Kin's
Blood

Dragon Kin's Blood

A Kingdom of Galahar Novel

Jo Gatenby

BALANCE OF SEVEN
Leavenworth, WA

To my husband, Bill,
who always thinks I can.

Contents

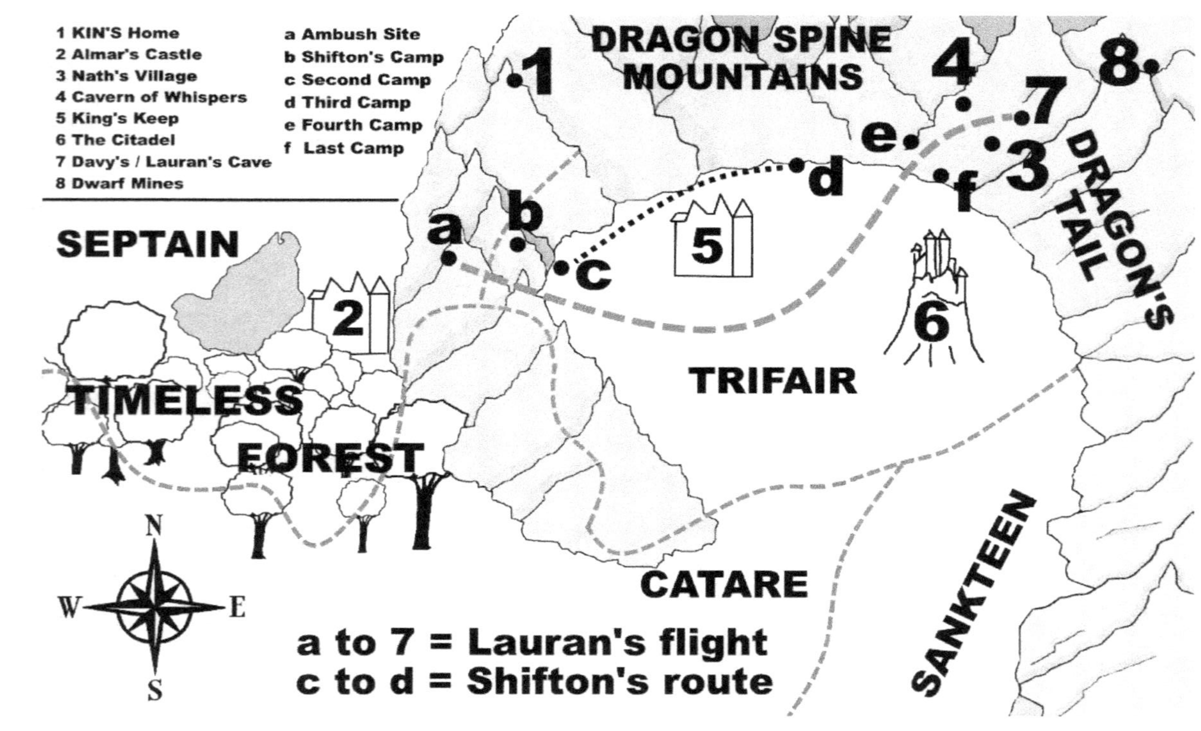

1 KIN'S Home
2 Almar's Castle
3 Nath's Village
4 Cavern of Whispers
5 King's Keep
6 The Citadel
7 Davy's / Lauran's Cave
8 Dwarf Mines
a Ambush Site
b Shifton's Camp
c Second Camp
d Third Camp
e Fourth Camp
f Last Camp
DRAGON SPINE MOUNTAINS
DRAGON'S TAIL
SEPTAIN
TIMELESS FOREST
TRIFAIR
CATARE
SANKTEEN
a to 7 = Lauran's flight
c to d = Shifton's route
N W E S

1

Spring
Dragon Spine Mountains
Kingdom of Galahar

A sudden gust of chill wind heralded the arrival of the huge, thirty-foot-long black dragon with brilliant green eyes that Lauran had been waiting for. As the cloud vapor parted, she yelped and ducked into a sheltered corner by the wide entrance to her father's aerie, muttering under her breath in annoyance.

[Did Ganther tell you why Maxim called a conclave?]

In dragon form, Marissa could only use mind-speech, but her question aroused Lauran's curiosity. She stuck her head out to watch Marissa change form. Her friend's forty-five-foot wingspan tucked neatly into place on either side of her dorsal ridges as she landed, dust scattering beneath her talons.

Moving forward, Marissa paused, rising to balance on

her tail and thick back legs. She stood with her shorter forearms lifted and her head bent.

The air around the draikana shivered.

Shimmering scales retracted, collapsing like a cascading waterfall to reveal supple skin the color of night. Her lovely tail curled and contorted, then shortened and disappeared above her rounded buttocks.

Lauran waited, tapping an impatient foot, as wings folded into themselves, absorbing into Marissa's arched back. Her hindquarters narrowed as her forearms stretched and thinned. Thick talons receded into long, tapered fingers. Her massive limbs sank seamlessly into the arms and legs of her emerging human form.

Her fearsome muzzle shrank, morphing into delicate features. Her flinty gaze mellowed, revealing intelligence and kindness. Spiny crests softened and flowed into waves of black curls.

Stunning green eyes, contrasting with her smooth ebony face, glittered with excitement. "Brrr, chilly spring days aren't meant for being naked!"

"Come on, Marissa." Lauran stalked after the older woman, who hurried toward the spare clothing kept near the entrance. "You know Ganther tells me as little as possible! What did my father conveniently forget to mention this time?"

Her friend grinned at her impatience. "Remember that peddler? Well, he's back."

"Is that all?" Lauran's face fell. "What does he want? More trade goods?" Her eyes shot wide. "Or are you saying he found the dragonhold?"

Her stomach clenched. The Kin had remained hidden for centuries, living in the most inaccessible part of the

Dragon Spine Mountains. *Did the Lowlander stumble across our home on his own? Or did someone lead him here?*

"No, no," Marissa hastened to reassure her. "He's camped in Frostveil Pass, same as last time. He waited two weeks before somebody flying over noticed him and told Maxim he was there."

She seemed impressed by the Lowlander's determination, and Lauran supposed he had shown great persistence. Winter still held sway this high in the mountains, causing cold, unpredictable weather. Storms could spring up from nowhere. He would have found it twice as difficult to survive as someone born there.

"Well, what is the peddler after?" Her eyes narrowed. "You know you're dying to tell me."

Marissa grew serious. "I guess he's some kind of nobleman in the Lowlands. He requested a delegation of Kin come down to meet Duke Almar in Septain Territory. That's why Maxim called the conclave. The Lowlanders want to formalize a trade agreement with us and set up regular meeting points."

Lauran's face lit up, her mind already whirling with ideas for persuading her father to allow her to go. After all, most Kin moved out on their own before their hundredth Name Day, yet she'd reached the age of 113 without ever leaving the mountains.

It was time she experienced more of the kingdom.

She noticed her friend's dubious expression. "What's bothering you? A delegation going to visit the Lowlanders, or setting up trade with them?"

"I'm not sure," Marissa admitted. "Maxim's more progressive than our past leaders. And I understand him wanting the Kin to be less reclusive . . . I guess I am not convinced this is our best option. He hasn't been Alpha long enough to have a track record." She shrugged. "And what ulterior motive could the Lowlander have for traveling this far? What's in it for him?"

Lauran laughed. "Well, trading with us may be his only chance to get his hands on dwarf-mined jewels."

"That's true. Didn't Ganther mention the peddler was interested in gemstones the last time he visited?" She gave an unladylike snort. "As if a dragon ever voluntarily gives up its hoard!"

"My father seems to have told you quite a bit." Lauran shot a sly glance her friend's way. "I did not realize you were so close."

"Ganther is interesting." Marissa's cheeks darkened as she fingered her sleeve and avoided Lauran's eyes. "Maybe the peddler wants us to negotiate with the dwarf king on his behalf?"

Relenting, Lauran allowed her to change the subject. "Father always says dwarves forge their resentment from the fires of memory. You know how they feel about Lowlanders!" Her forehead creased at this reminder that she'd never actually met a Lowlander, only heard Ganther's stories.

Even when he had taken her on one of his buying trips to the dwarven enclave three mountains over, all she'd seen were more snow- and ice-covered peaks.

"He could also trade with the Anishinabe over on the Dragon's Tail," Marissa pointed out.

Lauran shrugged. She'd never visited those distant foothills either, which only strengthened her determination to join the delegation and see something of the kingdom.

"Come on." She hung her outer wrap on a hook. "We have every right to be part of this. Everyone should have gathered by now. Let's go before they make a decision without us."

She grinned. "Watch this. I've been practicing." As Lauran shimmered with the change, she stretched her neck and slimmed her body. She oozed out of the wide collar of her tunic, expanding and morphing into her lovely golden dragon form outside her clothing.

She ended by tossing her clothes back onto a peg with her tail.

The maneuver took a great deal of control. She'd worked on the trick for weeks, hoping to impress a certain copper-skinned member of their Wing.

"Nice!" Marissa laughed. "But I just got dressed."

Lauran only rolled her eyes, huffing impatient smoke from her nostrils until the other woman sighed and undressed again. Without waiting for her friend to shift, the younger Kin launched herself from the ledge outside the cave. The larger dragon soon caught up with her and led the way to Conclave Hall.

The pair fought against fierce wind currents as they ascended to the craggy mountain peak, where what appeared to be a solid, unbroken expanse of stone was actually a concealed entrance. Lauran and Marissa flew up over the outcropping of weathered granite, which blended into the rugged terrain.

They glided behind the sloped rock face and down along a narrow hidden passageway, before plunging through an unassuming opening just wide enough to accommodate the largest wingspan.

The corridor widened, then suddenly the ground

dropped away. Overhead, the stone ceiling soared upward. The draikanas slipped into the grand hollow heart of their mountain cathedral.

The light from thick, glowing lichen reflected off the mineral-laced stalactites adorning the cavern's roof. The gentle luminosity bathed the vast subterranean chamber in a kaleidoscope of colors, from deep blues and purples to soft golds and silvers. Even after a hundred years, the sight still made Lauran's breath catch.

Marissa landed, and the golden dragon hurried to join her. The young women resumed their human forms, shivering as they pulled waiting robes over their heads.

Lauran sighed and rolled up the sleeves of her robe as they slipped on sandals before moving deeper into the cavern. Unless she brought her own clothing, there were seldom items available in her size. Although she stood a respectable seven foot six in human form, most female Dragon Kin—including Marissa—topped eight feet, while their men ranged from nine to twelve.

Lauran scanned the floor of the great hall, which sloped downward in a series of wide, terraced steps, looking for her father. But it was impossible to pick him out. The hundreds of Kin gathered below in their human forms indicated just how significant this conclave was.

They paused, allowing their vision to acclimate to the softer light. The tiers created a natural amphitheater, and the gallery echoed with murmured chatter.

Lauran nodded to a member of her Wing who remained in dragon form. Spaced out around the hall's perimeter, they and other volunteers kept stones heated by dragonfire, warming the massive chamber. In exchange for their service, they would have been given the first opportunity to express their opinions.

Maxim must have sent out a mind-call to the entire clan! Lauran shivered. Only the Alpha could project a powerful mental summons everyone could hear.

Excitement curled in the pit of her stomach.

Small groups of Kin might live in proximity—like her Wing—but most preferred the privacy of solitude, although females stayed in smaller family units until their dragonets were old enough to join the clan. She'd never seen so many gathered in one place, and she recognized less than half of them.

She and Marissa had received the call, of course, but Ganther had told her it would be boring and she didn't need to go. A rush of annoyance flared. *He's just trying to keep me from getting involved, as always.* If her friend hadn't explained, they might've missed all the fun. It was time he stopped being so overprotective!

As the young women slipped through the crowd, drawing closer to the front, Lauran tightened control of her mind-speech. It would be embarrassing to leak her thoughts here. Verbal dialogue was the only form of communication permitted during a conclave. Without that rule, the strongest mind-speakers—such as her father—could have easily dominated everyone else.

Only one person spoke in turn for the same reason.

The line of those wanting to speak was gone, so they'd timed their arrival well. As they settled in place, Zyre still stood at the council stone, grumbling and complaining as usual. Lauran rolled her eyes. She didn't need to listen, already aware the pessimistic gray would find negatives in any proposal.

She lifted onto tiptoe, annoyed at having to stretch her neck to see over those in front of her. A raised dais several tiers below made it easier for her. Cut from the rock and adorned with intricate carvings telling the clan's stories, it was flanked by towering stalagmites—each carved in the shape of a fearsome dragon.

The council of elders was already seated there, upon ornate thrones signifying their authority and wisdom. Alpha Maxim sat in the center of the Elder's Row, with the oldest Kin on either side of him. He was one of the largest deep-ocean-blue dragons, and his size carried over into his human appearance. In the flickering light, the bluish tinge to his skin and the dark teal of his hair were barely visible.

She grinned, as even Maxim's renowned patience wore thin. He cut Zyre's rambling tirade off with curt thanks and prepared to render his judgment. Although he considered and valued each clan member's opinion, the Alpha's word was final.

Lauran leaned forward, as eager as everyone else to learn his decision.

Maxim rose and stepped to the front of the raised platform.

"I am aware many of you are fearful of change. 'We have always done it thus' is the cry of the complacent. I refuse to allow us to become rigid, hidebound, insular. Join me in celebrating as Dragon Kin move into the wider world."

A low rumble arose, the majority approving, but with an undercurrent of discontent.

"We will take this small step." The edge of anger bleeding into his raised voice produced attentive silence. "However, that doesn't mean we'll reveal our secrets. This modification to previous policies does not extend to letting the entire kingdom discover our true nature."

The cries of approval became louder now.

He motioned for quiet. "We know there are other shifters in Galahar, though not everyone welcomes or accepts them. What people do not understand, they fear." His gentle smile teased them. "Even peoples such as us."

Some uneasy murmurs erupted as this insight sank in. Lauran grinned, noting those around her who looked chagrined.

Maxim continued speaking. "I believe a party of ten will be sufficient: five riders and their dragons. We are much larger than the Lowlanders. We don't want them to fear an invasion." This drew a weak chuckle from his listeners.

But having spoken, his word became law. The Kin would work together, doing as he decreed, regardless of their opinions on his ruling.

"Ganther has agreed to lead the delegation."

Lauran—and several others around her—gasped as her father rose and stood below the dais. Everyone knew he blamed Lowlanders for her mother's death. She shook her head in astonishment. *I wonder how Maxim talked the old curmudgeon into it.*

"I would like nine more volunteers," the Alpha continued. "Nobody will be forced to go. If you're uncomfortable with the idea, please refrain from volunteering."

Lauran's hand shot into the air before he finished speaking. She nudged Marissa, who sighed and followed suit. A few other hands rose, including Zyre's.

She glanced over at Ganther and caught him rolling his eyes. Though he frowned at her raised arm, they shared a conspiratorial grin at the gray's expense. Zyre might not approve, but he couldn't stand being left out.

When Maxim counted them off, there were nine volunteers, as he'd requested. She almost cheered in her excitement at being chosen. Aware her father would object to her participation, she kept quiet, hoping a mature response would work in her favor.

As the conclave filed out, conversing among themselves in hushed tones, Ganther waved their group over in front of the dais to await the Alpha.

Lauran tried not to look smug when anyone looked their way.

She turned back to their group, most of whom she recognized, although she hadn't interacted with many of those who'd volunteered. She and Marissa stood beside Kellin, another draikana with an opalescent dragon form. Her slender white body shimmered against the dark stone walls.

Two other women lingered nearby, whispering together. Callie and Audra boasted lavender and amber dragons, and their human forms reflected this. Callie's arms retained a pale purple sheen, and her hair tumbled in a rich, bold plum down her back, while Audra's burnt-orange mane falling around her shoulders gave away her draconic coloring.

Zyre slouched nearby, everyone studiously ignoring him. Everything about him appeared as slate gray as his dragon's hide. Dram remained to one side, his warm loam-brown skin color fitting considering his dragon wore rich chestnut scales.

Lauran tried to avoid looking at Davint, but the large copper-skinned man met her gaze and gave her a laconic nod. Her stomach jumping, she bobbed her head before jerking her attention to the last person waiting for Ganther to begin.

Staton was the least familiar to her. She vaguely remembered him visiting with her father . . . maybe fifty years ago. His sun-tanned arms and face reminded her his dragon sported a deep, weathered tan hide, the color of the cliffs behind Ganther's aerie in the sunshine.

Before she could do more than nod in greeting, Maxim approached, and the eager delegation turned toward him.

"Thank you for volunteering. This is an exciting new venture, and we're trusting you to represent us." He met each of their eyes in turn, and Lauran wasn't the only Kin who stood taller, proud of his faith in them.

"However, as a precaution, I must insist you pair off to play dragon and rider. Those playing dragons will remain in that form for the duration of your stay."

They nodded. This was their current policy whenever they interacted with outsiders.

"Ganther and I have discussed this," Maxim continued. "By using pseudonyms, we can keep each Kin's identity secret while giving you the option of appearing in either human or dragon form in the future."

He waved a large hand. "We suggest 'La' and the end of the rider's name for a female, 'Ta' for a male. Since dragons only use mind-speech, half of you won't need to remember everyone's names. But it's simple enough; just recall who's riding whom. For example, if Ganther rides Marissa, he and the other riders will refer to her as La'ther."

His sudden grin made him look younger. "And of

course, if you are chosen to play dragon, be sure you answer to your new name!"

Quiet chuckles rewarded his small joke.

"I'll leave it to your delegation leader to assign your roles." He paused, meeting each of their eyes. "Thank you again for volunteering, and good luck."

Once he departed, their attention turned to her father, who cleared his throat and frowned. "I guess I should decide who does what, as Maxim said—"

Marissa interrupted, stepping closer to lay a hand on his arm and peer up into his face. "Please, Ganther, if *you* make the selections, there may be some grumbling about partiality or prejudice. Couldn't we draw for it?"

Drawing stones was a traditional Kin method for settling disputes where both parties held equal claims to the result. Totally impartial, the black and white rocks were impossible to accuse of favoritism.

Rumbles of agreement helped Ganther tear his eyes away from the lovely young woman. Lauran hid a smile. Marissa might only be a century older than her, but she suspected her friend wanted Ganther for a mate. She chuckled to herself. It would take a harder man than Ganther to resist Marissa. Her poor father didn't stand a chance.

Ganther finally nodded, and Lauran swallowed another cheer. If her father chose, no doubt she would be in dragon form for the entire visit. The stones gave her a fifty-fifty shot at greater participation.

Kellin often acted as runner and carried a pouch of stones with her. They passed the bag around, each keeping their fist closed around their stone. Everyone drew except

Ganther. As their leader, he had no option but to remain human.

They formed a semicircle. Stretching their fists into the center, they turned their palms up and opened them.

2

Atlantic Coast
North America

Jenny turned to stare at her grim, pale reflection in the glass of the bay window. "I'm not a child, Frank." Her throat was tight with frustration. "I don't need you watching my every move."

"This isn't about me, Jenn." Her stepfather sounded as if his patience was wearing thin. His voice rose. "This is about you and your attitude."

"My attitude? Are you serious?" She gave a bitter laugh, shaking her head. "You're not exactly the picture of understanding."

He lowered his voice, visibly fighting the urge to shout. "I'm trying to be patient, but you make it very difficult."

It seemed pointless to argue. She retreated into silence, letting the rest of his words wash over her unheard as she stared out at the gray storm clouds.

"You know what, Frank?" she interrupted. "Just leave me alone."

He took a deep, frustrated breath. "I can't do that, Jenny. I care about you, whether or not you believe me. But you need to start taking some responsibility."

At last, she turned to face him, her eyes sharp and unwavering. "For what? Living my life? Or not wanting to be under your thumb?"

Frank's expression softened. "No, for your role in making this situation work. It's a new experience for all of us. Your mother and I only want what's best for everyone." He sighed, lifting his hands, palm up. "Jenny, we're a family now. We're in this together."

"Yeah? Well, I'm nineteen. An adult. And maybe I don't want to be part of your family."

Her stepfather's face fell.

She turned back to the window, her stomach twisting with anxiety. Their arguments followed a familiar pattern. He found her ungrateful, rude, and immature. She considered him arrogant, overbearing, and worst of all . . . not her father.

Her jaw clenched. *Mom never asked what I thought about Frank and Davy's intrusion into our lives. She just went ahead and married him.*

Jenny had been happy to escape to university, but she would barely be scraping by on Dad's life insurance. Taking Frank's money made everything worse. It was a constant reminder that she owed him.

It infuriated her to be indebted to him—no doubt contrary to his expectations. He didn't get her at all. So Jenny goaded him, half hoping he *would* cut her off. *Perhaps then Mom would acknowledge what he's really like.*

The rain lashing against the glass mirrored her frustration as she fumed in silence. Jenny's gaze flicked right, catching the reflection of the almost-nine-year-old boy behind her on the couch. She experienced a twitch of guilt at Davy's alarmed expression, his wide eyes obscured by thick glasses reflecting the lamplight. Her stepbrother sat curled in a corner, as if he wanted to disappear into the cushions. *Looks like I'm not the only one suffering here.*

Frank stormed off to find his new wife, although he knew Mom hated being pulled into their fights.

Jenny stifled the urge to shout, "You can't tell me what to do. You're not my dad." Such a juvenile reaction would not help establish her as a mature adult in his eyes.

But it was awfully tempting.

Movement in the glass caught her eye once more, and she watched Davy take this opportunity to escape. *He'll lose himself in a book up in his room or play that stupid video game he loves. We won't see him again until suppertime.* She smirked. *He's such a geek.*

She pulled her phone from her pocket, and something fell to the floor. Jenny sighed, bending to retrieve the small figure of a man riding a dragon. Despite being a daily annoyance, Davy could sometimes be surprisingly sweet. That morning, the kid had noticed her moping. He'd given her his favorite game character's minifig, as if it would somehow make her feel better.

Jenny stuffed it back in her pocket and checked for messages. Nothing. *The reception here sucks.* She'd barely heard from any of her friends all week. The rain didn't improve signal quality—or her mood.

Raised voices emanating from the kitchen made her grimace. Her mother would resist getting involved, claiming their battles gave her a headache. *She'll give in, though . . . and take his side.* Jenny scowled. *She always does!*

Tired of arguing, she considered her options. If she retreated to her postage-stamp-sized room under the eaves like the brat, Frank would invade her space with another lecture. It made her claustrophobic just thinking about them all crammed in there. And Mom might follow him, crying because they weren't close anymore.

Well, whose fault is that? I didn't forget about Dad and move two strangers into our home. Jenny blinked away hot tears, always near the surface when dealing with her new so-called family. *I gotta get out of here. I won't let them gang up on me again!*

Shoving the phone in her back pocket, she grabbed a raincoat and flew out the door. She pulled the front halves of the slicker across each other for warmth as she sprinted toward the rocky beach.

Within moments, Jenny caught the faint sound of someone shouting her name over the blowing wind but didn't turn to look. She judged herself far enough away to ignore them and feign surprised innocence later. If Mom called her cell, she'd pretend she didn't hear her ringtone over the noise of the whitecaps crashing against the rocks.

Even the beach is lame. She kicked at the thick layer of pebbles. *Why did I let them guilt me into this alleged vacation? I could be in Florida with my friends!*

Discontented gray waves slapped sullenly at the rocky shore. The rain slackened to a dull drizzle, but the chill breeze slipping through her plastic coat made her shiver. She remained somewhat dry, although far from comfortable.

Jenny rubbed her arms and half ran down the scree in

a vain effort to get warm, careful not to step wrong and twist an ankle. Running track was one of her few joys these days. She scowled at the idea of being benched for the remainder of the season.

Despite being noon, clouds obscured the sun, making the day overcast and gloomy. Seagulls sounded raucous appeals overhead, their plaintive cries suggestive of lost children. Loneliness welled up inside her in response to their calls. She missed her friends, she missed her father, but most of all, she missed the way things used to be.

She and Dad used to sit on either end of their old porch swing on rainy days such as this, with their feet tucked up under blankets, rocking and talking for hours.

Jenny tilted her head back, letting the occasional spit of rain run down her cheeks like icy tears. Wind pressed against her from behind, pushing her forward.

Should I turn around? She hesitated, shivering, then continued walking away from the cottage, disinclined to listen to another lecture because she was underdressed for the weather.

All too soon, she reached what she expected to be the end of their section of the scree. Here, the ocean cut inland, separating a wall of cliffs from their side of the cove.

At least it had, the only other time she'd ventured this far.

Today, she discovered that when the water receded, a small drop-off and short stretch of additional beach became visible.

She'd ignored most of Frank's droning about 'flood tides' and 'ebb tides' when they'd first arrived. But apparently, some of it had stuck. If she remembered right, this bit of shoreline would remain exposed for about six hours.

As Jenny stared down at the uncovered span, she felt an odd tingling on her skin. The hairs on her arms stood up; her curls plastered to her face and clung to her hood. "What the hell . . . ?"

A YouTube video shown in science class flashed through her mind: several young men laughing at the same phenomenon. She gasped. Didn't that mean lightning was imminent? The voice-over had claimed they'd been lucky not to be killed.

Without hesitation, Jenny threw herself down the incline, frantic to get lower. The descent proved easy, though slippery.

She flinched and cowered as a crackling bolt cut through the air, its afterimage seared into her vision. *One, one thousand . . .*

Her dazed eyes registered the unusual deep, shadowed fold in the rocks before her brain interpreted what she was looking at. Had she discovered a hidden cave? If so, water probably submerged the whole thing whenever the tide came in, making it uninhabitable.

Two, one thousand . . .

One hand shielding her gaze from the rain, the other clutching the neck of her slicker, Jenny hurried across to the base of the cliff.

Three, one thousand . . .

She stared upward. The hill leaned away from her and the cave stood within reach. But thoughts of crawly things with hairy legs and beady eyes made her hesitate.

A concussive explosion of thunder sent her scrambling into the dubious shelter with a shriek. She immediately pulled her cell phone out, activated the flashlight, and shone it in a circle, her uneasy gaze scanning every corner for movement.

Light reflected off a mica-speckled ceiling, spreading diffused sparkles throughout the cave. Fortunately, there were no signs of life. Unable to shake the image of spiders lurking out of sight, she shone the beam around once more, double-checking for cobwebs.

Telling herself to stop being ridiculous, she took a deep breath, leaning toward the entrance to check on the weather. That single massive lightning strike seemed to have worn the storm out. Smaller flashes sparked behind clouds, but the accompanying thunder grumbled in the distance, moving away.

Relieved, she turned to inspect the small chamber, glad it opened tall enough for her to stand in. If she stretched her arms wide, she could touch both sides at once. A perfect space for one person.

Jenny pushed her hood back and gave her short curls an impatient shake, surprised by how much warmer she was out of the wind. Sliding her raincoat off, she hung it on an outcropping to dry.

She spotted a rock with a concave top worn smooth, as if by generations of backsides, leaving the ideal spot for her to sit. The peacefulness of the place soothed her agitation. She didn't even mind the dank odor of earth and brine.

Her hunched shoulders relaxed, and Jenny sighed. *Mom keeps saying what a nice guy Frank is. Perhaps if he were someone else's stepdad, I'd like him just fine.*

She shifted, trying to get more comfortable. *But he isn't. And pretending everything is okay is getting harder.*

Her shoulders drooped. She should head back. But faking a smile and apologizing or starting another fight seemed to be her only choices.

The close quarters of the cramped cottage made matters worse than if they'd been home. Circumstances were difficult enough without having to block out the sound of Frank and Mom getting busy when they thought everyone was asleep.

Jenny pushed this uncomfortable picture from her mind. She picked at her chipped nail polish, trying to decide what to do or say to improve the situation with her stepfather.

Then a faint, all-too-familiar voice called her name from outside the cave. Startled by Davy's shout, she lifted her head. Concern that the brat was out in the storm quickly dissolved into annoyance that he'd followed her.

Jenny groaned. *Are all little brothers pests? Or*—she grimaced—*are stepbrothers a special pain?*

And she'd been enjoying the peace of her tiny sanctuary.

She hesitated, considering her options. After all, the overhang hid the cave entrance. What if he didn't realize where she was and had called for her, hoping she would answer? The storm was passing, so he was safe enough. *If I stay quiet, perhaps . . .*

A loud, cheery peal sounded. Jenny fumbled with her phone and silenced the ringtone, but the noise would already have revealed her position. She stood with a sigh. *Might as well get this over with.*

As she turned to reach for her raincoat, her flashlight beam caught a narrow, shadowed line etched from roof to floor beside her coat. She leaned closer, shining the light into the crack. The crevice appeared to lead to a small cavity, just large enough to conceal her.

Jenny's mouth quirked. *If I get in there and stay quiet, I can hide until he leaves.* She glanced over her shoulder at the light coming through the entrance.

The sound of a foot scraping against a rock near the opening sent her leaping for this unexpected concealment. She shoved her slicker through the gap, twisted her body sideways, and wriggled into the crevice.

It proved tighter than Jenny expected. The stone scratched her arms and snagged her clothes. Her head got caught as the top of the narrow passage tapered, and she froze, dismayed at the thought of getting stuck. She tried to pull back, but the irregular edges dug in, making retreat difficult.

Her muscles tightened as she fought panic. An uncomfortable weight pressed against her neck, leaving her no choice but to go forward. She forced her way through headfirst, hissing in pain when a jagged protrusion scraped her ear.

Jenny began to regret her impulsiveness. She tried to make herself smaller as the fissure tapered, pressing against her ribcage. The cold, damp walls tightened around her, raising goosebumps on her arms. With a determined push, she squeezed through, ignoring the discomfort.

Pain flared again when a sharp outcropping ripped her shirt. She scraped her shoulder blade as she fell out of the narrow opening into a tiny second chamber.

Cursing under her breath, she wiped at the blood trickling down her neck from her ear. But since she'd come this far . . .

Turning off the light function, she tucked her cell phone in her back pocket.

Jenny sat on her discarded raincoat, unable to stand upright in the confined space. She leaned forward against the wall, pressing one eye to the crack as the smell of damp earth tickled her nostrils. Davy's dad wouldn't let him have a phone until he was twelve, but like a good Boy Scout, he was prepared. His flashlight beam flickered in the outer cave. Heart pounding, she waited, willing him to leave and allow her to escape these cramped quarters.

"Jenny? Are you in here?"

Her ear ached, and her shoulder burned. *What the hell am I doing?*

She sat back, chagrined. *This is stupid! I'm playing some juvenile game of hide-and-seek. I'm hurt. I've ruined my favorite shirt. What if I get stuck again getting out?*

The idea of being trapped in this closet-sized hole caused a flutter of panic. What if Davy left, and she needed his help prying herself free?

She leaned forward, prepared to admit defeat and call out, when a brilliant light flared behind her. Startled, Jenny jerked around in time to witness the burst fade into a warm glow. Tiny orbs brightened the surrounding darkness. Her stepbrother forgotten, she squinted in surprise at a whirling sphere of sparkling lights drifting down a widening passageway.

Her breath caught. *How beautiful . . .*

The surrounding walls shifted, expanding into a spacious tunnel. The swirling apparition pulsed, beckoning her forward. Fascinated, she stood, experiencing a powerful urge to touch the glittering orbs. Yet some primal survival instinct made her tuck both hands into her back pockets. Her fingers brushed against her phone and a small, hard object resting beside it.

She blinked, confused, as a minifigure came out with her cell phone. The physical sensation of holding the minifig grounded her. She flushed with sudden shame, recalling that morning's incident. *He tried to be kind, and I grabbed the toy and stuffed it in my pocket. Did I even thank him?*

Jenny recalled his voice calling her name. She half turned. *Davy . . .*

The sphere pulsed, whirling lights recapturing her attention, soothing her worries, and luring her closer. Dazed, she slipped the phone and minifig into her back pockets. Her wide eyes never left the dancing circle of light. She took a step nearer its swirling invitation.

Overwhelmed by a sense of wonder, Jenny reached out a finger. The whirling slowed, becoming a soft glimmering mist, spreading and moving just out of reach. Fascinated, she stretched out her hand, consumed by the need to touch its elusive beauty.

She hesitated as warmth filled the passageway. A faint whisper, like the rustle of birch leaves in a gentle wind, sent delighted shivers down her spine. Still, a tiny, alarmed voice in her head clamored to be acknowledged. *How did the space grow larger? It's unnatural!*

Jenny faltered, struggling to wake from the fog clouding her mind. The iridescent twinkling pulsed and swirled hypnotically, recapturing her gaze. Her shoulders relaxed as her reservations dwindled. Blood dripped from her ear unnoticed, darkening the shoulder of her t-shirt. Her hands dropped to her sides.

The dancing orbs radiated a sense of welcome and

peace—no family drama intruding—drawing her closer. *How* this had happened no longer mattered. An overpowering sensation of belonging enveloped her.

It's marvelous. No wonder it came to me . . .

Jenny took an eager step forward, reaching out to the haze. The lights scattered, as if shy and avoiding her touch, only to re-form a little deeper down the tunnel.

Wait. What tunnel? That wee nagging voice wouldn't shut up.

"Are you leading me somewhere?" She'd meant to sound amused, but her nervous whisper quivered.

"Where are you, Jenny? Answer me!" Davy's shout disrupted the light's compulsion once more.

She shook her head, confused, and mumbled, "Davy?"

As she lurched and spun around, an errant spiderweb wafted across her face. The viscous strands caressed her cheeks like sticky fingers, covering her nose and lips.

With a horrified shriek, she jerked back, smashing her skull into a low spot on the ceiling. Her body sagged. Just before she lost consciousness, the cloud surged forward, enveloping her in its welcoming folds. As her eyes rolled upward, the world went dark.

Davy shoved his way through the crevice, into the tunnel, and saw her. His bouncing flashlight cast crazy shadows on the walls as he ran toward his sister.

For a moment, the dim gray outline of her slender figure was silhouetted within the haze. Then the mist swirled, the sparkling lights flashing a bright glare. He cried out, throwing his arms up and covering his eyes.

When the radiance dimmed and he turned back, Jenny had vanished.

Davy pushed his glasses up his nose, staring at the spot where his stepsister had disappeared. He shivered, his thin t-shirt soaked from the rain. When he'd looked out his bedroom window and saw her running down the beach, there had been no time to grab a coat. He'd had to follow her immediately if he'd hoped to catch up. He'd seen her silhouette in that last lightning blast, but when he got to the scree, she'd vanished.

The foggy iridescence twinkled and sparkled at him, moving closer, as if beckoning him to join her. He shifted his gaze, refusing that hypnotic invitation. He gulped, stepping back.

"Jenny?" His voice quivered, and his hands curled into fists.

She failed to reappear, and the glittering sphere started to shrink.

He felt a strange, surreal familiarity with what had just happened. It was like moving between worlds via portals in his favorite video game, *Realms of Destiny*. The parallel seemed so obvious, he didn't even question it.

Jenny wasn't simply gone. She was somewhere else.

I should get Dad.

Yet he stood, stepping from one foot to another, half caught in the mist's mesmerizing rotations.

Davy had always devoured fantasy books—from Peter Pan to Narnia, to more grown-up ones, like Stephen King's *Fairy Tale.*

He'd harbored a secret hope that real magic still existed . . . somewhere. Now the proof stood in front of him, and all he could do was worry about Jenny.

He bit his lip, shoving his sliding glasses back into place again. *I should run to the cottage and get help. But if I'm too slow, it might be gone by the time I get back. I can't let her go by herself.*

Davy touched his pocket before remembering he'd given her the Commander's minifig. Feeling small and alone, he experienced a pang of longing for the familiar weight of his treasured mascot. He took a shaky breath, sending out a silent wish for his talisman to keep her safe.

Dad insists family is the most important thing. So I need to find my sister and protect her.

The sparkling fog faded and thinned. A surge of panic urged him forward. "Wait! You gotta bring her back."

The mist paused at the sound of his voice, as if listening to him. Encouraged, he pleaded, "Please! She belongs here, with us."

To the desperate boy, the hesitant shimmering seemed to pulse for ages, although only a few minutes passed. Near despair, he regretted not getting his father.

Then, with agonizing sluggishness, the small circle of sparkling orbs grew larger once more. Davy waited a while, hoping Jenny would reappear, but nothing happened. The circling lights pulsed outward, as if beckoning him.

He edged nearer the mist. "Okay." He gulped. "Take me where you brought my sister."

Closing his eyes, he stepped into the light.

3

The Dragon's Tail, Galahar
Seven Days until Summer Solstice

No matter how early Nath rose, Marden always seemed to be up before him. He yawned, squinting at the old shaman sitting at the table in the common room, reading by the light of the magicked orb floating above him.

"Good day, Master." He stretched as another yawn overtook him. "Sorry."

Marden's dark eyes twinkled as he peered over the top of the book at his apprentice. "Perhaps avoiding late night dice and drink with friends might make morning more bearable."

"Just getting better acquainted with my neighbors." Nath grinned.

His master snorted. "I am not yet so decrepit I forget you were born here." He shook his head with a mock frown. "I trust they are familiar with you by now. Happy

Name Day, my boy. It is hard to accept you are forty-two today. How did that happen?"

His youthful-looking apprentice gave him a cheerful shrug.

Marden rose with a groan, his timeworn bones protesting. He opened the door in their entryway, allowing the fresh morning breeze to frisk through their cave. The soft glow of the rising sun glinted off the mountain peaks and filtered through the opening.

Nath crossed to the fireplace, squatting to poke the coals and add a log. The crackling flames released a comforting scent. The blaze settled to red-hot embers by the time their neighbor, Marta, bustled in, bearing breakfast through the tunnel from an adjoining cave.

She held a tray with a pot of herbal tea—steam rising from the spout—and a covered bowl. Her granddaughter, Polina, followed, carrying a cauldron of porridge. Like her grandmar, the young woman wore her straight hair in a single thick braid down her back, although Marta's showed more gray than black.

Marden smiled a greeting.

"Come, sirrahs, fortify yourselves for the day ahead," Marta advised. She moved gracefully around them as she poured each a cup of kaffee.

"Thank you." The old shaman wrapped his gnarled fingers round the warm mug. "A touch of honey this morn, if you please." As she attended to his request, the hot sweet aroma scented the air.

Her gaze shifted to Nath. "And you, young master. I have not forgotten what today is." She gave him a hug. "Your mam would have been proud of the fine man you've become." Her eyes filled with tears. "I still miss her."

He leaned his forehead against hers. "Me too." They stood for a moment, then she pushed him away. He sat as she lifted the cloth, revealing a bowl heaped with fresh berries.

She bent and kissed his cheek. "First summer fruits, all for you. Blessings on your Name Day."

"Gooseberries!" He flushed with pleasure. "My favorite. Thank you, Auntie. How kind of you to remember."

Polina hung the cauldron over the fire, then slipped back out into the hall. Nath pretended not to notice. She returned, holding out her gift with a confident grin.

He accepted the basket of wild mountain flowers, acknowledging her gesture with a solemn smile. "Good morn and thank you. Your blossoms will brighten our humble cave." Their strong perfume mingled with the aroma of heated honey, making him glad the door stood open.

Undeterred by his reserve, she peered up at him from under lowered eyelashes. "I hoped they might bring a touch of nature's splendor to your Name Day."

Marden sipped his honeyed tea, hiding a smirk. Nath frowned as the shaman and Marta shared a rueful glance behind Polina's back.

He inclined his head and shoulders in a stiff half bow. "A kind gesture, though the presence of two such special women is gift enough. The beauty of nature is indeed all around. May these remind us of that while we work."

Polina stepped toward him. Anticipating her movement, he kept the basket between them, thwarting her attempts to kiss him.

"Life is not all about duties, Nath," she persisted. "Magic exists in more than rituals."

He hid his irritation with a polite smile, affecting not

to understand her innuendo. "I appreciate that, but I am content focusing on my studies."

A flash of annoyance crossed her lovely face. "Perhaps someday you will discover there are everyday magical connections, like those between people."

Her grandmar took pity on Nath, clapping her hands and shooing her granddaughter toward their own home. They lingered at the doorway to offer further Name Day blessings.

"It is difficult to imagine you are over forty." Marta shook her head. "You look so youthful!"

Nath nodded gratefully as Polina's smile dimmed. He hoped their age difference would finally register.

Magic extended the user's life, bestowing both a blessing and a curse. Despite his true years, he already looked several years younger than the lovely young woman—an imbalance destined to worsen with each passing decade.

He frowned as the women disappeared. If Polina did not search elsewhere for companionship soon, she would end up alone, and he did not wish that for her. He pushed the problem away to deal with later and turned his attention to his waiting berries and cream.

He took a big mouthful, exclaiming over how good they tasted. Marden eyed Nath's dish with wistful longing. Nath burst into laughter at his expression and generously split the fruit between them. Layered with Marta's wonderful porridge and a bit of honey for sweetness, they created a breakfast fit for the High King himself.

When they finished, his master washed their dishes, while he swept the floor and banked the fire. In unspoken accord, they headed outside to enjoy the early summer sunshine.

As the sun painted the mountain peaks with gold, the shaman led his apprentice through a series of mystic exercises on the village common.

Listening as the mountains whispered their secrets, Nath experienced a sense of peace and belonging. After his parents' passing, the older man had become more like a second father to him.

Even catching sight of Polina—who watched him from the open door of the cave she shared with her grandmar—couldn't dull his enjoyment of this time they spent together.

When they finished, his master excused him. "It is your Name Day. Go do something you enjoy."

Nath accepted with enthusiasm. "After such a hard winter, our supplies of herbs and potions are getting low. I want to search the slopes for early buds. And with the Summer Solstice approaching in a week, we require them for the ritual. This warmer weather permits camping overnight, and I will return before nooning tomorrow."

Marden gave his blessing to this outing. "It pleases me that my apprentice chooses to combine practicality with pleasure."

Nath's smile dimmed as he reached out to grab a walking stick and warm wrap.

Did the shaman forget that today was supposed to be his last day of apprenticeship? He'd been studying for the agreed-upon thirty years . . . but what if he wasn't ready?

Troubled by his thoughts, Nath strode up the mountain. He might have to nudge Marden's memory—softening him up before broaching the subject, of course. And he knew just how to do that.

There was a special location a hard day's walk from

their village that produced the best mushrooms: large, white, fleshy monsters that Marden loved.

The problem lay with the unnatural nature of his intended destination. Strange noises and odd winds inside this particular cave system had prompted the old shaman to forbid the villagers from entering the Cavern of Whispers. Nath experienced a twinge of conscience whenever he disobeyed.

He cleared his mind of concerns about his future and haunted caverns, lengthening his stride to a ground-eating pace.

Nath's footsteps slowed as he approached the small, somehow ominous entrance. Caves didn't bother him; after all, they lived in one.

But something seemed . . . wrong . . . with this place. The world appeared different after being inside. Even outside, that gaping hole stole some of the brightness from the remaining sunshine.

Yet by forbidding access to this dangerous cavern, Marden had ensured that every boy in the village got dared to enter as a rite of passage.

When they reached their thirteenth Name Day, boys undertook their first overnight hunting trip. A small group of similarly aged cousins or friends camping together would just happen to pass this way.

Accidentally on purpose, as Auntie Marta would say.

Most youths ducked in, hid from their companion's sight for a moment, then ran outside as if chased by ghosts.

Nath assumed only he had ever ventured beyond the first chamber. As a young and overeager apprentice shaman, he had felt compelled to surpass his hunting pack. That was how he had stumbled upon the hidden trove inside. For years, he had kept the discovery of the huge mushrooms to himself and only visited the site occasionally.

His master never asked where Nath went 'shrooming, although he suspected Marden shared his secret. If he returned home with lesser-quality fungus, he risked facing disappointment in Marden's eyes.

His lips firmed in a determined line. He inhaled, then bent over to duck through the short opening. He forced himself to step forward, then halted, allowing his eyesight to adjust.

The first chamber yawned high overhead, the ceiling lost in gloom. Behind him, the rock overhang at the entrance swallowed the sunlight, leaving only a small pool around his feet.

He lifted an unlit brand from the ground and respectfully whispered, "*Ishkode.*" Fire flared, chasing away looming shadows, if not quite as far as he wished. Somehow, using magic in this place seemed dangerous, or he'd have set some orbs floating. Lighting the torch used the most wizardry he dared try in here.

Nath raised the flame and moved forward, surveying the walls, already knowing what he would find. Although the mushrooms picked during his previous gathering were regrowing, they remained too small to harvest again.

He would need to go farther in.

His throat grew dry, and he tried to suck some soothing moisture from his tongue. Reluctant footsteps took him toward the far end of the chamber. *Get on with it! The faster you finish, the sooner you are out of here.*

He squared his shoulders, casting one longing glance back at the bright spot of sunlight, which had already shrunk to a sliver in the distance. He marched forward before his resolve could give out, holding the flaming brand high.

When he shone his torch around the next chamber, light reflected off dozens of thick, white mushrooms. He sighed in relief, knowing he need go no farther.

Nath stabbed the end of the torch into the ground, letting the glowing lichen on the walls brighten his workspace. He pulled the knife from his belt and began the expert cutting and filling of his sack. Yet as he worked, he caught himself straining to listen. Sure enough, faint moans and whispers came breathing down the connecting passages that led deeper into the cave.

He swallowed, but it didn't ease the tightness. *This happens every time.*

Nath did not accept the tales the elders told around winter campfires. *No thank you, sirrah.* Outside—in daylight—he had grown too old to put stock in haunts, regardless of his youthful appearance. But here . . .

'Tis only the wind blowing down rock chimneys or echoes from my own movements.

But he worked faster . . . just in case.

Almost finished, he turned—and froze. He had been certain the chamber ended here. Yet now, a new passageway beckoned—one he swore had not been there previously. Cold sweat prickled his skin.

You are being ridiculous. Lack of observation on your part does not mean this tunnel didn't already exist. You should be ashamed, suffering youngling fantasies at your age.

He tried to tell himself it was only his overactive imagination—or a trick of the light—that made it appear that tendrils of fog snaked along the floor of the passage and into this chamber.

It was no use. Though he detected no breeze, mist swirled from the tunnel, as if blown around the corner by a strong wind. It coiled about his ankles like the long, sleek body of a furrtail. He felt a momentary longing for the company of one of the inquisitive little creatures.

Movement jerked his thoughts back to the cloud. He strained to see through the darkness. A vague white shape began to form.

Nath gasped. *Run!* his mind screamed. However, his feet seemed to be glued to the ground, his body frozen in place, unresponsive.

The specter inched closer, taking on more substance.

Nath worried his pounding heart would break through his ribs and burst out of his chest. The thing approached, dim limbs growing visible. Two arms . . . a pair of legs . . .

With a blinding light sparkling behind the apparition, and the mist shrouding the flames from his torch, he only glimpsed a vague outline.

The torch.

Though loath to take his eyes off the phantom, he wrenched his head around. Relieved, he caught sight of the weak flame—flickering, but still alight.

He whipped back around, fixing the approaching creature with his stare.

It drew closer.

Nath saw a face without discernible features. Somehow, that blank, undefined visage terrified him.

He startled as a high-pitched whine echoed through the chamber. Shame filled him as he realized the noise came from his own throat. Nath's eyes opened wider than he imagined possible, and he trembled, but still his frozen legs refused to obey his mind, which gibbered and screamed, *Run, run, run!*

A ghostly arm reached for him.

Cold white fingers clamped onto his shoulder. A body pitched forward; impulse made him catch it, just as instinct forced him to recoil in horror.

He stared.

Not a specter.

A young woman collapsed at his feet, blood staining her clothes and matting her short, blonde curls.

Aghast, Nath knelt beside her.

Her eyes opened as he lifted her shoulders, and she clutched his arm. She leaned against him, her eyelids fluttering. She lost consciousness again, going limp in his arms.

4

Septain Territory

Lauran swooped low, trailing the tip of one golden wing through the chill water of the bay beside Duke Almar's castle, sending spray arcing over the delighted younglings anchored on her back. They squealed with glee, and she chuckled—a muffled, gravelly thrum that vibrated deep in her belly.

The tiny humans fascinated her. She'd badgered Davint—who acted as her rider—until he'd agreed she might offer short flights to the villager's little ones. At least until he needed to attend the reception in the formal garden.

These Lowlanders were holding it in the Kin's honor, after all.

While Duke Almar had made the castle grounds accessible to the local townsfolk today, the peasants only caught brief glimpses of the regal visitors who roamed the gardens, towering over the nobility. Though most seemed satisfied to gape at the wondrous creatures perched on the walls above them, getting this close to one of the Kin *and* his beast provided an unexpected thrill.

The astonished parents had jumped at the chance for their younglings to ride a dragon. As they rushed to line up, Lauran had *sensed* their fear that a noble would notice the proceedings and claim the rides for their privileged offspring. She was determined not to let that happen.

One of the waiting fathers gathered his courage and sidled up to them as she waited to change passengers. "Right purty beast ye got there."

"She certainly is." Davint winked at Lauran, making her glad dragons couldn't blush. Though she wasn't sure if she was embarrassed or pleased by his comment.

"'Spect riding such a creature takes a might o' gettin' used to."

"Oh, she's a challenge to ride, true enough, but worth the effort."

The intimate tone of Davint's voice caught her off guard, sparking a flicker of annoyance at his casual familiarity. He had no right to speak about her that way. They weren't even courting yet! Yes, she was interested in him, and she couldn't deny the warmth spreading through her at his flirtatiousness. But she wouldn't be toyed with.

She gave a sharp huff, and the smaller man, sensing the change in her mood, shot her a wary look before backing away. As he rejoined his friends, his confusion at Davint's suggestive manner was evident. With a mischievous snort, she launched herself into the air, deliberately soaking her grinning companion's face with a playful splash—much to the amusement of those watching.

A while later, Davint caught the Lowlanders sneaking

back into line for a second turn. He announced, "Last flight," to good-natured groans and jeers.

At his mind-call, Lauran landed, sliding into place alongside the wharf as gracefully as any ship. She held her wings out to either side, providing a platform for stoic parents to retrieve their protesting young.

After the younglings had disembarked, she tossed her head impatiently, eager to be free of the restrictive riding harness. If only she were allowed to shift forms and untangle herself! Being forced to rely on others made her crest bristle.

When he finally released her, Davint stood on the dock beside her, laying a too-familiar palm on her chest. Annoyed that he hadn't taken her previous hint, she snapped her head toward him, baring her teeth. He snatched the offending hand away, dropping the gear and stumbling backward.

He turned his startled gesture into a wave. "Well done, La'vint. Go join the others."

Lauran gave Davint a blank stare, then recalled her alias. She nodded, glancing up at the four clan members in dragon form who perched on the rampart, staring down at the commotion below.

It amused her that the dragons' interest made some people nervous—the same people who cast anxious sideways glances up at the handsome Kin who dwarfed those around him. Not that she blamed them. He was well worth looking at.

Imposing and broad-shouldered, he stood half again as tall as the tallest Lowlander there. She enjoyed the view from behind as he strode off the dock, his deep-reddish skin glowing in the sunshine.

His dragon boasted her favorite shade of copper . . .

She stifled a snort of laughter, wondering how they would respond if he went draconic right there in front of them.

She moved toward the shore. As her powerful hind legs gripped the edge of the wharf to climb out, a nail protruding from under the dock dug into the tender skin around a talon. Heaving herself from the water, she smothered a hiss, not wanting to scare any of the younglings. Despite having near impenetrable scales covering her body, Lauran's toes, eyes, and even her taut leathery wing membrane remained vulnerable to injury.

Green blood dripped from the minor wound before it healed itself. She launched into the sky, snapping her wings open well above the heads of the crowd. Many ducked anyway at the sharp crack of displaced air.

Although they'd drawn stones to determine who would play rider, Lauran swallowed a resentful growl as Marissa shifted to give her room to land on the wall. Lauran had wanted to meet the Lowlanders the most. Instead, she was stuck up here. It wasn't fair. While she knew it might be unreasonable, she even wondered if her father could have rigged the drawing.

Her friend gave her a fond bump on the shoulder. *[You're leaking, dear,]* the stunning black dragon sympathized with a toothy smile.

Embarrassed, Lauran dampened down her sulky thoughts. She hadn't meant to broadcast her discontent. As the youngest of their group, she strove to prove herself, exercising as much self-control as possible.

The other draconic Kin sat on her opposite side. Kellin giggled, and the two drakes, Dram and Staton, seemed more amused than annoyed by her slip. *La'ther, La'lie, Ta're, and Ta'dra,* she thought, reminding herself of their temporary pseudonyms.

Lauran found adapting to their phony nicknames the most challenging aspect of their mission so far, given the myriad of more interesting events happening. She sighed, rubbing muzzles with Marissa. *[I guess I'm lucky to be part of this delegation at all.]*

Her friend snorted, steam rising from her nostrils. *[Ganther sure wishes you'd stayed home.]*

[That's true!] Her huff of agreement sent fine ash floating over the crowd below. *[If Father had his way, I'd be guarding his hoard or writing his memoirs right this minute.]*

They hissed laughter, mouths opening to reveal enormous teeth. Several more-timid humans in the courtyard below seemed to decide they should be elsewhere and scurried away.

[I can't wait to be back in human form.] Lauran shifted restlessly. *[I miss having hands.]* She sighed. *[I expected this to be fun and exciting. How much time does it take to come to an agreement?]*

Marissa shrugged one great shoulder. *[As long as it takes, I guess. They've already met with the duke, and the initial discussions seem to have gone well. There's this garden party event this afternoon, then dinner and a secondary gift exchange this evening. Ganther said we'll be heading home tomorrow morning.]*

Angling her neck around to her wounded foot, Lauran tried to get comfortable on the wall as she licked dried blood from the healed scratch.

Despite her boredom, she loved it up here on the

thick, straight, uncompromising stone ramparts. The high walls reminded her of the sheer gray cliffs that harbored the Kin's aeries.

However, seeing her people entering the enclosed spaces in Duke Almar's castle made her nervous. No dragon—or even a human-form Kin—could easily escape those tiny doors and windows!

Since it possessed the best vantage point, the dragons had appropriated this section, which the soldiers had hurriedly vacated. Armed men huddled on the adjoining battlements on either side. They leaned against the crenellations, pretending to study the crowds below, though she assumed they were meant to monitor the visiting Kin's "wild animals."

Lauran filled her massive lungs with air, her sensitive nose sorting through the scents of blooming flowers, perfumed women, and roasting meat. Her stomach rumbled in anticipation as she filtered out the less-pleasant odors of sweaty, unwashed bodies, dirty nappies, and stale ale.

She sent her mind ranging among the Kin at the party. Her father, deep in discussion with the noble who had played the peddler to act as intermediary between their peoples, didn't acknowledge her. She moved on before Ganther could reprimand her.

Davint entered the garden. Lauran was relieved when he accepted her presence in his consciousness, amused by her curiosity. At least he did not seem to resent her peeking out through his eyes. She tried to be patient, but he never paused to investigate things that appealed to her— such as the noblewomen's attire.

The duke's daughter, Lady Avila, greeted him, and the golden dragon examined her with interest as Davint bent down to answer her. She wasn't jealous of them speaking; comparing the huge Kin to the diminutive young woman confirmed how ridiculous their being together would be.

Lauran heaved a sigh, stirring up dust in the courtyard beneath her and blowing off hats. Several Lowlanders scurried after them.

While she appreciated Davint allowing her light touch on his mind, listening and seeing what happened around him, it wasn't the same as being there herself. It would have been so much fun to stroll into the party arm-in-arm with the copper giant in their usual human forms. She could have spoken with the delicate lady, compared dress styles, and truly taken part in the festivities.

Disgruntled, she pulled out of Davint's mind and turned toward the water. She studied the Lowlander pleasure crafts playing on the lake, until the strange behavior of a tall, thin man caught her attention.

His guards blocked everyone else's access to the wharf, so she knew he had to be important. Curious, she tilted her great head to watch him.

She gaped when he pulled his robes aside, dropped to his hands and knees, and crawled to the dock's edge— right where she'd exited the water. He used a cloth to wipe the wood, even reaching around and underneath the decking.

He must have noticed I hurt myself. She blinked in surprise. *When I tell Father of their concern for a dragon's well-being, perhaps he'll reassess his opinion of them.*

No matter that these specific Lowlanders weren't responsible for hunting her mother. Ganther held them all accountable for her death. He had told her about Mirelle so often, Lauran sometimes felt she remembered a woman she'd never met.

Her thoughts faltered as the lanky man turned and she caught his gloating expression. Uneasy, she tucked the incident away to mention to Davint or her father later.

As the nobleman rushed off, she dismissed his odd behavior and gave herself over to indulging her interest in the many statues and fountains lining the streets below.

In dragon form, the Kin found shiny objects almost irresistible. *Perhaps that's why we spend most of our time as humans. Otherwise, our caves would be overrun with worthless glittery trinkets.* She snorted in amusement.

Ganther's own hoard featured artwork and priceless treasures, nestled in beds of cheap gilded trifles he'd gathered as a drake. He also owned an extensive collection of armor, relics from the days when knights still hunted dragons.

Although she appreciated jewelry, Lauran's own tastes ran to sculpture, which she enjoyed in both her forms. Her gaze kept returning to a particular fountain, where a pod of carved-stone dolphins leaped from the water.

They're so lifelike, you'd expect them to whistle and click.

Lauran *shielded* her mind from the others, before allowing herself to picture how Davint's well-defined muscles would translate to a statue.

Now *that* treasure she would pay good coin for.

5

Shifton charged up the tower stairs to his chambers, ignoring the astonished servants who leaped out of his path. The crazed grin on his face caused everyone he met to turn away, fearful of catching his eye. Several made signs to ward off evil behind his back.

A tall scarecrow of a man, he wore lengthy, pointed sideburns in an attempt to look more mature. He appeared to be in his twenties, despite being much, much older—one of the few things he resented about practicing magic. His apparent youth prevented others from showing him the respect he so richly deserved.

Shifton's long, gangling legs took the steps two, sometimes three, at a time, and his robes flew around him in an undignified manner he would have abhorred under normal circumstances.

He held a soiled cloth in front of him as if bearing a holy relic.

As he entered his workroom, a miasma of musty parchment and ancient tomes, with an undercurrent of rotten food, struck him. The heavy smell hung in the air, doing battle with pungent odors that stung the nostrils—a concoction of exotic herbs, rare minerals, and unidentifiable substances.

The scrabbling of tiny feet drew his attention to the dirty dishes covered with spoiled victuals that were scattered amid the evidence of his life's work. Startled by the sound of his entrance, rats fled their interrupted feeding.

Pulled from contemplation of his treasure, he stared at the squalid scene in dismay. Sunlight flickering through grimy windows cast eerie shadows on the walls, revealing a cluttered space where confusion reigned. How had things gotten so bad?

He scowled, all too aware how it had happened. He'd driven the servants away, screaming at them not to bother him, too wrapped up in spellcraft to care about his surroundings. Though if anyone deserved the blame, it was Duke Almar, always demanding results. As if magic were brewed like tea and youth could be bottled on command.

Shifton stared around him in disgust. Tall bookshelves sagged under the weight of dusty grimoires and weathered leather-bound books. He was so close now. Once he succeeded, he would order the servants to scrub his chambers from top to bottom.

A dark cabinet hunkered in the corner, secretive as a private guilt. He paused to admire an arm's-length wooden shaft holding pride of place atop it. Tapered in the middle like an hourglass, it was layered with carved enchantments, crystal shards, and other more-exotic precious stones.

I need more jewels. His lips pinched in frustration. *I've used up everything I had on this one control rod. How will I create more?*

His eyes traveled down the lengths of several dusty wood tables to a solid door of ancient, blackened oak centered on the back wall. It was covered with intricate carvings that writhed and shifted at the edge of his vision.

Embedded deep within the doorframe, a thick, weathered plank was bound in place by heavy chains. Secured by a braided iron lock, it kept the mysteries of the room captive.

His gaze dropped to the haphazard piles of tattered scrolls and disheveled parchments lying scattered, mixed with pages crawling with alchemical symbols and arcane diagrams. Magic implements—tarnished silver athames, glass vials, and carved wands—were strewn about, adding to the chaos, and he grimaced.

I suppose I should allow the servants in here to clean. Under strict supervision, naturally.

His eyes returned to the door, and he fancied he heard a moan. Impossible, of course. The spells he'd cast on that chamber prevented screams from escaping.

No. I can't permit it. Nobody can be trusted to enter. Not yet. There are too many secrets. Not until my work is successful.

Shifton lifted the fabric he held, reminded of the dark stain upon it and all it signified. Excitement rekindled, driving out all other thoughts. He dismissed the filth around him and pushed aside the secret hidden behind the locked door.

Success is within my grasp. I stand on the very edge of greatness. Nothing else matters.

He turned and strode to the nearest table. With a sweep of his arm, he cleared a space—heedless of the thuds and crashes as the displaced overflow fell to the floor.

"There isn't much here," he muttered. "I'll have to adjust the potion."

A whispered spell and flick of his fingers lifted a substance from the cloth. Liquid floated in the air while he scrambled for a small glass bottle, then descended into the tube with a graceful swirl.

Shifton held the vial up, squinting in the dim light. He admired how the green blood moved as if alive, even outside its host. Now he would prove all his theories correct.

His lips tightened. "Those who persecuted and criticized me will learn what a great wiz-wi-w—"

A sharp pain stabbed his stomach, making him double over. He grabbed the table for support while almost dropping the precious liquid.

"I'm a warlock. A bloody warlock." He forced the words through gritted teeth, tears blurring his eyes as the twisting anguish released its hold on him in slow, agonizing increments.

Damn those sharding sorcerers to the netherworld. Hot fury burned away the last of the pain, and Shifton straightened.

Not content to banish him—no, they'd had to curse him too. To strip him of the wizard title he'd worked thirty long years to earn and ensure he never used that designation again without suffering. *Well, let them call me warlock. I'll prove whose magic is stronger. They will all bow before me one day.*

He held the fragile container with both hands to stop them trembling, then set the vial in a rack and focused his attention on the task at hand.

To make the potion, I must modify the quantities.

Once he verified the accuracy of his adjustments, Shifton moved to the cabinet and selected the herbs and essences he'd been gathering and distilling for months.

A quick wipe of a bowl with the now-clean cloth, and he began measuring and stirring, muttering and grumbling to himself as he worked. With so little base compound, he only needed miniscule amounts of the other ingredients.

With the last step completed, he poured the final product into a sterile vial and stoppered the top. He held the potion up to the light and frowned. The added ingredients didn't seem to make any difference. Pale-green liquid still shifted and gleamed as if alive.

Yet he remained confident his creation would work. In fact, he would describe himself as almost positive. Nonetheless, a tiny niggle of doubt ate at him.

Perhaps he should test it? Though having such a minute amount, he hated to waste any. *No, let Almar try it,* Shifton decided. If the potion worked, he'd claim the credit.

If not . . .

Well, the chances of permanent damage were minimal. He tucked the bottle in a hidden pocket in his robes and left his chambers without a backward glance.

6

The duke slumped on his throne, exhausted by the morning's audiences. Today's first trial had been their unusual visitors: the Dragon Kin. Almar resented being forced to be diplomatic, but he refused to ruin long-term plans in a fit of pique.

He'd greeted them with insincere smiles, welcoming them to Septain Territory. They did not fool him, pretending to be human. Although he refrained from calling them unnatural freaks of nature, their looming bodies and ancient eyes staring down at him from behind humanoid masks made his skin crawl.

However, he would play along until he got what he needed. Shards, how he hated guarding his speech. Few enough pleasures remained to him, and his acid tongue was one.

Afterward, he'd had to deal with a trickle of petitioners. *Parasites and leeches.* He yearned for the days when crowds of courtiers filled this hall, eager for a chance word from him. Nowadays, they avoided his presence unless absolutely necessary. The nobles feared his cutting words more than they desired his favor.

Each morning, the ones who had to see him shuffled in one after another, stating their business with downcast eyes, ever wary of his uncertain temper. After receiving his judgment, they scuttled away like homeless curs with their tails between their legs.

Almar scowled at everyone and everything inside the large, almost empty room, looking for someone to vent his ill-humor on.

His gaze swept over the soldiers positioned nearest his dais. Ostensibly, they protected him from attacks by approaching supplicants. However, he'd heard rumors his guards drew lots to determine who must stand at the doors facing him, and who could take these prized closer positions with their backs to him.

Nothing happened in the castle he didn't know about.

He rolled his eyes across the audience chamber, prepared to make someone flinch. But the sentries flanking the entrance kept their focus on the step below him, careful not to meet his gaze. A snarling smirk lifted one side of his mouth. Oh yes, he remained in charge despite his advancing years.

The duke glared around the room, hating all those healthy, youthful bodies. He sensed himself aging just sitting next to them. That timeworn saying told the truth of it: "youth squandered what age treasured." He straightened, shaking himself from his self-pity. There must still be time. He would succeed.

His Captain of the Guard stood nearby. Rudolph's watchful eyes wandered everywhere but Lady Avila. Yet that didn't fool Almar.

The girl displayed less caution. He saw how often her glance slid toward the handsome young man. The little slattern better watch her step. He would have no by-blows in his court.

He shifted, his scowl deepening. Damnation, he needed to pee again. His sharding bladder seemed smaller every year. He leaned sideways, and the sharp crack of a fart filled the room . . . although everyone pretended not to notice. He straightened, biting his lip at a jab of pain. His joints ached if he moved but stiffened up if he didn't.

Almar blamed that damned warlock for his suffering. *After years of backing that charlatan, what results has he provided me? Certainly not my lost youth.*

Indignation and jealousy coiled in his chest, fueling him with their combined outrage. It irked him that Shifton appeared little older than when they'd first met.

How unfair that magic extended the lives of its users. That this power—granted to even the lowliest peasants in Galahar—was denied him, despite all his potential.

His stomach roiled as the past engulfed him. He half closed his eyes, just for a moment, but memory seized him, dragging him back.

Unable to accept that he, who possessed so many talents and special qualities, would be refused this single element he desired most, the duke approached the wizards at the Citadel.

Their headmaster, the Prime, remained patient as he repeatedly explained how the pretesting every youngling received around their twelfth Name Day worked. How the team of sorcerers conducted their infallible tests.

Lady Avila shifted behind him, the rustle of her dress annoying him. She stilled before he could reprimand her.

All the useless women in his life disappointed him. None of his wives had given him a son, and the only daughter who had lived past four Name Days hovered beside him.

Almar's grip tightened on the arms of his throne. He'd stood there himself, next to his own father. Witnessing the old man wasting away had filled him with horror. He'd sworn it would never happen to him. He'd lied and manipulated, bullied and bribed . . . yet here he sat, afraid that every breath he took might be his last.

Against his will, the past pulled him back to his youth.

Young and headstrong, Almar insisted on being allowed to try the stones. In the end, they granted his request. He fought a sense of awe when he stepped into the Crystal Chamber. The huge gemstones, hundreds of times larger than the small focal jewels each wizard used, stood on pedestals, ranked from the weakest power, rose red, to the strongest, azure.

The Prime invited him to step forward and begin. Confident in his undoubted superiority, he approached with youthful vanity and rested his hand on the first crystal.

Nothing happened.

He couldn't believe it. Ignoring the wizard's chiding, he lunged from one stone to the next, trying them all.

None of them responded.

With age, he came to understand—but still rejected— the Prime's attempts to be kind to him. The man's sympathy burned like vinegar in a wound.

Humiliated, he stormed away from their mountain fortress, swearing he would prove them wrong, no matter the cost.

Almar lifted his head, surfacing from his memories as

weariness overwhelmed him. His lips twisted in a sneer. *And if someone else pays in my stead, why, that's even better.*

He noted those around him awaiting his pleasure and reached for the sharding cane he loathed. He'd had enough for one day.

Avila sprang forward, ready to assist. She didn't touch him, aware he hated showing weakness in public but prepared should he choose to take her arm.

He waved her away, using the cane to help him rise.

As he paused, setting his balance before he tried to move, a new thought struck him. He would have been about her age when he inherited the throne. Recalling his father's untimely death, he shot her a sharp glance.

Would anyone dare share old rumors with her after all this time? He searched her lovely face and saw nothing but concern for his welfare. *No,* he decided. *No one would risk their indiscretion getting back to me.*

"I'll retire to my chamber to prepare for the ceremony this evening."

As always, his brusque tone bordered on rudeness. Almar never said, "I'm going to rest." They might both understand that's what he needed, but he wouldn't admit it aloud.

"You may represent me at the garden party this afternoon."

Her eyes lit up, but she controlled her reaction.

He nodded grim approval of her composure as she inclined her head. "Send him to me there. We have matters to discuss before tonight."

Her lips tightened, but she gave a curt nod.

She didn't have to ask who he meant.

7

Shifton stepped into the darkened room and paused, blinded by the change in lighting. A slight movement and shaft of light caught his eye. He spotted the duke standing near the balcony, half-hidden by a curtain, staring down at the festivities.

Almar's gaze remained fixed on the garden below as he lifted his hand, beckoning the warlock forward.

The offhand gesture irritated Shifton, but he kept a pleasant smile frozen on his face, reminding himself not to underestimate the old man because he appeared worn and frail. He'd seen the duke shrink with each passing season, clinging to a cane, hunching over it as he moved with short, painful steps. Yet his gaze remained piercing, his will as strong as ever.

Shifton stepped closer, folding his arms to clasp his wrists, hidden inside his sleeves.

Almar still didn't turn around. "Well? What progress?"

The abrupt demand made the warlock stiffen.

Though he stood behind the old man, he worked to keep his face expressionless. *But after everything I've done—all I have become—he might at least express some sharding appreciation.*

The duke countered his thoughts as if he'd heard them. "So much time . . . and money—*my* money. And what have . . . you achieved?" His words came in breathless wheezes as he waved a gnarled hand at the glittering company in the garden below. "A lot of abhorrent . . . strangers befouling . . . my castle—turning my . . . people's heads."

Shifton fought to control his indignation, keeping his eyes downcast and his expression carefully neutral. His mind raged, the nails of his hidden fingers biting into his palms as he struggled to suppress his frustration.

I spent decades searching for the knowledge you desired. I broke every rule at the Citadel, combing restricted books without permission. I managed to avoid Stilling when wizards caught me, though they branded me a warlock. Yet you dare ask what I've achieved!

Shifton fought to keep his tone even. "Yes, the money you provided paid for bribes and bought stolen manuscripts, which afforded the inspiration for my potions. Despite the knowledge I gained through years of arduous study, Your Grace, many difficulties persisted—"

"Yes, yes!" Almar snapped, interrupting him. "I am aware of all that. You've been working . . . nonstop, blah, blah. Get . . . to the point." He waved at the strangers towering over the crowd of nobles below. "They're here . . . What's next?"

Shifton gritted his teeth, resolving to make the duke acknowledge his efforts. His voice rose as he warmed to the task of listing his successes. "I spent months orchestrating an 'accidental' meeting with a dragonrider in the mountains. These bedamned Kin hide themselves away like sequestered monks. It was our good fortune that their leader turned out to be that rider. Weeks of diplomacy led to their attendance at this festival."

"Bah. I am familiar with . . . these justifications. Stop telling . . . me things I'm already aware of. What's . . . taking so long? I am not . . . getting any younger." Almar swayed, clutching at his cane for balance. "You've been . . . promising this would work . . . since you trained as . . . an apprentice wizard. I . . . grow weaker each day. I yearn . . . to be strong . . . again." He inhaled with short, harsh breaths as his rant exhausted his waning strength.

Used to Almar's rages, Shifton stepped forward to stand beside him. Ignoring the duke's momentary weakness, he peered down as sounds of merriment rose from the garden. He scowled, catching sight of Lady Avila speaking with one of their remarkable visitors—a well-proportioned, if oversized, red-skinned male.

As the giant knelt so their heads were level, she gifted the stranger a brilliant smile. Shifton's fingers curled into fists, and his lips tightened.

The warlock inhaled deeply, invoking calm, as he turned away to focus on appeasing her father. "We're close now. Everything we've worked for is at hand. It won't be much longer. Yet even preparing the amulets for tonight presented a monumental task. You must understand what complex spells I devised."

He frowned, releasing his hands to give his chin a thoughtful stroke. "Are you certain, my lord, that we should squander all the gems on this one dangerous gambit? It took me years to gather so many flawless—"

"My jewels, you mean?" Duke Almar interrupted with a threatening glare, his unshakeable will a tangible force between them. "You convinced . . . me that this . . . was the . . . best option . . . So be it."

Shifton's exasperation pushed him to be indiscrete. "Yes! Through painstaking research, I answered the riddle of the dragonriders' kinship with their dragons—"

Shards! The warlock caught himself before he divulged the knowledge that consumed his every waking moment. That secret was his.

Not that it really mattered. The old man's obsession with everything magical stemmed from his complete lack of talent. The fool always tried to provoke him into disclosing mysteries of the craft.

As if he could ever use them.

Shifton's voice took on a cajoling note as he quickly changed the subject. "The noble who lured them here managed to cut one of the Kin during his visits and make it look like an accident."

Almar turned to face him at last, an eyebrow raised in interrogation.

The warlock shrugged. "There is a magical . . . *connection . . .* between them and their dragons. I thought it best to test all possibilities." He shook his head. "Their blood was no more effective than any other humans, including my own. The potion requires dragon plasma to work."

He pulled a tiny vial from a hidden pocket and held it out to the duke. "A sample of what is to come."

"Is this . . . ?" Almar's eyes lit up.

Shifton nodded. "One of the beasts scratched itself. A few drops of its lifeblood, mixed into an elixir I've been working on, should improve your strength. However, the effect will be temporary. A few hours at most. When I have a greater quantity, I will produce an additional potion to adjust your body chemistry, ensuring it makes the enchantment permanent. Supplementary infusions will contain less spellwork and more blood, but it's a delicate balance."

The duke reached for it, hesitating as the warlock frowned. "What's wrong?"

"Maybe nothing." Shifton shook his head. "While the unscaled hide of a dragon's inner thigh is a vulnerability, it's hardly easy to access. So I hoped the unprotected skin around the beast's talons would prove equally vulnerable. And so it was." His scowl deepened. "But the creature scarcely bled at all. Perhaps their healing powers are stronger than I anticipated. I'd best adjust the spells before tonight—"

Almar cut his musing short, seizing the vial with shaky hands. He held it up and stared in awe. The green liquid inside roiled and shifted as if alive. Steadying his trembling fingers, he pulled the cork and downed the solution.

At once, he gasped, drawing a shuddering breath that shook his frail body.

Shifton watched in fascinated disgust as the duke's head snapped back and his face rippled.

The old man's skin bulged and churned. His wrinkles faded before the warlock's eyes, until the duke looked ten years younger. He stood taller, and his shoulders straightened.

"It works!" His voice sounded firmer. His hand shot out to clutch Shifton's arm. Even his gnarled fingers were less clawed, and the warlock winced at the strength of his viselike grip. "If your plan succeeds, I will give you any reward you ask."

Shifton strove to sound modest as he turned away, staring at the partygoers below. "I have every confidence I can fulfill my part of our bargain."

His eyes sought Lady Avila, and he leered. "I shall consider what token of appreciation your humble servant might request."

8

Ganther excused himself and retreated from the elderly gaggle of overpowdered and highly perfumed matriarchs who—much to the annoyance of the men he assumed were their husbands—had swarmed him the moment he entered.

At first, he'd enjoyed their blunt questions and sharp tongues. They reminded him of the older draikanas at home.

However, as the generous application of alcohol turned their queries sly, their innuendoes about his size had begun to annoy him. Prolonged periods of tactfulness always grated on his nerves.

Claiming he needed to check on his companions, he left them gossiping comfortably among themselves, ruefully confident he was the main topic of conversation.

Simply opening his mind would have allowed Ganther to contact the others. However, it would have also left him vulnerable to the clamoring of the surrounding crowd. Lowlanders had an appalling lack of control over their thoughts. He'd had to double his shields since they'd arrived.

Servants circulated, offering glasses of wine on trays, though some had been tasked with ferrying outsize containers he suspected were originally large glass vases for the delegates. Some people looked askance at the size of their drinks, but Ganther knew his team could hold their liquor. It took several vats of ale to get a Kin tipsy. These wee drafts wouldn't do it.

He carefully picked his way toward the rear of the hall, where tables with gleaming white cloths groaned under a vast array of foods. Most of it was tiny for someone his size. However, he was pleased to see some larger tarts at the far end.

Choosing a berry-filled one, he tilted his head back and ate it in two bites, licking juice from his fingers. When he lowered his chin, he found a stout, bearded Lowlander gaping at him. A slice from another dish sat on the man's plate, and Ganther realized what he had taken for a tart had actually been a full pie.

Refusing to acknowledge he'd done anything uncouth; he nodded politely before moving away. He was relieved this far-too-long diplomatic exercise would soon conclude. The earlier they retired for the night, the quicker morning would arrive and the sooner they could return home. He yearned to sleep in his own bed again.

Not that their quarters weren't comfortable. They'd been given rooms in the oldest quarter of the castle, where the ceilings rose to gracious heights that let them stand without hitting their heads.

Three large beds had been pushed together for each of them, and he suspected the local seamstresses had been rushed to get so many sheets and quilts stitched together, forming bedding for them all. He appreciated the quality of their work.

In any case, they couldn't gracefully retire until Duke Almar made an appearance.

His eyes wandered about the room, picking out the other Kin delegates, tall as stalwart trees scattered across a field.

The ballroom, though spacious, was so full of sharding Lowlanders, he was almost afraid to move. They were so much shorter than his people, he feared he would crush someone every time he turned.

Ganther's gaze landed on the wizard, who stood out among the gaudy costumes like a black crow in a tree filled with songbirds.

Of all those they'd met here, only three—Shifton; the duke's seneschal, Edwards; and the duke himself—had any sort of mental shields. And they kept their thoughts locked down tight.

He would have been suspicious if he hadn't been doing the same thing himself!

The past few days had been spent in the seneschal's chamber, hammering out the details of a trade agreement. He appreciated Edwards's dry humor, and the two men had worked well together. More than one servant had tried to hide smirks at the sight of his huge body crouched beside the diminutive seneschal as they talked, but Ganther had ignored them.

He thought they had the basis for an acceptable arrangement to present to their respective leaders. If everyone agreed, Maxim would journey to the castle himself, where he and the duke could sign a formal contract.

Ganther wondered idly how Lauran was handling the onslaught of undisciplined minds when he felt the familiar touch of her mind sliding past his shields with the ease of long practice.

[How's everything going?]

[I'll admit, I do not enjoy being surrounded by non-Kin. They don't belong to our clan,] Ganther grumbled.

[Get through tonight, and you can request Maxim choose someone else to come back with him.] Humor colored her thoughts. *[You could always recommend Zyre!]*

He grunted in agreement. *[I'll have you know, it's entirely possible there will actually be a return visit.]*

She chuckled at his admission, and he gave a mental sigh. *[Well, I had my doubts when we first arrived. But our people avoided making any gauche mistakes, and Edwards and I have reached a workable arrangement. It just needs to be ratified by Maxim and Almar.]*

He refrained from mentioning the pie incident and thickened the shield surrounding that particular memory. Then he let her peer through his eyes at the event, feeling her mental laughter as his scrutiny rested on a single sullen member of their group standing isolated in a far corner.

Those surrounding him avoided eye contact and kept their distance. Zyre stood alone, like an island in the center of a calm sea. He could've put his thick arms out and swung around without hitting anyone.

[I wish I could say no one has been rude.]

Lauran agreed, trying not to laugh while offering sympathy. *[Perhaps that was expecting too much.]*

The gray-skinned Kin glared as excited humans surrounded others in their group while snubbing him. He gave an aggravated huff as a brave server approached him with a tray of drinks, including an oversized option, which Zyre grabbed. The obstinate man scowled with such ferocity that the servant yelped and practically ran in the opposite direction.

Ganther sighed, but Lauran wasn't about to let him accept the blame for the gray Kin's ill temper. *[It's not your fault Maxim bypassed him and chose you to lead the delegation.]*

[I know, but he can't even be civil. I don't understand why he was allowed to be part of our mission. The Alpha knows Zyre better than anyone.]

Her giggle tickled the back of his mind. *[Perhaps this is Maxim's way of making him someone else's problem for a while.]*

[I knew I should have assigned roles.] Ganther glared at Zyre's sour expression. *[It's unfortunate he ended up drawing black. And regrettable that being a rider puts him in direct contact with the Lowlanders.]*

The pair shared a silent laugh. Davint caught their mutual vision and smirked, rolling his eyes in the gray's direction.

[Despite Zyre, things are going well,] Lauran insisted.

[You're right,] Ganther decided. *[Everyone has stayed in character—even him. Our* shifting *abilities remain a secret, and tomorrow we return home.]*

[So,] she teased, *[improve your damn attitude, old man.]*

Ganther turned his snort of laughter into a smothered cough, inclining his head when an elderly Lowlander glanced around at him with raised eyebrows.

[Fine,] he agreed affably. *[After all, I am representing Dragon Kin.]* A wave of amusement emanated from him,

making Davint and Dram cast curious glances his way. *[Besides, I promised Maxim I'd behave.]*

He *sent* her an image of him straightening to his almost ten feet in height, a polite half smile pasted on his face. Before she could approve, a trumpet's blare caught them off guard.

Ganther's sensitive hearing made him cringe and clap his hands over his ears. Lauran cried out at the backlash of his shock, her startled roar from the top of the wall competing with the blast.

When he looked up, their shared vision showed the duke standing before his throne on the dais, awaiting them.

The other Kin began moving forward, shaking their heads to ease the ringing.

Ganther eased past his people to reach the front of their group. *[Leave me alone now, young lady. I believe I have a final piece of protocol to perform.]*

He *sent* a loving caress after Lauran as she slipped from his mind.

Almar stepped to the edge of the platform, glancing upward with a puckered brow. He appeared uncomfortable having to look up at them. Ganther guessed any Lowlanders being presented before the throne would stand several steps lower than the duke.

Their host smoothed his expression as he faced the crowd. If the duke's smile looked forced, he sounded pleasant enough. "We have gathered . . . to bid farewell to our guests. It has been an eventful . . . few days getting acquainted . . . with our new friends. I hope that relations . . . between our two . . . peoples . . . grow closer with the passage of time."

Ganther bowed, and the others followed his lead.

Almar's breath came in loud, heavy inhalations by the end of this brief speech. He lifted his hand. In response, five servants hurried forward, each bearing an elegant medallion and chain lying on a satin pillow with golden tassels, raised high. The medallions featured massive glowing gems in their centers.

The Kin had tendered their own gifts when they arrived. Careful consideration had gone into the decision to present a matched pair of resonant scales, offered up by their Alpha himself, although that knowledge had not been shared with the Lowlanders. The set was a stunning ocean blue so dark, it bordered on indigo. Faint threads of silver shimmered when they were tilted against the light—like moonlight over deep water. Intentional focus on the first scale allowed the holder of the second to appear in its depths, enabling long-distance communication. It was truly a worthy offering, signifying honor and trust by the Kin.

Maxim had forewarned them to expect a gifting ceremony in return. Yet a hush settled over them when Almar presented the delegation leaders, Ganther and Davint, with the largest and most elaborate emerald and ruby pendants they'd ever seen.

Ganther's eyes widened, and he stiffened in astonishment. Dwarf gems of this size and quality were rare indeed. He suspected few jewels of such clarity and beauty existed outside royal vaults.

The duke honored the rest with smaller, more subdued sapphire, yellow citrine, and deep amber versions, also set in intricate smithwork. The others remained polite, though Zyre let out a low, pleased growl at the sight of his huge blue stone. The duke's smile faltered at the sound, but he quickly recovered with the ease of experience.

[Stop that noise right now,] Ganther snarled silently. He *sensed* the older Kin's resentment at the reprimand and reinforced his command with a fierce frown. They would not act like uncivilized savages in front of the Lowlanders.

Despite some jealous glances from Zyre, all five seemed pleased to receive a token, and even the belligerent gray looked gratified when Almar hung a pendant around each neck himself.

The ceremony concluded with Ganther's brief, well-mannered speech of thanks. Relieved their visit was ending on a high note, the delegation made their final courtesies and slipped away from the ballroom.

They finally retired for the night, restless with anticipation and eager to get home.

9

Six Days until Summer Solstice

The twinkling cloud enveloped Davy, warm and tingling on his skin. It was like swimming through heavy salt water without getting wet.

He floated, holding his breath, weightless and shielding his eyes from the brilliance surrounding him as he drifted through the glow.

Several moments later, he landed hard and stumbled forward down a short, dark tunnel. The light behind him dimmed. As he spun around, the mist collapsed in on itself, swallowing the shiny sparkles and leaving him alone in a large, silent chamber lit only by the soft, glimmering radiance of thick, brittle-looking lichen.

Davy gulped, pushing his sliding glasses up his nose.

He was still inside a cave . . . just not the same one. This place appeared much bigger and smelled different. Huge mushrooms, unlike anything he'd ever seen before, sprouted from the walls amid the lichen.

His nervous fingers touched the small flashlight tucked in his waistband, but he left it there. No point wasting the batteries while it was light enough to see.

"Jenny?" His voice mocked him, echoing throughout the cave.

He regretted calling out, as odd whispers vibrated long after they should have stopped.

No one else answered.

Davy disliked the eerie greenish tinge the glowing lichen gave his skin. The whole space gave him a creepy sensation, as if the shadows were watching him.

He bolted toward the only exit, tripping on a cloth bag on the floor and almost slipping on crushed mushrooms.

As he darted into a larger chamber, he was grateful for a tiny patch of sunlight beckoning from the far wall. He nearly ran outside but forced himself to stop and explore.

"To get home, we gotta remember where we landed." His face screwed up as he tried to recall any stories involving travel to other worlds. "When Lucy went through the wardrobe, she discovered a winter landscape." His stomach rumbled, reminding him he'd missed lunch. "But she also made a friend who gave her something to eat."

Davy examined the mushrooms, which were smaller out here. He glanced over his shoulder. The entrance behind him now loomed black and ominous. Green streaks from the glowing lichen quivered across the dark gap.

I wish it didn't look so spooky. He took a nervous step toward it.

Voices seemed to murmur from the opening, growing louder as he drew nearer.

Davy shivered. *It's only my imagination.* But he

skittered backward, annoyed with himself for not grabbing that bag he'd tripped on.

He sighed, pulling his t-shirt out of his jeans. Good thing Mom bought his clothes a size too big. If he held up the front edge, it would let him carry stuff.

A quivering smile quirked the corners of Davy's mouth as he began harvesting the mushrooms. Carol wasn't used to being his mother yet, and he'd overheard her tell Dad she worried she knew nothing about little boys. But he guessed she was doing pretty good.

Focusing on Mom and Dad helped him ignore the sighs and mutters whispering from the next chamber. After filling his makeshift bowl, he headed outside.

Davy squinted as the rising sun's glare struck his eyes, blinking until tears smeared his glasses. He fumbled to wipe them clean with the hem of his shirt, careful not to drop the mushrooms.

But he couldn't stop gaping at the world spread before him.

He stepped away from the entrance, captivated by the most beautiful mountain scenery he'd ever seen. Every direction revealed huge rocky slopes and distant white-capped peaks.

"But, you see," he muttered, "the Land of Oz has never been civilized." It was a line from Carol's favorite book, which had always delighted him.

This place looked massive. How would he find his sister?

"JENNY!" Davy shouted as loud as possible. Only a faint echo of his own voice replied. *Where is she?* His eyes widened. *What if going through the portal separately means we arrived in different places?*

In his panic, he forgot to watch his step and walked into a pile of melting snow. It covered his shoe, filling his sock with cold, wet slush. Davy hopped away, shaking his foot and muttering, "Always winter and never Christmas," as Mister Tumnus said.

But despite some snowy patches, green things grew everywhere he looked, although he didn't recognize many of the plants. The few twisted trees had silvery bark that shimmered in the sunlight, and he'd never seen anything like the odd dandelion-like flowers, their fluffy, cotton-candy-pink heads nodding in the morning breeze.

Where was he?

His wild gaze darted about, and he saw a footprint in a patch of mud. The smeared tread mark made it hard to swear it belonged to Jenny . . . but who else would be outside this particular cave?

He spotted another print further down the slope. That gave him a bearing. He hurried forward, trying not to stumble on the uneven ground and drop his meager food supply.

This plan worked—until the footprints crossed an expanse of stone and ended. Davy continued anyway, trying to line up with his previous steps. By the time he looked back, the prints were gone—and so was his sense of direction.

And all this walking made him hungrier. He nibbled as he hiked, wishing Mom or Jenny would appear to cook them for him.

The mushrooms soon vanished.

It did not occur to him that they might be poisonous until after he finished them. His dad always knew what was safe to eat in the woods. He worried for a bit, then decided they must be okay. At least he didn't feel sick—yet—though his hunger persisted.

Davy spent the next hour wandering up and down the mountainside. He was disoriented, and it was getting darker . . . but without a clear destination, he couldn't be considered lost.

Could he?

10

Lauran and the other impatient dragons waited as Gan-ther led his delegates out of the castle at midmorning. She *sensed* him chafing at the layers of protocol, just as eager to be off.

As instructed, she and the others landed in a spacious field outside the walls, designated as their embarkation site.

A sizable crowd gathered to bid them farewell. The sorcerer, Shifton, stood behind Lady Avila, who repre-sented Duke Almar. She once again made his apologies.

Lauran regretted not getting acquainted with the duke's daughter. *[For one so young, she carries herself with confidence. And she has a lovely smile.]* Marissa *sent* her agreement.

The golden dragon leaned down to inspect the lady as she drew near, blowing a soft jet of warm breath that puffed Avila's hair into the air. The handsome Captain of the Guard standing by her side tensed.

But Avila just laughed and even stretched out her hand to bravely stroke the dragon's muzzle.

Lauran's eyes whirled yellow with pleasure. *[I like her!]*

[Daughter.] Her father glared at her. *[Behave yourself.]* She withdrew, chastened but unrepentant.

The human Kin mounted their dragon companions. Lady Avila signaled the guards to push the people back.

When everyone was clear, Ganther *sent* a mental command. The impressive assemblage rose into the air as one. As they beat their wings, the rumbling of alternating wing strokes boomed and cracked, causing many of the spectators to cry out and even fall to the ground.

Lauran suppressed a laugh. A gathering of dragons had earned the name *thunder* for a reason. Flying in formation, they circled the field, then headed toward the mountains. The cheering Lowlanders disappeared behind them.

Not long after the abominations had flown away, Shifton raised his head to follow the entrance of Rudolph, Captain of the Guard, to the audience chamber. Torches flickered as an errant breeze followed him into the room. Though bright sun shone outside, heavy curtains covered the windows. The duke found the dim light more soothing.

Shifton scowled at the young soldier's confident stride as he marched forward—his muscular body controlled, his eyes clear and keen.

Nor did the warlock miss how Lady Avila brightened. His teeth clenched as the young man nodded at her, standing in her place just behind her father's throne. At least Almar forbade her from bringing her yappy little dog into the audience chamber.

Sharding thing growls every time it sees me. I would enjoy silencing it one day. Shifton's glower deepened, and he straightened, pulling his thin shoulders back in an attempt to appear more imposing.

Rudolph bowed deeply before His Grace, the duke, and gave the sorcerer a wary nod.

"Leave us." Shifton gestured to the guards standing at their posts. His mouth tightened in annoyance when the men looked toward the captain, who gave an almost imperceptible nod, granting them permission to march out. The doors closed with a hollow, echoing bang.

Again, the torchlight flickered, sending tendrils of light into darkened corners before steadying to bright spots against the shadowed stone walls.

Almar sat forward, appearing withered and shrunken once again.

Shifton pursed his lips. The small amount of potion he'd prepared had barely gotten the man through the closing ceremonies.

The duke's reedy voice never rose above a loud whisper, each word a gasp for air. "I'm giving you and . . . your men into the . . . command of Wizard Shifton."

A faint echo of pain stabbed the warlock's side. *That wasn't me. I didn't say anything!* He repeated this mantra until the discomfort faded.

The captain raised a questioning eyebrow but remained silent as the duke continued. "I have received credible . . . infor . . ." He paused as if gathering strength, his breath coming in strangled wheezes. "Information . . . that the Kin plan to send . . . their dragons to attack . . . now, while we least expect it."

Surprise flooded Rudolph's face. "But, sire, they just

left. Are they not our allies, our trading partners? We spent the last three days celebrating our new friendship."

Almar's heavy eyebrows drew together in a fierce frown. "Are you doubting my word? You'll do . . . as you're told. This information comes from . . . a reliable source . . . one I trust." He sank back, his face lined with fatigue from his outburst.

"But, Father." Lady Avila stepped closer to his side. "There must be some misunderstanding. They seemed such honorable men. I talked to them. I don't think—"

"No, you do not," the duke snapped, causing her to recoil. "It is a ruler's . . . job to decide what . . . the truth is. To . . . protect his territory." His ire caused a coughing fit. She started forward again, but he scowled, waving her away. "Take yourself off. Allow . . . the servants to care for you. Have a meal and . . . leave . . . important decision-making . . . to those best equipped . . . to deal . . . with matters of state."

Avila's shoulders stiffened, and she colored at his rebuke. Her lips pressed into a thin line. When he sat glaring at her and did not relent, she dipped her head in a wooden nod.

"As you wish." She stalked from the room, her neck and cheeks flushed and her spine rigid, pausing only to incline her reddened face to the captain as she passed.

Shifton regretted seeing her so angry. It also infuriated him that she did not turn to acknowledge him. Everything about Rudolph annoyed Shifton: his calmness, his youth, his looks, even the way echoes of the torch flames danced on the man's armor and gilded his dark hair. He shot a jealous glare at the soldier, who now dared speak in Avila's defense.

"Lady Avila's words have merit, Your Grace. Dragon Kin are renowned for their honor. I discussed the codes they live by with them." The soldier gave a bewildered shake of his head. "What does High King Romar recommend we do?"

Shifton didn't wait for Duke Almar to reprimand the man. "Enough!"

His curled fingers reached out, as if grabbing Rudolph's neck, though they stood five paces apart.

The soldier gasped, clawing at his windpipe. His boots scrabbled against the worn stone floors as an invisible hand lifted him onto his toes, cutting off his air.

"We're not asking for your opinion. It is our duty to protect Septain. By the time this news reaches Romar and he travels from his keep in Trifair, he'd be too late." Shifton squeezed his fingers, savoring the resistance of the young man's throat against his empty palm. "You will listen to your duke's orders and obey."

Almar, smiling in amused approval, watched in silence. His gaze flicked between the two as the captain gagged and scratched his neck with both hands.

"Am I clear?" The warlock tightened his grip a fraction more.

Desperate, Rudolph tried to speak but made only gargling sounds. He jerked his head in frantic agreement, his bulging eyes wild with panic.

Shifton reluctantly dropped his arm, accepting that he needed the man alive . . . for now.

The captain fell forward, dropping to his knees. Coughing and choking, he rubbed his swollen throat.

"Gather your men. We leave within the hour."

Rudolph climbed to his feet, chest heaving as he

sucked in air. He gave another, much less polished bow to the duke. He hesitated, avoiding the warlock's eyes, then jerked his head toward him in acknowledgement before pivoting on his heel and marching from the room.

Avila went to her suite as ordered. She paced around her elegant salon, clenching her fists and stomping her feet. "'Allow the servants to care for you.' As if I'm a youngling who needs to be coddled."

Her little white dog, Pepper, followed her movements with adoring eyes. She came to sit beside him, absently rubbing his ears. He laid his head on her lap, only to have her push him away, jump up, and resume pacing. The confused pup sat up, then lay back down at her abrupt hand signal.

"'Leave important decision-making to those best equipped to deal with matters of state.' Ha. Who will rule Septain Territory once you're gone, Father?"

She suddenly found her spacious quarters stifling, the soothing, muted colors smothering. Avila threw open the balcony doors and marched to the balustrade, slamming her palms down on the smooth marble rail hard enough to make them sting. Pepper ran after her, pushing past her skirts to poke his nose out between balusters.

She wanted to scream—but a duchess never let her aggravation show. Her grip on the railing tightened until her hands ached.

Avila prided herself on being able to read people. It was what she had trained for all her life. One could not rule a territory if they were unable to intuit whom to trust!

She both liked and trusted the Kin she'd met, and from the little she'd gleaned from her tutors, they were committed to their codes of honor. They seemed incapable of being as duplicitous as her father suggested. She'd heard their sincerity when she spoke with them—something Shifton and the duke seemed to lack.

Who had provided this so-called trustworthy information? Her pacing took her back inside, where she strode to and fro, trying to dispel her agitation.

The servants didn't mention any spies returning to the castle in the past few days. Where did his news come from?

The sorcerer's smug face flashed in her mind. *Shifton! I'm certain he's behind this. But what conceivable motive could he have?*

Unable to sit still, Avila left her suite and hurried down the stairs, ignoring Pepper's indignant barks at being forsaken. She waited, concealed in the shadows near a suit of armor, until Rudolph left his interview with her father.

The young captain appeared, rubbing his throat as if in pain. He drew closer, his broad shoulders throwing her into shadow as she stepped out to meet him. His face was a dark silhouette against the torchlit hallway.

He shifted to her side and dipped his forehead in a respectful nod. "Milady."

She waited, but he remained silent. Avila frowned. "Have you nothing to say about this ridiculous order?"

The captain pursed his lips and shook his head. "It is not my job to evaluate my orders. I carry them out to the best of my ability." He straightened his shoulders.

She refused to accept this. "Sometimes one must take

a stand for one's convictions. Do you trust this news to be true? Are the Kin our enemies? Do you consider them capable of such treachery?"

"Anybody can practice deceit with proper motivation." Rudolph shrugged. "Perhaps they have a strong justification, convincing them of their right to attack us."

Avila started to object, but he held up his hand. She wouldn't have tolerated such impertinence from anyone else, but she bit her lip and allowed him to continue.

"We will soon discover if the threat is real. We have a specific location to await their attack, and we'll be in place and ready by nightfall."

He pointed in the direction of the courtyard. "We have archers and spear throwers, though we're more used to castle walls. I fear we do not train to fight an enemy that strikes from open skies. No one has ever employed dragons in warfare before." He caught Avila's frown, and his mouth twitched. "Yes, always assuming they attack us at all."

She sighed, and her shoulders drooped. "You're right, of course. You must do as Father commands. I will expect no less obedience when I am duchess."

Rudolph smiled for the first time. "I look forward to that day, Your Grace."

Surprised, she glanced up at the warmth in his voice, and they locked gazes. Avila's eyes widened and her heartbeat sped up as the moment stretched. Her breath caught in a small gasp, breaking them out of the moment, and he pulled his gaze away.

Shaken by the unexpected intimacy, she blurted her concern. "Beware of Shifton. I've never trusted him. Once crowned, I shall ask the Citadel for another advisor that very day."

"Be careful, Avila." Rudolph scowled. "He's more dangerous than you imagine."

He had never spoken her name aloud before, always calling her *milady*. A quiet thrill ran up her spine, though he didn't seem to notice what he'd done.

He stared into the distance, once again rubbing his throat.

She reached out to touch his arm. "Are you unwell?"

"No, why?" He became aware of his actions and dropped his hand. "It's nothing. I'm fine. I must resume my duties now. There is much to prepare.

"Don't worry, milady." A slight tremor betrayed his formal tone. "I will inform you as soon as we return. Although I'm hopeful the duke's fears are unfounded, we will still be prepared for any possibility."

With a quick nod and without waiting to be dismissed, he hurried toward the courtyard, leaving her staring after him.

11

A bright light woke Jenny.

"Mom," she complained, throwing an arm over her face, "it's too early. Close the drapes."

An unintelligible male voice mumbled apologetically. Surprised, she moved her hand and opened drowsy eyes, staring up at an unfamiliar white ceiling. A sculpture loomed overhead.

She frowned. *Where am I?*

Someone lifted her wrist and fastened something there. *A hospital ID band? What's the matter with me?* She turned her head and met the kindest gaze she'd ever seen.

"There, that should be better. I am afraid your mam is not here." The young man gave her a warm smile, and she found herself smiling back.

She took in his unbound past-the-shoulders, straight hair. And something about his clothes struck her as odd. Jenny sat up, the sudden movement making her dizzy.

"Whoa!" She squinted, one hand to her head, as she surveyed the unfamiliar room.

Her mouth dropped open. The rough white walls were painted to look like rock. She twisted to stare upward. Not a sculpture but a kite, intricately decorated to resemble a giant bird poised for flight. It seemed so delicate, it might have been floating above her, rather than hanging on the wall.

Okay, what sort of hospital is this?

Bewildered, she turned back to the stranger sitting on a low stool beside her bed. The guy appeared to be about her age. She envied his straight hair, having given up and accepted her own short, blonde curls ages ago. His was so black, dark-blue highlights shimmered in the flickering firelight.

Wait, what? Jenny stopped her scrutiny long enough to confirm that, yes, a fireplace with a cheerful fire warmed the chamber. The flames cast shadows over his golden-brown face, sharpening his cheekbones and aquiline nose.

Her gaze moved to his strange clothing. Some sort of leather tunic with intricate embroidery covered a linen undergarment.

"Where am I?" She frowned. "What is this place? I didn't realize this area had native reservations. How did I get here?"

He looked uncomprehending, and she blushed. "Oh, is that not what they're called anymore? I'm not sure of the politically correct term for a First Nations . . ." She hesitated, searching for a word that wouldn't offend him. "Reserve? Settlement?"

"Eya, we are Anishinabe, 'the People.'" He stated this as if it explained everything.

Jenny raised her hand to push her hair behind her ear, catching sight of the woven band he'd attached to her wrist. She'd expected a plastic patient ID but instead saw a bracelet tied in place. A beautiful tiger's-eye gemstone with distinctive markings was braided into the middle.

She lifted her arm, peering at it. "What's this?"

The young man shrugged. "You spoke Lowlander while unconscious. I suspected you would not understand our language, so I created a translation stone for you."

"A . . . uh-hunh . . ." *Okay, he's a little delusional. Is this some sort of mental facility?* Uneasiness shivered down her spine, but there was no way Mom would have allowed Frank to put her in a loony bin. *So where the hell am I?*

She narrowed her eyes, staring at the young man. *He can't be too bad off, or they wouldn't let him wander around alone. I wonder if I can get some answers out of him.*

Annoyed by her confusion, Jenny glanced down at the bed for clues. It seemed to be a mattress sitting on a low wooden frame. Her gaze shifted, and she gasped, pulling the blankets up to her neck. She only wore some sort of thin linen nightgown, and a quick shift of her body confirmed she had nothing else on.

"Where are my clothes?" She glared at him, though she couldn't blame him for her state of undress—she hoped.

"You sustained injuries." He flushed and lowered his eyes. "One of our women removed your torn and bloody clothing. She cleaned and mended them for you." He waved at a table across the room, where a folded pile caught her attention. "She also treated the scrapes on your shoulder, eya. But my master repaired the more serious wounds to your forehead and ear."

His cheeks darkened. "I should have healed you myself. However, your appearance in the Cavern of Whispers was so unexpected, I just wanted to return you to Marden as quickly as possible."

Jenny ignored the nonsense about him healing her. He must have delusions of being a doctor's assistant or something. *A head injury? Okay, I think I remember that.*

When she strained to recall recent events, her memories scattered like minnows in a pond. She adjusted her position until her back pressed against the wall. Cold bled through her thin garment, making her jerk forward. She turned to check behind her.

Not painted walls imitating stone. The pallet, or mattress, she lay on butted up against an actual wall of whitewashed rock.

How the hell had she ended up in some sort of cave? She frowned. Something about that tugged at her memory.

A frail-looking elderly man shuffled into the room, leaning on a carved wooden stick. She stared in surprise. He also had long, straight hair, though his was silvery gray and tied back with a leather thong. Wrinkles seamed his face, and Jenny suspected he might be the oldest person she'd ever seen.

He peered at her, tilting his head with bright, birdlike interest. She got the oddest impression he knew exactly what she was thinking.

"Our guest is awake. Good morn and well come. We are pleased to offer you shelter. Nath, she will be hungry after her ordeal. Be so kind as to fetch food and drink for her."

Jenny made a note of the younger guy's name. He rose to his feet in a fluid, graceful gesture, and she noticed he wore deep-blue woolen trousers and leather boots. *Well, what did you expect? Fringe and moccasins?*

Nath astonished her by bowing to the old man. "Eya, Master Marden."

She watched him go, struggling to hide her astonishment at such antiquated behavior, then turned to face his so-called master.

"Where am I?" Her fingers tightened on the blankets. "What happened to me?"

His voice reflected his gentle smile. "We, too, have questions. First, what is your name?"

She sighed, rolling her eyes. "Are you some kind of doctor? I guess you need to check my memory, right? Fine. I remember that much anyway. My name's Jennifer Peters, but I go by Jenny."

"Hello, Jenny." He beamed at her, and she caught herself smiling back. Why did she feel safe? It wasn't like her to trust strangers this easily. She should stay on her guard; for all she knew, they might be kidnappers! "The cavern where we discovered you is forbidden. Who are your people? The style of your clothes is unusual, even for a Lowlander."

She pressed the heel of her palm to her forehead. "Everything's sorta foggy." Her mouth tightened in a stubborn line as she dropped her hand and looked up. "What is this place? Who are you?"

He moved to the stool abandoned by the younger man and sank down. An expression of pain flitted across his face so fast, she wondered if she'd imagined it. "I am Shaman Marden. You already met my apprentice, Nath.

You are in the portion of the Dragon Spine mountain range some call the Tail."

He shrugged. "That is who and where we are." He smiled again. "And we want to help you."

"I've never been good at geography." Her scowl deepened. "Mom always says I'd get lost driving to the mall. We're on vacation on the coast at some cottage. But I never learned the names of any mountains nearby. Nothing you're saying is familiar. How far is it to the nearest town?"

"Oh, we are several days' walk from any Lowlander villages. Eya, that is why we wondered at your presence here."

"That's impossible." She straightened, her eyebrows rising in alarm. "Mom will be going spare. I have to get home."

"And we want to help you return. Be at peace now." He patted her hand, and a feeling of calm flowed over her. "Tell me what you recall of your journey here."

Jenny's eyelids drooped. "The last thing I remember . . ." Her eyes flew open. "The cave! Those sparkles . . ." Her memory of events remained murky. Something odd had happened. "I located a hidden passage . . ." She touched her injured ear, expecting to flinch—but she experienced no pain.

She patted harder and twisted it. *Nope, no cut.* Yet she would have sworn . . . Her fingers moved to her scalp. Hadn't she hit her head too? Hard?

Jenny shot a sharp glance at the old man. "That Nath guy, he said you fixed my injuries. How long have I been here? What did you do to me?"

The shaman blinked at the panic in her voice. "Did

you not wish to be healed? I apologize if I acted against your beliefs. I appreciate there are those who refuse magical assistance. However, it did not occur to us that you might be one."

"*Magic?*" she yelped. "Nobody said anything about magic! Don't be ridiculous. Just tell me where on Earth I am, and I'll figure the rest out myself."

His puzzled expression deepened.

Jenny's agitation grew, making her lash out. "Come off it. Our planet . . . you know, that blue ball circling the sun. We must still be in North America. So are we in Canada? Or the States? If you took me across the border, you'll be in big trouble. Kidnapping is a serious crime."

"We remain in the Kingdom of Galahar." He ignored her growing hysteria. "Though we are unable to ascertain which of the seven Lowlander territories you hail from. Anishinabe have limited dealings with outsiders."

Jenny frowned in confusion. He sounded sincere, yet his answer made no sense.

Seeing her bewilderment, he tried again. "I understand Lowlanders name us Mountain People." Marden gave her an encouraging smile. "This settlement is of the *Makwag*—what you would call Bear—tribe."

He shrugged. "However, I am not well-traveled and do not recognize the names you mentioned. As for magic . . ." He muttered, "*Waasaa,*" and gestured.

Some echo in the back of her mind that she refused to acknowledge whispered, *Light.*

A radiant ball popped into view. It hung in the air, brightening the chamber.

The old man smiled. "I would never lie about that."

She stared at him. *They're both delusional, him and*

the younger one. Though now that he'd pointed it out, Jenny saw similar orbs sitting in the room's far corners. They emitted a soft light. Suitable for a sick room, she supposed.

But she intended to find a logical explanation for everything she saw. Anyone would go a bit nutty living alone in the boonies. Perhaps these guys belonged to some survivalist camp hiding in the hills above the cottage. Well, if so, she would soon find a way to escape.

In the meantime, she would humor them and their fantasies.

Jenny returned to her initial question. "So, how did I end up here?"

The shaman, or whatever he called himself, seemed happy to answer her questions. Too bad the answers didn't make sense. "Why, as you told me yourself: through the gateway marked by the sparkles." He waved his hand again, and the ball of light vanished.

Jenny licked her lips, her eyes darting around him. "That's an excellent trick, but one any good magician can do." *Davy would be in his glory here,* she thought fleetingly.

But nineteen tended to be more skeptical than almost nine. She had no intention of falling for whatever sleight-of-hand tricks they decided to play on her.

A tickle of unease prickled her skin. Something about the brat . . .

Marden sat quiet, letting her proceed at her own pace. Jenny had never met anyone so still before. Yet that calm, unruffled manner, soft voice, and serene expression seemed familiar . . .

"Yoda!" She reddened as Marden's eyes widened in

surprise at her exclamation. "Sorry, that's who you remind me of."

He offered a polite smile. "This is a friend of yours?"

"No! *You* know . . . the Jedi Master. The movies? Mom loves Oz, but Dad preferred Star Wars. We must have watched the franchise a hundred times." She took in his baffled expression and sighed. "How long have you been living here?"

"I have lived in these mountains all my life." Marden tilted his head. "For the past one hundred five years, this village has been under my care."

Jenny made a rude noise, then blushed at his raised eyebrows. He did look really old, so she supposed it was possible. "Um, you look great for your age."

His eyes twinkled. "You misunderstand. Though I have been this village's shaman for over a century, I have seen three hundred fifty-two Name Days."

She gawked at him. "Birthdays, you mean?" *Does he really believe he's over three hundred fifty?*

"Birth days," Marden repeated with a radiant smile. "What a charming term. Is that what your people say?"

She refused to be sucked down another rabbit hole. *Damn it, magic and parallel worlds do not exist. Don't get caught up in their delusions.*

"Perhaps you might explain the purpose of this device." He laid an object on her knee.

12

"My cell!" Jenny grabbed it and pressed the power button. She half expected to find they'd tampered with it, but her password screen came right up. And her battery life still sat at 75%, though as she'd suspected, she got no signal.

She glanced around the room, noting the absence of electrical outlets. *Wow! Do they seriously have no juice at all? Even off-gridders have solar panels!*

"Sell? I do not wish to purchase the item." Marden sounded doubtful. "I only want to understand what its function is."

This surprised an uneasy laugh out of her. "Boy, you are out of touch. I guess you would say communication, for the most part. I just about live on mine." She frowned again at the lack of bars.

No movies, no TV, no electricity. But everyone recognized cell phones . . . didn't they? Perhaps they were homesteaders, living off the grid, rather than survivalists—but those guys always stockpiled tons of supplies . . . right?

"Ah!" Marden brightened. "Similar to a scrying mirror or dragon's scale."

Jenny stared. *And we're back to nuts.* "Okay, sure, like that."

Her hand crept up to her ear as she reached the only logical explanation for her healed injuries. "Seriously, how long have I been here?"

If she had been gone for a couple of hours, Mom might be annoyed. If she'd lost enough time for her cuts to heal, her mother would be worried sick.

The young guy, Nath, reentered the room before the shaman could respond, bearing a tray with bread, cheese, and fruit. Her eyes fixed on the food, and to her embarrassment, her stomach rumbled.

However, Nath must have overheard them talking, for he answered her question. "I found you yesterday, right around sunset, Jenny, and brought you here. You have been unconscious or asleep since then."

Focused on her meal, she only half listened, though she did like the little lilt he put in her name, pronouncing it *Jay-nee.* As he set the tray on her knees, she looked up, wondering about his accent. Their eyes met, and once again, she was struck by the kindness and warmth in his. She found it impossible not to trust him.

The old man's quiet cough interrupted them, and Nath pulled away with an awkward glance at his master. She dropped her embarrassed gaze to the food, grabbing a piece of bread and shoveling some into her mouth.

"OMG." Jenny stared at the remaining slice in her hand. "That's the best thing I've ever tasted." She grabbed a wedge of cheese, took a bite, followed by a swallow of warm milk, then closed her eyes, groaning with pleasure.

And then Nath's previous words sank in.

"Hold on." A patch of her foggy memory cleared, and she remembered Davy's voice calling, *"Wait for me."* "My bro—stepbrother, is he here too? Did he follow me?"

Marden's knowing glance marked her correction, but he shook his head. "Nath saw only you. He ran far into the night carrying you by the shortest path." His tone was sharp with disapproval as he glared at his apprentice. "A most dangerous journey in the dark. Anything might have happened." He turned back to her. "Perhaps the boy did not pursue you."

"Yeah, or maybe he followed me after you"—she waved at the younger man—"took me away." Jenny pushed the tray off her lap and flung the blankets aside. Both men averted their eyes as she swung her bare legs free of the bed. "He may have been sitting there alone ever since, waiting."

Nath nodded. "I will go check on him."

"I'm coming too."

He glanced back as she stood, the long gown falling to cover her feet.

When he opened his mouth to object, she overrode him. "He's my responsibility. Besides, you're a stranger; you might frighten him." She folded her arms across her chest and scowled. "I am going!"

He looked to Marden, who nodded. Nath sighed and shrugged his agreement. He motioned for her to follow him, leading her out into a short tunnel lined with those glowing orbs. Since she'd insisted, Jenny had no choice but to follow him as he turned right.

She assumed if they'd gone left, they would have reached the shaman's quarters or possibly a way out.

"Do not stray from the lit paths," he warned, pointing as they passed a dark opening. "We have many unused passages full of pits riddling these mountains."

She scuttled along behind him, the stone floor cold on her bare feet.

He guided her deeper into the mountain, stopping at a side chamber where water pooled in a large, deep tub.

"At the peak of summer, we enjoy bathing in the cooler waters. Of course, given the current weather, it would be too cold for that today."

"Of course," she mocked in a low murmur.

Nath shot her a startled glance, as if unused to being teased, and continued. "If you would like a bath, I can heat it for you."

Jenny shook her head, uneasy at the idea of being naked and vulnerable.

"Then I will bring a container full to your room and warm it for you. Once you have washed, dressed, and finished your meal, we may go." Nath grabbed a bucket, which he filled and set in the hallway to collect on his way back.

He led her farther down the tunnel. "This is the water closet." He opened a door to what she would have described as an indoor outhouse.

An open-bottomed chair covered a hole, and a pile of fresh leaves seemed to serve as toilet paper. It should have smelled dank and fusty, except herbs—hanging from the ceiling to dry—filled the air with a clean, spicy scent. He showed her a large barrel of dirt, miming sprinkling the latrine when done with one's business.

By the time he finished, these intimate instructions left them both red faced.

"Okay, what's down that tunnel?" She turned away, pointing to another lighted passageway.

"We share these amenities with our neighbors. If you hang this garland"—he pulled a wreath from the wall between the two rooms, which she'd assumed was a decoration, and placed it on a peg by the water closet—"it warns others the chamber is in use."

He paused. "Remember to leave the bracelet on, or you will not understand us." With a quick nod, he headed back the way they'd come, scooping up the bucket as he went.

When she returned to the bedchamber, someone had made the bed and laid out her clothing for her. The washbasin was full and the water hot, as Nath had promised. She clutched the neck of her gown and shot nervous glances over her shoulder, wishing for proper doors on their rooms instead of hanging blankets.

Jenny moved to the other doorway and peeked out. A second tunnel accessed a larger room, judging by the corner of an enormous fireplace. Murmurs echoed down the passageway. She recognized Nath and Marden's voices and experienced unexpected relief when a woman answered them. At least she wasn't the only female here.

She hurried to wash and dress, keeping one eye on the door curtain. Despite her concern for Davy, she enjoyed getting clean. She searched the room for her missing shoes but didn't find them. She did find Davy's minifig standing on a table and slipped it into her back pocket.

Turning her cell phone off, she slipped it into her other back pocket. She would check for a signal along the way and call home when she could. *In the meantime, I better save the battery.*

Jenny fidgeted with the bracelet but humored Nath by leaving it on. Unable to resist the food any longer, she returned to the abandoned tray.

None of this made any sense, but the boy took precedence. He might be a brat, but if he had followed her, he was her first priority. Frank could stick his jibs about her "irresponsible behavior" in his ear. If Davy was here, she'd find him, then sort out the rest.

Assuming she believed Marden—and somehow, she did not believe he'd lied—the largest inconsistency was how she had come to be several days' travel from home.

Jenny felt like she held the puzzle pieces. She just needed to make them fit together in a logical pattern. *I recall finding that cave . . . and hitting my head . . .* Her mind shied away from further memories, other than brief flashes of sparkles. The bare tail end of a daydream or nightmare . . . nothing more.

Anxious to search for Davy, Jenny crammed the last of the bread into her mouth and carried the tray down the hall to a small kitchen / living room arrangement. *Bet they call it a common room or something archaic like that,* she sniggered to herself.

But when she entered, the men sat at the table alone. She paused in the doorway as a little brown creature leaped and squealed, then vanished behind the fireplace. *A mouse, right?* she reassured herself. *I did not see a tiny . . . whatever . . . in a leaf robe and acorn cap. That would be impossible.*

Her hand went to her temple. *Perhaps I hit my head harder than I realized?*

Nath hurried to take her tray. Although he'd given her

back her clothes, he appeared flustered when she emerged wearing jeans, as if unused to women possessing legs.

Jenny gave him a distracted smile as she sat. "I heard a woman's voice."

"Oh yes, my auntie." He smiled with obvious affection. "You will meet her soon. She is the one who mended your clothing."

"Okay, but she didn't have to make my bed. I would have done it."

Marden chuckled. "Marta cooks for us, but 'tis the brownies that tend the house."

Jenny sighed. *Great, we're back with the fairies.*

Not wanting to argue, she offered a vague smile and stared around with interest. A structure built to cover the entrance surprised her. *Like that cave hotel we stayed at in Spain. They're set up to live here all year.*

A fireplace filled the center of the far wall, a cheery fire snapping and crackling on the grate. A pair of worn leather armchairs sat on either side, facing it. A black pot hung from a hook over the banked coals. The remaining furniture comprised a table, four chairs, a woven carpet, and a bench beside the door.

By now, her feet were freezing, and she kept lifting them off the cold floor. Convincing herself this was all a dream would be easier if everything didn't feel so damn real.

Nath fetched her shoes and socks, which sat drying on the hearth. "I must attend to other visitors. Please excuse me; I will return shortly." He disappeared, leaving her alone with the old man.

Marden seemed fascinated as he watched her put her

runners on. She shrugged off his comments about their ingenuity and his admiration for their Velcro straps.

Her hands stilled as another idea occurred to her. Might her end of the tunnel she'd discovered lead into that cavern he'd mentioned? The one where he'd found her? Was it possible her sudden appearance had sparked their belief in all that nonsense about doorways to other realms?

Jenny finished fastening her shoes. Maybe, but none of that mattered. If Davy had followed her, perhaps he still awaited her in the cave. Nath had to take her back there.

The shaman held up a large volume he'd been studying when she entered. He seemed concerned, tapping his fingers on the table and frowning down at the thick, leather-covered book.

"I have been seeking information on portals," the old man began. "There may be a serious issue—"

She stood up, cutting him off mid-sentence. "No time for that now. And it might be a moot point. If your portal is there, I'll go home." Her anxiety increased whenever she focused on Davy. If something happened to him, Frank would never forgive her. She needed to be sure he was safe.

Fortunately, Nath chose that moment to return. However, seeing Marden's posture, he grew still at once. His attentiveness to his master made her uneasy.

"We can discuss it later, all right?" Jenny gave them both a bright smile and motioned the younger man to lead the way.

Again, he waited for his master's reluctant nod before he moved. Nath's deference was getting on her nerves. Did he never think for himself?

He picked up a sack, threw some sort of blanket, or

ruana, over his shoulders, and selected a tall walking stick from a collection leaning against the wall by the doorway.

She tapped her hand on her leg, impatient to be off. At the door, Jenny glanced back. The old man watched her go, his expression troubled. A niggle of guilt poked at her. *I didn't need to be rude to him.*

But finding Davy was more important than good manners. If she ended up returning . . . well, she would deal with his delusions then.

She turned to survey the outside area, and her step-brother vanished from her mind. Her conviction that she wasn't far from home got a devastating blow, as she stared up . . . and the mountains swallowed everything else.

Jenny stood on a steep slope, surrounded by enormous peaks on every side that grew larger as they marched into the distance. This increase stunned her, as perspective demanded they decrease in size the farther they receded from her.

These resembled nothing she'd seen pictured on Earth. Confused and unsettled, she touched her head again.

What is this place?

Disoriented, she turned to speak to Nath, but he was gone. Jenny shaded her eyes and squinted. She located him talking to three children . . . except . . .

They all had beards—even the one with large breasts.

She squeezed her eyelids closed, and when she opened them, the small, sturdy figures were disappearing around the side of a hill. *And are those pickaxes on their shoulders?*

Nath rejoined her, and she pointed to where they'd been standing. "You have little people here?"

He frowned, following her finger. "Is that what Low-landers call dwarves? I am uncertain they would appreciate such a designation."

She held up her hand. "Nope. No more. I am officially done."

Jenny turned away, and other anomalies fought for her attention. Dozens of similar tiny huts sat tight against the surrounding inclines. She presumed they fronted other cave homes. Additional doors appeared to be set right into openings in the mountainside.

And then there were the people. The shaman and his apprentice weren't just a couple of recluses living in the backwoods.

A whole community lived here—all with straight, black hair that was shoulder length or longer, tanned copper skin, and the same odd clothing. Well, the men wore leather tunics, same as Nath and Marden. However, the women's long skirts—with bodices that tied up the front and shawls in every bright color of the rainbow—resembled costumes in a Shakespearean play. The children were little miniatures of their parents.

The scandalized stares the women threw at Jenny's jeans confirmed a suspicion that had lingered following Nath's reaction.

Fashion here did *not* include females wearing pants.

13

Jenny faced Nath, overwhelmed and struggling to make any of her theories fit the evidence before her eyes.

He led her toward a common area, where villagers ran forward to offer supplies—including more bread and cheese. One of the children even filled Nath's canteen from a nearby well. Another brought him an assortment of small stones. The apprentice chose a few, making a show of tucking them into a pouch on his belt.

The girl who provided them looked delighted and scampered off.

Before she could ask why he needed them, Nath touched Jenny's arm and pointed to an older woman hurrying toward them with a bundle of fabric in her hands. "Eya, I want you to meet someone special."

Reining in her impatience, she plastered a smile on her face.

"Auntie M is the one who tended your wounds and mended your clothes." He turned toward her. "Marta, this is *Jay-nee.*"

Nath's introduction took her by surprise, and Jenny burst out laughing.

"You're joking, right? Marden tries to tell me I arrived through some sort of wormhole, and then you come up with Aunt Em? Are you kidding me?" She waved her hand around the village. "Okay, definitely not in Kansas anymore."

The incomprehension on their faces annoyed her. "Go on, everyone knows that story. L. Frank Baum? Over the rainbow, and all that? It's Mom's favorite book, and she makes me watch the movie, like, twice a year."

Jenny rolled her eyes. "And each time she points out that they changed the silver slippers to ruby so they'd show up better on the big screen, and that nobody remembers Dorothy says that line about Kansas twice in the film, although it wasn't even in the novel."

Nath frowned, so she sighed and turned politely to face the woman. "Um, thank you for mending my clothes. You did a great job."

"You look a sight perkier than when I last saw you, eya." Marta smiled, handing her the bundle of knit wool fabric she'd brought. Pastel colors swirled like clouds: pale pink, soft blue, faded yellow.

Jenny gasped in delight as she shook the ruana out. "It's beautiful."

Auntie M beamed, showing her how the front half of the long rectangle split up the middle.

"My mom has one of these, but hers isn't as pretty." Jenny twirled the wrap around her shoulders, snuggling into its warmth, before impulsively hugging Marta.

Pleased, the older woman laughed. "You visit me anytime you tire of those two great lugs, eya? I be right interested to hear about your world." Without waiting for a response, she nodded and bustled off.

Nath proceeded through the village, greeting people along the way. Some of Jenny's former impatience returned. The sooner she found Davy, the less trouble she'd face at home, where she expected to get blamed for this little adventure. She grimaced, not even wanting to imagine Frank's reaction.

She amused herself watching how many young women went out of their way to intercept Nath's path. Although the apprentice smiled politely at them, she found it odd that he didn't encourage any of them. His reserved responses made her smirk. Perhaps he was just shy. But they weren't making very quick progress leaving the village.

Jenny had the sudden sensation of being watched—which was ridiculous, with the villagers all openly gaping at her. Uneasy, she glanced around and saw a beautiful woman about a year or two her senior. Her dark hair was gathered into a single thick braid, and she stood a few feet away, frowning at Jenny.

Anger flashed in the young woman's dark eyes as they flicked from Jenny's new wrap to her face and back down.

Jenny nudged Nath. "Who's that?"

Although people surrounded them, he seemed to understand who she meant. His lips thinned. "Polina, Marta's granddaughter," he said shortly, returning his attention to the children.

Ah, I bet she expected to receive it as a gift on her next . . . Name Day. That explained her bitter stare anyway. How kind of Marta to give a stranger something so precious—although her granddaughter didn't appear to share the sentiment.

It didn't help that the lovely woman's rounded curves made Jenny all too aware of her wiry runner's frame.

Self-conscious now, she ran a hand down her beautiful ruana and tucked an unruly short, blonde curl behind her ear—drawing Polina's narrowed eyes to Jenny's wrist.

Jenny tried a sympathetic smile, but Polina sniffed. She leaned toward the girl beside her, making a show of pointing at Jenny, gesturing at her short curls and whispering an aside that sent a flood of giggles through the others.

Nath caught the incident. He gave the jealous woman a hard stare, and she reddened. Undeterred, she muttered a few more words. Whatever she added shocked those listening. Then she stuck her nose in the air and flounced away.

I've never seen anyone flounce before. Jenny stifled a smirk. *Maybe it's the clothes; you can't do proper flouncing without long skirts.* She grew wistful as she viewed the whispering girls. *It doesn't look like I'll be making friends with them.*

As the muttering spread to their mothers, she moved closer to Nath's side. Several of the women watched her with narrowed eyes, though some faces appeared more concerned than judgmental.

She tugged on his arm. "Is it my pants? My short hair? What's their problem?" She jerked her chin in the villagers' direction.

Nath tilted his head, a gesture that reminded her of the old shaman. He stared at the disapproving expressions of the older women, then comprehension dawned on his face.

He turned toward her, dismayed. "That is not the issue. It disturbs them that I am accompanying you."

Confused, Jenny frowned. "You're the only one who knows where my stepbrother might be. Don't they want you to help me?"

"That is not their concern. They fear for your reputation." Nath reddened. "We are an unwed couple going into the mountains together. And we are likely to be gone overnight."

He cast a helpless look around. "Perhaps we should ask Polina"—Jenny gave him a look—"or one of the other girls," he hurried to add, "to accompany us. To chaperone."

Her frown deepened as he struggled to explain. "If you belonged to our tribe, your father would forbid this trek alone with me."

Jenny didn't bother concealing her annoyance. "First, we are not a couple. Second, I've been living on my own at university for two years. And third, I am not one of your people."

She held her temper with difficulty. "Among my . . . tribe, I am an adult and quite capable of making my own decisions!" She lifted an eyebrow. "I can certainly control myself. Should I be worried about you?"

"Of course not," Nath spluttered. "I would never—"

Jenny took pity on him, cutting him off. "Good. I guess we don't have a problem, do we?" He looked dazed as he shook his head and led the way past the curious villagers.

She was pleased to find the younger men showed less prejudice toward her than the women had. They touched fingers to foreheads, nodding with shy smiles as she passed.

However, Polina, making sure she stayed in full view

of their visitor, glared at her as they walked the entire length of the village.

Jenny's tight smile gave warning as she tilted her face toward Nath. "Is there any reason for her to assume you and she are an item?"

He seemed startled by her directness but firmly shook his head. "I never courted her nor paid her more attention than any of the others."

She smothered a giggle at his old-fashioned wording.

"However," he continued with obvious reluctance, "she likes to imagine there may be something between us one day, because her grandmother takes care of the shaman and me."

Jenny sighed. Okay, not her problem. She waved him onward, breathing easier once the crest of a hill hid the settlement from view.

"How much farther?" she asked an hour later. Despite a chill breeze, the warm sun and exercise made her hot. She gasped for breath from the steep climb, irked he didn't seem the least bit winded.

"Another three hours." His long legs covered the ground quickly, and she half ran to keep up. Nath noticed her struggling and slowed to match her pace. "Perhaps four."

She gave him a sharp look, and he grinned. Her lips twitched as she tried to suppress a return smile.

When they approached a particularly steep section, he moved ahead. As she scrambled up the loose shale behind him, her feet slid out from under her. Nath reached back and grabbed her hand, steadying her before she could tumble backward.

Jenny let out a breathless laugh. "Thanks!"

As they walked, he told her he'd been born in the village, which at least explained his lack of knowledge about the modern world. She wondered how long they'd hidden in these mountains, and probed for inconsistencies, hoping to trip him up. It was no use. She grudgingly concluded he believed everything he said, no matter how outlandish.

"Marden took me in as his apprentice when I turned twelve." He glanced back over his shoulder. "I have served him for thirty years now."

Jenny tripped, gawking at him. "Are you seriously claiming you're over forty?"

Nath shrugged. "Magic use slows one's aging. I may look eighteen, but I have celebrated forty-two Name Days."

She retreated into silence. Even if she couldn't explain some of the surrounding anomalies, that didn't mean she was ready to buy into all their magical mumbo jumbo.

He suggested stopping, but Jenny resisted, impatient to reach their destination. By midmorning, however, her legs ached from the unaccustomed climb. When Nath announced a halt for something he called nooning, she was grateful to rest, and she couldn't suppress a moan as she lowered herself to the ground.

Running and climbing use very different muscles—or I'm more out of shape than I realized! She tried to recall when she'd last gone jogging. With all the rain they'd experienced during their "holiday" at the cottage, she figured it must have been at least a week—plus however-many days since she'd ended up here.

Despite the proof provided by the village's existence and the length of this hike, Jenny persisted in clinging to the hope that she'd wandered into their cave network from that little side passage. If the shamans deluded themselves about *how* she had arrived, perhaps they'd also misjudged *when.* That would explain her "miraculous" healing.

Which left Davy wandering the tunnels, or alone on the mountainside, since who knew when. Her stomach clenched, and she bit her lip. *Poor kid. He must be scared stiff.*

Nath distracted her from her circling thoughts by sitting beside her, pulling food from the bag he'd carried all morning, and handing her the canteen. They drank from the same flask, Jenny sternly repressing all concerns about germs. She nibbled some bread, but between the big breakfast and her concern for her stepbrother, she could not manage much.

As they sat, her body stiffened, and when it was time to go, she found standing difficult. She groaned in pain, and Nath moved behind her. He paused, wordlessly asking permission before he touched her. She assumed he intended to rub her neck, so she shrugged and nodded, accepting the intimacy.

To her surprise, he just rested his hands on her shoulders. Startled, Jenny looked around at his closed eyes. He mumbled something halfway between a song and a chant, and warmth passed down her body. When he stepped away, her muscles no longer hurt.

She turned, wide-eyed. He ducked his head, smiled

shyly, and walked ahead. She hesitated before stumbling after him.

The sun clung to the treetops like a rebellious child refusing to go to bed by the time they reached the entrance to a large cavern. At first, it appeared much the same as others they'd passed. Yet something about this one seemed . . . off. It made the hair on her arms prickle.

Ignoring Nath's suggestion that she wait outside, Jenny followed him in.

Gloom enveloped her, the atmosphere more dismal than she'd expected, though a faint glow from lichen-covered walls surprised her. "Where did you find me?" she whispered. It felt like the sort of place one stayed quiet. As if there might be . . . something . . . listening.

He held up a torch she hadn't noticed him lighting. The first chamber appeared empty, except for the stubs of broken mushroom stems sticking out of the ground.

Nath nodded at an opening ahead of them and murmured, "In there."

He took the lead again, and she followed. The largest mushrooms she'd ever seen filled the second space. He bent down to retrieve a bag. The way he kept eyeing a side passage made her nervous, but when she checked that tunnel, it ended in another dead end.

So much for her theory about linked caves.

In accordance with his account of events, she saw an unlit torch laying on the ground and the cut mushrooms that had spilled from his dropped sack when he caught her.

Jenny lifted her chin, ignoring this evidence. His stuff on the floor proved nothing; he might have arranged that. Although offhand, she couldn't think of any reason why he would.

Her obstinance weakening, she recalled the odd vegetation she'd refused to acknowledge on their way here. True, she possessed minimal knowledge about plants and herbs, but shouldn't she recognize *something*? She'd never seen hot-pink dandelion fluff before!

And what about those impossible mountains? And the way he'd healed her aches?

What if Marden's claim . . . ?

No! Don't be ridiculous! I'm being influenced by mass hypnosis or self-delusion or a similar phenomenon.

Jenny shouted, "DAVY!"

Nath winced as her voice echoed through the cavern. Whispered reverberations came back, lingering and repeating longer than she expected.

She spun in a circle, checking every corner. If the brat had followed her here, he hadn't hung around.

And, she thought sarcastically, *if some sparkling mystical object brought us here . . . it's vanished as well, leaving no indication it ever existed.*

14

By nooning, the Kin were halfway up the mountain whose peaks harbored their aeries. Their home remained hidden from view, concealed by banks of clouds.

As they soared higher, Davint leaned forward to whisper, "You know, flying with you like this is almost too easy." Her sensitive ears caught his murmurs, and his warm breath against her scaled neck made her shiver. "You're so steady, I may as well be sitting on the ground."

Lauran suspected he meant it as a compliment but didn't care for his comparison. *[Oh, is that so?]* Her words dripped with mock offense. *[I'll have to make it more interesting for you, then.]*

With an impish growl, she veered sharply to the left, banking into a tight turn that made Davint cling to her back.

His laughter mingled with the rush of wind.

[Careful now, don't lose your grip,] she taunted, her voice laced with amusement as she righted their course. Glancing over her shoulder, she caught his grin.

"Never mind me. I can handle anything you throw at me." His tone dared her to try again.

[Are you challenging me, my dear rider?] Lauran chuckled, a deep rumble that vibrated through her chest.

"Perhaps." A smirk played on his lips. "Though I warn you, I'm not one to back down."

[Well, then, challenge accepted.]

With a swift flick of her powerful wings, she plunged into a steep dive, hurtling toward the earth below with breathtaking speed. Davint whooped, gripping tighter and urging her on.

[Will you two please save your flirting for another time?] Her father's irritated voice cut their fun short, and the embarrassed pair circled back to rejoin their smirking companions.

The weary delegation arrived on the ledge of Ganther's cavern in the early afternoon. Riders dismounted, moving aside to allow room for the others to land. The air around the five dragons shimmered, as their enormous bodies underwent their remarkable transformations.

Unfazed by their nudity, the newly shifted Kin collected tunics from a row of pegs filled with similar garments to ward off the chill of the damp mountain aerie.

It pleased Lauran to be back in human form—and since they'd landed in her father's lair, clothes that fit her. Her short robe, with its plunging neckline, left just enough to the imagination. She noticed Davint's gaze lingering on her shapely legs and hid a satisfied smile.

She moved deeper into the cavern, slipping through a side entrance draped with heavy tapestry and down a twisting tunnel designed to thwart any winds curling through the open mouth of the aerie. It opened into a vast gathering hall, broad enough to host a dozen towering Kin.

Pale, glowing lichen etched the walls like miniature trees, casting a muted luminosity; sufficient enough to reveal the banked oil lamps hanging at intervals around the perimeter of the room. The others crowded in behind her.

Ganther called for their attention. "You all did an excellent job." He avoided looking at Zyre as he made this claim, and she exchanged grins with Marissa. "I must report to Maxim, but then we celebrate. Everyone, grab something to eat and bring it back here in an hour. Our *dragons*, at least, will be hungry after a sojourn with the Lowlanders' hospitality."

Laughter and growls of agreement met his sarcasm.

Lauran stayed quiet, having found the castle staff most generous in their estimates of what a dragon ate. She and the others might not have shared the fancy meals their riders indulged in, but the succulent meat provided them had dripped with blood and juice.

Just thinking about it made her mouth water. *I think there's time to hunt for my contribution to the feast.*

The others brought so much food, Lauran decided to wait and bring out her raw, bloody tahr after they'd finished. When she did, the women declined to indulge.

Undeterred, the men transformed, devouring the meat as if they were starving and hadn't just eaten. The drakes shifted back to human form, groaning and rubbing their bulging stomachs as they slipped their tunics on. She and her friends teased them for their gluttony.

The sun's long rays reached into Ganther's cave by the time everyone had eaten and drunk their fill.

"Here now," Dram called. "Let's have a peek at those baubles the duke gave you." He winked at Lauran. "You might have mentioned your dragons liked jewelry too."

Shouts of laughter met his teasing, although Zyre scowled as if taking his words to heart. The others soon busied themselves passing around the faux riders' medallions and admiring their delicate beauty. Designed to mimic wizards' crystals—though significantly larger—each displayed an ornate silver filigree holding a faceted gem in place.

As she stood close to a group examining one, Lauran rolled her head back against her hunched shoulders and rubbed the base of her neck, trying to ease an odd tension riding there.

A snippet of conversation caught her attention. Zyre had sidled over to flash his sapphire pendant at Kellin and Staton. "Pretty trinkets are all well and good, but a real leader would have gotten a better deal out of the old man. And notice who snagged the choicest gift." The younger Kin looked uncomfortable and wouldn't meet his eyes.

Lauran glared at the gray-skinned man. Her father had done an excellent job, and no one—especially not Zyre—could have done better. She caught his eye, and he broke off, sitting back with an unrepentant sneer.

She rolled her eyes, turning around in time to witness Ganther presenting Marissa with his medallion. *Well, I guess she's succeeding faster than I expected.* The dark green of the emerald matched her friend's eyes. Lauran smiled, pleased for them both.

Davint came over and took her arm before she could

join them, drawing her away from the group. "I want you to have this." He slipped the chain of his own medallion over her head.

His closeness startled her, and after a quick glance at his face, she looked down, admiring the pendant. She was delighted by his generosity and its implications.

"Are you sure?" Lauran turned it, appreciating the way its blood-red ruby caught the light. She'd never seen a perfect gem as large as this one.

"Of course." He snorted at her instant possessiveness. "I understand how much you wanted to explore the Lowlanders' castle. It's not fair you didn't get to. Next time, you can be the rider, no matter which of us draws a white stone."

Her eyes sparked yellow, thrilled by the suggestion that they would be paired on future outings. She found him kind, fun, and gentle, and she cared for him.

So why was she hesitating? Why not just tell him how she felt?

I refuse to be rushed; after all, I'm only one hundred thirteen. I am not ready to be tied down.

She kept her gaze lowered, admiring the ruby. The gem shimmered, reflecting the flickering firelight. There seemed to be hints of hidden depths inside it.

Lauran smiled, remembering their playful flight. She pictured the jewel resting against her scales as she soared beside Davint, imagining what it would be like to finally be together.

Perhaps they'd start in dragon form, since flying was almost as exhilarating as sex. *I'll tease and mock him for being too slow as I head straight up into the sky. We'll race above the clouds until the air grows rarified—even for dragons. We might circle, tantalize, swoop, and play, an intricate dance of togetherness.*

As I tire—she smirked—or pretend to, I'll slip closer, and he may seize my talons in his. Wrapping our wings around each other, we can plummet toward the ground.

At the last moment, Davint should flare his pinions to catch the wind in his wings and land us at his aerie. But dragon mouths aren't made for kissing, so our eyes locked as we change, we will transform in unison . . .

Perhaps he'll cup my breasts, maybe lean down and brush my nipples with his tongue, before pulling me closer. Lauran's breath caught as heat surged through her. The flush of sensation made her shiver, as if in anticipation of his touch.

With our naked bodies pressed together; we'll share a slow, hungry kiss. After he scoops me up in his arms, he'll carry me into his inner chamber—

A low growl made her start. She looked up, suddenly reminded of where she was.

Davint stared at her, his eyes whirling red with desire.

A deep blush burned from her chest to her forehead. Mortified, she realized he'd received part of her erotic daydream—or at least *sensed* the lust behind it. She turned and bolted across the room, pushing her way past the other Kin as she headed for the tunnel.

Bursting out into the launching chamber, Lauran shimmered as she ran, stretching her neck and slimming her body as she'd practiced. She oozed out of the wide collar of her tunic, expanding and morphing into her dragon form outside her clothes.

She had hoped to impress Davint with the maneuver, but now she rushed through the change, fleeing from him in embarrassment. Her throat and head widened, and she suffered a sudden sharp bite around her neck as the chain tightened.

Oh no, I forgot about the medallion.

Lauran resisted the urge to look back. She couldn't face Davint.

Metal rained to the ground, accompanied by a tinkle and sharper clink from the pendant. Her tunic fell to the floor as her body convulsed, wrenching itself through the change.

A searing burn at the base of her throat made her gasp. The scorching intensified, until she cried out against the pain.

She halted her frantic rush, catching herself on the lip of the outcropping, whimpering. Tears streamed down her scaled cheeks, forming viscous pools at her feet as she finally turned.

Davint pushed the tapestry aside and rushed toward her. "Don't cry; I can fix the chain. Please stop crying. It will be all right."

She shook her head, in too much torment to speak. He didn't understand. Her suffering increased, twisting tighter, sharp and sickening. The pressure building inside her chest threatened to split it open, and the pain was becoming unbearable. With a roar of anguish, Lauran hammered her ribs with massive forepaws, then collapsed to the floor.

The others exited the tunnel and stood staring at her trembling form crouched in the aerie's entrance.

Unnerved by her distress, Davint tried to move closer, but her body writhed in agony, her lashing tail keeping him at bay.

Callie stooped and picked up the broken medallion, frowning as she held it up. "The ruby's fallen out."

Ganther lumbered over, glowering at the two of them. "What's happening? What did you do to my daughter?"

Zyre looked around for the missing gemstone as Davint protested his innocence.

Again, something twisted inside Lauran. It moved deeper, tearing through muscle and tissue—unnatural and relentless. She gasped, staggering on trembling limbs.

Each new onslaught brought fresh suffering and disorientation. With a growl of frustration, she forced herself to focus. Though her body trembled, she grew still, and as she did, Lauran made the connection between her torture and the ruby's disappearance.

[It's here.] She pointed a talon at her chest. *[FA-THER, pay attention! It is inside me. Davint didn't do anything wrong. Somehow, the ruby is trapped within me.]*

She tried shifting back to human form, hoping to separate herself from the jewel.

Nothing happened.

Stunned, Lauran tried again. She put her entire will into the transformation, struggling to control her shift, fighting against unseen bonds that made a prison of her own body.

But her efforts proved useless. She remained trapped in dragon form.

[I CAN'T CHANGE!]

Her frantic *sending* made everyone turn toward her in alarm.

Panting, Lauran tried to push through the agony. As the sharp-edged ruby penetrated deeper within her, each advance heightened her excruciating pain. She gave a thankful moan when the gemstone stopped moving. Her anguish eased, replaced by a burning ache.

As she regained a scrap of control, she experienced a subtle pulsing emanating from the cursed jewel inside her.

15

G anther stared at Lauran as she stood trembling, her forepaws pressing against the pain in her chest. He took in the broken chain in Davint's hand and the pendant missing its ruby. He reached out and touched her mind, reading her knowledge.

Though he couldn't fathom how, he understood what had happened. "Get them off."

Heads swung his way, surprised and questioning.

He raised his voice. "The pendants. Take them off. NOW!"

Ganther's thoughts touched them, and the others understood. He rushed to the shelves on a side wall and grabbed a small chest. He opened the lid and held it out to the other Kin. Most of those wearing the duke's gifts hurried to remove the chains, dropping the medallions inside as if they were red hot.

Zyre hung back, his hand clutching his pendant. When Ganther frowned impatiently, the gray-skinned man reluctantly lifted it over his head, dangled it over the open box, and slowly deposited the sapphire medallion inside.

Ganther closed the box. Frowns eased as they lowered their shoulders, stretching and twisting their necks. He caught Lauran's suspicion that they'd all been suffering the same tension she'd noticed in herself earlier.

Marissa rested a hand on Ganther's arm. "I feel different . . . better. Is that chest silver?"

He nodded, raising his heavy brows. "Yes. And it seems to stop whatever energy these gems are giving off. That might be helpful . . ."

Zyre interrupted, that ever-present sneer marring his face. "How can we be certain it isn't just her?" He flicked a careless hand at the golden dragon.

Davint's soft snarl made the gray-skinned man take a nervous step backward.

Ganther's eyes narrowed. His voice remained calm despite the rage building inside him. "That's a good point. Why don't you put one of the pendants on and attempt a shift? That way, we can be certain it affects all of us."

Zyre scowled, looking away as Davint snorted.

Ganther nodded. "Then we'll assume the spell applies to any Kin." He stared at his daughter. "But only in our dragon form."

Catching Lauran's thought that the irritation they'd all experienced from the toxic jewels affected even those already shifted to human form, the green man gave her an impatient frown. "To fix this, we need to trace the source of this jewelry."

Ganther gave the chest a rough shake, and a chatter of metal protested. "So our first step is a return visit to Duke Almar. We must discover where he acquired them."

His rising fury started affecting the group. "Let us hope he didn't realize the effect they would have—our shifting abilities are a secret, after all—but if he did . . ." His lips tightened as his voice trailed off in a low growl, echoed by those surrounding him, even Zyre.

Struggling to control his anger, Ganther set the box back on the shelf.

His fear over what had happened to his daughter was exacerbated by his disdain for Lowlanders. The brief time he'd spent in their company couldn't eradicate that.

Lauran's eyes whirled orange like the others. He'd tried his best to teach her control, to be slow to show anger. Being larger and deadlier than everyone else, Kin learned caution from the egg. But once roused, their explosive wrath left little standing. Their inner dragons took over, becoming single-minded with destructive determination.

This outrage could not stand. He had to express the fury gripping him.

Ganther's whirling red eyes met each of theirs, drawing them in. Their outrage fed and built on his, like a fire. One after another, their orange eyes deepened, flaring crimson in response.

"Come on," he snarled, and the others responded to his command with low, vicious growls. "Let's go get some answers."

Without waiting for their shouts of agreement, Ganther leaped from the ledge, shifting to his green-scaled dragon form in midair.

Lauran moved to the side as their Wing jostled for

position; the cave filled with enormous dragons eager to follow her father.

Only Zyre hung back. "We should take this with us," he suggested, retrieving the silver chest.

No one argued.

Quickly shifting, he launched himself after the green dragon, chest clutched in his front talons.

The others rushed after them. Their incensed minds joined and solidified their intent in a typhoon of anger, which roared through their ranks, consuming them.

I have to clear my head . . . Lauran struggled against her father's influence. *Gotta remain in control . . . need to recall something important . . .*

Davint shifted into his drake form but hung back, waiting until she moved forward to join him on the out-cropping before launching.

With her father already some distance away, the influence of his stronger mind eased. More objective thoughts pulled at her as the cloud of emotion thinned. Something bothered her—besides the ruby inside her. But with Ganther clouding her mind, she couldn't analyze the situation.

Some buried instinct urged her to call the others back. Yet how would she explain this impression of dread when she didn't understand its cause?

Not seeing another option, Lauran leaped into the air after Davint.

She gave a terrible roar of pain as she stretched her pinions and pumped her wings up and down. Every movement caused her chest muscles to twist around the sharp gemstone, producing agonizing stabs deeper inside her body each time she flapped. How could she fly without using her wings?

Lauran fell behind as she struggled to find a comfortable method of flight. She soon settled for gritting her teeth and flying upward at a steep angle. When the torment became unbearable, she spread her vast wingspan wide and glided straight ahead for as long as possible, trying to slow her descent to the ground.

Davint circled protectively, matching her slower pace. The last to leave the cavern, this restricted style of flight further slowed their progress. Yet as the distance from her father increased, her mind cleared and her reservations about their actions intensified.

Davint drew closer. He looked concerned, *sensing* her suffering and confusion.

To distract them both, she reached out, struggling to define her misgivings. *[We shouldn't rush into this. Perhaps we should have spoken with Maxim . . .]*

Her eyes widened as the cause of her unease finally rose above her pain. *[We're in dragon form! All of us. A thunder of dragons charging in! If we change shape in front of them, we'll expose our shifting to the Lowlanders. The Alpha has forbidden sharing our secret. We have to stop my father before he defies that edict.]*

She *sensed* Davint's shock as his blood cooled and his mind cleared too. He *shared* his agreement. Lauran tried to increase her speed, but the pain became too intense.

Alarmed, he moved closer, but she shook her head. *[You've got to reach Ganther. You must make him see reason before he gets us all banished. If he wants to confront the duke, he needs to do it in human form. Those becoming riders will require clothes, so I'll return for a travel bag.]*

Though she *sensed* his reluctance to leave her, he

didn't have a better plan. With a distressed glance at her over his shoulder, he sped away.

A few powerful wingbeats later, he disappeared.

She turned her aching body toward her father's aerie and struggled back to their starting point.

Lauran gripped the travel bag in her hind talons, grateful they hadn't yet had a chance to unpack from their trip. At least she didn't need to dig through Ganther's belongings and try to fill a sack with clothes using her forepaws and claws.

Clenching her teeth so hard her jaw hurt, she beat her wings. After a few strokes, she admitted defeat and held herself in a glide. She opened her mind, straining to listen for the group ahead, squinting to see them with the setting sun in her eyes.

A sudden familiar outburst of annoyance and anger told her when Davint confronted her father. Ganther might be strong, but the younger drake showed great determination.

It took some persuading, which gave Lauran a chance to draw closer. She sensed the group's fury fading to a more controlled indignation as Davint's reasoning got through.

Her anxiety lightened, somehow making the pain easier to bear.

When half the thunder volunteered to act as riders, she swelled with pride at their ability to control their passions. She crooned her approval as the volunteers soared above their partners, shifted to human form in midair, and dropped onto the backs of the hovering dragons below.

She closed the distance between them during this maneuver. As they continued westward, she tried to alert them to her presence. Seeing them slow and begin circling near the top of a mountain, she inferred they awaited clothes for the naked Kin.

But as she approached, Lauran found their attention fixed on the opposite slope. Her enhanced eyesight picked out a group of men huddled among the rocks.

Are the Lowlanders under the impression they're being attacked? Can't they see we're unarmed? Why aren't they listening to the riders calling to them?

Her bewilderment turned to horror as a cloud of projectiles shot upward at the hovering dragons, causing them to scatter.

As the soldiers rose to fire another round of arrows, she recognized their uniforms.

Why are Duke Almar's men shooting at us?

Most of them huddled behind boulders, but one man stood alone amid the cowering militia. The presence of the court sorcerer added to the puzzle.

She flew closer, finding her slow speed infuriating. Dragons dived and wove among the spears and arrows. Those playing riders hunched low on their backs, calling for the men to stop firing.

It seemed incredible that no one was injured yet. But Lauran feared what might happen if her father lost his temper again. Were the Lowlanders prepared to stand against dragonfire?

Surrounded by soldiers, Shifton held a long stick with elaborate carvings in his hand. It was thick at either end but tapered in the center where he gripped it, and he pointed the strange device at one dragon after another. Whatever result he expected, his obvious frustration showed in the way he shouted and leaped about.

Lauran's breath caught. Marissa was dodging an arrow, unaware of a spear being thrown at her.

Lauran bugled a warning, and the black dragon managed an awkward twist that almost dislodged her rider, Ganther. Though the kill shot missed its mark, it pierced Marissa's thigh. The wounded Kin screamed, and Ganther cried out in unison.

Another soldier stood to take aim at her. Lauran watched the second spear release. As if in slow motion, she dived, calculating its angle of ascent. If unchecked, it would shear through her friend's shoulder joint and pierce Ganther, more vulnerable in his human form.

She flung herself into the spear's path. The lance pierced the taut membrane of Lauran's wing.

At that same moment, the sorcerer pointed his stick at her.

A shriek of pain froze in her throat. Her eyes flew wide as he shifted the rod and her immobilized body followed where he gestured.

16

A dart of fear pierced Lauran's rigid figure as she stared down at Shifton's gloating red face.

With her wings already spread, she managed a rough landing where his magic forced her down on a tiny plateau amid the soldiers. She struggled but lacked any control over her frozen body while he pointed that rod at her. The spear dangling from the cut about halfway down her wing, beside the center finger joint, flapped around, tearing at the delicate membrane.

Lauran almost fainted when the lance jostled free upon impact. *He wants a dragon for some reason.* Pain from her injury throbbed in unison with the burning in her chest. Tears leaked down her frozen cheeks. *And now he's captured me!*

He was so much smaller than her, Lauran had to strain downward to keep him in view as he pranced in front of her. Legs spread for balance, she'd managed to come to rest on her hindquarters and tail, forearms in the air, frozen with her injured wing stretched out to one side.

Unable to turn her head, she rolled her eyes up enough to catch sight of the others escaping over the crest of the mountain, toward home.

Shocked to discover she could no longer *hear* or *sense* them, her attempts to mind-call reached no further than her own ears. No matter how she fought to snap and snarl, she remained silent, immobilized.

Shifton retrieved her dropped bag and stalked forward with a smile. "My, aren't you a pretty thing? The duke *will* be pleased." He scanned the sky, frowning. "Though I'd hoped more of your kind would succumb to the jewels."

Apparently unable to resist boasting, he met her glare with a triumphant smirk. "At first, I thought to rely on your renowned dragon greed. But I decided to speed things up with an addiction spell. It's rather ingenious, actually. The longer the holder wears the gems, the less likely they are to recall even having them on."

He shrugged. "It appears you're more resistant to my spells than I'd hoped, since I only caught *you*. But one is all I require. For now." Her glare seemed to amuse him.

"So, what have we here?" He opened her discarded travel bag. "Clothing? Why would a dragon need clothes?" He chuckled, as if he'd made a joke.

"You may be aware I am . . ." His mouth worked for a moment. "Warlock Shifton," he forced through gritted teeth.

A warlock? Her heart stopped, then began pounding. *Why is a dark wizard interested in capturing a Kin?* Lauran's vivid imagination churned out one horrible suggestion after another. He could use the healing ability of her blood in spells, make relics from her bones, employ her scales for communication—not to mention profit. And if he could control her, he'd have power enough to blacken a territory.

Perhaps he suspected her dread. "Oh, you have nothing to fear. I won't harm you." He waved a dismissive hand. "It's a living dragon we want, not pieces of it."

She didn't trust the sly sideways glance he gave her.

"No, we need you in this form. *Not* pretending to be human." The warlock nodded in satisfaction when her eyes widened in shock. "Oh yes, I am well aware of your little pretense. How you hide your animal shapes. The gall—assuming you're the equal of humans."

Equal! Lauran fumed. *Far superior, if you ask me. We would never pretend to be friends with someone, only to betray them the moment it suits us.* Her heart sank. *How could he know about the Kin? Who has he told?*

The warlock, caught up in his own rhetoric, ignored her pathetic attempts to project scorn. He strode back and forth, unable to resist bragging to a—literal—captive audience. "You don't understand what I've sacrificed for this knowledge. No one else has the capacity to achieve what I have."

Shifton faced her. Even frozen, Lauran's skepticism finally managed to pierce his self-importance. He scowled. "Bah, I'll show you. I will prove everyone wrong." He lifted the thick rod. "Those cowards at the Citadel do not recognize the power I can access."

Lauran stared as he raised the heavy stick in front of her. The intricate carvings were more detailed than her initial impression had suggested. Lines of color led to exquisite miniature jewels set into the wood. Words and patterns intertwined everywhere, except where he held it at the unadorned, narrowed center. It glowed with inner power, beautiful and mesmerizing.

Evil warped the surrounding air, causing a shiver of revulsion to ripple across her scales. Enthralled, she found it impossible to look away.

Shifton waved the rod, and his abrupt action broke its thrall. With a grateful exhale, she closed her eyes—the only part of her she seemed able to move.

"It's curious, though. If you're not wearing the medallion, then how am I controlling you?" He eyed her speculatively, then stepped into the shadow of her massive head. Her forearms hung useless in the air, quivering as she felt him reach up and press his hand to her chest.

Everything within her rebelled at his touch. Though she was frozen, the scales beneath his fingers gave a faint, involuntary rasp—like teeth clacking in a cold wind.

Shifton stepped back into view and opened his eyes. "Oh, this surpasses my expectations. At least where shifters are concerned." His lips pulled back in a triumphant smile. "I hoped for control, but this . . . this is exquisite."

He waved his free hand. "As soon as I figure out another delivery system, I will create my own army of obedient servants—dragons, trolls, giants—and Galahar will kneel before me."

Lauran kept her eyes averted, not wanting to lose what little autonomy she still possessed. With rising anger, she forced herself to focus on every word, desperate to discover something useful in his ranting. *He doesn't even know what this . . . thing . . . he's created is capable of!*

"The Kin's shifting abilities gave me a path to deliver my bespelled gems. I'll need to create alternate methods to control other races."

She fought against the pull of the engraved rod, feeling the answering call from the ruby inside her, attacking her will.

He half turned, letting the stick dangle at his side, hidden from sight by his leg. If she'd been able to, she would have sagged with relief.

"I expected you, as you saw, but it wouldn't have mattered if you failed to come."

Shifton nodded in satisfaction at the questioning glance she was unable to resist. "Yes. This magic rod allows me to track my gemstones. I can find them anywhere. And once they penetrate a host, it's an easy matter to track my creatures down too. You'll never hide from me again!"

No! That makes me a danger to my people. I can't return home; I'll lead him right to them. Appalled, the remaining bespelled jewels filled her thoughts. Would the silver box be enough to stop Shifton's magic from locating them?

The warlock paced in front of her and continued his boasting. "The longer you are near the rod, the more control it gains. After a full day, you'll be mine completely, and you shall obey me without question."

Lauran's struggles against the binding spell were proving futile. She could feel a creeping numbness as the dark magic battled her will. She blinked back useless tears, determined not to display her despair before this horrible man.

Shifton paused, frowning. "I need more jewels, of course. That fool Almar gave away everything it took me years to collect." He looked at her with a smug grin. "But once you are subjugated to the rod, I'll send you to visit those damned dwarves and acquire whatever I desire. Why, you can even fetch your friends too!"

The warlock pulled a wicked-looking knife from his belt, and her heart pounded. Though he'd promised not to hurt her, she knew better than to trust him. "But first, I must fulfill a promise and claim a wife."

He moved forward, angling the blade so the sun reflected off its deadly edge.

She lost sight of him as he stepped beneath her muzzle. Her eyes strained to see past her thick hind feet and glistening talons, catching only the dark edge of Shifton's swaying cloak. She tensed, feeling exposed and vulnerable with him so close to her belly and having no way to stop him.

A sudden jab to the unscaled leather of her inner thigh sent a searing ache lancing through her. Warm blood trickled down her leg.

Lauran could feel her body trying helplessly to heal the wound, the cursed gemstone pulsing in beat with her heart, blocking her power. But that weapon must also have possessed magical properties, for the edges of the poisoned injury burned, refusing to close.

Zyre crouched beside Marissa, who keened in pain. Her wing would heal on its own, but that didn't make it hurt any less—and it would take time to fully recover.

He slipped into her shadow and eased the silver chest open. There it was. His beautiful sapphire—finally. He hooked the chain and pulled it out, shutting the lid and hiding the pendant under his foot, as Ganther called the others in.

"Where's Lauran?" her father demanded.

"The wizard has her," someone shouted back.

Zyre added his voice to the growl of outrage, but his thoughts clung to the prize beneath his foot.

[Shift back, now.] Ganther's order rang out, and his plan blasted into their minds.

The sly gray shook his head, resisting the command, even as he shifted. *[Wait, we need to get Marissa out of here. If she shifts, I can take her back to the dragonhold.]*

Zyre knew Ganther fancied the wounded dragon, and sure enough, the green hesitated, then gave an abrupt nod. *[Do it. Then report what's happened to Maxim.]*

A faint *sense* of contempt slipped through with his words. Zyre didn't care. Let their sanctimonious Wing leader think he was a coward. All that mattered was getting his beloved jewel away—far from here and safely hidden.

He didn't even object when Ganther spotted the chest and grabbed it before launching into the air.

Shifton leaned closer with an eager leer, pulling an empty vial from inside his robe.

Then something enormous hitting the ground to their right interrupted him. He cowered against her as dirt and rocks exploded into the air.

Lauran strained her eyes toward the blast and saw a large boulder, half buried in the earth. Movement flashed at the edge of her vision. Colors swept past, a rainbow of jewel tones dominated by green, copper, brown, and opalescent.

Her spirits soared. *They've returned for me.*

The concussive thuds and snaps of leathery wings echoed against the mountains as they passed overhead.

More rocks landed, preceding the Kin with thumps and crashes, and flames roared from above. Her clan all flew in dragon form now, no pseudoriders in sight.

A burst of fire above their heads made the soldiers duck and stumble backward. Lauran fought her rising hopes. *If I'm bewitched, how can they free me?*

As if in answer, another large rock landed near her, missing the warlock but grazing his leg. Shifton yelped and jumped, his startled leap sending the rod flying through the air. It rolled down the slope and tumbled into a crevice.

As the warlock's connection with the weapon broke, the spell snapped, and she was free of its control.

Lauran jerked her muzzle forward, giving her captor a hard shove. He fell backward over the dropped boulder with a loud squawk. She snarled, barely resisting the urge to snap her teeth at him. Despite a strong urge to bite his head off, she was no killer and certainly not a cannibal. Just the thought of tasting human flesh made her ill.

Instead, she turned, half rising on her hind legs as she bugled in delight. *[You came back,]* she crooned, as her companions' love flooded over her in response.

Davint dived down and snatched up the fallen travel bag. She *sensed* his relief at seeing her freed. Ganther circled overhead, his flames keeping the Lowlander's heads down.

Lauran dragged her wounded wing over to the narrow crevice. Unfortunately, it tapered too much for her head or forepaws to fit in. A rough estimate of the crack's depth confirmed she wouldn't be able to reach the rod, even in human form.

Frustrated, she attempted to launch herself into the air, ready to follow her fleeing clan. The stabbing pain in her injured wing mirrored the shooting agony in her chest, and she sank back to the ground.

But that wasn't the only thing making the golden dragon hesitate. Though overjoyed to see her fellow Kin, Shifton's threat echoed. He could track her anywhere. Lauran couldn't return to the dragonhold with them. She would not lead him to her people.

Davint looked backward, questioning her delay.

She *reached* out. *[Keep going. My injuries aren't that bad. Father needs your help getting Marissa to safety, and I will only slow you down. Go, I'll join you soon.]*

He hesitated, but the soldiers began rallying around their captain, so he gave her a reluctant nod and followed the others.

Shifton lay on the ground behind her, the wind knocked out of him, wheezing and gasping for air.

She exhaled in relief as the other Lowlanders continued to ignore her. They seemed more concerned with watching the thunder of marauding dragons depart than the one dragon they assumed the warlock had already immobilized.

Lauran stared after her friends, then sighed. She launched herself in the opposite direction, heading southeast, with the setting sun at her back. She was grateful to discover it was easier to take off downhill.

Yet with the sharp-edged jewel cutting into her chest muscles, trying to fly was agony. Now, with the wind whipping through the cut in her damaged wing, ripping the tough membrane a tiny bit more with each stroke, every movement pushed her pain past agony to pure misery.

She shuddered at the involuntary twitching of exposed nerves.

But she didn't stop.

Tears streamed in her wake as she fled, coasting down the ridge toward Trifair Territory, leaving behind the only home, and family, she'd ever known.

17

With the dragons retreating, Rudolph hurried across the crest to the duke's wizard.

"You let them escape," Shifton accused, angrily pushing the young man's helping hands away and brushing his robes off as he stood. He stamped his feet in frustration as he stared after the golden dragon disappearing down the mountain.

"We didn't *let* them do anything." The captain frowned. "How can we fight a force with aerial superiority? We wounded some of them and drove the others off. What more should we have done?"

"What matters is that it escaped." Shifton stalked over to the crevice and extended his hand. "To me." The rod shot up, snapping into his grip.

Rudolph itched to wipe the smirk off the wizard's face as murmurs of awe came from the surrounding soldiers.

"The objective, Captain, included capturing or killing one of them. Though our preference is for a live specimen." Shifton rounded on the unsmiling man. "Your men did not succeed in accomplishing either of those tasks."

Rudolph's scowl deepened. He opened his mouth to argue. Shifton held his gaze, and the captain's hand crept to his throat. He clamped his lips together, dropping his eyes.

The sorcerer didn't bother hiding his scorn as he turned his back. "It's good to know you've learned to shut up and follow orders, at any rate." He pushed the rod forward and began muttering to himself.

Tamping down his anger, the captain watched curiously as Shifton rotated in a slow circle. The top of the stick twitched to the east. His muttered curses made the men shift uneasily.

Rudolph found himself hoping things continued to not go the wizard's way. Guilt for betraying his duty washed over him.

At last, Shifton spun around. "That damned beast has quite a head start, but it's injured. It will have to land soon, then we'll be able to track it." He faced the captain. "Get your men together. We're moving out. Leave the wagons. Load our supplies on the mules."

He strode through the troops, who cast fearful glances in his direction as they hurried to step aside. He mounted his horse and sat, making his impatience clear by twirling the rod in his hand as Rudolph marshaled his soldiers. By pure chance, they'd only suffered minor injuries and were soon prepared to march.

On horseback, Shifton set a grueling pace for the marching troops.

Yet the young captain clamped his lips together and

didn't object. Behind him, the men glared at the sorcerer's rigid back and cursed under their breath.

The second moon had risen high overhead before Shifton called a halt. The soldiers dropped their packs and fell to the ground where they stood, groaning and rolling their aching shoulders.

"Position my pavilion over here." Pointing to the only flat space in the area, Shifton stalked over and seated himself on a rock, apparently absorbed in studying his rod.

The captain directed the men to make camp. Rudolph set troops to raise the shelter. Then he assigned others to tend the animals, gather firewood, and start a meal.

Once Shifton's tent was raised, he disappeared inside.

Before long, the pleasant aromas of burning logs, kaffee, and roasting meat made the hungry soldiers lift their heads, sniffing in appreciation. The men divided naturally into groups, settling beside three flickering campfires.

These would burn throughout the night, providing warmth and protection from wild animals while ensuring no attacks caught them off guard. A duty roster kept the fires tended and allowed everyone to get some sleep.

Rudolph observed the separation with some concern. He worried these divisions might cause problems if they needed to respond as a unit during this mission.

At the first campfire, where he'd laid his own bedroll, dancing flames illuminated the faces of men he had grown close to.

He could see the youngest, least seasoned recruits at the center fire, glancing toward the more experienced soldiers. They were clearly not yet sure enough of themselves to join the veterans. This group had sustained most of the troops' minor injuries, so he paused to check on them.

Rudolph then assembled a plate of food and strode toward the smallest faction at the third campfire. This older, jaded unit troubled him the most. Because they had achieved the top ranks they could ever hope to attain, his own quick rise to power at such a young age disconcerted them.

Though he hadn't purchased his commission—he came from a poor family and had worked hard for his promotions—they remained envious of his abilities and scornful of his youth.

Aware of their feelings, Rudolph was determined to prove his worth as their leader. But that would take time. He compared the dingy state of this overweight, disheveled group with the tidy appearance of the newer recruits—despite the dust and dirt of their travels—and sighed.

"Make a note of young Ardal's injury." He stared hard at Jareth, their loud and opinionated ringleader. "His arm is sore but doesn't appear to be broken. Give him light duties for the rest of the week, then we'll look at it again."

The captain had hoped assigning the sluggard log duty would instill a sense of pride and responsibility in him. But he showed little sign of improvement.

Ignoring Jareth's loud exhale, he waited as the log-book was located. A dull quill began scratching across the page with exaggerated slowness before he moved away.

Rudolph was confident he could win over this resentful group given time. He just hoped he'd get the chance.

He felt the weight of their glares on his back as he entered Shifton's tent, carrying the plate of food for the sorcerer. He set his mouth in a grim line and straightened his shoulders.

No matter what the wizard did to him, these were his men, and he would do what he could to protect them. Even from his superiors.

18

As the sun disappeared behind a neighboring mountain, Davy's stomach growled in a steady complaint, expressing its annoyance with the food situation.

Despite his hunger, he admired the brilliant orange and purple reflections, until the growing shadows and dying sunlight dropped the temperature. Earlier, walking had kept him warm enough, though he only wore a t-shirt and jeans. But the cool evening breeze gave him goosebumps, and he rubbed his arms, trying to chase away the chill.

Although grateful he wasn't wearing sandals, he was limping now. His wet sock, rubbing inside the damp shoe, had formed a throbbing blister on his heel.

And Davy really regretted not grabbing his jacket when he left the cottage.

As he shivered, contemplating his limited options, a large creature half his size leaped out of the bushes. He yelped in surprise and fell on his backside with a painful thump, making him say a word Mom would not have approved of.

He scooted back as the animal sat up. It stared at him with curiosity but made no move to attack. Its four legs and paws and plump furry gray body reminded him of a rabbit—if rabbits were the size of collies. Yet dark feathers covered its head, rising to a tufted top, and it sported a beak and beady black eyes like a bird.

Since it didn't immediately charge him, he hoped it wasn't dangerous. Thinking of Narnia again, he sat forward with a hopeful smile. "Are you a talking . . . whatever you are?"

The creature cocked its crown to one side, as if judging him. It suddenly startled, twitching around toward something he couldn't hear.

It has no ears, but birds don't have any, do they? Not ones that stick up, anyway.

The odd animal darted back into the underbrush and disappeared.

Davy stood, pushing his glasses up as he scanned his surroundings for any sign of approaching danger, while rubbing his wounded bottom. Nothing else jumped out, but everything in this place looked unfamiliar.

Although he was cold and tired, hunger bothered him the most. He just wanted to locate Jenny and go home for supper.

He swallowed a sniffle. *You're going to be nine soon. Stop being a crybaby!*

With the sun setting, it became harder to see his way. He filled his shirt-bowl again with a furry moss he found growing in abundance. It smelled nice, kind of minty—like medicine—but should he eat it? He'd been lucky with the mushrooms, but did he dare take another risk? His petulant stomach suggested yes, but he resisted.

The moon rose yet provided little brightness. He pulled his flashlight out of his waistband, then hesitated. Maybe he should save the batteries.

Davy stumbled along for a few hours, until he noticed the darkness fading . . . but it couldn't be morning already. He glanced at the sky and stopped short, gawking at a second moon glowing above him. A weary grin greeted this unusual sight.

He took advantage of the new illumination to examine the slope ahead. He spotted another cave entrance. His smile faded as he slowed to a halt. The night kept getting colder, and he needed someplace safe to sleep—and hide.

What if something's living in there? He recalled the odd creature he'd seen earlier, and a shiver ran up his spine. *Something dangerous.*

As he hesitated, an enormous shadow slipped across him. With the buried instincts of a prey animal, he leaped into the shelter of a tree as he peered upward. Several large shapes flew overhead.

Dragons!

His breath caught. He stared in wonder as their silhouettes carved slow arcs against the glowing moons. A thrill shivered down his spine—until they began circling back his way.

Did they see me? Are they hunting for food?

Suddenly as frightened as he had been thrilled, Davy darted up the hill, toward the dubious safety of the cave.

19

Ironically, Lauran had always yearned to explore Galahar. Now she was forced to reconnoiter the kingdom
against her will.

This side of the Dragon Spine Mountains encircled
the vast plains of Trifair Territory, where she coasted
across endless miles of waving grasslands. The rich, clean
smell of growing things soothed her.

With throbbing pain as her constant companion, she
flapped her wings just enough to remain airborne.

To the northwest, a castle appeared in the distance,
glinting in the setting sun.

Ganther's lessons had included knowledge of King's
Keep, but at present, Lauran trusted no Lowlander. Not
even High King Romar, whose companions were rumored
to come from among all the magical inhabitants of his
realm.

With daylight waning and evening pressing close, the
flat, featureless steppe offered no hiding places. Leaving
the stronghold behind, she skirted further south.

A solitary black mountain loomed in the southeast. From her studies, she recognized the Citadel, proud training ground for Galahar's wizards and sorceresses. If the warlock expected them to oppose him, they might help her. However, since meeting Shifton marked her first encounter with a sorcerer, she felt justified being leery of them all.

Lauran shuddered, angling between these landmarks, hoping to cross the plains unnoticed. She intended to put as much distance between herself and any sorcerers as possible. She set as her goal the foothills at the curved end of her beloved mountains, which Lowlanders called the Dragon's Tail.

By veering northeast across Trifair, she hoped to return to the high reaches and find shelter, while distancing herself from her clan, who lived far to the northwest, on the other side of the mountain range.

Cursing under her breath, Lauran gritted her teeth, forcing her injured wing to lift her above the rising slopes. As she reached the flatter peaks of these buttes, she passed over the scattered tiny villages of the Anishinabe.

As the first moon rose, sparks of light flickered to life in the settlements. Torches, lamps, or magic orbs, she assumed. Lauran might have spent more time admiring the way their homes nestled into the sloping foothills . . . if she hadn't been so busy struggling to stay aloft.

She tried to distract herself from the persistent pain fogging her thoughts. *Why haven't the Kin ever considered building fronts on our caves? It'd be so much warmer in winter.* She stored the idea to share with her clan when— if—she returned home.

The steady drip of blood from her leg weakened her.

The second moon glowed in the sky, picking out objects below while shadows lengthened. Her flying became more erratic. Waves of dizziness blurred her vision.

When she *sensed* the brush of a familiar mind, Lauran clamped down on her shields, cutting herself off from her searching Wing. She needed a place to hide—now!

She forced herself to focus on the foothills below. The double moon's rays picked out a dark opening high above a settlement. There appeared to be a safe distance between the village and the cave, and she hoped it would accommodate a smallish dragon.

Lauran landed with a heavy lurch. She had reached the limits of her endurance. This would have to do. She limped forward, holding the injured wing open. The very idea of trying to fold the wounded span of membrane made her cringe and whimper.

The exhausted shifter dragged herself across the ground, stopping at the entrance. She gave a deep grunting growl. From the echo, she estimated the cave to be quite long but narrow. It seemed intended for her. She puffed out a weary blast of smoke. *It's about time being petite—for a Kin—proved an advantage.*

As Lauran used slow, careful movements to maneuver through the low tapered opening—pressing against one side to avoid jostling her injury—she *heard* her thunder drawing closer, calling for her.

Desperate to protect them, she dived through the narrow entrance, twisting to keep from knocking her damaged wing. Once inside, though, she *sensed* what she'd missed earlier. She wasn't alone.

[Lowlander!]

Lauran rose on her hind legs with an angry hiss. At the instinctive mantling of her wings, the spar bones of both pinions slammed into the low ceiling.

A shock of anguish shot along the wounded leading edge, past the finger joint, through her shoulder, and up her neck, flooding her brain with piercing agony. She staggered deeper into the cave, dizziness throwing off her balance. The chamber whirled as her eyes rolled up, her vision blurring into darkness. She felt herself falling and lost consciousness just before she slammed into the floor.

[Hold up.] Davint spun on his tail in midair to look behind him.

Ganther backwinged, gliding to hover beside him. *[Did you hear her?]*

The younger male cast his mind around. *[I thought I did . . . for a moment.]* He shook his head in frustration. *[I can't sense anything now.]*

[We've already circled over this area twice. Could she have made it this far? Maybe she went further south. I just don't understand why she didn't come with us.]

Davint shared Ganther's annoyance. He, too, wondered why she'd failed to follow as she'd promised, but he felt compelled to defend her. *[I'm sure she has a good reason.]*

[Humph. Let's try over the next ridge. If we fail to find her, we should circle back and track the Lowlanders. We must beat them to her.]

The dragons fell into formation, their wings beating in deafening unison as the thunder rose into the sky.

20

Jenny watched Nath as he searched the area around the Cavern of Whispers.

"Eya, I found something," he called, dashing Jenny's hopes that Davy hadn't followed her. "If he continues following that trail, he will end up in our village."

She ran over, staring down at the small muddy footprints heading down the mountainside. They were smudged but could be running shoe tracks, so they must be the brat's. She glanced down at Nath's leather boots. No one else she'd met so far wore modern footwear.

Jenny peered at the ground dubiously, not seeing any path. "We didn't come that way."

"No, we took the shortcut. The route I carried you down when I found you. The climb is difficult yet faster than the easier trail." He stared up at the sky. "Sunset approaches, and it smells like snow. Let us follow his tracks until we find a good place to camp." Nath shot an uneasy glance over his shoulder at the cave. "I have no desire to spend the night nearby."

She shivered, thinking of the risks he'd taken to get her help. Though annoyed there was an easier path that would have saved her aching thighs, Jenny admitted to herself that she would have chosen the shorter route too. She followed him, glad to leave the creepy Cavern of Whispers behind.

They traced Davy's meandering trail until Nath's prediction proved correct and a few snowflakes heralded the arrival of an early-summer snowstorm. He pulled out a slingshot as he walked and brought down the strangest-looking creature she'd ever seen, which he called a sqwabbit.

That's what those stones were for! The weird-ass thing looks like a cross between a rabbit and a chicken. She sat with her back turned while he cleaned their supper.

It amazed Jenny how fast Nath created their shelter. Walls of cut branches, interwoven with lower limbs, formed a windbreak. In minutes, he'd transformed a tree that reminded her of an oversize spreading pine into a refuge.

When she followed him in, crawling underneath the boughs, she discovered that the tree's own branches began growing high enough for her to stand upright near the center. It created a tent effect, with a wide-open space around the trunk.

Nath started a small campfire by muttering and pointing his finger. Despite her suspicious gaze, she couldn't catch him using flint or tinder. He looked amused when she made him roll up his sleeves, convinced he was hiding some trick.

Afterward, he braced the skinned meat on a spit. Jenny felt squeamish, having seen the animal being hunted, but gave an appreciative sniff once it started cooking. She slipped her silent phone from her back pocket and set it on the ground beside her as she sank down to sit cross-legged.

The dancing flames drew her gaze. Smoke worked its way up the trunk and escaped out the top of the tree, while the strained branches groaned under the weight of wet snow.

"*Songiton.*" Nath waved his hand, explaining he'd thrown up an invisible dome.

Jenny refused to believe him. Although she reluctantly admitted that the space got warmer and the melting snow-fall stopped drenching their camp, she still held out hope for a more logical explanation than his ridiculous insistence on "magic." When he suggested she touch it for herself, she pretended not to hear him.

Then he made a tossing gesture and whispered, "*Waasaa.*"

An orb blossomed, and the shadows brightened. "Let me see that thing up close," she demanded, determined to spoil the illusion.

He obliged, setting it on her palm.

She sensed no heat or weight, nothing tangible to catch hold of. "Turn it off and on . . . please." He did as she requested—several times—then floated the ball of light into the air. It was obvious there were no strings.

Jenny stood and pressed against the force field. That was no trick. It really was there.

Shaken, she sat back down, staring up through the thick needles, struggling to accept that Nath had the ability to do genuine magic. Last week, if anyone had claimed she'd be camping in a tree-tent with a wizard, she would have dismissed the idea as ludicrous.

Alright, say magic exists here. Does that mean we did come through a portal, as Marden suggested?

Jenny reached toward the orb, which hovered just beyond her fingertips. "Is this weird for you? Force fields, instant fires." She pointed. "Floating lights. Or is it normal?"

Nath chuckled. "It is usual for a shaman, yes." He twirled his finger, making the ball of light spin lazily. "Although becoming a master of such vast amounts of knowledge requires patience. Remember, I told you magic slows aging, which is good, as our training lasts decades."

She frowned. "You weren't kidding when you said you'd been Marden's apprentice for thirty years?"

"That is the length of time it takes to become a shaman." A frown crossed his face. "Yet Marden has not indicated I am ready to advance. Perhaps he thinks I am not."

She opened her mouth, then decided to stay quiet. It was none of her business, and she hadn't known Nath long enough to suggest he stand up for himself and demand an answer.

He tossed another stick on the fire. "I am lucky, I suppose. Shamans learn by doing. Though we all use the same range of five crystal strengths, the Lowlanders teach their wizards differently; they sequester their apprentices for just as long."

She shook her head and grinned. "And I thought four years of high school was excessive." Of course, she then needed to explain their education system to him as he turned the sqwabbit on the spit.

Their conversation wandered to their respective child-hoods, and they marveled at how their disparate cultures provided similar experiences. Both had learned to swim in a creek. They'd each grown up with a beloved pet: dog for her, wolf for him. And they both had had a best friend living next door. This last seemed to sadden Nath, though he didn't explain.

She assumed they wouldn't be able to talk about books or music because they lived in different worlds. However, when she mentioned it, they enjoyed trying to sing to each other. Since neither possessed a strong singing voice, their lame attempts met with mixed success, but their laughter, at least, was in perfect harmony.

Jenny marveled at how comfortable she felt around him. It seemed like they'd been friends for years, rather than a day.

"So, what's the deal with Polina? She's sort of stunning. Why aren't you interested?"

Nath sat silent for a moment, and she wondered if she'd overstepped the bounds of their blossoming friend-ship. When he began speaking, his answer didn't appear to match her question.

"A great plateau lies southeast of us, about halfway between the eastern and western tribes, that is large enough to host every tribe. Winter's desolation prevents anyone from claiming and settling the location—a blessing."

Jenny raised an eyebrow but listened without inter-rupting.

He explained how the Anishinabe assembled for *Kakandawin,* "the Gathering," to celebrate the end of each summer. It provided a chaperoned situation for young folk to socialize and court. Many handfastings were arranged during the two-week celebration.

"This intermingling ensures the People do not become inbred." Nath grimaced. "Part of a shaman's duties is to memorize the marital roles so nobody handfasts a close relative."

Jenny nodded her understanding.

He ducked his head and continued. "A girl named Haven was my best friend. Her family lived in the cave next to mine, and we became inseparable almost from birth. With our fathers being as near as brothers, everyone hoped we would marry and join our families once we were older." He hesitated, and Jenny leaned forward, resting her chin in her hand, her elbow balanced on her knee.

"But Marden assesses all younglings in our tribe on their twelfth Name Day." He paused. "When tested, my power flared and hers did not. Our lives changed."

Nath lifted his head, meeting her gaze. "I became the shaman's apprentice. As I told you, it is the blessing and curse of magic that it slows its user's aging to about one year for every five of a Common's life."

She gave him a sympathetic smile but stayed quiet, feeling there was more to come.

"Over time, Haven aged into a beautiful young woman. She turned eighteen while I lingered in the body of a boy of thirteen. We grew apart." He shrugged. "How could we not?"

He looked away. "One year, she and her family attended *Kakandawin*, and she came back with a husband. He was of the *Mahigan*—the Wolf—tribe." Nath sighed. "Busy helping the shaman with potions and healing, I didn't even find out until we returned home. However, our paths had diverged long before, and I loved working with Marden. I was happy for her when she handfasted. It seemed the spirits understood where we belonged."

He added a log to the fire and turned the spit. "After a few years, she bore him a daughter. They named her Polina."

Jenny gasped softly but didn't interrupt.

"Sometimes, I watched the youngling from afar. Spied on them as a family. To glimpse my life's alternate path—if only." Her eyes widened, and he hastened to clarify. "Oh, not often . . . I am sure they never realized." Nath snorted. "Although I suppose Marden did. The man sees around corners. He said nothing but kept me too busy to get obsessed."

"What happened to them?" she asked quietly.

He sighed. "When Polina turned five, they tried to enlarge their dwelling by digging through to another chamber. It is possible they hit a fault line, causing a cave-in. In any case, Haven, her mate, and three friends died. By lucky happenstance, the youngling was with her grandmar when the accident happened, so she escaped unharmed."

"Marta," Jenny whispered. "And the others? Did your parents . . . ?"

"Yes. My mam and da and Marta's husband. All laughing and working together one moment, gone the next."

They sat in silence, listening to the hiss and crackle of the fire. She understood his pain, having lost her dad. But to lose both of them . . . Her heart ached for him.

"Marta never expected to outlive her own daughter. Or to be without her mate too." He shook his head again.

"I think having Polina may have saved her life." He sighed. "But since her grandmar has always taken care of us, the youngling spent many hours in our company."

Jenny bit back a grin. "And she developed a crush on you?"

Nath nodded, looking rueful. "Eya. Endearing at six, much less so at sixteen. She has now celebrated over twenty-three Name Days." He shrugged. "If she does not look at someone besides me, she will end up alone. I do not wish that for her. However, I am uncertain what else I can do to make my position clear."

He turned his earnest expression her way. "I did my best to explain that we have no future. I would never mislead her."

Jenny nodded. "I believe you."

"To me, she is still a youngling . . . and Haven's daughter. When I contemplate being with her . . . the whole idea feels wrong. If the spirits had guided us down different paths, I would have been her father."

Nath pulled the cooked meat off the spit with a practiced hand, appearing glad of the distraction. He cut the sqwabbit in half and split it between them, adding a thick slice of bread from their provisions.

Her stomach growled. Yet after only a bite or two, her meal sat forgotten on her knee. She understood Polina better now, but her thoughts kept returning to Davy, buzzing like flies against a windowpane. When had he last eaten? Was he sitting in this storm, cold and afraid? Would she be able to find him? If she did, could they make their way home?

She took comfort in Nath's calm presence. As they sat staring into the fire, Jenny found herself talking about her family too. How hard she'd taken it when her father died, the unexpected news that her mother planned to remarry so soon. What a tagalong brat Davy could be. How she chafed under Frank's strict rules after being used to her easygoing dad. She sighed, recalling her escape to university and how she counted the days until she could return to school after every holiday.

Nath listened without interrupting, leaning over to bump his shoulder companionably against hers.

"Everything has changed." She heaved a dramatic sigh. "My life will never be the same."

He nodded. "But is that not the nature of existence? Always changing, never constant. How boring things would be otherwise."

"I suppose." Annoyed by his lack of sympathy, she shifted away so they no longer touched, then mocked herself. *I wanted a pity party, not a Zen lecture.* Even more aggravating: he made sense.

Jenny finished eating in silence. She threw her bones into the fire, following Nath's example. "Anyway, Mom must be pretty concerned about me." Her mouth formed a little moue. "And Frank will be worried about Davy too."

"I am certain they are fretting about you both."

"I guess." She shrugged. "I'm not Frank's kid—but the brat is. It's only natural for him to be more anxious about his son."

She frowned, staring into the flames. "But Davy's only a . . . a youngling, you know? I mean, his dad takes him camping and stuff, but that's different from being alone in the woods at night. I bet he's scared." Jenny pointed toward the sky, hidden from view by their shelter. "And with this snow obliterating his footprints, we won't be able to track him anymore."

"We will find him." Nath reached over and squeezed her arm. "And if anyone can get you both home, I would trust Marden. He is the strongest shaman I have ever met, and the wisest man."

Jenny slumped to one side, unconvinced, and something uncomfortable jabbed her backside. She checked underneath her, but the layer of pine needles seemed soft enough. Then her fingers brushed the bulge in her back pocket. She pulled out the minifig of Davy's hero riding a dragon and clutched it tightly. She swallowed hard around the lump in her throat as she rubbed her thumb over it.

"What is that?"

She opened her hand. "This is my stepbrother's favorite thing. It's one of the characters in a game he plays with his friends." Her voice quivered. "He gave it to me the morning we came here because he wanted to cheer me up."

"This was with your clothing. We thought it was a talisman. It belongs to the boy, eya?" Nath's sharp question startled her.

"Yes, why?"

He snatched up the minifig. "If I cast a finding spell using this object, we can track him." Nath shot her a triumphant grin. "I told you we would find him."

21

Davy's mind gibbered in fear as a monster pushed into the narrow cave. He cringed, backing up against the stone wall, rocks poking his back. His frantic glance confirmed what he already knew: There was no place to hide.

Glowing red eyes turned his way, and an alien thought touched him. *[Lowlander!]* the beast hissed. Rage and a pain not his own washed over the boy as the beast rose on its hind legs.

Davy shrank back, twisting his face away from those dreadful claws.

He heard giant wings fanning the air and a loud *thwack*, followed by a crash as the creature slammed to the ground. A shower of loose dirt rained down on the body. He stayed still, holding his breath, too frightened to move. *It might be a trick.*

After a few moments, he became convinced the thing was unconscious—or dead.

Davy pushed his glasses up his nose and stared at the massive form. After the hours he'd spent battling creatures like this in *Realms of Destiny,* he certainly recognized this one.

A real, honest-to-goodness dragon!

He held his breath, waving his hand as a trickle of smoke rose from its nostrils.

Okay, not dead. A real, *live,* honest-to-goodness *fire-breathing* dragon . . . who definitely wasn't happy to see him! Davy made himself take several deep breaths.

It seemed to have knocked itself out cold. Now might be his chance. He forced his trembling legs to move, inching his way around the beast, clinging to the walls.

He wished more of that glowing lichen grew here. The tiny patches scattered on the damp rocks only brightened the dim interior enough to silhouette the body. He considered using his flashlight but feared the glow would give away his position if the dragon woke.

He edged along the opposite wall, eyes fixed on the huge mound's slow, undulating movements. The entrance to the cave glowed in the moonlight. Almost past, he began to hurry, which turned out to be a mistake.

Davy slipped in something wet and landed hard, scraping his knees as he fell onto the slick, stony floor. He hissed in pain and wiped his slimy hands on his jeans.

He stared at the massive body, worried the noise of his fall might have woken the creature. In the dim light, he saw a dark trail of liquid oozing down the dragon's leg, running across the ground, and forming the puddle he'd fallen in. *Oh no. It's wounded.*

Maybe it got speared by a knight or fought another dragon. Recalling how majestic the thunder had looked as they'd flown overhead, Davy regretted the dragon's injuries, though he was still afraid.

As he climbed back to his feet with a painful grimace, half bent to hold his injured knee, he spotted the dragon's shattered wing. It looked as mangled as a kite caught in a tree. With all those rips and holes, hitting the cave roof must have hurt.

Davy understood he should run, escaping while he could. But he lingered, his thoughts churning. For one thing . . . a freaking dragon, bro! He had never expected to see that outside his *RoD* game.

And he remembered how it spoke. No, not it—she. *She* had talked to him. Nothing else he'd encountered so far had communicated with him. Should he pass up this opportunity? She might talk, but he got the distinct impression she did *not* like people. Was there any way to change that?

Dad always warned him how dangerous wounded animals could be. But if Androcles helped the lion . . . Davy licked dry lips as he shifted from foot to foot.

"Please, please, please don't eat me," he whispered.

Taking a cautious step over the pooling blood, he tried to locate the source of the bleeding. A thick line of sluggish, dark liquid led him to a leaking gash high on her thigh. He looked around, feeling helpless. He only wore a thin t-shirt and his jeans. When the dragon had burst into the cave, he had even dropped the moss he'd collected.

But detectives on TV always put pressure on bullet wounds to stop them bleeding . . .

The dragon's head lay curled in a half circle, so the boy tiptoed inside the curve of her neck, between the injured leg and her cheek, to reach the cut. He stretched out a tentative hand to press against the wound.

Davy sensed movement behind him and froze. Still pressing on the injury, he twisted to look over his shoulder.

A huge eyeball stared at him, a thin rim of fiery-red iris showing around a large black pupil. The brow ridge above the eye slid forward into a scowl, and the lip below it lifted in a snarl. A low growl vibrated the ground beneath his feet.

"M-m-my name is David Andrew Smythe. I'm eight and th-th-three-quarters. H-how old are you? I-I am l-looking for my sister, and . . . and . . ."

Suddenly, it was too much. Cold, hungry, lost for hours—and now frightened of being eaten when he'd only tried to help . . .

He burst into tears.

The dragon drew back, eyes widening as they faded from red to orange, until they settled into a deep blue. *[Hush, youngling.]* The growl cut off, and the snarl softened. *[Where is your sister?]*

That female voice spoke inside Davy's head again. He also caught a sense of indignation at such negligence. "She's lost too." He blinked his tears away with another sniffle.

[My name is Lauran. Please stop crying, or I may start too.] She waited patiently until he quieted.

She sniffed at him. Before he could retreat, an enormous, very warm tongue licked the cuts on his knees. A tingling sensation tickled his leg—not uncomfortable . . . more of a vibration—and the pain disappeared.

He experienced a fleeting moment of wonder. *She healed my scrapes.* But he pushed this aside in his eagerness at finding someone who could help him. "I followed her through the sparkles, but she'd vanished by the time I got here. Now I can't find her nowhere."

Davy tried to keep pressure on the dragon's wound as he spoke, ducking his head in embarrassment at bawling like a baby. His first aid efforts proved unsuccessful, and green blood trickled between his fingers.

Lauran sounded amazed when he explained his attempts to stop the flow. *[What a sweet youngling you are. However, I doubt your hands are large enough to supply adequate pressure.]*

"So what can we do?" He'd calmed down, but now his voice rose as the idea of her bleeding out horrified him anew. "We can't just give up."

[Do I smell humbridge moss on your shirt?]

This sudden subject change confused Davy. "What?" He glanced down at his stained clothes. "That stuff I gathered? Maybe. I don't know what you call it. I got awful hungry, but I wasn't sure if I should eat any." He jerked his chin toward the back of the cave. "I dropped it all when you scared me."

[I'm glad you didn't try eating some. That moss is quite poisonous when ingested. But it has healing properties, and packing the cut with it may help.]

Davy needed convincing before he would remove his hands from her injury. After some discussion, they compromised. She used her large forepaw to apply pressure while he scrambled to gather the spilled moss in the semi-darkness. He hurried back, squeezing around her in the narrow confines of the cave.

The boy followed her instructions, stuffing the wound as full of moss as possible. He winced as she gasped and whimpered. Davy knew his efforts were hurting her, so he tried to distract her. He talked the entire time, telling her how his video game had prepared him for his visit to the kingdom.

In turn, Lauran explained that he was in Galahar and told him how she'd come to be injured. The boy grew outraged on her behalf, but she soon brought the conversation back to his world, which she found fascinating.

[So you don't have dragons, but you can fly? Are your wizards so powerful, then?]

Davy giggled. "No, we use planes—big, motorized machines with spinning propellers." He shrugged. "I can't explain how they work. We didn't study that in school yet. We also drive cars with motors too; my dad said they used to be called 'horseless carriages' when they were originally released."

Even with the cut packed as full as possible, green blood seeped through. Although it was better than nothing, Lauran needed a doctor. He suggested this, but at first, she didn't understand what he meant.

[Ah, a healer. Yes, if only I trusted someone nearby.] She moved slightly, then groaned. *[But I doubt anyone can help me.]* She nudged him with her muzzle. *[Thank you for your thoughtfulness and assistance, but . . . I'm getting . . . lightheaded. Perhaps . . . I . . . may . . .]*

She fainted before she could finish speaking, her head thumping on the ground beside him. Davy feared she might never awaken if she lost too much blood. He stood there, feeling helpless.

He sighed. Although no longer scared or alone, he still lacked food, and the only drinking water trickled down the damp walls. He added exhaustion to his list of complaints.

Davy removed his glasses, rubbing his eyes and yawning. Then he curled up in the curve of Lauran's neck, huddled against the warmth coming off her scales, and fell asleep.

22

Five Days until Summer Solstice

Lauran drifted in and out of consciousness. Pain woke her, and blood loss dragged her under again and again.

When Davy's hunger woke him before the sun rose, her empathy and his lack of shielding let her feel every pang. She lacked the energy to strengthen her own shields. From what he'd shared of his meandering journey, he hadn't eaten since that unsatisfying meal of raw mushrooms before nooning the day before.

She peered at him from under half-closed eyelids as he fumbled with his glasses. He shifted away from her with slow, careful movements. Touched by his thoughtfulness, she pretended to be asleep, though his empty stomach's rumbling reminded her she was hungry too.

He cupped his hands, attempting to catch some of the dampness dripping down the wall, and she smothered a chuckle when the gritty taste caused a disgusted expression.

Lauran lifted her muzzle—too quickly. The world spun. Davy said something, but her slurred reply barely made sense.

He tried carrying water to her, but it trickled through his fingers. However, the narrow cave allowed her to twist her head around and lick the wet walls herself. The moisture helped, but she soon became lightheaded and passed out again.

When she next woke, Lauran *sensed* his concern. *[Fetch some fresh moss from the hill below the entrance; it's one of the first things to grow each summer.]*

Davy rushed outside, eager to be helpful. She tensed at his sudden yelp—relaxing when it turned into a hoot of delight.

He came running back in. "It snowed while we slept." He lifted his hand to suck on a handful of slush. "Brrrr, brain freeze!" Though she protested, he insisted on bringing some to pack on her wounds.

[Thank you.] Lauran gave a relieved sigh. *[The cold does numb the pain a bit.]*

When he'd filled a shirt-bowl full of the mossy vegetation, he returned to change her dressing. His nose wrinkled and his lip curled in revulsion as he worked, his mouth twisting as if he wanted to gag as he removed the bloody packing. "This is totally gross."

But he persevered, applying fresh moss after using the last of the fast-melting snow to clean the wound. His grimaces as he gingerly removed the wadding from her injury, made Lauran turn her head, a snigger escaping before she smothered it.

He looked up at her, then grinned. Another chortle burst free, and he chuckled in reply. Before they knew it, the pair began laughing so hard that Davy leaned against her to stay upright. She started repeating, *[Ow, ow, ow,]* as the jiggling from her laughter disturbed her damaged wing, which only made them laugh harder.

When they composed themselves, he insisted she apply pressure to try and stem the flow of blood, though she hissed through her teeth at each fresh wave of pain. They both lied, assuring each other her cut leaked less than before, although the glowing green pool grew steadily larger.

To keep him distracted, Lauran showed him how to turn over rocks and dig out the fat grubs underneath. He picked up a slug and sniffed.

Amused by his caution, she assured him they were edible—if perhaps a little chewy.

But even though his belly grumbled, he couldn't bring himself to put the wriggling thing in his mouth. "Yech, I'm not *that* hungry yet!"

With few rocks in the cave, he went outside and dug around, returning with a dozen larvae, carried on a large leaf. He didn't want to squish them, so he kept jiggling the edges to stop them from escaping.

Lauran used her long tongue to scoop up a thick, slimy maggot, slurping with enthusiasm, and he hastily looked away.

After her meal and another sip of water, she dragged herself into the weak sun at the cave entrance, though this risked reopening her wound. After shifting her wing, she paused, bending her muzzle close to her chest and squeezing her great eyelids shut, trying to hide the agony this simple movement caused her.

Despite her efforts, she *felt* his growing concern over

her blood loss. As the sunshine warmed her, reflecting off her scales and brightening the inside of the cave, Lauran *sensed* a strong emotion from him. She looked over to find him staring at her with tears in his eyes.

"You're the most beautiful thing I've ever seen." He spoke with such awe that she would have blushed if she'd been in human form.

She drifted, half asleep in the warm sunshine. However, Davy's restlessness kept waking her. His hunger and his anxiety for both her and Jenny made her fretful and uneasy. She sensed the depth of his longing to look for his sister, yet he feared she might die if left alone.

Lauran faded in and out of consciousness all morning. Whenever she woke, they argued about his leaving. *[I'm doing much better. You should find your sister,]* she urged.

Despite her growing fondness for the boy, he couldn't heal her. A constant throbbing pain pulsed from the gemstone inside, but her shattered wing worried her more. If it wasn't mended soon, she might never fly again.

Yet Davy refused to abandon her. He scouted the area outside the cave to gather more of the medicinal moss and repeated her dressing change. Despite all their efforts, the blood pool below her spread, drop by drop.

The morning dragged on. By nooning, his need for food drove him to try the grubs. He screwed up his face and closed his eyes. Lauran managed a weak chuckle as he dropped the chubby, wiggling larva into his mouth. He chewed and swallowed, his entire body shuddering with disgust. But he got enough of them down to quiet the hunger raging inside him.

[I grow weaker, and I may not make it.] She sighed. *[That might be for the best. My clan would be safe, then.]*

"Don't you say that." Davy scowled, finally convinced he had to leave her. "I'm going to find someone who can fix you."

[There's a village below us. Head in that direction. Do not talk to anyone but your sister or a healer. And if you see any soldiers, hide.]

He promised, waiting as she crawled back inside the cave and sank down, her eyes drooping closed. He leaned forward and planted a gentle kiss on her muzzle. The corner of her mouth turned up. "I'll be as quick as I can," he whispered.

She slipped into an uneasy half doze, keeping a light touch on his thoughts. Their connection grew weaker as he moved farther away, down the mountain, until he was out of her mind's reach.

23

Duke Almar continued his slow pacing in front of the dais, aware of his daughter's watchful eyes from her place beside his throne.

He moved his gold-headed cane forward with a thump, took a step, and stopped to rest, both hands clutching the top knob. *Damn it.* When had it become impossible to take two steps without catching his breath? *If that sharding warlock doesn't hurry, my time will run out.*

He shuffled his back to Avila and lifted one gnarled hand. It shook as he stretched his fingers, no matter how fiercely he willed it steady. As the trembling increased, he dropped it, using both hands to steady himself on the handle of his cane. He inhaled and continued pacing.

Memory of his body's reaction to Shifton's concoction taunted him. Strength that had been lost to him for countless years had straightened his hunched shoulders. He swore the wrinkles in his skin had stretched and smoothed. He'd felt twenty years younger. Recalling the delight of those exquisite moments, a smile played on his lips.

Then his mouth tightened. The effects had only lasted about an hour. After experiencing that brief respite, the heavy weight of his advancing age pressed on him harder than ever.

Shifton kept promising the elixir would be ready soon. *Is he stalling for time, hoping to gain the upper hand by delaying treatment?* The warlock insisted this initial potion, with just the tiniest amount of dragon blood, marked the beginning. Additional concentrated infusions of the beast's plasma would be necessary. He claimed adjustments to Almar's body chemistry must occur to prepare him to accept the serum.

That much seemed to be true. Already, the duke detected changes within himself. Occasional sporadic tingles he'd never experienced before spread through him. Sometimes, they even stirred him below the belt in ways he anticipated enjoying again.

As Almar paused to rest, he eyed the round bottom of a servant woman, bent over to lay a new fire in the audience room fireplace. *Nice to discover there's some life left in my old pecker.* An amused snort escaped him, drawing Avila's inquiring glance.

"Get away with you, girl." The duke scowled. "I'm going to my chambers. I won't need you anymore today."

Stone-faced, she inclined her head and exited the hall without a word.

No doubt she's still annoyed at my outburst the other day. Well, what did he care? She was always spying on him. As if he needed a nursemaid.

If only he'd fathered a son. Someone strong to follow in his footsteps . . .

His eyes narrowed. *No . . . perhaps it's better this way.*

If the warlock fulfilled his promises, Almar would avoid dealing with an impatient heir waiting to inherit the throne. Yes, having a biddable daughter to care for him remained the safer option.

Almar ignored the niggle whispering in the back of his mind—the one troubled by the girl's lack of compliance. She would follow his commands or face the consequences.

He admired the servant woman's backside once more before turning to go.

Perhaps a comely young wife would be even better. She would be his third—no, his fourth. Avila's mother had been number three. The stupid bint had died birthing her and saddled him with the girl.

He shuffled across the broad entrance hall, pausing to rest halfway.

Yes, if Avila complained or misbehaved, he would make her marry Shifton. Another dark chuckle burst free. The warlock imagined Almar didn't notice how the fool watched her. But the duke saw everything.

He began his slow, careful journey up the stairs. He peered around, ensuring he remained undetected. His obstinance drove him to visit his destination alone—and in secret.

He had no intention of returning to his chambers to rest, whatever that stupid daughter of his expected.

The sorcerer's empty suite had haunted his thoughts ever since Shifton and Rudolph left with the soldiers yesterday. His difficulty lay in the long flights of stairs between here and his objective. Of course, calling for porters to carry him would have solved that problem.

At each wide landing, Almar took advantage of the benches set against side walls to sit and regain his strength.

He distracted himself by listing several reasons to do this alone.

First, servants talked; better the warlock never discovered his visit.

And just as bad, Avila would learn of his excursion. She displayed an annoying level of friendly relations with their retainers, who kept her apprised of any gossip. While this had proved useful in the past, he preferred she keep her attention on the domestic side of his life and not ask questions he didn't want to answer.

His mouth firmed into a grim line. But foremost in his reasoning . . . it would be humiliating to admit he required assistance. Bad enough to face his growing feebleness himself; he couldn't stand pity on the faces around him. His sharp tongue kept everyone dancing attendance and fearing his wrath. And that's how he intended to keep things.

One step.

Since the servants used the back stairs and Avila had disappeared somewhere to pout, Almar planned to take his time and make the journey unobserved.

All wizards are buffoons, acting so superior. Look how easily I fooled Shifton's masters at the Citadel all those years ago.

Two steps.

He sneered, lost in memory. *Shifton only needed to continue researching my pet project without alerting his superiors. And he couldn't manage that much. When he got caught, I talked the convocation of wizards out of Stilling him. It would have served the clumsy oaf right to lose his power, but I convinced them of his repentance.*

He reached another landing and sank onto a bench to rest, his pulse pounding in his temples. *Ha! Talk about naive and gullible! They even allowed me to take him into my castle to 'supervise' him.*

Almar stood and repeated his climb. One step.

The fools fell for my honeyed words like baby birds. Mouths wide, they swallowed all my lies, and I got myself a wizard turned tame warlock.

His thoughts kept him entertained until he arrived at his destination. Weary and breathless, he reached for the handle of the door, then hesitated.

What if Shifton set a spell to repel unauthorized visitors? Or an alarm to notify him of an intrusion? The man had forbidden the servants from entering—a stricture they happily complied with. Would he be arrogant enough to consider that sufficient defense?

Only one way to discover the answer.

Almar planted his feet, gripped his cane, and opened the door. He braced himself . . . but nothing happened. *Ha! As I suspected, the proud idiot presumes his reputation is all the protection he needs.*

Shifton might have set a magical alarm, but no point fretting over maybes.

The duke shuffled inside.

Dim and shadowy, the only light in the room came from half-covered windows. He made his way across the suite, weaving around furniture and piles of books, to push the curtains open. Sunlight poured over the worktables, exposing litter everywhere. Dirty dishes piled high, rings from wet mugs, dust on every flat surface . . .

Almar's nose wrinkled. If the warlock refused to allow the servants access, he should at least clean his own mess. Almar glared around in disgust. How did Shifton locate anything in this pig's wallow?

Even the floor seemed gritty underfoot as he walked to the table holding the largest concentration of debris.

He kicked an abandoned plate. The sudden sharp clatter, followed by the scurrying of vermin, made his heart catch and pound hard enough to leave him gasping.

Almar inhaled, held his breath, and exhaled, calming himself. He turned his attention to the scrawled notes scattered and piled across the tabletop. These proved useless, however, since the warlock used his own coded style. Shorthand, initials, and meaningless symbols filled endless pages.

The duke ground his teeth in frustration, throwing the papers down. *There must be something I can use . . .*

He hobbled along each table, examining the books lying open with little interest. An ominous black door with a chain and lock attracted his attention. Almar eyed it, his curiosity aroused. What secrets might the warlock keep hidden there? But he had neither the strength nor patience to break in.

Resigned to his lack of success, the duke turned to go. His eye fell on a discarded vial, similar to the one Shifton had given him, on a table near the entrance. He pounced on it, lifting and tilting it, squinting with farsighted intensity.

Yes! A small amount of green liquid sat glowing at the bottom. Almar attempted to insert his forefinger into the ampoule, but his enlarged knuckles proved too thick. His little finger fit, though he worried for a moment it might get stuck.

He forgot his concern when his fingertip touched the elixir. He pushed in deeper, then twisted the tube to wipe up every bit of excess before pulling it out, begrudging each drop of moisture clinging to the sides.

Almar lifted his trembling hand to his mouth and sucked his finger. A warm glow coursed through him, and he gasped, lifting his chin. The ampoule dropped and shattered as he shuddered with pleasure.

The sensation diminished . . . fading far too fast. His dull eyes peered out from under drooping eyelids. Head bent, he sighed, staring around with indifference.

Time to leave. Nothing else here interested him.

Broken glass now littered the floor, and the curtains sat open.

Almar vaguely recalled his concern that Shifton would discover he'd been in his rooms. Anger stirred him from his lethargy. Who cared if the warlock learned of his visit?

He owned the castle. He would go where he liked.

His brief rage passed, and his shoulders slumped. Even that small fit of temper had exhausted him. After a pause, Almar began the weary journey down to his own chambers.

He needed that rest now.

Avila hid in the shadows, her back pressed against the cool stone wall behind a suit of armor as her father made his way down to the second floor. He shuffled past her hiding place and continued down the hallway.

Her eyes rose to the stairs he'd just descended. The ones leading to Shifton's quarters. Those two wily schemers were planning something, and she intended to discover what.

She listened, waiting for the thump of his cane and thud of his footsteps to be cut off by the hollow thunk of heavy doors closing, before running swiftly up to the top level.

Avila turned, her bright eyes checking for witnesses, before she slipped inside, shutting the door behind her.

24

The smell of hot kaffee woke Jenny before sunrise. She and Nath ate a meal of cold sqwabbit and bread with the delicious brew, sweetened with a little honey.

Though she now believed in his magic, when he snuffed the fire with a gesture, she still poured sand over the coals—just to be safe.

They emerged from their tree-tent into a white world, though bright sunshine already worked to melt the light snow.

Jenny watched Nath lift the minifig and mutter a spell. At first, nothing happened. Then he stood it on his open palm. The front of the tiny figure twitched, then twisted to face down the slope. She shivered. It was kind of eerie seeing the commander moving on his own.

They spent the morning following its direction, changing course every time the spelled object shifted. Although she didn't see any difference in their surroundings, Nath seemed to. He smiled and advised her that Davy's trail now headed downhill toward his village.

"He is this way. Come!"

They began to run, the minifig held out in front of them.

They hadn't gone far when Nath stopped short, pointing at several familiar footprints in a patch of mud.

She clutched his arm. "It's him. He must be close. DAVY."

From the distance came a wail, "JENNY? HELP!"

Nath took off running again before she could react.

"Hey!" She raced after him and soon caught up. They jumped over a puddle of melted snow, slipping in the muck, though neither fell. Holding each other up, they slid and staggered around a huge thicket covered in fruit that reminded her of oversize blackberries.

As they rounded the corner, they came to an abrupt stop. A bearlike creature sat eating berries from the bushes only a few yards ahead. She gulped in fright, having only seen bears in zoos, though it looked smaller than she would have expected.

The bear's head lifted, its nose twitching. Nath pushed her behind him, and she braced to run in case it charged at them. Instead, it favored them with a disinterested glance, let out a huff, and returned to scarfing all the fruit within reach.

They took slow, careful steps backward until the beast vanished from sight.

"Jenny? Is that you?" The bushes rustled, and a reedy voice appealed, "Make it go away!" Nath used a stick to shift the branches, revealing a small boy with berry juice dribbling down his chin, staining his already dirty hands and t-shirt.

"Davy!" She pushed forward. "Are you all right?"

"Watch out." The young shaman grabbed her shoulder. "The brambles are sharp."

Jenny glanced down and saw the wicked barb of a long, curved thorn poised to prick her arm. Its tip glistened, making her shiver. She retreated. "How did you get in there?"

The boy shrugged, stuffing more berries in his mouth as he talked. "I crawled. I was eating from the outside branches when that"—he pointed—"showed up. Dad always said to never run from a bear, so I dropped and slithered underneath." He twisted his arm to show a red welt running up the back. "I scratched myself good getting in here."

"Can you climb out the same way?" Jenny beckoned him, but Davy's eyes widened.

He gave a vehement shake of his head. "I'm not coming out till that thing is gone."

She argued with him, but he refused to budge.

All their noise had made the bear curious. It began walking in their direction, making little growling sounds. Nath stepped forward to confront it, waving his hands and *pushing* a burst of magical light from his fingers, which exploded before its face. With a yelp of surprise, the frightened animal startled backward, turned tail, and ran.

Davy wriggled out from under the bushes, earning another scratch on his cheek. He straightened his glasses and threw his arms around his sister, who gave him an awkward hug.

"You shouldn't have followed me," she scolded.

Nath tied a second translation-stone bracelet to her brother's wrist.

Jenny nodded at his thoughtfulness. However, in her

relief at finding her stepbrother, she forgot to introduce her companion.

"Dad would have wanted me to," Davy protested, earning a dubious frown from her. "How did you find me? I've been looking for you everywhere." His arms pinwheeled.

Nath held up the toy figure, and the boy snatched it.

"The Commander!" He grinned at Jenny. "I knew he'd keep you safe." His face grew puzzled. "But how did he help you locate me?"

She'd been examining him, reassuring herself he was unharmed. Now she ignored Davy's question in favor of her own. "What's all over your clothes?" Before he could answer, she recalled she had a surprise. "Forget it . . . I have so much to tell you."

The boy glanced down at the moss-colored stains.

Jenny said, "There's magic here!" as he replied, "It's only Lauran's blood."

They stopped talking and stared at each other.

He responded, "What? For real?"

At the same time, Jenny asked, "Who is Lauran, and why is her blood green?"

Davy grinned. "Me first. I guess I should have expected this world to be magical. I mean, if I met a dragon . . . oh, yeah . . ."

He frowned, but before he could continue, Nath gripped his shoulder. He turned the boy to face him. "What did you say? Where did you encounter dragons?"

Davy's eyebrows rose, startled by his intensity. "Who are you?"

A bit of Jenny's old impatience leaked out. "He found me in the Cavern of Whispers. He's a shaman in a quaint little village near here." She suddenly remembered something. "And I saw real dwarves there!"

Her stepbrother ignored her as he stared at Nath. "That's, like, a healer, right?"

"I am an *apprentice*." But he nodded. "In time, I will assume the shaman's role within our tribe."

Davy grabbed Nath's sleeve, his lower lip trembling. "Please! You gotta come with me *now*. She's going to die!"

"Who is dying?" Nath raised his hand, calming the excited youngling. "Where?"

"The dragon!" The boy danced excitedly from foot to foot. "Her cave isn't far. Hurry!"

The other two exchanged looks, and Nath nodded. "Eya, lead on."

25

The wounded dragon shifter regained consciousness as a familiar mind and voice reached her in unison.

"Lauran? Are you awake? It's me, Davy."

She opened her eyes to view his anxious face. *[I'm here. You returned faster than I expected. And I sense you aren't alone. Did you find your sister?]*

"Yes, she's with a healer who saved her, which is great, 'cause we need his help. Jenny says he's a good guy."

The dragon *felt* the impatience of the couple waiting outside, and a shiver of trepidation shook her. Did she dare trust Lowlanders again? But she trusted the boy, and he seemed willing to vouch for the others . . .

She allowed herself to be convinced, and Davy returned to the entrance to wave them inside.

The man paused in the opening.

He must be the healer. Lauran *felt* his wonder and ducked her muzzle shyly. Behind him, the boy's sister gasped, staring at her sprawling form in wonder. Their admiration made her self-conscious, and she tried to straighten up, but agony overwhelmed her. She slumped back to the ground with a groan.

Even lying down, she towered over the man's head. She *read* his thoughts and understood her curled body made the cave look smaller by comparison. This disconcerted her since she was accustomed to being the smallest of her kind.

As the healer surveyed her injuries, Lauran *felt* his growing concern outweigh his delight in meeting her. Nervous, she snorted, blowing soft smoke over them. Her eyes stayed half closed, and her breathing sounded strained, even to her.

She waited, helpless and exposed, with one wing folded at an awkward angle under her body and the other stretched out across the cavern floor.

Though the man made a slow approach, holding his hands wide to show he meant no harm, Lauran tensed. Her breath came in fast, short puffs.

"Greetings, milady. My name is Nath. I am an apprentice shaman." He bowed.

When she inclined her head in response, the sister's mouth dropped open. "Whoa! She understands you!"

"Of course she does." Davy frowned, indignant on the dragon's behalf.

[Yes. Your minds are quite . . . simple.]

The young woman blushed at the tired sarcasm in Lauran's voice. "Sorry, no offense intended. We don't have dragons on Earth, so I didn't realize you talked. My name's Jenny." She blinked. "Hey! You weren't speaking aloud! I heard you in my head. Are you telepathic? That is so cool."

[It is I who should apologize. Your brother explained

how he followed you here. I'm not being very gracious to a visitor to Galahar.]

Lauran snorted, puffing out another small cloud of smoke. *[Although I am unfamiliar with this terminology, you speak the truth. My kind can communicate mind to mind. What I don't understand is why such talk is cold in your world.]*

Jenny and Davy laughed. "Not cold—cool. That's slang—a figure of speech—where we're from." Her eyebrows lifted. "But I'm not sure why."

Nath interrupted impatiently. "I am concerned about your injuries, milady." He gave a sympathetic hiss as he leaned in to inspect the large slash in the center of the membrane of her damaged wing, most of which hung in tatters. Then he frowned, studying the seeping wound on her thigh.

[You suspect the cut is the more serious, if less painful, injury.]

Nath nodded, waving at the pooling liquid below her. "Indeed. You have lost too much blood. You cannot afford to lose any more." He leaned forward, nodding in approval of the moss packed into the gash, though his scowl deepened when drips fell as they watched. "May I ask why your body is not healing itself? I have a distinct memory of my master describing the almost mythical curative powers of dragons."

Lauran shook her head, weakening from the exertion of communicating. *[That is a . . . tale I will share. But I fear I am too . . . fatigued right now. Your assessment . . . is correct. I . . . fear the wound . . . has been poisoned, but I cannot afford to lose more . . . blood. Do you suppose . . . you can help me?]*

"We should fetch Marden. He has more experience than I." Nath hesitated. "Although I am not certain we have time." He shifted his head and shoulders from side to side, his indecision needing action. She *felt* him make up his mind, and he bowed. "I will do my best."

Davy's face lit up as the healer summoned a bright orb, allowing him to better examine her injuries. He sent the others to gather more moss. Lauran was amused at the confident way the boy instructed his sister on what to pick.

Nath pulled Lauran's attention back inside the cave by removing the packing from her wound. The bleeding started again at once. He placed both hands atop the cut on her thigh, ignoring the thick green blood staining them.

Despite the pain, Lauran held still, watching as he closed his eyes. Swaying gently, he intoned a healing chant. The injury resisted, which seemed to perplex him, though she'd already told him something wasn't right. Her body's own magic should have repaired her long ago.

But the wound refused to heal, even with Nath's help.

Unexpected heat from his hands made her gasp as he increased his efforts, pouring magical healing into the sliced skin. Reluctant as a cat taking a bath, the puncture drew together, pulled back, sealed over again, then inched closed bit by bit. The flow slowed to a trickle, then a drip, and finally stopped.

She bore his ministrations without complaint, though her body shook in reaction to his spellwork. Nath inspected the incision, and she *sensed* his puzzlement that the scar failed to heal. It glowered, red and angry, against her scales. Lauran didn't care about being disfigured; she was just happy something had stopped hurting.

But the stress and constant blood loss had taken their

toll. She grew lightheaded, and as the siblings returned with fresh moss, her eyes rolled upward.

Jenny yanked Nath out of the way as Lauran's body sagged and her massive head thumped to the ground. The impact sent dust swirling into the air.

He shifted the orb, adding a second one, while inspecting the shattered wing. "She will suffer less if I work on her other injury while she is unconscious. Someone did a nasty job on her."

The torn edges would not be easy to repair. Nath's sure, gentle hands made a thorough examination of the pieces. "Can you clean the healed wound using the dampened antiseptic moss you collected?"

Jenny grimaced but agreed.

"Come with me, Davy, and I will show you a plant we'll need. If you give it a quick slice, it produces a thick, sticky substance . . ."

The pair disappeared outside, where Jenny could hear Nath instructing the boy on what and how to cut. A few minutes later, they returned. Davy looked proud of himself, carrying a broad leaf full of gooey material.

Nath dug through his travel sack. "I use mesh to bundle various herbs and other forage I gather as I wander. But perhaps the netting might serve another purpose here. Aha!"

He held up the roll, cutting a length with his belt knife.

Then he sent Davy crawling underneath Lauran to smear the goo on the underside of her wing in a rough circle around the damaged section. "That is sufficient. Now stretch the mesh"—he handed the boy a large square—

"and press it into the sap. We will have to work fast before the sap dries."

As her stepbrother worked, the healer explained, "This will create a lightweight, sturdy base on the bottom side of Lauran's wing that should support the tattered fragments."

Nath laid the shredded skin out. Working with swift, sure movements, he repositioned the pieces as best he could. He sent Davy for fresh "glue" and applied sap to each membrane section, securing them to the fabric one at a time.

Then he dived back into his sack. "I hope Marden repacked that small container of salve in my supplies."

Jenny watched in fascination. Her stepbrother stood on tiptoe beside her, trying to get a better view.

Nath smiled at their curiosity and explained as he worked. "Healers carry essential medicines like this in case of emergencies. If we add some water from my flask"—he saturated the injury—"and use the lightest touch to spread cream over the area, that should seal the moisture in."

He looked up at them. "Now comes the hard part." He inhaled, then muttered, "I wish Marden were here." They stood silent as he laid his hands on the damaged membrane and began a barely audible chant.

Jenny patted Davy's hand, which had tightened on her arm. She didn't see any glow or shimmering light—though she did experience a faint tingling on her skin as Nath fed healing power into the pieces.

Her eyes widened as the ragged edges shivered, stretched, and joined together.

But the apprentice shaman frowned. "Although there is less fight in this wound than with the cut on her leg, something within the dragon seems to be protesting my intervention." His face reddened with effort. "It cannot be her own magic fighting mine; I've never encountered anyone's power working against its holder's best interests." He fell silent as he concentrated.

When he finished, Nath examined his work. "This section will be thicker, but that should not hinder her flight."

Jenny thought he looked exhausted. He was panting from his efforts and wiped sweat from his forehead. The moment he stepped away from Lauran, his knees buckled and he staggered sideways.

She rushed forward and caught him. He slung an arm around her shoulder, murmuring his thanks for her support as she helped him to a nearby boulder to rest. Davy brought him the flask, and he drank the last of the water.

In unison, they turned to watch the gentle movement of Lauran's chest, verifying the unconscious dragon lived.

26

Shifton tried to ignore the men as they broke camp, annoyed by how quickly they jumped to obey Rudolph's orders. Despite his anxiety, he found himself entertained by one oily miscreant's open mockery of the young captain behind his back. While it would never do to encourage such behavior, the warlock enjoyed the man's sarcastic facial expressions and mimicry of the captain's walk.

Impatient with the business of breaking camp, Shifton moved to the edge of the small plateau, which overlooked the Trifair plains below. He concentrated on the rod, urging the spell to seek its target. The bejeweled wood twitched in his grasp. The dragon still lay ahead—some distance to the east—across this sharding grassland.

His gaze shifted slightly northeast toward High King Romar's castle. *I should have brought a far-seer.* Though he assured himself they remained unobserved, he would have preferred to verify it.

Shifton regarded the grasslands with contempt. Their only advantages lay in their inability to conceal a dragon and how much easier they would be to traverse than these damn mountains.

His sullen, brooding eyes cut southeast whenever he relaxed his control over them. He detested being so near the place he'd called home for thirty-five years. He had made his choices long ago, and he considered regrets an annoying waste of time.

Yet his gaze kept shifting toward that dark, looming mountain. The Citadel. It dominated the landscape, towering against the distant snowy peaks of the Tail.

Memories stirred, unbidden and unwelcome. *A speechless Master Dargan, staring at him in horror. A sqwabbit's headless body sprawled at Shifton's feet. Blood on his hands. The master's shields faltering for a single moment before he regained control—just long enough for his revulsion and disgust to inundate the young warlock.*

Shifton shuddered, forcing the recollection away. *Everything that went wrong was Almar's fault. I was so naive when I first met him.*

How innocently his debasement had begun. He'd returned to Septain for his da's funeral—one of the rare occasions an acolyte was permitted to leave the Citadel during their initial thirty-year apprenticeship. His lip lifted in a snarl, recalling the small, drab affair.

Then came Duke Almar's invitation to the castle. How Shifton had preened, boasting to his mam and friends. The duke had just celebrated his twentieth Name Day. Handsome, not yet in his prime, he had inherited the title after his father's unfortunate fall from a horse.

Shifton had only questioned that accident years later.

He scowled at the youthful vanity that had led to his downfall. Almar had given him his first forbidden book.

He still remembered the greasy texture of the cover, the growing certainty it was human skin. *Oh, the duke pretended ignorance and flattered me, claiming only someone as brilliant as me could decipher such complex writings.*

Many envied his current position. But they did not know the things he'd endured. *Almar himself journeyed to the Citadel when my work was discovered, ostensibly to plead my cause.*

Shifton's mouth twisted. No need to imagine that conversation. The duke took great pleasure in recounting it for him.

"Have pity on the poor, uneducated son of a dead merchant. He lacked the understanding to recognize the danger. He's not bad—just overzealous. A passion for knowledge—even forbidden learning—led him astray. Your righteous anger has shown him his failings. He is eager to atone. Have mercy . . ."

Bah. Shifton swiped the rod through the air, almost striking the head of a startled soldier standing nearby. The man flinched, but the warlock ignored him.

The silver-tongued liar spun them a tale where I didn't recognize myself.

Almar had smuggled the rest of Shifton's forbidden books out of the Citadel. Those idiots trusted him when he claimed Shifton had just owned the one . . . that he'd only just started his studies.

The duke's intervention had not fully succeeded. They didn't restore Shifton's honor or his title as wizard—the thing he valued most. But they didn't Still his magic—Almar's primary concern. Instead, they'd agreed to revisit his case . . . in fifty years.

The approach of that expiring time limit provided

Shifton with a convenient excuse if they got caught trespassing. With both High King Romar's castle and the Citadel in sight, he'd best be prepared. Galahar might be a peaceful kingdom, but its dukes monitored everything occurring within the borders of their territories.

On Shifton's orders, his troops had worked their way down the opposite side of the mountains from Septain. It would take the rest of the day to descend out of the foothills, but today they would enter Trifair.

He hoped that by keeping to the northeast and hugging the foothills behind King's Keep, they pass without being discovered. Their next two camps would be the most dangerous. They dared not light any fires, which could be seen for miles on these flat stretches.

It turned his stomach to consider the groveling he would be required to do if they were caught trespassing. But if apprehended, he would claim to be seeking reinstatement.

One did what needs must.

As for the soldiers—well, his duke supported him and wanted to ensure his safety on the journey.

Shifton jerked, becoming aware he'd been staring in the direction of the Citadel again, tangled in old emotions. A strange mixture of loss and hatred twisted inside him.

He flew into a rage and whirled, storming through the camp toward his horse. The uneasy sideways glances of the men soothed his prickly ego. Impatient, he mounted his gelding, with his back to the imposing mountain fortress, pushing away his memories.

Shifton hauled roughly on the horse's bit. Turning, he was prepared to rail at the soldiers, only to find them ready and waiting, cutting his rant short.

With an unimpressed scowl, he settled for scrutinizing the mule carrying his pavilion. He was proud he rated covered sleeping quarters while his men slept in the open air. *Am I not the undisputed power in Septain Territory?* His glare flicked in the Citadel's direction. *Perhaps even the most powerful sorcerer in the entire kingdom. We shall see.*

To his further annoyance, the tent appeared securely stowed, giving him no excuse to complain. He pointed in the direction the rod indicated and gave the order.

"Forward march."

Rudolph moved to the front of the column, falling in behind Shifton. The captain obviously disapproved of their current location, but Shifton didn't care, ignoring the man's thinned lips and glowering expression. Cold rations and a hard march would give him something else to whine about.

The dragon's escape still rankled. Yet this delay might be useful. By the time he returned, Almar should be frantic with worry. The duke's desperation to reclaim his youth would make him easier to manipulate.

Shifton permitted himself a smug smirk. Besides, even younger men had accidents. Avila would be his, and should something untoward happen to her father, she would become Duchess . . . and he, of course, would be Duke.

His smile widened at these pleasant thoughts.

If she became intractable, well . . . he'd be sorry, but she might just follow in her father's footsteps. Once she bore him a son, naturally. A legitimate heir was important, even if Shifton was likely to outlive any Common youngling.

Distant thunder rippled across the clear sky, startling him out of his daydreams, sparking memories of dragons in flight.

The dragon held the key to his success—quite literally. Without its blood, none of his plans would be possible.

But his luck persisted. It had sustained a serious wound.

As he recalled that damaged wing, Shifton assured himself it would be impossible for the beast to fly any great distance. It amazed him it had gotten this far. It must have stopped to hide by now, so he should find it soon.

His speculation that it had gone to ground grew into certainty. He would not return to Septain empty-handed.

With his goal feeling within reach, the warlock increased his speed, once more setting a punishing pace for the foot soldiers.

27

Lauran woke with a groan just before sundown. Climbing to her feet, she swayed to one side, then slumped back to the ground. *[Shards, I'm so tired and weak.]*

"You lost a lot of blood." Nath stepped closer, though he could not have supported her weight if she'd fallen toward him. He sent Davy to collect some rocks. He and Jenny used them to dam a shallow pool beside her, collecting water before the puddle drained into the dirt floor.

Lauran drank her fill, giving them a grateful nod, then laid her muzzle down next to the boy. His sister sat on her other side, soothing her by stroking her neck.

[Thank you for your help, healer. I am in your debt.]

"Only an apprentice shaman. But honored to have been of assistance." Nath ducked his head. "Are you up to telling us how this happened to you?"

Given Lauran's exhaustion, it took her some time. She told them everything—except the truth about the Kin and her inability to shift. It sufficed to say the warlock hunted her for her blood.

Jenny shuddered. "So, this ruby inside you works as a tracking device and also as a means to control you?" The healer sat silent, a troubled frown marring his handsome face.

Lauran nodded. *[That's what Shifton said, and I believed him. A lie served no purpose at that point.]* She hung her head. *[It's why I never answered when my Wing called to me. I hope they've given up looking and gone home.]*

She stared at Nath. *[You've done so much for me. I hate asking more of you . . . but would you consider removing the gemstone?]*

Jenny and Davy looked hopeful, but he hesitated. "That may be impossible since I cannot say what the nature of this warlock's spells are. I hesitate to undertake such a task when the magic might pose a serious risk for you."

[Oh, I beg you, please!] Lauran pleaded. *[Won't you at least try? I don't know how long I can stand living like this—hunted and unable to return home.]*

Nath tried to persuade her to let him contact Shaman Marden, though this seemed to annoy Jenny. "We need to get someone more experienced involved," he urged.

Lauran remained adamant. *[The warlock is too dangerous. It's bad enough I'm endangering you three. I ran away so I wouldn't put anyone else at risk. The fewer people who know where I am, the better.]* She assured him she understood the process would be painful and might fail.

He reluctantly allowed himself to be convinced.

Lauran faced the cave entrance, braced her forelegs against either side wall, and lifted her chin. *[I'm ready.]*

Nath swallowed hard, inhaled, and began. Pressing his

hands against the spot at the base of her neck, he chanted a spell, trying to draw the gemstone out with slow, gentle coaxing.

She winced, tensing against his hand. Pain coiled out from her chest to her shoulder joints. She panted, struggling to breathe past the anguish.

[Faster,] Lauran urged. *[Get it . . . over with. I will . . . suffer less.]* Agony wracked her body, cutting off her thoughts.

He acknowledged the sense of this with a nod, making his chanting quicker and louder.

She kept a light touch on his mind, *sensing* how the ruby fought him. Its malevolence strained against his commands, leaving no doubt of the reason her wounds refused to heal.

Lauran groaned, and he broke off with a guilty start. In the sudden silence, the muted sound of distant thunder reached them.

[Don't . . . stop . . .] Tears leaked down her cheeks and splashed him.

Nath gulped and wiped his forehead but renewed his efforts, raising his voice and commanding the ruby to obey him. She lifted her muzzle and screamed.

Davy clapped his hands over his ears and buried his face in Jenny's lap.

Lauran caught Nath's wince. He hunched his shoulders toward his head, though he continued the incantation, shouting over the cries she could not repress.

A sudden deafening roar reverberated through the narrow cave, stunning them all.

Nath quit chanting and whirled around, staggering

back in disbelief. He gaped as he fell back against the golden dragon.

Lauran's scream cut off when he stopped pulling on the ruby. She stared in shock as Ganther's enormous emerald-green body struggled to push its way through the constricted entrance. Fortunately, his broad chest and shoulders wouldn't fit through the opening her slimmer physique could. His cavernous mouth snarled, and giant teeth snapped at the healer. She took a moment to be grateful the cave's narrow entrance was too tight for his immense body.

Jenny shrieked, and Davy cried out in fright.

Her father pulled back. Lauran caught Nath as he sagged with relief—until Ganther's huge talons began scraping the sides of the entrance, trying to enlarge it.

Tears still streaming down her face, the golden dragon shoved the young man aside. He sprawled on top of the others, sending them all tumbling in a pile as she stepped forward.

[FATHER!] Lauran *sensed* her new friends' shock at her mind-call. *[Listen to me! He's a healer. He was trying to help me. STOP. He healed my wounds!]*

The other dragons outside the cave stayed closed and unresponsive. She kept yelling until the sounds of chaos died away. The talons retreated, and a deep, heavy voice rang in their minds.

[You screamed. If this Lowlander is helping the warlock, I will rip him into tiny pieces, starting from his toes and working my way up his body. Then I'll stomp the bits into pulp and use them to fertilize my garden.]

Lauran rolled her eyes at this menacing speech, trying to ignore Nath's thoughts buzzing in her mind. He seemed uncertain whether to be concerned by the details of the threat or fascinated that dragons cultivated gardens.

When it grew quiet outside, her new friends crept forward to stand beside her.

A moment later, Ganther, in human form, muscled his way into the cave, dipping his head to avoid striking the ceiling. He wore a simple robe that left the green-tinged skin of his legs and feet bare below the knees. He towered over Nath.

Lauran caught an odd thought from Jenny. *[Who, or what, is a 'jolly green'? No, forget it.]* She closed her mind to the trio. Instead, she concentrated on her father, who scowled at them.

The healer moved up beside her and rose on tiptoe to peer around Ganther. "W-where did your dragon go?" He stepped back as several more dragons—smaller than the enormous one attacking them earlier, but still a good head taller than Lauran—peered through the entrance. He heaved a relieved sigh when their size prevented them from forcing their way in.

Lauran swallowed a chuckle as Ganther's glare dried up her amusement. *[Father—]*

He interrupted her, casting a meaningful glance at the non-Kin. "I sent *him* to tell the others we found you. It's best to let *your father's* temper cool before he reappears here."

Lauran dipped her head, acknowledging his warning. *[This is Nath, a healer. He isn't a Lowlander; he's of the Mountain People. We can mind-talk with him.]*

The apprentice shaman frowned, perhaps catching the hint of caution in their voices. But a huge hand reached out and enveloped his, distracting him.

"I am Ganther, in charge of this group of Dragon Kin. We thank you for aiding one of our own." His powerful grip tightened, and Lauran shot her father a disapproving look.

Nath liberated his trapped fingers, wincing and patting the thick fist. "I did my best. However, the ruby remains in place, so she is not yet free." He moved aside, allowing the golden dragon space to walk toward the entrance. Ganther backed out, and she followed.

The smaller humans shuffled after her, huddling at the opening and gaping at the colorful dragons. Lauran checked on Davy, who stayed half hidden behind his sister. The boy never stopped smiling. He just stared, his eyes huge, as the great beasts pressed forward.

Dragon Kin jostled together as they all tried to reach her. They settled for rubbing muzzles with her, as if needing to assure themselves she was safe.

Touched and humbled by their concern, she crooned at Davint, who stood apart from them. His wings were half open as if he couldn't decide whether or not to stay. The copper drake snarled and turned his back on her, his tail flicking like an angry cat. Her excitement faded, and her shoulders drooped.

Lauran faced away from the furious drake and caught the other Kin up on everything that had occurred since the thunder parted ways, including her reason for leaving them. Davint continued to stay apart, scowling, yet close enough to listen.

[I didn't have a choice,] she said to the entire group, though she peeked over her shoulder at Davint.

Lauran shrank back when he turned his glare her way. *[Of course you did. And you chose not to trust us to help*

you. You chose,/—heavy sarcasm emphasized the word—
/*to leave your Wing alarmed and uncertain of your fate,
rather than trusting we would do everything possible to
save you.*/

Aware of everyone watching them, he moved aside,
snapping his powerful jaws.

Jenny flinched and tightened her hold on Davy.

Ganther cleared his throat. His bright tone suggested
his intention to lighten the mood as he launched into an
explanation of how they'd located her. "We watched the
Lowlander camp and saw which direction they headed
when they set out. Then we flew above the clouds so they
wouldn't spot us and went ahead of them. But we didn't
sense you when we passed over here. From what you've
said, I suppose you'd fainted by that time."

He shrugged. "We just kept circling around until we
heard your screams and assumed you were being attacked."

She leaned forward, eager to discover how Marissa
fared. He reassured her. "I sent that ass Zyre home with
her. Someone needed to accompany her and fill Maxim in
on what's happening." Ganther snorted. "With all his
moaning and griping, he didn't contribute much anyway."

Lauran sighed, relieved no one else had serious injuries. The rest had escaped with scratches and bruises,
which had soon healed. Despite taking a few days to mend,
even Marissa would recover from her severe wound. The
Kin admired the healer's repair job on her wing and agreed
she would be able to fly again.

"But that does not solve her problem." Nath's face
grew grave. "If we do not remove the gemstone, anyone

using the control rod could force Lauran to do their bidding."

Ganther's green skin darkened as he glowered, and the dragons growled in unison—a low, dangerous sound that made Jenny and Davy hug each other nervously.

"Please," Nath begged. "Let me fetch my master. He is much wiser than I am and may succeed where I failed."

The golden dragon still refused to involve anyone else, so it surprised her when Ganther overruled her, agreeing to meet with Marden. "We need someone more skilled to help us."

Accepting the wisdom of this, Lauran grudgingly agreed.

Nath ran down the mountain, leaving Jenny chatting with the giant. Davy, staring with wide-eyed wonder, leaned against Lauran as she talked with the other dragons.

Though the small cave she'd sheltered in stood high above the settlement, his long legs turned an hour's hike into a twenty-minute run.

By the time he reached the village, his lungs burned. As he neared his home, he leaped over shrubs and swerved around villagers. He barely heard Polina's sharp call over the pounding in his ears.

Nath waved her questions away, ignoring her glare. He burst through the front door, gasping, "Master!"

Marden emerged from his room, shuffling forward with both hands grasping his walking stick. He stared in alarm at his red-faced, puffing apprentice. "Calm yourself, boy. Excessive haste gains nothing."

"You must come . . . they need our help . . ."

The shaman frowned. "Who requires aid that has you so agitated? The younglings from the portal?"

"No." Nath gulped for air. "The dragons!"

Marden's eyes widened, but he asked no further questions. He moved to the table and wrapped the two worn journals he'd been studying in oilcloth, placing them high on a shelf. After throwing a wrap around his shoulders and taking a fresh grip on his walking stick, he gestured for the younger man to lead the way.

Torn between rushing back and proceeding at his master's pace, Nath was surprised to find himself struggling to keep up. Of course, he'd already made this journey at breakneck speed, and now they were repeating it uphill!

They did not speak. The old shaman focused all his energy on haste.

28

Jenny retreated into the narrow cave, pulling Davy with her, as the sun set and the temperature dropped. Ganther pulled up boulders just inside the entrance, where they sat protected from the cooling night breezes.

Still weak from her injuries, Lauran joined them. The larger dragons remained crouched in a semicircle outside.

With the great beasts to collect logs as easily as a youngling gathered sticks and dragonfire to light them, a nice bonfire greeted the two shamans when they arrived.

Despite Jenny's reassurances and Lauran's size, her tail curled tight around her forepaws as the old shaman approached. He looked so tiny beside her, yet she cringed away from him.

Marden stopped, panting and winded, and beamed at the waiting dragons with delight. He nodded at the golden dragon, before bowing low to Ganther and mind-speaking his greeting. *['Tis many years since I last met one of the Kin. We are honored to be of help.]*

Ganther's bushy eyebrows rose, and he inclined his upper body in a partial bow.

Jenny hid her grin as Nath beamed with pleasure at seeing his master shown respect by the green giant. He threw a few orbs in the air to light their conversation, and Ganther hurried to pull up more boulders for the newcomers.

Marden sank down on one with a grateful nod. His apprentice hovered and chided him for exerting himself, until the old man irritably waved him away and bid him hush.

Jenny put her arm around Davy as the exhausted boy slumped against her, half asleep.

At Marden's request, Lauran repeated her story. His smile faded as he listened, and his expression grew grave.

Nath shifted, restive and scowling. When she finished speaking, he burst out, "From my first day as his apprentice, my master taught me this basic tenet: 'harming one harms all'. I had assumed all sorcerers, Lowlander or Anishinabe, lived by the same code."

He shrugged, lifting his hands in the air. "I find it incomprehensible that a wizard would choose to renounce the light and become a warlock. That he set out to capture and enslave another living creature . . . ?" He paused, as if at a loss for words. "It seems so senseless."

Marden shook his head. "Everything has a purpose, my young apprentice. You should comprehend this by now."

Nath stared at him, wide-eyed with disbelief.

"Evil must exist," his master continued. "Yes! Wickedness occurs so good may vanquish it."

The younger man looked unconvinced. For a moment, Jenny expected him to argue, but he shrugged, deferring to his master's wisdom. She narrowed her eyes, irked by his submissiveness.

The old shaman peered around at the Kin. "Can you describe this object the warlock called a control rod?"

"It's a thick stick, about two dragon claws long," Ganther said. "He kept pointing it at us, but not a single dragon or rider reacted, except Lauran."

Lauran nodded. *[Yes, it's about the length of Jenny's arm, tapered to a plain center area where he gripped. Sort of like a long, thin hourglass. Scribbles and tiny gems covered the rest of the shaft, both above and below his hand. I couldn't see them all—and none of them well enough to recall.]*

Her entire body shuddered. *[While its curse controlled me, I could move nothing except my eyes. I was frozen, paralyzed, with no will of my own.]* She snapped her jaws in distress. *[A horrible aura of wickedness surrounded it.]* She gave Marden a shy, hopeful smile. *[Nath said you might be able to help us. Can you remove the ruby?]*

Jenny wasn't the only one who held her breath, awaiting his answer.

"Such a device would be unique, sharing a deep, personal connection with the sorcerer who fashioned it." The shaman pursed his lips. "Shifton will have spent months creating his, using magic to strengthen the enchantments and the links between the rod and the gemstones themselves. Those smaller stones may be shards off the larger ones used in the pendants."

He leaned forward. "Can you recall any of the runes or incantations on it? We must decipher those clues to break any spells and take control of the ruby ourselves."

[I'm afraid I can't provide enough detail to recreate it.] Lauran's shoulders slumped. *[I escaped too quickly to study it closely.]*

"And you're the only one who's ever seen the thing." Ganther's heavy eyebrows drew together. "The rest of us wouldn't stand a chance of getting near it."

Nath looked around at the others. "Even if she supplied all those details, the best artisan in our village would need several days to recreate it. Then we would still have to decipher it." He shrugged. "Do we have that kind of time?"

Ganther smashed his hand onto a rock, breaking it apart and startling Davy awake. Jenny patted him reassuringly, and he sat up, blinking blearily.

"The enemy approaches. We must take action now." The green man growled.

Marden's dubious expression warned them of his answer. "Lauran may be forced to flee this madman. To live, dreading this might be the day where he finds her . . ." He shook his head, his ancient eyes full of sorrow. "It is no life for the young draikana."

"We'll continue to monitor the warlock." Ganther's scowl deepened. "I suppose I could try to talk one of our dragons into eating him . . . although they'd have to get past the soldiers first."

The old shaman ignored the sarcastic suggestion. "Deciphering the symbols and reversing its spells are not impossible tasks,"—he shrugged—"but ones we cannot begin without that knowledge."

[Well,] Davint snarled, *[like Ganther said, Shifton won't be inclined to let someone waltz in and take his weapon from him. He'll be even more vigilant now he knows he only trapped one of us. How will we get anyone near it?]*

Everyone tried to imagine a way to acquire or at least examine the rod. The only sound breaking their glum silence was the hissing of heated logs as they released moisture, punctuated by sharp crackles and pops as pockets of sap boiled and exploded.

Jenny fidgeted, turning her phone over in her hands. She regretted that things seemed hopeless for Lauran, but she hoped they would soon turn their discussion to the portal and how to get her and Davy home.

The more she considered it, the more concerned she became that not a single sparkle had lingered in the Cavern of Whispers. Suppose the gateway only worked one way? Would they be stuck here?

She refused to give up hope. *We'll have quite a story to tell. Mom won't believe it.* Perhaps when they finished talking, the dragons would let her snap photos of them. *Without proof, nobody will ever—*

She gaped at Lauran, who sat facing her. Her phone! The dragon lifted a questioning brow ridge.

"I can do it!" When everyone looked her way, Jenny blushed at the sudden attention but held up her cell phone. "What if I use the zoom to take photographs? Getting close enough unnoticed should be easy."

Davy hooted. "That's a great idea, Jen."

Faced with a sea of puzzled expressions, she frowned impatiently. "Okay, let me show you." She turned her phone on, then peered across the clearing.

"Nath, can you send an orb down that way?" She waved her hand toward a tree, and he complied. "What about that owl sitting near the top branch?" Jenny lifted the cell phone, used the zoom, and snapped several photos.

She opened the gallery, turning the camera to allow Ganther and the others to see. "Zoomed images can get blurry. But it's clear enough to decipher the markings, right?"

When everyone saw the miraculous pictures, they got excited about the possibilities.

Nath grinned at her. "That might work. However, I should be the one doing this. It is too dangerous . . ." He hesitated, taking too long searching for a reason that wouldn't offend her.

"For a girl, you mean?" Jenny snapped. "Well, it is my phone, and besides, it's password protected, so you couldn't use it anyway. Stop being such a macho jerk, and I might let you come along."

The four draikanas agreed with her—once she explained what *macho jerk* meant.

Lauran glared in Davint's direction. *[That's becoming quite common around here.]*

Voices rose as the apprentice and the offended drake protested.

Davy covered his ears and cringed, but that couldn't block out the noise inside his mind. Jenny didn't stop objecting, but she looped her arm about his shoulders, knowing how much he hated loud arguments.

The quarrel might have lasted all night if their elders hadn't intervened.

Ganther gave a mental roar that silenced the entire group and made the boy yelp. The shaman acknowledged

Jenny's right to take the photos, given it was her plan and her phone. Nath yielded to their authority and asked to accompany her, and Davint agreed to transport them.

Should I mention that my battery is down to sixty-four percent? Jenny flicked her eyes around the company. *No, they wouldn't get it. Anyway, that should be more than enough. I hope!*

She gave a start as Marden clapped his hands together. "Very well. We should part for the night. Many tasks await us on the morrow."

Once the non-Kin headed down the mountain, Ganther called a pair of dragons over. "We must locate the soldier's camp. Dram, you fly reconnaissance. Mark their position but don't get spotted. Kellin, please return to the dragonhold and give Maxim an update. While you're there, I need a few things from my cave . . ."

29

Jenny led her exhausted stepbrother on the long hike down the mountain, following the shamans' dancing orbs, which lit their way.

When they reached the village, they laid another pallet on the floor in the chamber where she'd woken up, which happened to be Nath's. Although she offered to move, Nath assured her he didn't mind sleeping by the hearth in the common room.

Davy interrupted to complain that he was hungry, and they realized they'd skipped dinner in all the excitement. But Marta was ahead of them. She had left a hearty stew warming over a banked fire. New bread with freshly churned butter and apple turnovers—still warm from the oven—completed their meal.

When the boy pushed his glasses back up his nose with a weary yawn and pronounced himself "stuffed and ready for bed," Marden requested they stay seated for a moment. He stood and pulled an oilskin-swathed package down from a shelf and set it on the table. They sat forward in their seats as he unwrapped a pair of battered books.

"I have done some searching through my master's journals." He looked up at Jenny. "I mentioned earlier that I recalled references to issues with gateways, but in your rush to reach your brother, there was no time to speak of it."

Chastened, she reddened, though he did not sound at all censorious.

"My memory proved correct." His gnarled hands stroked the ancient book. "Our histories are full of these doorways. Are they a natural phenomenon caused by Galahar's magic? Or did someone create them? And if so, why?"

He shook his head. "Even my master found them a mystery. He only knew one thing: Such openings were growing rare."

Marden flapped his hand, seeming to indicate the unimportance of history at the moment. "These books confirm that different portals, as you call them, lead to other worlds. To return home, you must find the opening you came through"—he nodded at his apprentice—"in the place Nath found you. They occur in short-lived bursts, disappearing as your gateway did."

He leaned forward. "But here is the crucial thing. They shift." He wagged his finger in emphasis. "Eya! We do not comprehend why. Do Galahar's moons influence them, or something in the other world? We do not know. Everything I have read suggests you must return before end of day on the Summer Solstice, in less than four days. The gateway should open again at that time."

He hesitated. "The journal implies no other doorway opens to your reality for a year, or perhaps longer. And since they appear to be decaying, I cannot guarantee the stability of this one, either now or in the future."

"What can we do?" Jenny looked stricken. "Should we go camp in the cave, in case the portal activates early?"

"That may be the best idea." Nath drummed his fingers. "If they have grown unpredictable, a gateway might well develop before the appointed time."

"NO!" Davy pushed his chair back, sending it tumbling as he jumped up. Startled, the others faced the belligerent boy. "We can't leave until we're sure Lauran's safe."

Jenny stretched a hand toward him. "Nath and Marden will protect her. I must get you home."

Her stepbrother moved out of reach. "I won't go! If you try to force me . . . I-I'll run away." His fists clenched as he glared at her. "She needs our help."

Davy's tone turned accusatory. "You said you would get the photos. You promised." His voice softened to a plea. "They can't manage without you. We have to stay."

She shook her head. "Circumstances have changed. That may not be possible now."

Jenny stared down at the table, finding it hard to meet the boy's eyes. He was right; she'd offered her help—insisted, in fact. Though maybe if she left them her phone . . .

She sighed. They couldn't remain here any longer. It would be irresponsible. Her curiosity wasn't as important as getting Davy home. Her thoughts reeled. She tried to imagine what Mom would say if she were here. Or worse, Frank.

Yet . . . part of her agreed with her stepbrother. *How*

can we leave before we see Lauran freed? Not knowing what happened will drive me crazy.

She looked up, meeting Davy's pleading eyes. "Ugh!" she groaned. "Fine. But as soon as the shaman removes the ruby, we're out of here."

Jenny gave him her firmest stare, cutting his cheer short. "But if he can't do it in four days or less, we gotta go. No matter what. And only if the dragons are willing to give us a ride. If we must walk, we'll need to leave earlier, because even taking the shortcut, it takes almost a full day to reach the Cavern of Whispers."

Davy hugged her. "You're the best sister ever."

"Yeah, yeah." Jenny patted his back. "And you're still a brat." She sniffed him. "Yech, and you stink." She demanded he have a bath before she would allow him between clean sheets.

Nath helped her fill a tub in front of the fire in their room, using a bit of magic to heat the water. The boy insisted she leave before he climbed into the bathtub, complaining the entire time.

Marden disappeared while Davy bathed and came back with fresh clothes for him, borrowed from the villagers. He only consented to wear the nightshirt after the men showed him theirs and assured him they wore them every night.

Once she'd put her weary stepbrother to bed, Jenny returned to the common room. She discovered the older shaman poring over a large map, which was spread across their table and hanging off the sides.

He greeted her with an eager smile. "Nath has gone to bathe himself, so I hoped you might wish to learn more of *millioke*—this good land—you find yourself stranded in."

She came and leaned over his shoulder, gasping in delight at the beautiful details. It looked like a piece of art, with miniature mountains, lakes, and forests laid out in full color.

The shaman pointed at two tiny red dots close together on the top right, on the northeast end of a curving mountain range. "This is our village and the Cavern of Whispers."

"Is this to scale?" She checked the distance. "Calculating six hours' walk between those locations . . ." Her eyebrows rose. "Galahar must be at least the size of Canada or the US."

"My map is the most accurate magic can produce," he said proudly. "You mentioned these names before. Are they in your kingdom?"

Jenny laughed. "We refer to them as countries. I'm most familiar with those two. They're broken into provinces or states—what you would call territories." She frowned. "There are dozens of nations of various sizes in my world, and some of them may consider themselves kingdoms."

She leaned forward. "What are those?" Jenny pointed to brown ridges bordering the north and east sides of the map.

"The Impassable Escarpment. Even dragons who try to cross them never return." Marden ran his finger down and across wave symbols indicating waters on the west and south. "The Lowlanders living down here, along these coastlines, are great fishers and sailors."

He shrugged. "Yet those voyagers who search for distant shores are never seen again. Some claim they sailed over the world's edge."

"They used to say that crap about Earth too." She snorted. "Until they discovered the planet is round." She made a circle with her hands.

"Indeed." Marden's eyebrows lifted so high, they vanished under his bangs.

Jenny pulled out a chair and sat beside him. "So, the Bear Tribe settled here." She touched the Tail, covering those dots to the top right. "And the Kin are located somewhere there." She shifted her finger to the west, across the Trifair Plains, to the curve of the Dragon Spine Mountains. "Who are these Lowlanders everybody talks about?"

The old man spread his hands. "They live throughout the rest of Galahar. Most are ordinary folk, without magic—what some call Commons, or nulls. They come in many distinct colors and statures. Our oral histories tell how everyone and everything entered the kingdom through gateways—as you and Davy did."

His voice took on a singsong, storytelling tone. She imagined him teaching or sharing stories around a campfire the same way. "In the before times, all creatures used these doorways to slip between their worlds and ours. Some fled persecution or inhospitable climates, while others wandered through unaware of their arrival in a new land."

Marden shook his head. "It is said my people escaped a battle with a stronger tribe attempting to enslave them." He shared a rueful smile. "We are obstinate. Sometimes too thickheaded. We do not easily tolerate anyone trying to rule over us." He shrugged. "That is why we sought what many consider the least hospitable lands that none would covet. We tired of fighting and settled here, away from others."

He gestured toward the outdoors. "The High Kings of Galahar consented to allow my people to dwell in peace. We came to love our mountains, and they protected us. The Lowlanders do not interfere with our lives, and we live in harmony with nature."

His finger moved to a thick representation of trees near the top center of the map. "Other creatures made similar choices. The elves and fairies prefer the unspoiled beauty of the Timeless Forest."

Jenny laughed in delight. "Whoa! No way! Elves—are you serious?"

Her enthusiasm prompted a smile. "Oh yes. If we had more time, I would introduce you to the dwarves. You would find their underground city fascinating." Marden frowned. "News of their gemstones' ill-usage will be most distressing to them."

Jenny looked puzzled. "Nath says they won't trade with the Lowlanders. How come?"

The old shaman sighed. "Eya, that is an ancient grievance. I am afraid they exploited dwarven labor in the past, and clashes over mining and logging rights drove the dwarf community to withdraw into the mountains. Over time, prejudices on both sides increased."

This seemed to sadden him, so she tried to distract him. "Are there other magical creatures?"

"Of course." His face brightened, and he nodded. "It is even rumored there are unicorns deep in the Timeless Forest. We also have various shifters, such as the wolves." He hesitated, as if catching himself.

She looked at him curiously, and his lips tightened. "There are more troublesome beings as well. Trolls, giants, goblins . . . and the Mer."

"Wait! You mean mermaids? Why are they trouble? I always pictured them as beautiful things."

"Nay. Their songs convince the unwary of their beauty, but they do not love landwalkers, as they call us. They can be vicious creatures, luring sailors to their deaths."

His vehemence surprised Jenny. "Wow, okay, avoid merpeople." She returned to the map. "Hey, does Galahar have a capital city?" She looked up and caught his uncertainty. "I mean, a center of government?"

He tilted his head in that familiar birdlike manner of his. "A duke or duchess oversees each territory, while the High King rules overall."

"Okay, we're sort of the same." Jenny smiled. "In Canada, each province has a premier, with a prime minister at the top. In the US, states have governors, with a president leading them. There's an important island country that has a monarchy, though they also have a parliament." She shrugged. "I'm not well-versed in international politics, I'm afraid."

Marden listened with interest. He touched a mark on the plains at the base of the mountains. "We, too, have a monarch. The High King's Keep is here, in Trifair Territory."

He moved his finger southeast about an inch, although it remained on the grasslands. A tiny dark triangle suggested a mountain in the middle of the flatlands. "The sorcerers' Citadel lies here. That is where the Lowlanders train their wizards."

Jenny sat up straight, gaping at him. "Get out. You have a Hogwarts?" She grinned at his bewildered frown. "A school for magic?"

"Ah, yes. Not shamans, but each wizard's training takes place there."

"Like that Shifton." She scowled.

But Marden shook his head. "He has given up any claim to such a noble title. He is not of the light. Having fallen, he is now of the shadows—a warlock."

Jenny tried to make a death mask breathing noise, intoning, "He has gone to the dark side." She laughed at how bad her Darth Vader imitation sounded. Not that it mattered, as the shaman didn't recognize the reference anyway.

"Eya," he agreed.

"What's the difference between wizards and shamans?" She lifted one foot onto her chair, hugging her knee as she cocked her head, unconsciously mirroring him.

The old man studied her face as if checking her level of interest. Satisfied, he smiled. "The Lowlanders' sorcery is based on five colored crystals of varying strengths. Blue is the strongest, next is green, yellow, orange, and rose red is the weakest."

He pulled a chain from around his neck and showed her a small sapphire. "Someone with a strong affinity for blue magic is an Azure Wizard, then Emerald, Citrine, Amber, and the least potent is Crimson."

"How do they figure out what color power somebody has?"

"Ah! When a youngling enters the Citadel, they are tested to discover which of the mighty gemstones residing there responds to them. That is their strength, and they concentrate on training to use that magical ability."

"But your magic is different?" Jenny dropped her foot

back to the floor, leaning forward with interest and resting her chin on her hand. "And are all shaman men?"

"Shamans work with all the elements. All five crystals. We do not separate them. I suppose a Lowlander would regard us as the equal of an Azure Wizard, since we handle all the colors. We use them in conjunction with the magic of the earth and the spirits."

He smiled at her inquisitiveness. "A shaman's female counterpart is a wise woman. Each tribe has one or the other. I cannot, in truth, say they never have both. But in all my years, I have only seen this happen twice. Eya! In each case, the couple bonded."

Before she could ask any more questions, Nath came out to join them. "Master, the hour grows late. And to-morrow will be a strenuous day."

Marden sighed and, leaning over, stage-whispered to Jenny. "That is my apprentice's polite reminder that it is time for his elderly mentor to be abed." He rolled up the map with slow, careful movements, as if his hands hurt. "I fear he is correct."

She stood, then stooped to plant an impulsive kiss on Marden's cheek. "Sleep well." He smiled and patted her hand.

As she slipped past Nath, he murmured something that sounded like "May you encounter the divine." His words kept her awake far into the night. In a place where magic existed, encountering some deity in her slumbers seemed entirely possible.

She rolled over and punched her pillow. *Why didn't he just say pleasant dreams?*

30

Four Days until Summer Solstice

Lady Avila closed the door to her suite, wedged a chair under the handle, and crossed the room as Pepper scampered around her feet in delighted circles. Satisfied with her precautions, she sank into her favorite seat by the window.

She lifted a layer of fabric and floss from the sewing basket beside her and removed the papers hidden underneath. Laying them on her lap, she smoothed the wrinkled pages she'd stolen from Shifton's workroom yesterday.

Avila shuddered, recalling the squalid conditions in his chamber. Although she'd been tempted to call a squad of servants in to clean up, that would have exposed her trespass. She planned to return the pilfered notes before the sorcerer returned and discovered their absence.

She'd noticed that most of the books were ancient tomes with obscure titles such as *Draconic Alchemy*, *Necromantic Transmutations*, and *Spectral Harmonics*. So

Shifton's interests included dragons, working with the dead, and ghosts, among other even murkier subjects.

In his disorganized records, she'd seen references to exotic creatures—basilisk, chimera, and manticore—as well as more common beasts, such as werewolves and Mer. She did not understand what her father wanted from Shifton. What could he be researching? And why?

Avila bent over the papers she'd stolen. His execrable handwriting appeared almost indecipherable, and he had created abbreviations that must be significant to him but, at first glance, seemed incomprehensible.

Even the title above the list of ingredients, *Serpentis Invigoratus,* held little significance for anyone but Shifton. She read the first line:

Three handfuls of Silverthorn Berries—brewed
for ess.

"Hmm, I suppose 'ess' might mean essence. I can't think of another word that fits."

Pepper jumped up on the couch and sat watching her as she read. Most of the time, Avila found his attentive listening and intelligent head tilt charming, as if he were trying to understand her. Today, she barely acknowledged him as she checked the next line.

One flask Starflower Nectar—hndpk under fm,
at peak pot.

"Shards . . . all right, huh-nd-pik—Oh! Hand pick under 'fm.' Perhaps full moons? 'Peak pot' is easy: peak potency, or maybe potential . . ."

She rose, tossing the pages onto a tabletop as she turned toward the dog. "Ugh. This will take forever to decipher. And what good is a recipe? I need some clue indicating its purpose."

Pepper gave a single bark, as if encouraging her.

Avila gathered the papers, returning to her chair and reading with renewed determination.

Moonstone Dust; a Phoenix Feather . . .

"'Sage's Tears'—I recognize that one. The Master Healer uses them. She said they amplified the potency of any elixir they were added to. If memory serves, they're collected from a weeping willow in the heart of the Timeless Forest."

She sat back, stroking Pepper absently, her lips pursed as she deliberated. "So, whatever he's concocting sounds strong." Avila glanced down at the last ingredient.

One vial of DB.

"That's it? Only the initials DB? No preparation hints?"

The actual procedure for assembling the elements looked even more difficult to read. As if Shifton's excitement had made his hands shake, resulting in splattered and distorted lettering. It didn't help that he'd spilled kaffee on the page at some point, washing out the writing in one spot and smearing the ink in others.

Avila moved to a window, hoping the afternoon sun would make the damaged parchment easier to read. She held the paper close to her face, squinting at the scribbles.

Prep initial treat. using 20 drops of DB in order
to prep the vessel.

The noblewoman scowled. "Damnation! Speak plain, will you? 'Prep' . . . prepare? Yes, that makes sense . . . 'Treat' . . . that's obviously treatment. Add those drops— they must be potent, if you require so little—to 'prepare the vessel.' A container of some sort? Why does it have to be prepared?"

Pepper whined, waving a paw in the air as her tone made him anxious. She began walking back and forth. The dog hurried to trot beside her, until she signaled him to return to the couch. He did as he was told, but his eyes followed her as she paced.

Her elaborate coiffure came undone as she ran her fingers through her hair, gripping the strands in frustration.

Begin rit. at midnight, under waxing sec. moon.

"Well, that one is easy enough. Start the ritual when the second moon is getting full. All right, let's hope he says something about the uses for this potion."

"'Stir widdershins'—Grandmar used to use that term. Let me see, she said it meant clockwise . . . no, counter-clockwise, that's right—'with the Phoenix Feather, until it glows green.'"

She skimmed down through the notes. "What's this?"

Store in a sealed vial, away from direct sunlight,
and consume with caution.

"Well, that sounds serious. And this recipe creates something you're supposed to take, like medicine." Avila frowned. "Wait. That could mean the vessel being prepared is the person consuming this concoction."

She leaned to one side, tilting the page toward the light.

Inc DB-Ess in add prep until desired balance is
achieved.

"All right, balancing is good—I hope. So, 'inc.'—increase whatever DB is . . . you only want the essence of that vialful for these 'additional preparations.'"

Her frown deepened as she squinted at the closing lines.

Excessive use of DB may have an unpredictable

*effect on the vessel and disrupt the natural
order.*

Pepper ran to her side as Avila sank onto the couch, and Avila pulled him closer. "Oh, Father, what have you gotten yourself into?"

31

Lauran rose with the sun the next morning. The constant agony caused by the ruby shifting in her chest remained bearable if she kept her movements small. She avoided looking at the ugly scars marring her skin—the last remnant of the stubborn gem's power fighting her body's natural resources—and flexed her wing.

The membrane was stiff. She'd have to get used to flying with one thicker center, but she felt grateful to be whole again, suffering no additional pain. Ganther kept wanting her to rest, but despite her ordeal, she had the resilience of youth on her side.

Curious to see how Jenny's scheme worked, her father planned to join them today to take her *fotos*. Since Lauran's new friends had met him in human form, he couldn't shift until they finished here.

However, Kellin returned before dawn. She was weary from her extended flight and burdened with the supplies he'd requested, so Ganther sent Davint alone.

Lauran pretended not to notice as her father waved him off, saying, "Away with you. I'll meet you at the shaman's afterward." She lay basking in the sunshine, watching from under half-closed eyelids, as the copper launched himself into the air.

They were still avoiding each other, although she knew he shared everyone's eagerness to see her set free.

Among the first to wake, Jenny heard the copper drake arrive and rushed out to meet him. She hadn't expected the dragons to pick them up, assuming she'd have to climb back up the mountain this morning. And his early arrival meant they didn't have a chance to warn anyone about the Kin camping nearby.

The sight of a huge dragon landing on the common alarmed the villagers. Women screamed and shielded their younglings, while men grabbed weapons and ran at Davint, who reared back in annoyance. Jenny waved her hands, trying to be heard over their panicked cries.

"He's friendly!" she yelled, but her shout was lost in the din, and no one listened.

Nath rushed out and, using magic to amplify his voice, bellowed, "STOP. HE IS OUR FRIEND."

This greeting did not improve Davint's foul humor. He answered their apologies with an annoyed grunt, though he allowed them to mount and instructed them where to hang on to his scaled hide.

Now that the actual moment to ride a dragon had arrived, Jenny kept picturing herself sliding down his spine and tumbling through the air. She swallowed hard, opting to sit in front of Nath, trusting him to hold her in place.

Despite her excitement, she yawned, wishing she'd been able to sleep in. After last night's anxiety, she was amazed she hadn't dreamed at all. Not that she remembered, anyway.

"I will not be joining you," Marden called from the doorway. "I must continue my research."

Jenny's jaw dropped. His coming along had never crossed her mind. No one else spoke, yet Davint and Nath's carefully blank expressions told her it had never occurred to them either. They each endeavored to hide their relief.

However, catching the twinkle in Marden's eye as he came forward, Jenny harbored a sudden suspicion that he'd been teasing—and perhaps repaying them—for considering him too elderly for this adventure.

Davy was the one who caused them trouble, throwing a tantrum worthy of a three-year-old when he learned he couldn't go. Only Davint's promise of a future ride elicited sullen agreement. Marden took him to meet some of the village boys, with the prospect of introducing them to Lauran cheering him up.

Davint crouched and launched himself into the sky with a jerk, making Jenny squeal and scattering the villagers who'd gathered to gawk at him. The snap of his wings, high above their heads, echoed off the surrounding slopes.

Her stomach lurched as the world dropped away beneath her. The wind tugged at her hair as they soared higher, each dip and surge of his wingbeats making her cling to his neck. Though the sun shone above the clouds, the chilly air made her grateful for Marta's gift of the warm ruana.

A few moments after Davint left, a shadow fell across Lauran. She tilted her head to peer up at Ganther looming over her. He slapped her shoulder with a massive hand. "Here now, I can tell you were only pretending to be asleep. Come help me."

Lauran rose and followed him over to an odd pile of metal objects, including a large cauldron. He lifted several items off the top, and she helped him spread out four chainmail shirts Kellin had brought—human knee-length hauberks.

"I acquired these intending to make a Kin-sized mid-thigh habergeon."

She gave a snort of draconic laughter, tickled by the idea of a dragon in a coat of mail.

He grinned. "Lucky thing I never got round to it!"

After explaining what he wanted, Lauran used a razor-sharp talon to cut away the arms. Next, she sliced each across both shoulder seams and down one side seam so they lay flat.

Ganther gave a satisfied grunt. "If I join them into a sort of collar you can wear, it should cover the base of your neck, where the ruby sits." His eyes flicked to the spot she kept rubbing, and his mouth tightened. "The silver chest limited the signal being broadcast by the other necklaces. Hopefully, this will do the same thing."

He used pincers and rings to join the sides of the shirts together, leaving the last side open. Then they laid the resulting sheet of metal flat.

[Now what?] she asked, as he turned to the remaining materials Kellin had brought.

He dumped out the contents of the heavy cast-iron cauldron, sending coins, thick jewelry, and silver dishes clanking and sparkling to the ground.

By this time, the other dragons had gathered, attracted by their unusual activities. Their whirling yellow eyes followed his movements with avid curiosity, excited by the proximity of so much treasure.

[This is for my daughter,] Ganther snarled.

They sank back, their hoarding instincts having driven them forward. Though lacking the ability to blush, shame at losing control reflected on their faces. Lauran understood their embarrassment since her eyes, too, whirled with excitement.

Her father nodded in sympathy. She *sensed* his own inner dragon howling at the suggestion of relinquishing any of its hoard. It humbled her that he soothed his beast just by staring at her. His love warmed and comforted her.

"I didn't find it easy sharing my stash's location," Ganther admitted as they settled into the tedious process of removing any jewels from their settings. "Despite knowing Kellin from birth, I struggled with telling her how to locate it." He cocked his head and grinned at his daughter. "I trust her with my life . . . and yours. But my treasure is another story! Anyway, she swore to only touch what I told her to and to keep its whereabouts a secret."

He shrugged. "In the end, having no time to fetch the goods myself, I confided in her." He gave Lauran an amused sideways glance. "Though I may move my stash when we return to the dragonhold."

As Davint flew, he shared the information Dram had

collected the previous evening. Lack of transportation had hindered the warlock's advance through the mountains. A few pack animals carried the soldiers' supplies, but only Shifton rode a horse.

Despite this, they were steadily progressing. Now having descended to the plains, leaving the rougher mountain terrain behind, they would move faster. If they quick marched across the open grasslands, it was possible they could reach the foothills of the Tail by nightfall.

The copper dragon stayed high, using his superior hearing and sight to locate their quarry, right where Dram's report had placed them.

[If I circle that small mountain and approach low through the valley, they won't see me. I'll set you down behind that peak. You can hide there and take your pictures.]

Without waiting for a response, he banked sharply to the left. Jenny grabbed Nath's arms, leaning back against him as he tightened his grip on Davint's scales.

The dragon coasted in, using his great pinions and massive span of membrane to stay inches above the treed mountain slopes. He glided in silence, with no telltale cracks of thunder. As promised, he landed on the back slope of a ridge overlooking the soldiers' camp.

The pair dismounted and he crouched down to wait for them. They scrambled to the top, where a series of boulders at the rim gave them cover and provided a clear view of the encampment.

Below them, Shifton strutted about, waving the rod as soldiers hurried to break down his tent. They kept their heads averted or stole sideways glances at him, their unsmiling faces those of men working for someone they didn't like.

Jenny slipped her phone out and pressed the power button. The warlock's constant movements made her frown. She decided a video might work better than photos. Marden could pause or go frame-by-frame to decipher the information he required.

"Where are the other tents?" she whispered.

Nath shrugged, examining the camp. "It looks like Shifton has the only one. The rest of them are using bedrolls beside the fires." He pointed. "See the fabric rolls tied to the tops of their packs?"

"Well, that doesn't seem fair." Jenny became indignant on behalf of the troops, but Nath just urged her to hurry.

The warlock brandished the rod, making her job easier. The video didn't take long. She glanced at the power level before turning her cell phone off. Only 45% left. They'd need every ounce of battery she could save.

They slipped and slid down the ridge and remounted the dragon.

Once Ganther was satisfied with the quantity of silver they had piled up, he scooped up huge handfuls of coins, jewelry settings, and chains. He returned them to the cauldron, then stepped aside, giving her a nod.

Lauran moved closer and blew dragonfire inside, making the items melt into a shiny, sizzling liquid as they discussed their next step. They agreed that pouring the silver onto the links would be the most wasteful method. Perhaps he should brush it on?

In the end, he curled the long sheet of metal into a C shape. He dipped the chainmail into the enormous cauldron using a pair of notched sticks hooked into the top row of rings.

Once they'd coated the collar with the molten liquid, Lauran accepted one stick, while Ganther kept the other. They lifted the heavy coated armor, allowing excess silver to drip and harden for a few seconds, before they laid the piece flat on the ground.

Without thinking, her father reached for the cauldron, cursing when he singed his hands on the hot iron. He dipped them in a bucket of water, holding them up to watch the blisters heal.

Lauran flinched. While Kin healed quickly, that didn't mean injuries weren't painful.

With a few slashes of her talons, she notched and curved a couple of logs to act as wooden potholders. He used them to raise the cauldron, pouring the tiny amount of leftover precious metal over the chainmail. Small patches pooled on the ground.

Ganther tossed the unsalvageable container to one side. He poured the water over the drying silver to speed up the cooling process. While the sheet was still warm enough to be pliable, he put it around her neck so they could mold it to her body.

Lauran's scales protected her from the heat, which she found comfortably warm.

Ganther only touched the hot metal for a few seconds at a time, hissing and dipping his fingers repeatedly in a second bucket of water Callie fetched for them, until the silvered sheet cooled enough to handle without fully hardening.

They had to make some modifications to allow her wings to move freely, but he insisted she be covered front and rear. "No point blocking your chest only to have the blasted ruby sending signals through your spine!" He stepped back. "But I think it's working." He sounded surprised

She snorted, blowing ashes into the air, making him cough.

Davint interrupted them. He flew overhead with their friends clinging to his back, waggling his wings before heading downhill toward the village.

Her father waved an acknowledgment.

Lauran stood, but Ganther shook his head. "You better stay here and rest. The shamans' house isn't large enough for dragons." He gave her a sly sideways glance. "Unless you want to wait outside with Davint."

Since she wasn't ready to forgive the copper and suspected he felt the same, she sank down on the grass with a snarl. Ganther turned and bounded away down the mountain, his long, ground-eating strides carrying him out of sight in moments.

Speed and caution—was that too much to ask?

Shifton rode in silence, untouched by the mud and fatigue that plagued the men behind him.

Captain Rudolph, sullen and stiff, picked a careful path ahead. They hugged the folds of the foothills, skirting the open grasslands and keeping them out of sight of King's Keep.

Perhaps they should have waited for nightfall, but the warlock was done waiting. His back ached and his thighs were sore, no matter how often he healed them. He missed his luxuries, so the sooner they reached the far side of this sharding plain and caught that thrice-damned dragon, the sooner he could go home.

He lifted the rod and muttered the spell that sent it seeking the gemstones. But instead of pulling forward, like a hound after sqwabbit, his beautiful weapon drooped toward the ground.

Alarmed, Shifton experienced a surge of panic. Had the signal vanished? *No!* That was impossible. His chest tightened. His entire future rode on getting a dragon's blood, and a wounded one had seemed an easy conquest. If it slipped through his fingers . . .

He struggled to conceal his agitation from the troops, convinced the soldiers wouldn't accept his authority if they harbored reservations about his abilities.

They hadn't gone as far as he would have liked, and hours of daylight remained. But he would call an early halt and let them set up camp. He needed time and privacy to figure out what had gone wrong with his spell.

Shifton passed on his order when the captain reported in, ignoring the astonishment on Rudolph's face. *All he does whenever he delivers my dinner is sharding whine about how hard I push the men. He shouldn't complain about a premature stopover.*

32

Annoyed at being excluded, Lauran began gathering up the remaining jewelry fittings, which she dumped in the cauldron. She carefully collected all the jewels they'd removed and carried them into the narrow cave in search of a container to keep them in.

Ganther had laid a bedroll in here, with their supplies piled neatly out of the weather. As she set the ruined pot down, she noticed the small chest containing the other medallions sitting beside his pillow. That was perfect! No one else would open it.

Quickly lifting the lid, she dumped the gems inside. Even that brief exposure caused the power of the jewels inside to dull her movements . . . drag at her limbs. Lauran slammed the lid shut, relieved to find the link between the gemstones cut off in turn.

Yet unease nagged at the back of her mind, and she frowned, struggling to bring her concern into focus. *Yes, silver seems to inhibit the curse.* Her eyes widened. *But when the signal suddenly stops, what's preventing the war-lock from continuing in the last-known direction?*

Her tail lashed in agitation. She stared at the chest, an idea forming. They needed a distraction, a way to delay Shifton until Nath could heal her. Though Lauran sensed the young shaman's doubts about his abilities, she had touched the power in him and was confident that between them, he and Marden would succeed.

She flexed her wings, wincing as the damaged skin and muscle protested. It seemed the gemstone had moved deeper inside her. A vision of the gem pushing itself into her heart made her shudder. She suspected her ribs were all that protected her from this.

With the stone buried near the base of her breast-bone, the ruby throbbed with every breath. It was painful—yet it didn't stop her wings from working. Lauran thought she should still be able to fly—though not for long and not without damage.

She was still weak from blood loss, and the flight would slowly tear her apart inside. But she was tired of being treated like an invalid—desperate to be useful.

Lauran decided to act—and add it to the list of things she needed to be forgiven for.

She took a breath and whipped the chest open, snarl-ing as the buzz of the additional gemstones deepened. Brushing through the jewels she'd just dumped on top, she snatched the chain of a medallion with the tip of a talon and slammed the lid closed again.

The buzzing from the contained jewels lessened, but the pressure grew. It was worse than before her transfor-mation, and she sensed the gem she held trying to over-power her.

Thankful for the silver breastplate protecting her, Lauran whirled toward the cauldron and shot a desperate flame along the upper edge. She hurriedly scraped off some of the softened excess silver. Her great paws shook as she formed a ball around the pendant before the two stones could overwhelm her.

Lauran's hunched shoulders relaxed as the noise faded. That had been too close.

With the resulting blob tucked inside the top of her silvered collar, she went outside, nodding to Dram as she sauntered up the slope behind the clearing.

Once safely hidden by the trees, she increased her pace. High atop the next peak, she found what she'd hoped: a sheer drop-off on the other side. Her lip pulled back in a fierce snarl. If she leaped from this height, it would make taking off less agonizing.

Her plan was to fly a distance away and locate a suitable cave to hide the jewel in. Once her dragonfire melted the silver off the second necklace, she would take off before the gemstones could combine their power.

She crossed two talons on one forepaw. If they were lucky, the warlock would think she had fled in that direction, and hopefully she would return before Ganther could miss her.

Lauran inhaled, stretched up on her hind legs, spread her wings, and jumped.

Jenny explained their concerns about Lauran's situation to Ganther and his companions as they gathered in the shaman's common room. The Galaharans marveled at the video she'd taken.

"The Septainians will only take a couple of days to reach her current position," she pointed out. "We're worried that she's still recovering and might need more time. What if she has to find a new hiding place. How far can she even fly right now?"

"I had an idea that may help with that." The arrival of a huge green-skinned man had shocked the villagers once again. Ganther wasn't as immense as the giants who menaced their tribe on occasion, but at ten feet tall, he remained a most unusual sight.

Davint had landed on the village common again, rather than making the shaman walk up the mountainside to them. He'd settled down to wait while the other four met to discuss their options.

"I had an idea for concealing Lauran," Ganther repeated, giving the chair he was offered a dubious glance before opting to sit on the floor, his tall, broad body dwarfing the crowded room.

"After Lauran's accident, we put the warlock's other pendants in a small chest. Silver appears to inhibit his spells." He frowned. "Should have brought it down with me. Anyway, that gave me an idea for creating a coated wrap, like a collar, to place around Lauran's neck. I'm hoping it will block the ruby's signal and slow the sharding bugger down some."

"That will require a large amount of silver." Marden looked anxious. "I doubt we possess the necessary quantity in the entire village."

"Don't worry about that." The big man waved an oversize hand, looking chagrined as Nath ducked to avoid being hit. "Sorry. I sent Kellin to report to our Alpha, and she brought back everything I needed. I created the collar this morning by repurposing several chain mail shirts, linked together to produce the size I wanted."

Jenny looked puzzled. "Wouldn't they be made of iron rings?"

"Yes, but I coated them with melted jewelry settings and coins—anything silver. Lauran helped with that part—dragon's breath melts metal far better than any forge. She's wearing it now."

He gave a smug smile. "We applied it while it was warm and flexible enough to wrap around her. As I said, I hope it warps the gemstone's magical signature."

Everyone complimented Ganther on his ingenuity. If the gemstone signal disappeared, the trick might confuse Shifton and buy them more time to reverse engineer his spell.

Though Jenny said nothing, her thoughts unwittingly echoed Lauran's concerns; she hoped the warlock would not just continue in the same direction.

Less than four days remained to save Lauran and return home. The responsibility of returning Davy to their world weighed on Jenny. She kept circling back to her decision, like a tongue to a bad tooth. Had she been selfish? Was she letting him stay because *she* was reluctant to leave? What if something happened to him? Could she live with that? Maybe she should force him to revisit the cavern with her immediately.

She pulled her wandering attention to Nath, who appeared enthusiastic about their chances of success.

"My master and I can decipher the spells now that we have pictures of the rod. We should finish by tomorrow night."

Marden raised his eyebrows at his apprentice's rash

promise and advised caution. "Let us take a closer look at these photos of Jenny's before we commit ourselves."

He smiled at Nath's chagrin. "It is a difficult venture we undertake." The old man included Jenny in his warm glance. "And we have not forgotten that Lauran is not our only concern."

She gave him a grateful smile, some of the stress lifting from her young shoulders.

Ganther agreed the dragons would continue to track the warlock and his soldiers. And they would only move the wounded dragon if absolutely necessary. Despite Nath's efforts to heal her external wounds, the spell still impeded her body's natural abilities, preventing Lauran from fully healing. A general weakness persisted, and she tired easily.

They were wrapping up when a woman's shrill cries, accompanied by the shouts and laughter of children, brought their meeting to an abrupt halt. They rushed outside in alarm.

While waiting on the common to carry Ganther back up the mountain, Davint had apparently decided to enjoy a nap in the sun. Returning from a fishing trip and in search of lunch—what his new friends called nooning—Davy had been delighted to find the copper drake dozing on the green.

With his encouragement, the village younglings had soon gotten over their initial timidity. Before long, they were climbing over the lazing behemoth and playing chasing games around his bulk. He let out occasional bursts of smoke, making them shriek and run away laughing.

The current disturbance was caused by a horrified mam searching for her youngling. She was terrified to find the wee boy nestled between Davint's muzzle and forearm, sound asleep.

Nath intervened as the hysterical woman threatened the amused dragon with a broom. The others laughed as she rescued her infant—who had slept through the entire affair.

The village younglings groaned with disappointment when Ganther, waving goodbye, mounted Davint. They leaped into the air with a mighty crack of thunderous wings.

33

Shifton was convinced Rudolph awaited any opportunity to strike back at him and would attempt to turn the soldiers against him. He assumed the young captain's ambitions mirrored his own: grasping, self-serving, eager to exploit any advantage against a rival.

His impatient pacing as they set up camp reflected his inner turmoil. Alone in his tent, he cast the tracking spell multiple times with no results. His anxiety rose, and his casting grew frantic . . .

Again. Nothing. Once more. It remained still.

He would lose his position. Avila. Everything.

Shifton lifted the powerless engraved shaft. *One last try—*

Without warning, the enchantment resumed working, and the weapon hummed in his hand. Relief made him giddy and lightheaded. He couldn't understand what he'd been doing wrong.

The control rod twitched and started to move. Although he expected it to resume its previous direction to the southeast, the tip nudged away from its last heading. It turned in slow increments, making him fear the dragon was abandoning the Tail and returning home.

His teeth clenched in frustration. If it did that, it would make their illicit trek through Trifair Territory a meaningless waste of time. Worse, they'd have to sneak past the High King's Keep again empty-handed, and he'd have to endure Rudolph's smug gloating all the way home.

Shifton breathed a sigh of relief when the rod stopped. It now showed that the beast lay to the northeast. True, they would have to climb the sharding foothills again, but they needed to do that anyway.

Moreover, he felt the strength of the gemstone's pull through the vibrating shaft in his hand, suggesting it must be nearer than before.

Perhaps the beast had moved through an area where something in the mountains blocked the gem's communication with the rod. He scowled doubtfully. *I'll look into that later . . . after we find the dragon.*

With some reluctance, Shifton decided to remain in place until morning. The men were preparing supper, and by the time they ate and broke camp, it would be night.

He gripped the shaft until his knuckles ached. *Damn it. With this strong a signal, it's close.* But stumbling upon a wounded beast without warning in the dark would be dangerous. No point in taking foolish chances.

Besides, he'd expended so much energy repeatedly casting the spell that he needed to replenish his power stores before he faced it.

Lauran staggered down the slope, returning to the clearing

as another dragon and rider soared in and landed. She glanced up and bugled a welcome—to her father.

Davint scowled at her.

She lifted her muzzle, turning her head away and refusing to acknowledge him.

Easing herself carefully to the ground, she tried not to wince as pain lanced through her chest. A dull throb echoed across her back from straining her partially healed wounds, but she clenched her jaw and bore it. They would soon learn what she'd done, but she hoped to be somewhat recovered before she had to face them.

Ganther walked over to where she lay. He sat beside her, slinging his thick arm around her neck. "How long are you two planning to continue this?"

[Until he stops being a macho jerk, I suppose.] Lauran sniffed.

Her father grimaced. "I suspect I will soon grow weary of that phrase."

She ducked her head, giving him a toothy grin, then sobered. *[We haven't talked alone since you arrived, and I wanted to apologize.]*

He flapped his hand, as if to dismiss her explanation, but she insisted. *[No, I mean it. I forgot all about Maxim's directive and gave the boy my real name. Although in my defense, I didn't have a rider at the time.]*

"*That's* what you're sorry for?" Ganther's bushy eyebrows lifted. "Not running away from home?"

[Don't you start. All I need is two macho jerks annoying me. What if we reversed the situation? Imagine an enemy's tracker locked inside you, capable of leading a madman to me and the rest of the Kin. What would you do?]

He struggled to be truthful. "I might have made the

same choice," he admitted. "But you are my only daughter . . ."

[Well, you're my only father!] He laughed at her annoyed reply, and she huffed before smiling back. *[So, we're good?]*

He nodded. "We are."

Davint stomped by, quite obviously avoiding looking in their direction. He gathered himself and launched into the air.

Lauran pretended not to admire his sleek lines.

"He's only angry because he cares about you." Ganther jerked his head after the drake. "Your leaving hurt him. But he'll get over it." A snort of laughter escaped him. "Although it may take two hundred years."

That didn't help, so she changed the subject. *[Jenny's been asking when my 'father' is coming back. I can't very well say you are him in human form.]*

"Humph. I suppose *he* would return to check on you, wouldn't he? We'll have to be careful, though." He pointed to some bushes at the edge of the clearing.

The budding underbrush provided a poor hiding place for the group of giggling younglings who'd followed Davint up the mountain and now peeked out at them.

Ganther *sent* an expanded mind-call, limited to include only the Kin. To preserve their secret, he instructed they do any shape-shifting somewhere distant from the village. This meant either hiking back to camp or working in pairs, as dragon and rider.

"I'm going to show Nath that silver chest next time I see him."

Lauran had been considering how to reveal what she'd done and was startled. Ganther seemed to have read her carefully shielded thoughts. She sighed. They'd just made up, and now her father would probably be angry all over again.

She cleared her throat. *[About that . . .]* With some trepidation, she filled him in on her afternoon adventure.

His face grew stony, and his frosty glare caused her to fidget nervously.

[I'm not a youngling!] she protested. *[Please stop treating me like one.]*

"I suppose you aren't." Ganther sighed. "And it was a good idea." He grinned suddenly. "Though I think I'll let you explain it to Davint."

34

A sixty-foot-long dragon in flight was quite an impressive sight. They watched until Davint disappeared up the mountain, then Jenny turned to Davy. "I need to talk to Marden about these photos. Can you entertain yourself for a while?"

"Go ask Marta to cook your fish," Nath suggested. "It is well past nooning. You must be starved."

She frowned as the boy picked up the slightly disreputable catch he'd tossed aside while they'd climbed on Davint and ran off. Should she have been the one to suggest he eat something? And what had he done all day while she was off riding dragons? Did boys his age need someone to keep an eye on them?

I am so not cut out to be in charge of him!

Jenny turned to find Nath and the shaman waiting for her.

As usual, Marden seemed to read her mind. "He is safe with his companions. They will watch out for him."

"It's nice to see him smile." She rubbed her tired eyes. "They moved in with us when Mom and his dad got married, and he had to change schools." Jenny shrugged. "He spends a lot of time alone in his room, so I don't imagine he's found it easy making new friends."

She reddened. *Did my resentment blind me to Davy's grievances?*

But there were more pressing matters to discuss with Marden than her past thoughtlessness.

"We have another problem." She held out her cell phone and told them about the battery running low. "The video took more power than I expected. But I still think it was the best option."

Nath watched with interest as Jenny explained how to pause and zoom in on the photos. "Make the drawings fast," she urged, pointing at the power indicator. "Once the battery's dead, it's useless until I can recharge it."

Marden thanked her. "You have given us quite a challenge, young lady. Although the warlock's approach has already provided a grave deadline."

He shrugged, waving his hand to indicate the village. "Our people are not warriors, though they will fight to protect themselves." He shook his head. "Yet this is not their dispute, and I cannot ask them to battle professional soldiers. When the warlock comes, we shall cast a spell to hide the village."

Jenny nodded. She smiled at how Marden handled the phone with caution, as if it were fragile. *That's fair, I suppose, since dropping it would not be a good idea.*

Inside, the shaman pulled out a stack of heavy parchment, and Nath fetched a quill and a bottle of ink from somewhere deeper in the cave.

She left them arguing over the translation of a blurry section of footage and searching through individual frames for a better angle.

Their easy acceptance of the phone still amazed her. *Although if you're familiar with magic, what's a little piece of technology?* Jenny chuckled as she let herself out.

She wandered around the village, nodding to those she recognized. On her way back, she spotted Marta sitting outside, peeling a potato-like vegetable, and joined her.

At the sound of their voices, Polina popped her head out the door. Her smile of welcome died. She glared, pinching her lips, before retreating inside without a word. Her grandmar sighed, then lifted a pot of pea pods from the ground and handed them to her young friend to shell. They sat working in comfortable silence for a time, the sun warm on their backs.

"Nath told me about his parents and your family," Jenny murmured. Marta's knife stopped moving. "I'm very sorry for your loss."

The older woman inclined her head. "Thank you. It happened long ago." She hesitated, then added, "And it feels like yesterday."

"He cared for Polina's mom."

"Oh, thick as cave mice, those two." Marta laughed, resuming her work. "From the moment they laid in a cradle together." She shrugged. "Marden chose Nath as his apprentice afore they were old enough to be more than friends."

Her smile turned sad. "*That* was a dream their parents shared. But their lives took different paths. She aged; he did not. Their diverging destinies led them in opposite directions."

Marta grew thoughtful. "I think losing their friendship hurt them the most." She slid a too casual sideways look at the younger woman. "It is nice to see him opening himself to friendship again. It is not good to close oneself off."

"He's like the big brother I never had." Jenny waved off the implication. "I'm going to miss him . . . and you too." She paused. "Davy and I must leave soon." She explained about the instability of the portals. "On the one hand, we don't belong here. We need to get home."

She sighed again, throwing the last of the shells in the discard bowl. "On the other, it's important to help free Lauran. And I did promise. But it seems as if I'm gambling with our futures by delaying."

Marta laid aside her potatoes and took Jenny's hands. "These are hard decisions to rest on such youthful shoulders, and no one can decide for you. You are grown now. The youngling is your responsibility. I am confident you will do your best to protect him."

She gave the younger woman a little shake. "Let us cherish our remaining time together. Give the women a day to get organized. We shall hold a Gather and show you how we celebrate." She chuckled. "Besides, many parents are as eager as their younglings to meet these Dragon Kin our shamans are helping."

Jenny brightened.

A farewell party might be fun, and it reinforced her hope they would make it home.

News of the pending celebration swept through the village.

Davy and his friends raced up the mountain, eager to tell Lauran and the others about the festivities.

The boys returned to the village with an invitation: Would they prefer to hold the event in the large clearing by Lauran's cave? The villagers agreed. So many dragons certainly wouldn't fit on the common!

With a speed that left Jenny's head spinning, the women organized everything.

She enjoyed the festive air of activity making everyone a little giddy. Younglings ran shouting and laughing, and nobody seemed to mind them underfoot. She overheard early-morning plans to fish or hunt, and mams boasted about the last of their winter spices, jams, and preserves, while setting their daughters the task of baking fresh bread.

Jenny giggled, eavesdropping on men wondering how they would sneak ale past their vigilant wives. She smiled as younglings asked her, in hopeful whispers, if they might ride a dragon.

Everyone retired to their beds early, though she suspected no one would sleep well.

Only the shamans ignored the upcoming event. Bent over the cell phone, they painstakingly re-created the rod line by line.

Jenny laid on her palette on the floor, staring up at the darkened ceiling. The lack of windows seemed more oppressive tonight. She wished she could see the stars.

The soft murmur of voices drifted in from the common room, where Marden and Nath worked, their orbs burning late into the night. She resisted the temptation to scold them for staying up. They were grown men, after all.

She tried to fall asleep, but the weight of uncertainty pressed on her, and her mind just wouldn't shut off. If only there were fewer reasons to worry. Somehow, having offered hope with the photographs, she felt responsible for their success.

Jenny considered her stepbrother's affection for Lauran. *He won't leave until she is healed. Should I try forcing him?* She rolled onto her side. *He's been dying to ride a dragon. I can ask one to fly us to the cavern. But what then?*

If Davy took off, could she catch him? *Am I strong enough to force him into the portal?* And what was to prevent him from jumping back, if—no, *when*—they returned home?

Her blankets seemed too hot, and she pushed them off. Then she grew cold and pulled them over her once more. Uncomfortable and frustrated, she tried rubbing her eyes and yawning. She tossed onto her side, then turned over on her back. But nothing worked.

Oh great. Now I need to pee. Of course!

Careful not to disturb Davy, she slipped into the tunnel. Focused on following the diffused light orbs along the edge of the path, she headed down the passageway.

35

As Jenny approached the water closet, the door swung open, and a figure in a white robe stepped out.

She squealed and jumped. "Oh! Polina, you scared me." *Wonderful, my least favorite person in the village.*

"You!"

The loathing in that single word made her take a shocked step back.

"Why are you still here? Why do you and your brother not return to your own world? You have caused enough trouble."

After hearing Nath's history with Marta's daughter, Jenny had resolved to ignore the dark beauty's attitude. Though stung by Polina's rudeness, she tried to hold on to her temper. "Marta wants us at the Gather tomorrow . . . or later tonight . . . whenever." *Why am I explaining myself? It's none of her business.*

"Ha! You might fool Grandmar and Nath, but it is clear to me you are nothing sharding special—a novelty who amuses them. Once you leave, they will forget all about you."

"Whatever." Jenny flapped her hand. "Anyway, we can't return without knowing Lauran is all right."

Still caught up in her own worries, she lacked the energy to deal with Polina's jealousy. *Should we stay, or should I get Davy home? Are we already too late? What if we're stuck here? And now I really gotta pee.* She tried to push her way past.

But reminding Polina that dragons, too, favored the interloper seemed to enrage her further. "Your arrival ruined everything. He does not even talk to me anymore."

No need to ask who she meant.

Jenny's fists clenched. "He and I are friends. That's all. His feelings for you are unrelated to me." She forced herself to speak quietly, although the way Polina glared at her and the woman's possessive tone made her bristle.

"I think it's time you started using your head for more than a hat rack, as my Nana says," Jenny snapped. "You're too smart to keep wasting your energy chasing someone who doesn't want you."

Polina's scowl deepened, contorting her lovely face into something hateful. Her eyes locked on the arm her rival waved through the air. "He will be mine. Why should you get everything I desire?" Her mouth twisted. "Grandmar gave you my cloak, and Nath gives you what should belong to me."

She grabbed Jenny's wrist and jerked it up between them, pointing to the bracelet with its translation stone. "Did you suppose I would not recognize the talisman you wear? I used to play with these stones when . . ."

As the older woman caught herself, Jenny tried being

sympathetic. "When you were a child . . . a youngling?" She yanked her arm, trying to free herself. "Haven't you noticed that you're aging but he isn't?"

"That does not matter." Polina tossed her hair, impatient and scornful. "We belong together. He will discover a way to keep me young too!" She snatched at the bracelet with her other hand. They scuffled, but the taller woman held the advantage, being both heavier and furious. She got her fingers around the talisman and yanked.

Jenny yelped as the knot came undone. The band ripped from her wrist, leaving a red welt on her skin. "Hey, give that back!"

Polina hissed something incomprehensible, before bolting down an unlit tunnel.

Great. Now we can't understand each other. Jenny snatched up a pale orb and took off after Polina.

The passage curved and continued deeper into the mountain. Polina's longer legs gave her an advantage, but Jenny was the star of her track team and quickly gained ground.

They raced through the darkness, twisting and taking random turnings, until Jenny feared she would never find her way back alone. This only fueled her determination to catch Polina, get her bracelet, and return to bed.

They grew winded, and their pace slowed. When they reached a long straight stretch, Jenny's hopes of catching up increased. She pushed herself . . . almost enough . . . just . . . a bit . . . more . . . She extended her hand, ready to grab Polina's shoulder, when the woman took a sudden leap forward.

Without hesitation, Jenny did the same, dropping the orb as her arms whirled. She was several inches shorter and had launched herself farther back from the drop, but she almost made it.

While Polina's longer legs cleared the far side of the crevice with ease, Jenny's stomach slammed into the lip, leaving her breathless and gasping.

Her upper body lay on the path, until she slid backward toward the gaping hole. Her hands scrabbled along the ground, seeking a grip, as she breathed in wheezing gulps. She didn't stop sliding until her fingers caught on the edge, where she jerked to a halt, her own body weight straining her shoulder joints. Her bare feet scratched and dug at the wall, searching for footholds without success.

Desperation made her dig her fingertips into the rocky path, splintering her nails.

"Polina, help me!" The cool, damp air filled with the echo of her rapid breathing. Her hoarse voice rebounded in the dark tunnel, dying to a quiet that settled like additional pressure, pushing down on her. Sparks danced as her eyes tried to see through the darkness. Only the distant glow of her fallen orb, casting light up from below, let her make out the wide, broken lip of the crevice.

"Come on, Jenny, you can do this," she whispered, the words barely audible. Her hands throbbed, and she could feel the cuts on her bruised feet.

The edge disintegrated beneath her grasping fingers. She shifted, clutching for a new hold. Her heart stuttered, then began pounding in her chest. Fear shuddered down her spine, making it difficult to breathe.

Is she still here? Does she understand me? Can she even hear me? Questions scurried around her mind like panicked mice.

"Polina? Are you there?" Her breathless voice

sounded weak and frightened to her own ears. Coarse rock scratched her skin, though adrenaline masked the pain in her feet and hands.

Despite muscles trembling with exhaustion, Jenny clutched at the collapsing dirt with a strength born of desperation.

Blood from her fingertips spread, making the fragile soil muddy, and her grip slipped.

The crumbling rim gave way.

She screamed as her feeble hold tore free. Her body twisted in free fall, arms flailing wildly as she plunged backward.

She stretched one arm behind her in a desperate attempt to catch herself—but she hit hard. Her shriek cut off as she slammed into the ground, the breath punched from her lungs. With a sickening snap she barely registered, pain exploded in her forearm.

Then her head smashed into a concealed boulder.

And the world went black.

36

Three Days until Summer Solstice

Nath groaned, lifting his face from the table where he'd fallen asleep, as Davy burst into the common room far too early. Marden, already awake, poked their fire to life and heated breakfast, but he didn't appear any better rested.

They'd labored late into the night . . . until they encountered a problem. After spending several more hours trying to find a work-around, exhaustion overcame them.

"Where is Jenny?" they asked in unison, smiling briefly at their simultaneous question.

"Maybe she saw you sleeping and went over to Marta's," Davy suggested.

Nath frowned. Jenny was considerate enough to do that, but he thought it more likely she would order them to bed instead. He rubbed his blurry eyes. "Eya. I must find her after I get washed and grab kaffee. If you see Jenny, tell her it is important we speak with her."

Marden filled the boy's bowl from the ever-present pot over the fire. For breakfast, Marta had replaced the stew with a thick porridge. Davy wished aloud for brown sugar, orange juice, and toast with peanut butter, but he settled for berries and milk on his oatmeal. The shaman also allowed him a cup of milky kaffee laced with honey.

While the boy prepared to join his new friends, Nath splashed water on his face and finished his kaffee. He followed Davy outside and waved goodbye as the boys sprinted up the slope, chattering about helping Lauran with her plans for the Gather that evening.

Nath hurried next door. "Auntie M, is Jenny here?" He scanned the cheerful kitchen, as if suspecting she might be hidden in a cupboard.

Marta looked up from kneading bread, her welcoming smile fading at the force of his greeting. "No, I have not seen her this morning." She frowned, brushing flour from her nose with the back of her hand. "Which is strange, because she asked me to teach her to make bread. I assumed you shamans were keeping her busy with that gadget of hers."

"None of us have seen her today. Davy went to visit the dragons. If she is there, he will tell her we need her." Nath picked up a spoon and began tapping it on his palm. "I find it odd she would leave without telling anyone."

His forehead creased. "I am certain she would have if she planned to leave for long." He turned for the door. "I shall search the village. Perhaps she is assisting someone else."

"Let me help you." Marta returned the bread to its bowl and dusted off her hands. "Jenny cannot have gone far on her own."

Starting from opposite ends of the village, he and Marta questioned everyone. However, no one recalled seeing her today. By nooning, Nath's anxiety had grown.

Where could she be? And why did nobody see her leave?

Davy showed up, full of news about a recent arrival—Lauran's father, a green dragon named Ta'ther. "He made me nervous at first," the boy confessed, "because he acted so scary last time we saw him."

Marden chuckled when he heard the new dragon's name. Nath found it puzzling that the shaman seemed so amused by it, but his concern about Jenny outweighed his curiosity.

"Is your sister up with the Kin?" He caught Davy's arm as the youngling headed toward the door, having grabbed a piece of bread and fruit for his nooning. "It is imperative we speak with her, eya."

"Nope. Haven't seen her all day."

Marta stopped in, confirming that no one on her side of the village remembered seeing Jenny this morning. As they talked, Nath realized she hadn't been sighted since the previous evening.

"She would not leave without telling anyone. Certainly not without Davy."

"I have spoken to everyone except Polina." Auntie M sighed. "I do not understand where that girl's mind is today. She knows I need her help, but she has disappeared too."

Nath shot her a startled glance, but the older woman laughed and shook her head. "Oh no, given her obvious dislike of Jenny, 'twould be a miracle if they were together."

He opened his mouth, but she forestalled him. "Fine, I shall go ask her right now."

Polina stood in the middle of her room, staring at the bracelet clenched in her hands. *Why did I hold on to this? I should have thrown the stupid thing into the water closet.*

But she could not do it. The stone belonged to her earliest memories of Nath. It might be all she ever had of him.

A sob caught in her throat. She had cherished the hope he would present the tiger's-eye to her one day, as a groom's gift to his bride.

He would be furious when he learned of her actions.

Taking the bracelet had been rash, but over the past two days, her anger and hurt had grown as everyone—Grandmar, Nath, even Marden—ignored her to fawn over that boyish little blonde . . . nothing.

Polina lifted her chin. She didn't regret her words. *Jenny is insignificant, a nobody.* Her dark eyes flashed. *If I am sweet and patient with him once she is gone, he may apologize for his friendship with the little chit.*

She raised her arms, as if reaching for his. *And declare he only loves . . .* Her gaze fell on the traitorous band entwined in her fingers, breaking her daydream apart.

Her hands dropped to her side.

What had prompted her to act in such a foolish manner? The girl would have been gone soon; she'd overheard Grandmar say so. She only needed to be patient a bit longer.

Her bottom lip pouted. *This is Nath's fault. Why did he give my favorite stone to that . . . that . . . interloper?*

This would never have happened. Who cares if the stupid bint has a sore wrist? It serves her right. Polina frowned. *How long before he forgives me?*

A treacherous corner of her mind tried to replay that cry—the one that cut off midway. Such a faint sound . . . mayhap she had misheard? Surely 'twas just the wind sweeping down a chimney in the stones, confusing her.

She thrust the memory away, squeezing her eyes tight, desperate for last night's events to be a bad dream. When she opened them again, her bleak stare fixed on the proof to the contrary in her hand.

The door curtain lifted, and Marta entered the room without her customary knock. "Granddaughter, have you seen Jenny since . . ."

She broke off as Polina thrust her hands behind her back—too late. Even before Grandmar saw the bracelet, Polina's guilty expression betrayed her. Just like it had as a youngling.

"What have you got there?" Marta's sharp voice sounded fearful, and the alarm on her face filled her granddaughter with shame.

With reluctance, Polina produced the stolen item. "I found this, eya . . ." Her grandmar's mournful expression stopped her.

"Oh, my darling girl. What have you done?"

37

Jenny moaned. *What an awkward sleeping position.* Her back hurt, and her head hung over the edge.

Then she moved her arm.

She screamed as pain shot from her wrist to her shoulder. The world lurched sideways. Her eyes rolled upward—then everything went dark.

When she next woke, the throbbing limb pressed against her stomach warned her not to move it. Jenny lifted the opposite hand and gingerly touched the back of her aching skull, hissing as her fingers came away sticky. She frowned.

"Where am I?" Every part of her bruised body hurt. "What did I do to myself?" She tried to lift her head, but the strain on her shoulders sent pain pulsing down the injured limb. She settled for putting her free hand behind her neck for support.

As the murkiness lifted, fragments of her confrontation with Polina came back to her. Their fight . . . the chase . . . the plummet into darkness . . .

Does she know I fell? Am I in one of those pits Nath warned me about?

Jenny tried to recall how far they'd run. They had taken so many twists and turns. How deep into the mountains had they gone before her accident?

A faint light illuminated her hands and the sides of the pit amid the shadows. Careful to keep the broken bone as immobile as possible, she twisted her head and glimpsed the orb she'd dropped, still giving off a wan glow in a corner, just out of reach.

Despite her misery, Jenny realized she had to reposition her body. Aside from the discomfort of lying on a pile of jagged rocks, dampness soaked through her thin gown, and the wet fabric clung to her skin. She grew more uncomfortable the longer she lay there.

The slightest jarring caused exquisite pain, but she needed to move. She braced her neck with her uninjured hand, groaning as she attempted a quick sit-up, hoping to get it over with.

She got herself upright and hunched forward, taking deep breaths until the pit stopped spinning. If she fainted, she might fall backward and bang her throbbing head again.

Jenny wiped sweat from her forehead. Her face was flushed and her skin hot, despite the cold stone at her back.

Has Polina gone for help? How long since I fell? Are they looking for me yet?

She patted the surrounding ground using her undamaged arm. A thick layer of something soft but damp covered a bed of stones. It felt rough and uneven, like clumps of tangled growth.

I guess I should be thankful that cushioned my fall. She shuddered. *How many fractures would I have if I'd landed on bare rocks?*

Easing back with slow, careful movements, she leaned against the stone wall, grateful for its refreshing coolness on her fevered body.

At least until a tickle of featherlight legs skittered across her face.

"Ack!" She squealed, brushing the insect away, followed by, "Ow, shit, ow, damn, ow!" as she jerked her injured arm. For a while, her entire world narrowed to this screaming agony. Tears ran unnoticed down her face as she began deep breathing exercises while begging for the pain to recede.

The cold wall stopped being refreshing, and shivers shook her body, jarring her broken bones and increasing her anguish. She wedged herself sideways against a boulder, before losing consciousness once more.

An echo of a familiar voice woke her. Was that her mother calling? "I'm right here!" Her throat closed around dry, raspy croaks. "Mom?" The call faded behind the sound of her chattering teeth.

"Get up, you lazy thing. What have you done with my son?"

"F-Frank?" Jenny's bleary eyes peered about. "H-how are you here? Is Mom with you?"

As she concentrated, the pit came into focus. Her fuzzy thoughts cleared. Nobody was here. They were in another world. Perhaps even an alternate dimension. If she died here, they'd never learn what happened to her.

More tears trickled down her cheeks. She licked at their salty moisture, which did nothing to quench her thirst.

"Stop acting sorry for yourself! Haul your scrawny ass out of this hole so you can get Davy home!" Scolding didn't ease her pain, but it got her moving.

Jenny ran her hand around the ground beside her again. She needed some way to attract attention. A round rock gave her an idea. She cleared the mushy vegetation off a large, flat boulder, gasping and wincing whenever she moved too fast and jostled her injured limb.

Pressing herself into the wall to brace her injury, she began pounding the smaller stone against the bigger one. Three short, three long, three short taps. Pause and repeat.

Anyone hearing it might not know morse code, but they should recognize an unnatural rhythm. She beat the cadence until her good arm ached and her vision blurred.

"Time for bed, hon."

"Mom? You aren't r-real . . . but I w-wish you were h-here . . ."

Jenny slumped to one side, bumping the broken bone and waking herself with a strangled scream. She held the hard, swollen limb close while she rocked and cried.

The dryness in her mouth and throat tempted her to lick the muddy walls. Fear of choking on the grit kept her from trying, though soon she might not have a choice. Heat made her cheeks burn, and dizziness washed over her as her fever spiked again.

Exhausted, her eyes drooped, and she did not bother opening them at the sound of Nath's voice. He wasn't real. Anyway, she couldn't make out what he was saying.

"S-stop talking," she muttered. "I c-can't understand you. P-Polina took my t-translation stone!" She sounded petulant, but he was just another delusion. So what did it matter?

"Jenny? Are you okay?" her stepbrother called to her.

"D-Davy?" Her dry lips cracked as she tried to smile. "C-course. The g-gang's all here, eh? I'm fine. Why w-wouldn't I be?" Her head throbbed in time with her injury. She struggled not to burst into tears. "S-stuck in a h-hole with a broken b-bone, hearing v-voices. I must be just d-ducky."

"We know, hold on."

"You mean, d-don't g-go anywhere," she mumbled. "Isn't that a b-better line?"

Something touched her injured arm. Jenny screamed. *No more.* She succumbed to the darkness clouding her vision, welcoming the release from pain that oblivion provided.

When she swam back to consciousness, Nath was crouched by her side again. That was nice. Or was it? Delusions getting stronger probably wasn't a good sign. But his presence comforted her, even if he would soon fade away.

"You should comprehend me now."

She nodded, too tired to speak.

"Your arm is broken. Have you any other injuries?"

Jenny coughed to clear her throat. "N-nothing s-serious. My b-body aches, my head is s-spinning, spots are d-dancing in fr-front of my eyes . . . oh yes, and this f-fever . . . I'm j-just fine."

Nath's nod was difficult to see in the dim light. This delusion was a vast improvement over those empty voices. It made her feel less lonely.

"All right. Let's get you to the shaman so he can heal your wounds."

Jenny let her mind drift, floating, as buoyant as a

balloon on a string. Soon she'd soar up out of this hole. "W-why d-do you always do that?" She blurted the un-censored question through chattering teeth. Perhaps this delusion would somehow satisfy her curiosity.

He cocked his head. "Do what?"

"D-defer to M-Marden." Her eyelids drooped as she prattled on. "If he's n-not available, you d-do what n-needs d-doing. But as s-soon as M-Marden's n-near, you don't t-trust yourself. You s-step aside 'n' let him t-take over."

"He is my master!"

Yeah, he'd sound all pissy like that if I challenged him.

"I un-d-derstand th-that! But you h-healed L-Lauran's wounds. You are a sh-shaman t-too, even if neither of you admits it. S-seems as if you're b-both t-too used to you b-being his apprentice."

Jenny drew a ragged breath. "And I g-get you are n-not r-really h-here, but if you d-don't heal my d-damn arm, I'm g-gonna use a s-stone on y-your imaginary h-head!"

The vision of Nath laughed and reached toward her. She tensed, anticipating the pain of contact, even as she chided herself for playing along with a delusion.

However, he kept his hands apart, holding them on either side of her forearm.

Well, duh! He can't touch me. He's not here, re-member?

As her eyes drifted closed, he began chanting.

The wound grew warmer, the same as when he'd relieved her sore muscles on their hike to the Cavern of Whispers. Then the sensation became more intense. It made her imagine dozens of ants scratching deep inside, right at the bone.

Jenny gasped, forcing herself to stay still. Perhaps an

illusion could heal in a magical realm, as long as you trusted it would.

Feverish and delusional, she thought, *Tinker Bell. Clap if you believe.*

She wanted to laugh but was too busy clenching her teeth against the pain. She pressed herself into the wall, careful to keep the injury immobile. A few seconds later, the buzzing subsided. The tingles decreased as he removed his hands, and the heat faded.

Cautiously, she twisted the arm. No discomfort, never mind agony.

Jenny's eyes flew open to meet his.

She reached over and grabbed his forearm. "You're real!" she gasped.

Nath tilted his head to one side and gave her a familiar grin. "Yes, I am certain I exist."

Her face flushed beet red as she replayed their recent conversation. Despite being true, and something she'd thought about, she hadn't planned to broach it with him, having decided it was none of her business.

"I shouldn't have mentioned anything," she blurted. "I'm sorry. I was running a fever and hearing voices, and I thought you were a hallucination . . ."

"You said nothing I have not pondered myself." He waved her apology away. "I should be a full shaman by now, eya. But Marden must feel I am not ready." He shrugged. "It is hard not to doubt myself when it seems he does too." He sighed. "Perhaps you are correct, and I need to discover the truth of the matter.

"Enough." Nath shook his head impatiently. "Let us help you from this pit."

Jenny winced as he pulled her to her feet. Even with

the broken arm healed and her fever gone, she felt miserable—stiff and bruised from the fall. When he noticed her discomfort, Nath placed his hands on her neck, and that wonderful healing warmth spread through her again.

With Davy hauling on the rope and Nath's magical boost, they pulled her up, then helped her through the arduous hike back to the occupied portion of the cave.

By the time they arrived, exhaustion made her grateful for their support.

38

Jenny got her second wind after changing out of her wet clothing. Now, seated at the table sipping the hot kaffee Davy fetched, she groaned with appreciation of the wonderful aroma coming from the bowl of stew Marden served up.

Her stay in the pit felt like days, and it amazed her to discover it had only been about fourteen hours. She'd been afraid she would miss the Gather, but it was still early afternoon.

While she ate, Jenny caught the two men exchanging worried stares, as if having a conversation only they heard. *Perhaps they are!*

She narrowed her eyes. "I recognize that look." Her sharp glance darted between them. "What's wrong?"

Marden's face was grave. "The drawings go well. Since we are not creating an original spell, simply translating it, the work progresses."

"But part of the weapon is hidden," Nath interrupted. "The warlock moves around so often in the video; the rod is difficult to see. Without that final section, the rest is useless." He sighed. "We have to try again."

Jenny cocked her head. "If we leave right now, will you have time to finish decoding the spell? Davy and I can't wait much longer."

"We may, with this last piece of information. It is easier to break an existing curse with known components than to create one from nothing." Marden's face creased with concern. "However, you have been through an ordeal already today. Can Nath not do this alone?"

She made a dismissive gesture. "I'm fine. He did a great job healing me. I've had kaffee and food; I'm as fresh as if I slept all night. Why risk him having a problem with my phone? Please, I want to do this."

"Then let us ask Davint to take us this minute." Nath grabbed her free hand and pulled her from her seat. She bolted the last mouthful of stew as she rose.

Outside, gray clouds gathered overhead, hiding the blue skies Davy informed her they'd enjoyed that morning. Cold, wet drops splattered her face.

Jenny stopped, staring up in dismay. "Oh no! The Gather is going to be ruined."

Nath tugged her forward, impatient to be gone. "Do not worry. In early summer, storms appear at midday, drop a smattering of rain in the afternoon, and dissipate by evening. It will have blown over before dinnertime."

They ran up the mountain, arriving winded and unable to speak. Breathless, Nath's mind-speech filled the copper dragon in on the situation, and Davint agreed they needed to leave at once.

Minutes later, they found themselves airborne. He flew them above the cloud base, where the heat of the sun made steam rise from their damp clothing. He employed the same techniques as before to approach the soldiers' last reported route.

However, the warlock's troops no longer followed their former course.

Davint filled the pair in on the dragons' pendant misdirection, and they shared his hope for its success. They flew in ever-widening circles until the dragon's sharp eyesight located Shifton's party.

[Lauran's gemstone ploy is working!] Davint's triumphant shout filled their minds. *[Shifton isn't heading toward our cave anymore. He's following a different route up the foothills, moving away from the village. He must be heading for the hidden necklace.]*

Jenny whooped, and Nath gave a shrill whistle as they shared the copper's elation.

Careful not to sound his distinctive wingbeats, Davint coasted in and settled at the base of a narrow elevation. His chosen hiding place wasn't ideal. Only a thin ridge of loose shale separated them from the soldiers. The hill's steeper incline, covered in gravel and stones, shifted under their feet as they climbed.

Ahead, the warlock's men approached a valley, so the trio couldn't get any closer without being seen. They couldn't wait for a better opportunity, since the sun was getting low.

Jenny and Nath crawled to the new slope's peak despite several slips and skinned hands. They were dismayed to find fewer hiding places at the top as well. She turned her cell phone on and checked the battery level.

Only 12% left.

Yikes! That will have to be enough.

She whispered, "I'm going to do photos this time. A video uses too much power." He nodded his agreement.

Rising up, she peered over the rim, searching for Shifton. "Remember, we need the bottom inside length," Nath muttered. She gestured for him to keep quiet.

The warlock led the approaching line of men, but the rod hung on his opposite side, facing away from her. She zoomed in on him, trying to keep him in frame, while the indicator counted down, raising her anxiety level.

11%.

Jenny frowned. *How can I get him to lift the device?*

Without warning, Davint broke cover. He landed on the ridge to their left, scrabbling to stay upright as the surface crumbled beneath his feet. He roared down at the soldiers, drawing everyone's eyes away from his human companions. Then he launched himself up with a thunderous crack.

He must have been monitoring my thoughts. She glared as the copper circled past them. *You need to be more careful!* she thought as hard as she could at him.

Under their captain's guidance, the men reacted with amazing speed. As Shifton pointed his weapon at the dragon with an outraged shout, arrows followed the drake.

Jenny leaned forward, braced the cell phone on a small rock, and took the picture. Then she shot several more, just to be certain. The warlock held the rod out at the perfect angle, as if he were posing for her photos.

Davint's bellow of pain snapped her head around in time to see him collapse backward, taking a dramatic tumble down the slope on their side of the ridge.

She froze, shocked, but Nath already moved toward him. Jenny jerked into motion, staying low as she half slid amid a landslide of loose shale to join them. *Lauran will kill us if anything happens to him.*

As they reached Davint, he sat up. An arrow stuck out of his face where it had slipped under his eyelid and pierced his eye. When he shook his head, it jolted free and fell away—but the eyeball came with it, dangling down onto his cheek.

Jenny turned aside, covering her mouth as she tried not to retch.

Nath stretched up to cover the wound with a healing hand, but the drake eluded his grasp. *[That can wait. I still have one working eye. Did I give them a good show? If Shifton thinks I'm wounded, perhaps he'll waste time trying to find my body.]*

Furious, Jenny rounded on him. "You did that as another delaying tactic? You scared me half to death!"

Davint used a forepaw to push the eyeball into place. *[Hey, they injured me for real. The rest involved superb acting. Let's go before they reach the ridge and discover I'm still alive.]*

They scrambled onto Davint's back, and he took off running down the gully, wings outstretched. When he leaped into the air, the currents carried him low through the narrow fold between hills. He glided until an updraft swept him around the next rise. He didn't risk the percussive sound of his wingbeats until several ridges lay between them and the warlock.

Blood drops blew back on his passengers, confirming the severity of his injury. Despite his healing abilities, which had started to close the wound, it was still seeping fluids when they landed.

Jenny feared he might lose his sight for good.

39

The dragon's signal had remained stationary all night, making Shifton anxious to arrive before it moved again.

When a big copper dragon showed up as they reached the final slopes, he took it as a sign, convincing himself the drake was warning them off to protect the female. *Animals are like that, aren't they?*

He'd hoped they'd killed it, but when his men cleared the ridge behind them, they only stumbled across a small pool of blood.

Shifton refused to acknowledge the possibility of not catching the golden dragon aloud. However, he collected a vial of the precious green liquid—just in case. He tucked it in his waistband and made them search for a while longer, despite his urgent desire to keep moving.

But wounded or not, the beast eluded them.

Annoyed, he quick marched the men straight to the source of the signal. A brief storm lashed them with winds and rain but died off as fast as it began. The sun kissed the tips of the mountains to the west as they arrived.

He dismounted, grateful for a chance to get off his sharding horse. *If only we'd prevented that thrice-damned creature from escaping . . .* He hadn't planned on riding so much when he took up this hunt. Every night, he had to heal his tender flesh, or he'd never have managed to mount again the next day.

Shifton gave Rudolph a triumphant smile as he pointed at the footprints leading into the cave. He held his arm out straight, and the rod bent right, indicating a passage that curved away from the entrance.

There was every indication his sharding search would end in there.

"Wait here."

"But, sirrah," Captain Rudolph protested his abrupt order.

The warlock lifted the weapon. "My magic tells me there is nothing to fear." Despite his brave words, Shifton floated several orbs up into the air, lighting his way. He had no intention of allowing the creature to ambush him.

The powerful signal from the gemstone beat a welcoming song from deeper inside. He waved the lights ahead of him. Holding the rod up, he advanced into the darkness.

"You might as well show yourself," he taunted. "Escape is impossible. You should already be experiencing the pull of the rod's spells taking over your body. Come forth!"

He paused, prepared to capture the dragon when it rushed him. When his gibe went unheeded, he frowned, moving forward again. The orbs floated ahead of him, lighting the walls and ceiling.

Shifton stared at the dirt floor, where huge footprints

sank into the otherwise undisturbed silt. A thick drag mark ran along the center. *Ah yes, the tail.*

Two sets of prints. One facing in, another coming out. His scowl deepened, and he paused. He would have expected a single set, or perhaps three. A pair implied the dragon had come and gone.

Shifton checked his talisman. *No, the spell is pointing straight ahead. It must be here.*

Waving the orbs in front of him, he approached with caution. After about fifty paces, he reached the end of the tunnel.

He stared wildly in every direction, but the trail stopped. He whirled around, searching for side passages. The rod in his hand tweaked down, but the dragon couldn't be underground unless another chamber lay below this one.

Shifton retraced his steps, looking for hidden offshoots he might have missed, but he found nothing. Standing at the entrance, he raised the device and repeated the tracking spell. Once again, the rod pointed behind him, deeper down the tunnel.

He turned and followed the control rod's pull back to the tunnel's end.

This time, when the rod's tip pulled down, he leaned over to confirm his suspicions. A pile of scattered rocks lay across the floor. Upon closer examination, the shifted indents in the ground told him somebody had moved them. He stretched out widespread fingers, urging the top stone to lift.

Shifton returned to the soldiers a half hour later, his face almost puce with fury. The chain of the medallion he'd uncovered coiled around his tight fist, causing white lines where it dug into his skin.

"They appear to be more intelligent than I anticipated," he snarled. "We'll stop here tonight and retrace our steps tomorrow." Glowering, he slipped the pendant over his head, giving it a fond pat.

The setting sun glanced off the emerald, shooting green sparks off the captain's armor.

Rudolph stood facing him, unmoving.

"Well?" Shifton snapped. "What are you waiting for? Do as you're told."

The captain rested his hand on the hilt of his sword, drew himself upright, and remained in place. The other soldiers, sensing a confrontation, gathered in a loose circle around them.

Shifton's face burned with humiliation. "Explain yourself!"

Rudolph's hair stirred in the breeze as he removed his helmet, tucking it under his arm. "We shouldn't be here." His expression was determined, and he took a defiant stance. "We have no authority to be in Trifair Territory."

The air held an ominous heaviness. Even the birds fell silent. The watching men exchanged uneasy glances.

"You can kill me." Rudolph faced Shifton, spreading his legs as if preparing himself for an attack. "But I cannot be party to this farce any longer. If the High King had sanctioned our mission, we wouldn't have taken such elaborate steps to avoid his notice. You may have Duke Almar fooled, but I harbor serious doubts about your motives."

His hand came up to his throat. He dropped it to his

side and lifted his chin, then spoke as if quoting someone. "Sometimes one must take a stand for one's convictions."

Shifton's lip lifted in a snarl. *Is the fool smiling? Does he not realize I could strike him down where he stands?*

But the young captain wasn't finished. He waved at the apprehensive soldiers hanging on every word. "I cannot lead my men into an unlawful confrontation. It seems quite obvious we are the aggressors. Those dragonriders never intended to attack. They called to us, questioning our conduct. *We* assaulted *them*. It shames me to have been party to such despicable actions."

Shifton stared at him, incredulous. He raised his arm.

Rudolph visibly braced himself.

The warlock's eyes shifted to the surrounding soldiers. The grim expressions on the men's faces changed his mind. "I won't kill you without my duke's approval," he announced pompously. "However, since Almar gave me command over you, they are *my* men, not yours. I hereby strip you of your rank for insubordination."

Shifton held out his hand.

Moving slowly, the stunned young man undid the gold circlet from the shoulder of his robe and dropped it into the sorcerer's palm.

"Return to the castle. Give this to His Grace." The warlock pulled the vial from his waistband. "Tell him what transpired here. Let *him* decide your fate." He stepped forward and thrust the vial at Rudolph, who took the small container.

"Now get out of my sight." Shifton flicked his fingers with a dismissive sneer.

The demoted captain ignored him, turning to confront the soldiers. "Men, you have a choice to make.

Accompany me back to the castle, where we may face reprimand by the duke, or worse. Or stay here, under *his* command."

He shook his head. "I cannot accept that our good Duke Almar would approve of these actions. I must obey my conscience, as you are obliged to follow yours." He met each man's eyes in turn. Some shifted their gazes away, unable to meet his.

Rudolph strode toward them, and they parted, letting him pass. Without hesitation, the group of seasoned soldiers fell in behind him. A moment of silent indecision followed. Then, one after another, most of the youngest troops trailed in his wake.

"You'll regret this, boy!" Shifton's chest heaved as he glowered after the departing men.

Nobody moved until those leaving had disappeared over the crest of the slope below.

The warlock stared after them, expecting the deserters to realize their mistake and return. When that didn't happen, rage filled him, and he regretted not killing the traitor when he'd had the chance.

He pointed at a disheveled older man standing in front of the remaining small group of soldiers. "You there, consider this a field promotion." He threw the gold circlet at his feet. "You are now Captain of the Guard."

"Me name's Jareth." The soldier scowled, bending to scoop up the trinket.

Shifton flapped his hand. "Whatever. Get the camp set up." He moved aside, stroking the rod fondly, while his new officer roared and bullied the remaining men.

It required double the usual time, but the warlock vanished inside the moment they'd readied his tent. Alone, he was determined to reacquire the gemstone's signal. He held the weapon out with one straightened arm and cast the strongest finding spell he'd ever created.

He was unprepared for the end of the stick to shoot back, smashing into his stomach. Pain exploded, doubling him over. "Shards!" he gasped, rubbing the tender skin. "What new trickery is this?"

Had the beast changed directions a second time?

Shifton spun around, holding his precious rod with both hands, and tried again. Once more, it pressed back against him, though he stopped it from striking him. He frowned, faced another way, and repeated the incantation more softly. His weapon kept pulling back toward him. The warlock tested every direction, casting and recasting the enchantment in vain, growing increasingly frustrated.

As night fell, he sent orbs up into the corners, lighting his private space. He laid the rod on his small table, staring down at it in disbelief. When the flap of his tent opened and someone entered without asking permission, the warlock whirled around, hands raised to protect himself.

His slovenly new Captain of the Guard gave a squawk of alarm and almost dropped the food he carried.

Shifton lowered his arms, glaring at the plate in disgust. Bits of charred meat and vegetables floated in a sea of grease. "Put it down and get out. From now on, knock before you enter. Next time I won't hold back." He moved around the table to sit, staring at the device, following each of the spells engraved there, trying to discern any reason for it to stop working.

He expected the fellow to leave, but Jareth just stood there, mumbling. The warlock lifted his head, turning impatiently. "What did you say? Speak up, you idiot."

"You're so beautiful," the other man crooned, yearning in his voice. The dazed soldier stared at him—or rather, his eyes locked on Shifton's chest with a half smile and strange expression—dreamy yet somehow greedy.

Following the man's gaze, Shifton looked down and froze, shocked to discover he wore the pendant he'd recovered. Its huge emerald stone seemed to wink in the mage light.

When did I put it on? He strained his memory but couldn't recall seeing it after he brought it out of the cave. Sweat broke out on his forehead that had nothing to do with the overheated tent.

I possess far greater strength of magic than those I'm targeting, he reassured himself. *It should be impossible . . . but what if the acquisitive spells I placed on the pendants can affect me?*

This supposition roused his fury, and sickening rage overwhelmed him. Shifton yanked the chain over his head and flung it across the room.

With multiple castings still activating it, the rod on the table twitched after it. He caught Jareth's eyes, too, following the arc of its trajectory, marking where the medallion smacked into the far wall and dropped out of sight.

A debilitating surge of jealousy seized Shifton. *Nobody else can have it. The jewels belong to me.* No one deserved his treasure but him. *And if I want to wear it, I sharding well will.*

"Get out. Get out!" he screamed. "GET OUT!"

He shoved the dazed captain through the flap of the tent, before scrambling along the floor to retrieve his precious pendant with its miraculous gemstone.

40

Lauran's head snapped in Jenny's direction, *sensing* her distress. *[Davint!]*

She bolted across the clearing, barely aware of her smaller friends as she closed the distance. His paw reached for her, and the limp, dangling eyeball swung loose.

A shriek tore from her throat, a piercing wail summoning every Kin within earshot.

Davint's hand slapped over the socket again, but Lauran was in a panic. She ran a few steps in one direction, stopped, changed course, and darted forward, only to once more jerk to a halt.

Her *sending* grew so loud and penetrating, nobody could reach her as she careened around the clearing, spiraling out of control. *[This is all my fault. I should have gone away. The others would be safe except for my foolishness. I am to blame. This all started with me. I made the correct decision when I left everyone. Oh, his beautiful face. I'm responsible . . .]*

An earsplitting, stentorian bellow caused Jenny to yelp in fright but silenced Lauran's raving. She flinched, her breath catching—the only sound in the sudden stillness.

Her father stared at Davint, his eyes whirling yellow with admiration. *[Didn't realize you had that in you, boy.]*

Lauran stood frozen, trembling at Davint's approach. He kept one paw over his damaged socket, but with the other, he reached for her, pulling her in. She refused to meet his gaze until he leaned down and his remaining eye locked on hers.

[I still maintain you made a mistake trying to go it alone.] His sending was firm, insistent. *[However, none of this is your fault. You can blame the warlock or the duke, but you cannot hold yourself responsible for any of this.]*

Lauran dropped her head, but he lifted it again. Her horrified stare kept shifting to the paw hiding his wound. *[And I appreciate you care about us . . . about me. But you can't protect everybody. We have to support each other.]*

His expression softened. *[Look at everyone who's prepared to help you. Nath healed your injuries—when he didn't even know you. Jenny risked her life to take those pictures—and she just met you.]*

She let him pull her close as his tone grew gentler. *[If strangers did so much, imagine what your loved ones are capable of.]*

He tapped the silver collar draped around her neck. *[Your father's idea to hide you from the hunters, Jenny's photos, and you hiding another medallion—those are only the beginning of what we can manage together. So forget this business of doing everything alone. Running away is not the answer.]*

A sob wrenched from Lauran's chest as she collapsed

against him. She let Davint's soft croon soothe her as he wrapped her in his wings and snuggled her close.

Jenny turned from the couple's reconciliation, wiping a furtive tear from her cheek. The large green dragon Davy had told her was Lauran's father, Ta'ther, stood beside Nath, watching them. She gave her friend a nudge.

At Jenny's prodding, the males exchanged guilty smiles and followed her over to one of the big stone fire-pits, where a pair of imposing women prepared a bonfire.

She stared at the towering females. *Wow! They're almost as tall as Ganther. That's as close to giants as I ever hope to get!*

Ta'ther mentioned that some of the female riders of the remaining dragons had arrived with him, while the green Kin returned home. Lauran's father introduced them to Audra, who rode Ta'dra, and Callie, La'lie's partner.

Jenny found their sudden name changes puzzling until they explained how their naming conventions worked. Part of their rider's name, with a "Ta" prefix for males and "La" for females.

"Okay, let me see if I've got this straight. Kellin is now called La'lie because she's a female and partnered with Callie? And Staton becomes Ta'dra because he's male and Audra is his rider? Don't you get confused using a different name every time you change partners?"

[Oh, it doesn't happen often.] Ta'ther assured her. *[But dragons have private names when not teamed up. So those are what they gave you, since they were unaware their riders would join them.]* He leaned his huge head closer.

[In truth, we don't bother much with this when we're at home. It's mainly a way to confuse the Lowlanders.]

He seemed to remember who he was speaking to. *[You are our friends,]* he hastened to reassure her. *[But our Alpha has mandated this.]*

Although Jenny wondered why Lauran and Davint didn't have riders yet, she supposed it might be impolite to ask. She cast about for another topic.

"Is Ganther coming back? I understood the collar was his idea. But I think someone just said you came up with it, Ta'ther?" For some reason, the women found her innocent question funny. Amid their laughter, no one answered her.

She tried again. "So, you and the dragons live together . . . is that why you call yourselves Dragon Kin?"

Audra nodded. "We are as one."

Callie, in the process of swallowing a drink, spluttered at this solemn utterance, spewing her kaffee over the fire.

Jenny's brow furrowed as she offered a small, uncertain smile—unsure why they found everything she said so amusing. Feeling like an outsider to private jokes among the tight-knit community, she smiled a farewell and walked away with Nath.

She jumped when lightning blasted overhead and began to count. "One, one thousand, two, one thousand, three, one thousand . . ." She reached eleven before thunder rolled.

"What were you doing?" Nath lifted one eyebrow.

Jenny blushed. "I used to be frightened of storms. My dad explained this method of counting told you how many miles away the lightning was." She sighed in relief. "I guess that wasn't very close."

He nodded but seemed distracted. "I want to heal that eye before it closes over with the eyeball misaligned. Can you find Marden and give him the photos while I do that?"

"My phone!" She stared at him, horrified. "With Davint's injury and the scramble to escape the soldiers, I forgot to turn it off."

41

They crowded together, focused on the black screen as Jenny jabbed at the power control. Nothing happened. Her eyes met Nath's. "The battery's dead."

Now she sympathized with Lauran's earlier reaction.

"It's my fault," she cried. "I've ruined everything. Why didn't I push the damn button? I told you and Marden about the depleted battery. How could I forget about it?"

She grabbed a handful of her short curls. "What are we going to do? There's no means to charge it here."

Nath gripped her shoulders, giving her a little shake. "We will not panic. There is always a way. Tell me of the energy this device uses."

"We need electricity." She shrugged, wishing she'd paid more attention in class. "I don't know the science. I plug a cord into an outlet, then I stick the other end here." She showed him the small slit at the bottom of her phone. "And the battery recharges."

Jenny waved her hand at the dark clouds hovering overhead. "Voltage, current, whatever—it's similar to the electrical charge in a thunderstorm, although not that strong. My professor claimed one lightning bolt could power an entire city . . . or something like that."

She sighed. "All I remember is Ben Franklin's experiment, where static from a storm collected on a kite and ran down the wet string, hit a key, and a spark jumped to his hand. I think it proved storms have electricity. That's not much help."

"You are wrong. That just might work." Nath nodded, his forehead creasing, as he glanced at the sky. "Run and fetch the flyer hanging on the wall in my room. Then stop by the blacksmith and ask him for the tiniest nail he makes; but have him flatten the tip to fit your device's slot. I must go heal Davint before he loses the eye." He winked at her. "I do not think Lauran appreciates his new look."

Jenny gave a shaky laugh, trying to be reassured by his confidence. She tucked the useless phone in her pocket and raced down the mountain to the village.

It felt good to be running again. Polina might not have outpaced her if she'd been in shape.

And she was grateful Marden wasn't home so she didn't have to waste time explaining her thoughtlessness. She grabbed the kite and ran.

Although the blacksmith gave her a funny look as she stood there holding the huge kite's frame, he did as she asked, handing her the flattened nail, which was not much thicker than a paperclip and about a quarter inch wide.

With a vague idea of Nath's intentions, she checked the fit in the recharging slot on her phone before giving the smith a fleeting smile. With a nod of thanks, she ran back up the mountain.

He had finished healing Davint by the time she returned, and the dragon bore his usual striking appearance. He and Lauran watched the proceedings with interest, their enormous bodies crouched on either side of the two young people. They commiserated with Jenny, assuring her the oversight might have happened to anyone.

Nath sank cross-legged to the ground, and Jenny squatted beside him. He indicated a set of painted rocks arrayed before him. "These represent the five power colors, from weakest to strongest. While wizards prefer actual crystals, all it really does is provide me with a focus. It is unfortunate I do not have any storage gems with me."

He met her blank expression, and a smile quirked the corner of his mouth. "Magic comes at a price," he reminded her. "Often, the cost is an exchange of energy, though not invariably. Eya, a shaman may use their own store of vitality, although one must take care not to overextend themselves and to replenish what they use."

Nath shrugged. "Or excess power can be stored in a gem or pulled from ley lines." He explained that he would invoke a ritual, petitioning the spirits of air and wind who dwelled in the center of any storm.

He tied the nail to the end of the twine on the kite's spool and instructed Jenny to get the flyer as high as the remaining string would allow, while he began beseeching the spirits' aid.

Though she felt foolish, she ran the length of the clearing with the kite bobbing along behind her. The wind caught it, and it flew up into the sky faster than she anticipated. Without her firm grip, the nail might have been torn from her hand.

The kite's resemblance to a giant bird in flight was remarkable.

Jenny heard Nath chanting softly as she jogged over to him. Lightning snapped and crashed overhead, and she shivered. "Be sure the bolt doesn't hit the kite directly," she shouted over the storm.

With an absent nod, he took the flattened metal, focusing on the sky above them, his chant growing faster and louder. Word of their problem had spread through the camp, so Kin and dragons now stood nearby, watching in silence.

Nath concentrated, his palms facing each other. He moved them closer, and energy crackled around the flyer overhead.

One hand reached out to her, and Jenny realized he wanted the phone. She hesitated, but if it got fried, they wouldn't be any worse off. She pulled it from her pocket and laid it in his outstretched palm.

He brought his hands together, encasing the cell. His face tight with concentration, Nath controlled the forces raging around them, and the kite began to glow. Jenny would have sworn she saw the current vibrating down the string.

When the power reached the nail, he slipped the flattened tip into the charging port on the phone. She half expected an explosion, so the resulting small spark seemed anticlimactic.

Nath released his end with a glad shout, expressing their gratitude and thanks. As the beautiful kite flew away, Jenny cried out, reaching to grab it. The cord fluttered against her fingers, before a gust of wind carried it out of reach.

He lifted his hands as if urging the flyer on its way. "I can always make another." He smiled.

She realized this loss was a necessary element of the ritual. The magic's price he'd mentioned. She still felt guilty for losing his wonderful creation, though. They watched it grow smaller, and as it sailed into the distance, the sun broke through, beating down on them like a benediction.

He handed her the phone.

Jenny took it with an uncertain squint, pressed the power button, and held her breath. To her relief, it booted up.

Nath moved closer, and they waited in silence until the indicator lit up.

"One hundred percent! That's incredible. Electric companies would love to get hold of you."

He laughed. "Go find Marden now. I require a brief rest after my exertions." Reassured he suffered from nothing worse than a slight weariness, she hurried off.

She met the old shaman struggling up the hill with the help of several villagers. With his walking stick in one hand, he leaned on Davy, who held his other arm. The boy's friends trailed behind, burdened with parchment, quills, ink, and even a small table and two stools.

Marden beamed. "Despite having work to do, I saw no reason to miss the celebration."

She agreed, handing him the phone.

"Ah, the last piece of our puzzle. When my young apprentice is ready, have him join me. There is much to decipher before morning."

42

Nath spent a few minutes in a nearby copse of trees above the camp, meditating and communing with the earth, replenishing his power, before he returned to the clearing.

He saw Marden working off to one side of the fire. The old man smiled a welcome as his apprentice approached.

A knot of resolve tightened in Nath's chest as he nodded. He couldn't delay this conversation any longer. He took a deep breath. "Why did you decide I am unqualified to be raised to full shaman?"

Marden's smile faded. He sighed, staring out at the milling Kin, then squared his shoulders and faced his accuser. "You *are* qualified." He grimaced, his words heavy with regret. "And more than ready. My own hubris has prevented me from either letting you go or stepping down." He looked away. An uncomfortable silence stretched.

Uncertain if he should speak, Nath shifted in his seat.

Marden lifted his chin, nodding, as though reaching a decision. "My health has been poor for quite some time. And I fear my condition worsens."

A cold shock washed over the younger man, and his hands shook. He wanted to argue, to refuse the bitter turn their conversation had taken. Perhaps the shaman tired more easily of late, but to hear him speak so calmly of his failing . . . It felt like Nath was back on that mountain slope behind Shifton's camp, with loose gravel sliding out from under his feet.

The younger man tried to object, but his master waved him to remain still. "Please, do not interrupt. It is past time I am honest with both of us." He took a deep breath. "In all likelihood, I shall not greet another spring."

Marden's expression softened as he peered at Nath's stricken face. "That is the nature of things, lad." He spoke in a gentler tone now. "The old impart their knowledge before passing on to their next great adventure. The young take that wisdom and add their own learning, thus ensuring each succeeding generation is wiser than the last."

He patted his apprentice's arm. "Trust in yourself, as I do. Have faith in the magic we share." Marden gave him a hard stare. "If you would be shaman, you know where you must begin."

Jenny looked up as Nath approached.

"Can you keep my master company while I take care of something?" From his grim tone, she suspected what—or rather who—he meant.

She agreed, though her mind buzzed with questions.

Marden smiled and set his work aside as Jenny came

and sat beside him. "Are you growing anxious to be getting home?"

She shrugged. "Sure, but I've met so many unique people here." She straightened. "That reminds me, I wanted to introduce Davy to the brownies, but they're so shy. I feel like I should give them something for looking after us, though. Any suggestions?"

The old shaman shook his head. "They are prideful and will not take kindly to anything that implies payment. A gift, though, might be appreciated."

They were interrupted by the villagers climbing up the mountain, each of whom must pay their respects to Marden. Even the most distrustful yielded to the triple lure of dragons, food, and celebration.

Everyone turned out except Polina and Marta.

Jenny smiled at the warm greetings of several young women, all wanting to show their disapproval of Polina's actions.

The Kin—in both forms—held back as they faced the approaching people. But the village younglings entertained no such reservations. With shouts of happy recognition, they rushed ahead of their parents.

One small boy clung to Davint's foreleg, grinning up at him with toothless adoration while his nervous mam stood watching.

An older girl reached up to touch Lauran's golden muzzle with trembling fingers. When the youngster spread her arms and threw herself against the draikana's chest, the dragon chuckled and her eyes softened.

But Jenny caught her wince, although Lauran hid her pain from the child.

Nath's long legs made short work of the run down the mountain. He'd taken the trail so often of late, he paid little attention to the path. He continued past the home he shared with Marden, heading for the only lighted entrance in the village.

Marta stood in the kitchen, wearing her best Gather robes, her head bowed and her shoulders slumped. His heart ached for his auntie, but he'd come with a purpose.

She heard him enter and turned. Fear hovered in her gaze, her cheeks flushed, and she looked down. "I must apologize for my granddaughter's conduct. I cannot guess what possessed her to attack Jenny like that. She has brought shame on our family. How can I make amends?"

"Do not ask for forgiveness. That is not your responsibility." Nath's harsh words startled Marta, who stared at him. "She recognized the wrongness of her actions yet did them anyway."

He gave her no chance to reply. "I do not suppose Polina meant to hurt her—and *maybe* she did not hear her fall." His tone made it clear he was unconvinced. "But stealing the translation bracelet so Jenny would not understand anyone? *That* she did on purpose."

"What happens to her now?" Marta's fingers touched her lips as she awaited his verdict.

"I will speak with her myself, but I judge it best if she leaves the village. Whether you accompany her is up to you."

"When her parents and her grandda died, she became my reason for living." Marta sighed. "Perhaps I spoiled her. I shall send her to her aunt, of the *Mahigan* tribe."

Her eyes flitted around the cave. "My home is here. I do not suppose I would have a place among them." Her lips twitched. "I am not a young, beautiful woman, ripe for a mate."

Her faint smile relieved Nath. "I am glad you are staying, Auntie M," he assured her. "We would miss you."

"Miss my pies, you mean." She teased weakly, blinking back tears. "She is in her room. I shall go to the Gather and make my peace with Jenny."

He realized it was pointless to repeat that she was not the one who needed to apologize, so he remained silent. Marta gave him a faint nod and left without another word.

Nath took a deep breath, bracing himself. He moved deeper into the familiar cave, stopping outside the curtain marking Polina's chamber. "Polina? May I come in?"

He heard her gasp, then a soft-spoken "Enter."

She sat on her pallet, looking up at him. "Are you here as my friend or as arbiter?"

"I hope I will always be your friend, but I am here to render judgment on your actions."

"It all happened by accident! I did not realize she fell." She flushed, dropping her eyes, unable to meet his steady stare. "Not for sure."

"But you attacked her and stole her bracelet, setting subsequent events in motion. You are lucky she only broke her arm. She might have sustained severe injuries. Your jealousy has grown stronger and has no basis in reality. I am not the man for you. We are fated to take different roads, you and I."

Polina stared at him, her lashes sparkling with unshed tears. "Just tell me my punishment."

Nath reached out and took her hands, pulling her to her feet. "This change is not intended to punish you but rather to create a fresh start. Your grandmar is sending you to stay with family in your da's tribe. Give over this youngling's fantasy. Use your head. Find someone who makes you happy. Promise me you will try."

Tears overflowed, sliding unheeded down her cheeks as she squeezed his hands. "I promise," she whispered.

Jenny also refused to let Marta apologize. "Polina is young and impulsive." Marta's eyes rolled, and the younger woman laughed. "No, I'm serious! I have some experience in that area; it's sort of how I ended up here."

Marta managed a weak smile, as fleeting as sunshine on a cloudy day.

Marden pretended not to be listening.

Jenny gave her a hug. "Maybe with the new tribe, she'll find someone to make her forget Nath."

"We can but hope!" Marta sighed, hugging her back.

The young shaman's return allowed the women to join the others in preparing food, leaving the two men to the task of deciphering the photographs.

The scent of roasting tahr, a creature Jenny deemed a cross between a cow and a mountain goat, made her mouth water. Taters and vegetables simmered over smaller fires, along with pots of kaffee.

Blankets were spread for families to gather and share in the feast. Anishinabe and Kin mingled. Excited chatter, punctuated by bursts of laughter, quieted as the serious business of eating began.

Jenny grinned, watching as some men furtively passed around skins of sour wine, avoiding their wives' glances of disapproval.

The shamans, however, continued working. They ate whatever they were handed, ignoring everything and everyone as they traced and debated the last symbols on the rod.

Though a guest of honor and welcome to sit with anyone, Jenny slipped into the shadows, distancing herself from the crowd. She experienced a pang of homesickness as she listened to those ranged around the bonfires and watched families laughing together.

She startled when a dark shadow loomed beside her before recognizing the golden dragon. It amazed her that a creature that large could move with such stealth.

[You seem lost in thought. Would you like some company, or do you prefer to be alone?]

Jenny smiled, waving to a spot next to her boulder. "Just thinking how much Chloe, my roommate from school, would enjoy this party."

[You must miss your family and friends.]

"Yeah, but I've made friends here too. It seems no matter where I am, I'll miss someone!" She looked up, and her face brightened. "Hey, Audra told me your friend Marissa is doing better. I'm so glad. Too bad she and Ganther couldn't be here. I'd love to meet her."

Lauran curled up beside her. *[Yes, I am happy for Da's sake as well. They will make a great pairing.]*

"Your dad and your best friend?" Jenny goggled at the dragon. "Is that weird for you?"

[Why?] The dragon tilted her head in puzzlement. *[My mam died before I hatched. Should I wish him to be*

sad and alone when he can be content with a wonderful mate? I am pleased he found someone.]

"Yeah, I get that." The conversation made Jenny uncomfortable, but curiosity compelled her to ask. "But that, like, makes her your mother, right? What if they have baby dragons? Will you be okay sharing him with his new family?"

Lauran laughed, wisps of smoke rising from her nostrils. *[I am beyond the need of mothering. However, she would never try to replace my mam. Marissa continues to be my friend and may also become my father's mate.]*

She hesitated, tilting her head as if considering the second part of the question. *[Dragonets are rare for our kind. Each is a treasure the entire Wing celebrates.]* Her muzzle nudged the young woman. *[Love is not halved by being shared but doubled. Should my father sire more younglings, his affection will grow to encompass us all.]*

"You sound like a greeting card." Jenny bumped her shoulder against the draikana. "My mom remarried a few months ago," she blurted, avoiding a discussion about holiday cards.

"Davy is my stepbrother, *his* son." She looked away. "You don't remember your mam, so I guess that's different. But I had a great dad, and Frank can't replace him." Jenny's voice quivered with unshed tears.

With surprising delicacy, the draikana curled her forepaw and gave a soft tap on the young woman's chest with a gentle talon. *[Your da will always be in here. This man won't ever take his place . . . But if you allow it, he might become a friend.]*

Jenny leaned against Lauran. "I almost ran away

shortly after Mom married Frank." She looked down. "I didn't go, because Davint's right. Running doesn't solve problems. It only creates new ones or makes things worse in other ways."

She sat up, making a face. "Of course, it helped that I was leaving for university not long afterward." Giving herself a shake, she rose to her feet. "I'll think about what you said. Now, however, I better find Davy and haul him off to bed."

Jenny stopped, looking surprised. "Wow, when did I become my mom?"

She joined Marta at one of the campfires instead, where the women shared stories and stole their husbands' wine.

The sight of the first moon rising acted like a signal. As Lauran moved to sit beside her, a man lifted something that reminded Jenny of a guitar or a banjo—though not either—into his lap. Someone began beating an insistent rhythm on a drum, and the stringed instrument joined in.

The younger villagers jumped to their feet, whirling and stomping in time to the beat. An older woman produced a series of reed pipes that increased in length, fastened together and stained a pretty shade of deep purple. Marta called it a syrinx, though Jenny whispered, "Pan flute."

Whatever the name, when the musician began trilling a counterpoint to the drumming, the infectious music became irresistible. Even the shamans looked up and smiled.

Someone's husband decided he was drunk enough to attempt to match the quick steps of the young folk. He dragged his protesting wife into the crowd of dancers. She gave in with little argument, and the couple started an intricate intertwined stomping romp, bringing shouts of encouragement and praise ringing from all sides.

The rhythm captivated the dragons, including Davint. He grabbed Lauran's forepaw, pulled her up, and whirled her into their own dance circle outside the main ring of dancers. They draped their tails over their forearms like elegant shawls to keep them out of the way while they swayed in time with the beat.

People gasped and fought for balance when tremors—caused by the heavy thumping of their huge feet—shook the ground underfoot

The musicians faltered to a discordant halt, and the enormous beasts stopped dancing, abashed, as the villagers stared at them. Then everyone burst into laughter and cheers.

As the music resumed, other dragons joined in, while the smaller people expanded their circle to dance in a ring around their larger companions.

The earth trembled with their enthusiasm.

Davy stood on the outskirts of the revelry with a group of boys his age. They hooted and stomped their feet in coltish imitation of their elders.

Nath responded to Jenny's wistful gaze, pulling the weakly protesting girl upright. Lauran pushed her forward, laughing as her friend whirled into the celebration with a delighted shout.

However, they hadn't danced for long when Marden appeared on the sidelines, concern creasing his seamed face. He beckoned Nath, who handed Jenny off to another villager and hurried to his master's side.

She watched over her shoulder as the men leaned close, the shaman pointing at the phone in his hand and making urgent gestures. They pushed through the crowd and disappeared.

Jenny gave her partner a distracted smile, trying not to worry as he twirled her around.

43

Are you certain?" Although Nath kept his voice low, he was unable to hide his urgency.

The two men ignored the revels and returned to their workstation. Several orbs floated around the table, attracting mothals that bumped lovingly up against the lights.

The older shaman shrugged, looking helpless. "I checked every photo. There is no doubt." His expression wavered between desperate and hopeful. "But my books may contain information that would be of assistance. Let us return to the village and continue our work there."

Nath collected their papers, and Marden tucked the phone in his tunic pocket before they headed homeward. As they reached the steep slope leading down the mountain, an enormous dark monster rose from the shadows.

Prepared to defend his master, the younger shaman threw up an orb.

He dropped his arms in relief when the moonlight resolved the shadowy figure into a green dragon, and Ta'ther stepped forward.

Lauran's father tilted his great head as he stared at them. *[You're leaving the party early.]*

"Yes." Marden nodded. "We must consult some of the texts stored in our home. Healing Lauran is more important than enjoying the festivities."

[I agree. Allow me to offer you a ride. You face a long walk down a steep hill in the dark. I am both safer and faster.]

Marden's eyes lit up, and he eagerly agreed. Nath nodded his thanks and helped the old man mount.

Ta'ther leaped into the air. Marden hooted with glee as they soared down the mountain. The excitement ended too soon, and he dismounted with obvious reluctance. He thanked the dragon for his help. The green assured him he would provide transportation any time the master needed.

The elder shaman patted his leg in thanks and tottered into the house, leaning heavily on his walking stick.

[Is something wrong?]

Nath realized Ta'ther had directed the soft query at his mind but not Marden's. He *sensed* the worry behind the dragon's thoughts. "Perhaps." He didn't want to cause panic, yet he wanted to be honest. "A situation has arisen we do not thus far understand. We are doing our best to discover the answers."

Hot breath bathed him as the dragon sighed. Ta'ther nodded his enormous head, not pressing for more information. He spread his wings and moved out into the common. After a brief run, he sprang into the air with sharp reports from his mighty downward strokes.

Nath lifted his hand against the whirl of dust and

leaves, then turned and went inside to continue their research.

The party wound down not long after the second moon rose. Jenny approached Lauran and Ta'ther to say good night.

"Everyone needs to get some rest." She smothered a yawn. "If Marden and Nath are done tomorrow, you may be freed from that." She pointed to where Lauran absently rubbed the constant ache in her chest.

At least Jenny hoped it would be that soon. They were running out of time.

She helped bank the fires and pack the food away.

The dragons offered rides down the mountain to any brave souls who climbed aboard. Although the village boys clamored to be allowed, their cautious mothers declined, preferring a sobering walk home. Good-natured eyerolls followed the men staggering downhill, singing and holding each other up.

Since the others didn't receive permission, Jenny thought it only fair Davy waited as well. Annoyed, he and his friends ran ahead. She stared after him in concern, relaxing as they began playing hide-and-seek in the dark and shouts of laughter reached her. The game soon devolved into trying to scare the younger girls by jumping out of the shadows and hollering.

When they arrived at the village, Jenny called good night to Marta as she shepherded her stepbrother inside the shaman's cave home. She was unsurprised to find Nath and Marden sitting at the table, poring over a battered text, surrounded by floating orbs and piles of books.

Davy jumped up and grabbed an orb, gave the two shamans a cheeky "G'night," and headed for the room he shared with his sister without being told.

"Be sure to wash before you crawl into bed," she called after him.

He waved a negligent hand in acknowledgment.

Jenny glanced at the men, noting their tired appearance. After a sleepless night spent studying the warlock's spell, they'd wasted hours searching for her before returning to their studies tonight. The stress showed. Marden's face seemed to have deeper lines, and the bags under Nath's eyes aged him.

She studied their bleak expressions and leaned forward to peek at what they worked on. "How is everything going?"

Marden gave a great sigh, confirming her concerns. "We are not giving up." She frowned at this ominous start. "But we came across a piece of the spell we cannot decipher. Without a solution, any attempt to remove the ruby might harm Lauran further."

Jenny dropped into a chair, stunned. She hadn't realized how much she'd been counting on them to fix everything. Coming to Galahar had felt like stepping into a fairy tale. And in a proper story, the good guys won. Right?

"What is it? What's wrong?"

Nath rubbed his forehead, as if getting a headache. "The rod features unfamiliar gems we have never seen before, worked in an unusual pattern. They seem to be a sixth power."

He sighed at her puzzled stare. "I told you about this. Wizards use five colors of crystals to work magic, ranging from the lowest, red, to the strongest, blue."

Marden interrupted. "We translated all the runes created using those powers . . . until we found one that made no sense. We hoped the blame lay in an error on the photo. Yet the second set you and Nath collected only confirmed our fears. It appears the warlock has discovered a sixth power." He spread his hands. "Unless these texts reveal an explanation of his find, we are out of options."

Jenny's stomach twisted, and the evening's joy drained away. She couldn't stand another setback.

Her plan had been simple: witness their new friend being healed and return home with fond memories of a wonderful adventure. Now, everything was getting complicated. If she and Davy were forced to leave while Lauran was still in jeopardy, he wouldn't handle it well.

"Can you show me the photos?" Even if she couldn't help, she needed to see for herself the obstacle killing their hopes.

Nath rummaged through the papers and books on the table and located the cell phone. He flipped through the pictures, found what he wanted, and handed it to her. She barely acknowledged the ease with which he now handled the alien device.

Jenny enlarged the picture of the area they meant. It was obvious what they referred to. Laid out in an unusual pattern, ivory globes stood apart from the other more colorful gems. They were round and cloudy—and familiar.

"You mean the pearls?" She frowned, not understanding.

The men gaped at her. Their matching incredulous expressions made her grin despite the seriousness of the situation.

Marden leaned forward. "Explain."

Jenny's eyebrows rose. "You don't know what a pearl is?" Both shamans shook their heads. "How is that possible? They form in mollusks, like clams or oysters. Layers of a hard, iridescent substance, covering an irritant in the shellfish." She pursed her lips. "I think they put a tiny bead or stone—something round, anyway—inside the ones they farm to create perfect cultured pearls."

"So they grow in the ocean?" Nath seemed confused by this.

"Sort of." She stared at them, puzzled. "If you have oysters, I don't understand why you wouldn't get them here."

He shrugged. "Lumprigs, I expect."

"Say what now?" She blinked. "You made that up."

He snorted. "Perhaps *they* do not exist in your world. They are tiny transparent creatures that live in symbiosis with mollusks. In exchange for keeping their shells free of dirt and algae, the lumprigs get a safe place to hide from predators." He shook his head. "I guess that means there are no pearls in Galahar."

"But there are," Jenny protested. "They're in the photos." She frowned again. "Unless they came from my world somehow?"

Marden had been sitting with half-closed eyes, seemingly lost in contemplation. Now he rose from his chair with a roar. "MERMAID'S TEARS!

He slammed his hands on the table, making the others flinch. "Eya! That immoral sharding warlock dared so much?"

Jenny shrank away, and Nath laid his hand on the shaman's shoulder.

The old man noticed Jenny's reaction and calmed

himself. "I am sorry, my dear, you did nothing wrong. *Nothing*," he emphasized. "I cannot believe even Shifton would go this far. One can always find evil artifacts in the shadow trade. Perhaps he purchased them."

Marden stared down at the photograph, still visible on the phone lying open on the table. "It would require a full-grown Mer and, from the size of those tears, a male."

She straightened, looking confused. "So mermaids cry pearls? That seems odd."

The shaman shook his head as he sank back into his seat. "They do not weep as we do. Since they live in salt water, what would be the purpose? The creatures fascinated my old master, and he often talked of them. Some of his knowledge remains with me."

He turned his face to the ceiling and closed his eyes. "As I recall, if they stay out of water for too long and start drying out, their scales begin to dissolve from within and their eye glands form these stones."

His sorrowful gaze met hers. "Like dragons, the Mer possess no magical powers themselves. They *are* magic, which gives their bodies special properties. It seems the warlock required the tears of a mermaid to help create the tools that seek the blood of a dragon, for whatever spell he hopes to cast."

His shoulders sagged. "To obtain stones of this size, you would need to capture a live merman. Not a simple task, I can assure you. Then one would have to torture him, letting him dry out by withholding the water he needs to survive. The longer he remains alive, the larger the gems . . . these pearls . . . that form."

Jenny shuddered. How could someone allow another creature to suffer just for a bit of profit?

As if reading her mind, Nath spoke up. "Men brutalize each other. Why should they care about a species they view as inferior or even an enemy?"

Marden clapped his hands to recapture their attention. "Enough wallowing in the misery mankind can cause. Now we understand what we are looking for, I am uncertain these books hold the answer." He gazed up at the cave's ceiling again, as if seeking the solution. "Let me fetch my master's personal journals, and we will hope the answers lie within."

He leaned forward and patted Jenny's arm. "Thank you, my dear. You give us renewed optimism."

44

Two Days until Summer Solstice

When Jenny and Davy entered the common room the next morning, Nath was twisting his neck, groaning, and rubbing his shoulders. His master seemed unbothered by their lack of sleep, yet dark circles under his eyes betrayed his weariness.

Although she offered to help, Marden waved her to a seat and busied himself at the fireplace.

The young man met her anxious gaze, alleviating her concerns with a nod. She leaned back, heaving a sigh of relief, trusting they had solved the puzzle of the spells. It would be good to see Lauran freed from her enchantment.

She looked at Davy. They were one step closer to going home.

Marden joined them, holding the cup he carried out to Nath.

Jenny hid a smile as he accepted the brew with

obvious reluctance, sniffed, and grimaced. "Ugh, I would rather be tired!"

The old man stared at him with mock sternness. "Drink all of it! You must be at your best today."

Nath gave a martyred sigh but obeyed. He breathed deep, held his nose, and threw the draft back in a single gulp. He pulled a face, and his whole body shuddered.

She exchanged grins with Davy, though by unspoken agreement, they resisted teasing him. After they ate, the young shaman read and reread his notes. He muttered under his breath and practiced hand gestures while they helped put all of Marden's books away.

Jenny was astonished to discover two additional rooms off the old shaman's sleeping chamber. Rows of texts and scrolls filled one room from bottom to top, while shelves packed with containers crowded the other.

She wandered deeper into the storeroom, reading labels. Earthen jars held seeds, roots, bark, and floral remnants of every variety—mandrake root and mugwort were instant favorites, calling to mind a well-loved book—while animal bones and feathers sat heaped in baskets. The fragrant aroma of dried herbs came from bundles hanging from the ceiling: sage, lavender . . . even roses and marigolds. The smell tickled her nose, and she sneezed.

Jenny jumped when Nath chuckled behind her. "Marden places spells around both these rooms that inhibit mice and insects. They also contain the odors so we can sleep. He renews the charms at Winter Solstice."

He began gathering ingredients and handing them to her as he went down the row. Once satisfied they'd collected everything he needed, they returned to the common room.

Nath placed a small cauldron filled with water over the fire to heat and set Jenny to chopping and crushing the components required for a potion. As he added each to the pot, he instructed Davy to stir. Sometimes clockwise, every so often widdershins—a word she found charming.

By midmorning, with the brew cooled and bottled, they prepared to leave.

She had just put on her wrap to follow her stepbrother outside when Nath drew her aside for a whispered exchange that left her nervous. Jenny hadn't anticipated being more than a witness to today's events.

Marden had ordered the villagers to keep to their homes today. Anishinabe stood at their doors, nodding in solemn benediction as the four passed.

They continued up the mountain in silence, each lost in their own thoughts.

45

Lauran awaited them in the clearing. She was nervous, and from Davy's reaction, the smile she tried to give him must have looked more like a grimace, with far too many teeth.

Nath moved to join her, nodding at Kellin and Staton, who shifted large rocks to flank her. They hoped the heavy boulders would anchor her when things got difficult.

In their conversations over the past few days, the young shaman had given Lauran some idea of what to expect. However, nothing like this had ever been done before. Besides the coming pain, she only knew that each curse element required separate handling.

But after experiencing the torture of their initial attempt at extracting the ruby, she admitted to herself that she dreaded the agony lying ahead. Despite that, she remained adamant, determined to proceed.

The quiet seemed unnatural. No birds called, and nobody coughed or shuffled their feet.

Lauran stood at the head of the group, and Nath stood

facing her. Ganther and Davint waited on one side, Marden on the other.

Jenny had her arm around the shoulders of a solemn Davy. She'd resisted letting him attend, fearing it would be too traumatic. But the boy had insisted, and with Marden's reluctant agreement, she had given in.

The siblings and the rest of the Kin formed a half circle in front of Lauran. She leaned forward to meet Nath's eyes. *[No matter what happens, promise me you won't stop.]*

His lips tightened. "I swear."

She removed the silver-coated chain mail and braced herself against the rocks.

He turned to face the witnesses, leaving her peering at his back. Beckoning Jenny to come stand beside him, the young shaman held out his hand. She gently pushed Davy to one side and came forward.

Lauran stared at her in surprise, then looked to Nath, who squared his shoulders, still facing the others. "The warlock added a magical component none of us has seen before." Those gathered murmured in shock and concern.

"Thanks to our friend from another world,"—he smiled down at Jenny—"we identified the component as Mermaid's Tears." His smile died as he looked out at them. "These are acquired through torturing an adult Mer."

Their friends who hadn't heard this news couldn't control their exclamations of dismay and outrage.

Nath waited for them to quiet before continuing. "These pearls, as Jenny calls them, do not afford the user magical abilities as such, but their innate magic acts to increase the potency of the other elements. Before I can sever the gemstone's curse, I must break the parts asunder."

He nodded to Davint, who also lumbered forward to join them.

All three—shaman, dragon, and Common—offered their palms.

The sun glinted off the honed edge of Nath's raised knife. It flashed down once, twice, a third time.

Without acknowledging the gasps of horror from those watching, he placed a bowl beneath their sliced hands, letting their blood mingle in the vessel. Marden stepped forward and healed their wounds.

The younger shaman bowed to the pair, who resumed their places. "Symbolic unity and shared sacrifice carry weight in ritual magic. Our hope is that this will release the essence of the captured Mermaid's Tears, weakening their potency and destabilizing the entire enchantment."

Nath inhaled deeply, then exhaled, long and slow, muttering what Lauran gleaned, through her light touch on his mind, to be a purification spell. He faced her, pouring their lifeblood into his cupped palm, then he pressed his bloodied hands on her scaled chest, over the embedded ruby.

He began chanting once again.

At first, she thought nothing was happening. Then a shudder rippled down her spine from neck to tail, before she grew still.

Lauran lifted her head. *[I feel . . . different. I'm not sure what happened, but the stone has stopped moving.]*

Nath exhaled, relief flickering in his eyes as he smiled up at her. "Then let us continue."

He bent to lift the clay jar containing the potion he'd brewed, removed the stopper, and held it out. "Each of the five magic powers is represented by a color."

His voice rang out, strong and clear. "We begin with rose red, the so-called weakest power. Crimson Wizards are known for their abilities with potions. Shifton used this talent to strengthen the binding enchantment on the stones."

He held the jar higher. "With this counterpotion, we weaken rose's subtle coercion, taking the first steps in making the spells susceptible to unraveling."

In a single fluid motion, Nath spun around and threw the liquid across Lauran's chest, covering his bloody handprints. Her muzzle rose as she arched her back, but she remained silent as the brew sank into her scales.

As the magics separated, they seemed to fill her chest. She experienced the strangest sensation. Their combined powers no longer compressed together; she *sensed* each one unfurling.

Lauran gasped. *[I can feel it working! It's like a tangled knot coming undone inside me.]*

He gave her an encouraging nod and stayed facing her. "Orange is a healing power. Amber Wizards *sense* the benefits inside plants and herbs and the rhythms of the body." His mouth tightened. "The warlock twisted this capacity to dominate his victims. I must disrupt this connection."

Nath placed his hands where her scales covered the jewel and began to chant.

Lauran moaned, gritting her teeth as she threw her muzzle skyward once again. She was determined not to cry out, but she couldn't suppress a groan. Yet as promised, he never paused or hesitated. His chanting swelled, becoming louder, more commanding.

The gemstone trembled inside her, resisting his magic. Her wings lifted, then resettled as she sank back down. Sweat shone on his forehead as Nath stepped away, breathing heavily.

"Yellow is also a healing power. But Citrine Wizards are empaths. They are often able to remove a person's pain as they heal. Shifton has woven this empathy into his curse, generating greater control over its victims."

He glanced over his shoulder. "I ask you to remain silent during this next step. Lauran and I must link minds and channel my empathic energy to reverse this emotional manipulation."

Nath placed both hands over her heart. She bent her great head forward, so he stood within the curve of her neck and his forehead touched her jaw. They closed their eyes.

She welcomed the warm rush as his magic surrounded her. His mind melded with hers. She rejoiced in his loyalty and compassion; he admired her honor and strength.

Her body tensed, resisting as he pushed the spell inside the gemstone. Unable to defend against him, the ruby twisted as if attempting to distract them and break their connection. She bit back a cry and concentrated on maintaining the link between them.

Despite their closed eyes, their heightened senses detected the intense focus of their witnesses, staring at their still figures. She had never experienced such an intense union with anyone before . . . not even Davint.

Lauran's shaking increased, but Nath never released

his grip. He pressed himself harder against her, and she dug her talons into the boulders.

When they broke apart, she sagged against one of the rocks, and he staggered back. Marden sprang to Nath's side, but the younger shaman straightened, waving Marden away.

Lauran panted, sending up billows of steam.

The young shaman took several deep breaths, faced the others again, and continued.

"Green enhances spellcasting. Emerald Wizards may be empaths, but their strength is in mind-speech. They sense the rhythms of the natural world and are often gifted with far-reach—the ability to move things with their minds. Shifton twisted this power to exert control over his victim's physical motions."

He turned sideways, patting Lauran on a great forearm. "I must perform quite a complex counterspell, which will disrupt this magic within the jewel. If successful, this should break any lingering force acting on your limbs and let you move freely again."

She nodded, huffing out a breath that ruffled his hair. Nath brushed it out of his face with a tired smile. He returned his hands to her chest scales and began chanting.

The invocation sparked like a static charge on her hide. Lauran gave a surprised growl when his incantation lifted them off the ground. United, they rose, hovering a few feet in the air, though her wings still lay flat against her back. She tried to struggle—but they stayed frozen together. Only Nath's lips moved.

Startled exclamations and gasps came from those observing, but they didn't interfere.

Nath had warned Lauran that as the power of each

color grew stronger, the enchantments would become harder to overcome. So she waited, trusting him, as his spell continued twice as long as the previous ones.

With an audible *pop*, they dropped to the ground. As the young shaman fell to one side, she widened her stance, grabbing the boulders to keep from falling on top of him. Ganther rushed to support her, and she reassured him all was well.

Marden knelt beside Nath, handing him a soft cloth. His former apprentice wiped his face and neck with a nod of thanks. After a few moments, he pushed himself upright and rose to his feet.

Lauran felt a tingling in her thigh and peered down at her half-healed injury. As she watched, the edges of the ugly scar from the knife wound began to slowly smooth out into unblemished hide. *[Do you see this?]*

Nath and Ganther leaned over, the large green muzzle dwarfing the man's smaller head. "The connection between the stone and your body has been broken!" Nath exclaimed excitedly. "Your natural healing powers are starting to reassert themselves!"

[Keep going!] She pushed her father back to the watching circle, and the young shaman moved closer.

"Thus far, fortune has favored us." Nath's expression grew grim. "But now the work grows harder."

A snort, halfway between a sob and a laugh, escaped Jenny from her place in the circle.

"Blue is the strongest power." The strain in his voice matched the exhaustion on his face. Yet he never faltered.

"Azure Wizards combine and strengthen the abilities of all the others. Shifton used this capability to forge a link between the weapon and the victim. Each of the spells cast today have weakened some aspect of the curse." Nath shook his head. "However, I cannot break the bond between ruby and rod."

Lauran felt a wave of disappointment. *Why are we even doing this, then?*

Nath raised his hand, forestalling the murmurs of protest. "But I can block the connection between the warlock's weapon and the cursed jewel by creating a shield around it." He turned toward her. "Ready?"

Still linked to him, Lauran *read* his concern that encasing the gemstone—inhibiting its ability to link with its controller—would be the most painful process of all. She lifted her lip in a snarl. *[Do it.]*

With both hands covering the stone's location, he began invoking a protection spell. Despite nullifying the lesser magics, the ruby clung to her like a burr, embedded in her flesh. His foot stepped back as he braced himself and pushed hard against her, demanding the magic obey him and encase the gemstone in a protective shell.

She roared, tossing her muzzle from side to side above Nath's head.

Pain sizzled along her nerves. She *felt* him use their bond to try and ease her suffering. Sweat soaked through his tunic, and his arms trembled from his efforts.

Ever since the jewel had entered her, its presence had pressed against her mind like an unwanted whisper in her ear. Even with the silver breastplate on, it had never been completely silenced.

Now, something shifted.

She sensed the torment dulling by miniscule degrees as the shield settled slowly into place around the cursed gemstone.

A wave of emotion uplifted them both. As Nath chanted, relief—or perhaps release—filled her as the gemstone's pulsing signal dwindled. The nagging pressure behind her thoughts faded. With it, tension she hadn't realized she carried drained from her shoulders.

The watchers could only wait in anxious silence. As the minutes stretched, they started to exchange nervous stares. Lauran wanted to reassure them, but holding still required all her focus.

Finally, Nath lifted his hands and sagged against her. "This task is complete." Lauran cradled him until he felt able to stand on his own.

The agony she'd been suffering had eased. She enjoyed the simple release of not feeling as if she were being torn apart.

46

Lauran's body slumped to the ground. *[Is that it? Are we finished?]*

Her friends drew close, their faces hopeful.

"We have neutralized the enchantments." Nath frowned. "However, the curse remains inside you. The warlock could still reactivate the incantation once he finds you and realizes what we have done. He is powerful enough to pierce my shielding spell. After you rest for a couple of days, we may proceed with removing the jewel, and—"

[NO!]

The others winced as her shout reverberated in their heads, covering their ears as if that would help. Embarrassed, Lauran lowered her mental voice. But she didn't back down.

[I don't want to wait. Take it out now.] She leaned down and nudged him with her muzzle, almost knocking him over. *[Please?]*

Marden frowned. "You are not the only one who

needs rest, milady. Nath has expended much energy already today."

Nath's raised hand stopped him. Marden pinched his lips closed but waited silently.

"You can expect more pain than you have endured thus far," the younger shaman warned. "And I am unsure I have enough strength remaining." He paused, then admitted, "But in your position, I would desire the same. I will try if you are decided."

Marden sniffed in disapproval but remained quiet.

Lauran huffed in relief. *[I'll take the risk. Get this thing out of me.]*

Ganther's brow ridge drew down. He looked mutinous. She stepped forward and put her paw on his foreleg in silent pleading. Her father sighed, his shoulders slumping, and he nodded. She leaned her forehead against his, then moved back into position, reaching out to clutch the boulders on either side of her.

Nath took several deep breaths, then placed his hand where the stone lay beneath her scales. In a low, firm voice, his chant began anew.

Lauran groaned as the gemstone started inching upward, tearing muscle and flesh as it went. Unable to remain still, she threw her head back, straining away from his grip.

As she'd requested, Nath never paused or hesitated. His chanting grew louder, more demanding. She snapped at the air above her, as if at an enemy.

He raised his voice a notch, calling the ruby forth.

The gemstone resisted, but she could feel it being forced to creep toward the surface. She tried to contain the anguish, but a growl burst through her clenched teeth. Her talons dug deep into the boulders, piercing them as if they were made of soft cheese.

Still Nath chanted, sweat running down his face. Lauran felt his arms tremble. His voice grew hoarse, demanding the ruby obey him.

The weapon remained inert, its magic sealed inside, but it was still attached to her body like a tick. The removal process proved as painful as promised, yet the ruby crept toward the surface.

She gritted her teeth against the agony, but soon her cries rose to anguished screams, reverberating down the mountain.

Dimly conscious of waves of concern wafting up from the village, closer at hand, Lauran *sensed* Jenny and Davy's distress on her behalf. Vague regret for causing their tears echoed behind Lauran's pain, but she couldn't stop. Not now, with freedom so close.

Yet as the struggle dragged on, her father's growing agitation pressed on her mind. She glanced over, locking eyes with the copper dragon, who nodded grim agreement.

[Quit it! You must give this up! You're sharding torturing her!] Ganther blared. Smoke flared from his nostrils, and his tears turned to steam.

Davint understood—and even shared—his anxiety, but he still grabbed her father and pulled him back. The other dragons piled on, keeping the green behemoth from reaching Lauran.

The young shaman stopped chanting but didn't release the stone.

She shook her head, flicking the tears streaming down her scaled cheeks onto the onlookers. *[Don't stop!]* she gasped between groans. *[I won't be a slave to the warlock or the ruby.]*

Ganther heard her over his struggling and subsided.

Nath's bemused glance viewed the salt water pooling on the ground at his feet and trickling downhill. He peered up and met Lauran's watery eyes. They exchanged grim nods, and his chanting resumed.

Throwing her head back, she roared.

A short time later, he looked around in despair. "I cannot move the ruby any farther. The jewel sits right below her scales, but they are too hard. I cannot pull it through this last barrier."

With the movement stopped, her screams reduced to anguished moans. She swayed, as if growing lightheaded.

"Hold on, Lauran. We need to try something else." He turned to Marden, who gave a helpless shrug.

She shoved Nath aside with a huge forepaw. *[Stand . . . back . . .]* She swiped a talon toward her throat.

A chorus of mental and verbal voices shouted, *NO!* But it was too late.

Nath glimpsed the ruby through her slashed armor and stared in horror as it disappeared, struggling to protect itself by burrowing deeper.

[Quick. Get that . . . thing . . . out . . . of me!] Lauran gasped.

He leaped forward, dragging the sleeve of his tunic out of the way, and plunged his hand inside the cut. His fist closed around something hard and sharp edged.

Nath yanked his arm out, holding the stone high in the air, shouting in triumph.

The slice on Lauran's neck healed as they stared. The last of her leg wound scar disappeared, and the patch on her wing smoothed and blended into the membrane.

As soon as the draikana's wounds disappeared, her scales started retracting. Lauran groaned, dropping to the ground, her forearms stretching and thinning.

Jenny and Davy's cries mingled with Nath's shocked gasp. He lifted his bloody hand, but Marden gripped his arm before he could begin a counterspell.

"Wait!" the old shaman commanded.

Nath gawked at his master in wild-eyed disbelief. But the dragons leaned forward, expressions of hope and expectation on their faces. Their eyes whirled yellow with excitement, and they crooned encouragement.

He stood watching as the changes continued to happen. Her body seemed to shimmer and pull in on itself. Long hair, pale as wheat, sprang out of her head, curling and twining down to cover full breasts.

A golden shoulder, the curve of her spine, a swelling hip flowing into a rounded bottom . . . This time he gasped in astonishment, finding a very large, quite beautiful, and completely naked young woman lying at his feet.

She gave him a sultry glance through a waterfall of pale-gold hair. Their eyes met, and his face flushed. He whirled about with his back facing her.

Hearing her chuckle at his embarrassment, his blush deepened.

To Nath's amazement, Marden appeared to have expected this. The old shaman skipped forward with a blanket and draped it over her.

Lauran nodded her thanks, peering shyly around at the others.

Jenny and Davy both wore stunned expressions. Jenny's hand flew to cover Davy's eyes—perhaps a second too late, given the boy's wide-eyed stare.

The golden woman laughed. "You have no idea how wonderful it is to be in human form again." Lauran's voice was husky from the abuse she'd put it through today. "Thank you, Nath."

The younger shaman peeked back over his shoulder, then wheeled around, still staring.

She gave him a grateful smile. "You succeeded!"

He was pleased yet bemused. "No, *we* did." He gestured to include everyone. "However, this"—he waved his hand in a circle encompassing her human form—"came as a surprise . . ." He turned to Marden with a raised eyebrow. "At least for me!"

The old shaman gave him an innocent smile, then winked.

Around them, the other dragons shifted, and Nath found himself surrounded by large, bare-naked people. He whirled away from Kellin, his cheeks burning once again, eyes almost as wide as Davy's. Audra and Callie, already in human form—and dressed, thankfully—seemed highly amused by his discomfiture.

At least Lauran tried to hide her amusement as Jenny struggled, uncertain where to look when confronted by a well-muscled, tall, and very nude Davint in his human form. She averted her gaze, only to face Ganther, Dram, and Staton—equally naked.

Marden took pity on the embarrassed young folk, handing out more blankets, until the underdressed Kin retired to the cave, where Callie handed out the additional clothing stored there. With breakfast long past and having missed nooning, she also suggested further explanations could wait.

Nath and Davy helped gather wood, filling one of the previous evening's firepits with branches. They wore identical stunned expressions as they watched Dram half shift his upper body, breathe flames to start the fire, and then change back.

"Cool!" the boy exclaimed with a grin, making Marden laugh.

Lauran heaved a relieved sigh at their acceptance, then asked Jenny to help her fetch the Gather leftovers the village women had placed in the cave for them.

They exchanged shy smiles, uncertain what to say to each other. Davy didn't have the same problem and circled the towering woman's thighs in a hug—as high as his reach allowed—every time he passed her.

As they watched the boy run to rejoin the men, Lauran sighed. "I'm still the same person inside . . . just in a different shape outside."

They stared at each other, then Jenny lunged forward to embrace her—very tall—friend's waist. "I really am glad you're free. But . . ." She shrugged. "This change sure took me by surprise!"

Laughing together, they resumed working in harmony.

Lauran found her happiness at returning to human form hard to contain. She couldn't stop smiling as she stretched her fingers and rubbed her arms.

The arduous task of overcoming the ruby left both her and Nath starving, and it appeared that watching had encouraged her friends' appetites as well. Everyone fell on the food as if it had been days, not hours, since their last meal.

When they finished, Lauran set her plate on the ground and leaned forward. "Let's talk."

47

Lauran filled in the missing pieces of the story while the fire died down to glowing embers. "It has always been our way to remain apart. We do not wish to share the knowledge that we Kin are shifters with outsiders. Whenever we're going into the Lowlanders' world, we pair off and play beast and dragonrider."

Nath grinned across at her father. "Only you played both Ganther and Ta'ther. Your mind-speech seemed familiar, but I put it down to a dragon growing to sound like his rider. The way people begin to resemble a beloved pet . . ." He blushed, hastening to add, "Not that dragons are anyone's pets!"

Lauran and the others chuckled as he backpedaled.

Marden caught Ganther's eye. "While aware of the Kin's existence and your abilities, since you chose to conceal them, I respected your wishes and did not inform my former apprentice of your true nature. Though I would have been duty bound to pass along this information at some point now that he is a shaman himself."

"I, too, shall keep your confidence," Nath added, glancing from Lauran to Davint beside her, to Ganther across the fire. "Shamans guard many secrets they do not share with the world at large." He shrugged. "This is simply one more."

Lauran bent down to kiss him on the cheek as the Kin murmured their gratitude.

Jenny leaned forward. "My stepbrother and I will soon leave, but you don't need to worry about us telling either. I can only imagine Earth's governments' reactions to finding out about Galahar, but I doubt their responses would be good. We're going to keep this place classified." The boy nodded his enthusiastic agreement.

When Davint insisted on kissing her cheek too, the embarrassed young woman retreated to Davy's side, blushing but pleased.

"My, this is quite the Seven-Day Quest, is it not?" Marden chuckled.

Ganther snorted. "Well, we've not reached the end yet."

Lauran shifted uneasily when Nath held up the jewel he'd removed from inside her. She didn't like being this close to it—even if it was encased in a shield.

"Eya, what shall we do about this?" he inquired. "And how should we handle the warlock—and his duke? Does anyone have any thoughts about why he wants to capture a dragon?" His questions began a debate that lasted until the second moon rose.

"We should go to the Council of Wizards at the Citadel." Nath smacked his knee. "The sorcerer is one of theirs. And Almar is a Lowlander. Why not let them deal with it?"

Ganther growled, sounding as fierce in human form as he did as a dragon.

Marden calmed him with a gentle touch on his arm. "That is an excellent suggestion, Shaman." He inclined his head. The younger man grinned at the honorific. "But if we go to the Council, we must tell them everything. If we did not reveal the Kins' secret, surely the warlock or the duke would. In either case, the Kin would be exposed. We have given our word not to betray them."

Nath sighed but nodded his reluctant acceptance of this reasoning. "But then what is to be done?"

At that moment, Davy gave a loud yawn. Lauran laughed, and everyone realized how late it was. He and Jenny had sat listening, not saying much except that this decision affected those who would remain in Galahar.

They looked up as Ganther rose, towering over them. "I sent Dram to reconnoiter. The warlock sits below us on the edge of the plain. He should arrive by nooning tomorrow. He did this vile deed to the Kin. Justice and retribution are ours to deliver." He announced this with a finality that suggested he would tolerate no further arguments.

Nath stood to face him, despite the difference in their heights. "That is true in the main. However,"—Ganther's grunt of satisfaction changed to a glower—"he has defiled the oaths we swear as sorcerers. He also turned to dark magic and has become a powerful warlock. You will need our help to defeat him."

Lauran was proud of how the young shaman defied her father.

"We achieved Lauran's freedom together, eya." Nath held the green Kin's gaze. "That is how we shall conquer Shifton. Together."

They glared at each other, and Lauran wondered if she should interfere. She relaxed when Ganther blinked, sat back down, and nodded. "So be it."

They spent a few minutes outlining a general plan for the next day, which included placing the rest of the medallions deep in the cave so their signals would draw the warlock to this place.

Ganther's sudden shift to dragon form left his robes sitting in a crumpled pile beside the firepit. *[Come on, let's get this youngling home before he falls asleep and tumbles off mid-flight.]*

To Davy's delight, the friends took advantage of his generosity by climbing aboard his broad back. Lauran called a soft *[Sleep well]* in their heads as they departed.

Jenny enjoyed a bath before preparing for bed. She smiled at her stepbrother's gentle snores coming from under a mountain of blankets. As she slid under her own covers, raised voices caught her attention. Startled, she climbed to her feet, trying to make out the muffled words.

She tiptoed down the tunnel toward the common room, hesitating as Nath spoke.

"No! I will not do it." Jenny blinked, surprised by the fury in his voice. "You cannot ask this of me. It is too much, eya."

"On the contrary, my boy." Marden sounded calm, though there was a sad undertone to his voice. "You are more powerful than you think. And far stronger. Only you can do this."

She'd never heard them argue. Her stomach clenched as she leaned forward to listen.

"You are wrong. It takes a convocation of wizards to Still a sorcerer's powers."

"Ah, but we do not need to suppress all his power." Marden sounded pleased, as if Nath had proved his point. "We must remove the strongest of the dark magic he has accumulated. To do this, a willing sacrifice needs to offer themselves as a conduit. You have read the spell; you know you can cast it."

"It would kill you." Nath's flat tone hurt Jenny's heart.

"That may be. It is dangerous, true. Perhaps my odds of surviving would be better were I still in my prime. However, I am nearly finished with this life. I am prepared for either outcome."

"If I am as strong as you say, it is unnecessary."

A long pause followed, and she strained to hear them.

"We share that hope," Marden conceded. "But he is far older and more experienced. You must be ready. Study the incantation. Just in case."

The young woman leaned against the wall, listening to them argue until Nath agreed to learn the spell. "But only as a last resort, eya."

Jenny slipped back down the hall to her bed. Until now, the coming battle had existed as a hypothetical. Something vague, like out of a story. Suddenly, it didn't seem nearly as thrilling as it had in a book. People she cared for might die.

"Magic always comes with a price," she whispered.

A long time later, she slept, her pillow drenched with tears.

The orbs circling Shifton's head cast dancing shadows on

the walls of his tent. His thin face twisted in frustration as he stared at the rod. Impatient fingers drummed on the small table.

He clenched his fists, squirming at the humiliation of being outsmarted. One hand snaked up to grip the pendant around his neck. The gems were his. He would have them all back, whatever it took.

However, the weapon refused to find any stone except the nearest gem in his possession. "Damn their sharding hides," he muttered. A dragon remained essential to his plans, though at the moment, his goal had shifted from acquiring dragon's blood to retrieving his darlings.

Although a small part of him knew he was in trouble, the overwhelming desire to claim the gems for his own silenced his howling inner voice. *Almar had no right to give them away! I found them, even if he did pay for them. What a fool I was to let him take them.*

For lack of a better idea, he'd marched his men back in their original direction and camped at the base of the foothills.

Now he wondered why the dragons had bothered planting the second gemstone. Just to delay him? To lure him into a trap? Why not move the beast . . . unless he had underestimated its injuries? Had his curse weakened it more than he'd expected? Perhaps they couldn't risk moving it without injuring it further.

Of course. Why haven't I considered that before? His hand tightened on the pendant as the idea took hold. It was so obvious now. But how would he locate it with the rod blocked? Shifton's rage simmered.

Very well. He would work through the night to create

a shield between his precious medallion and his weapon. Then he would retrieve what belonged to him.

However, care was required. He couldn't afford to underestimate them a second time. His mind raced. They might be clever, but he would show them he was more cunning. They wouldn't catch him off guard. If it was a trap, he'd spring it.

First, he needed that shield. He would not let the dragon slip through his grasp yet again.

48

Avila sat in silence at the opposite end of the table as Almar slammed his silverware down and pushed his plate away. He sneered at her, petulant as a youngling, then stood and began pacing. Her watchful eyes followed him.

The door crashed open, and he whirled, ready to roar his displeasure. But when the Captain of the Guard stepped forward, her father halted, seeming to swallow his harsh words.

Avila sat up straighter, staring at the young man.

Rudolph was covered in a layer of dust and grime. His frayed cloak bore stains and tears from his journey. His thick hair hung in disheveled strands, while the stubble shading his jaw and dark circles under his eyes exposed his fatigue.

Despite his exhausted state, he bowed.

The duke stopped, leaning forward over his cane. Avila didn't like the avid expression on his face. His lips parted and his gaze locked on something clasped tight in the captain's gloved fist. "What do you have for me?"

Rudolph held up a vial. "Do you mean this?"

Almar shuffled closer, snatching it from him. He twisted away to examine his prize. "Why are you bringing the dragon's blood? Where is the warlock?"

Avila gasped. "DB!" Fortunately, her father ignored her involuntary murmur.

"Warlock?" the young captain questioned softly.

Her eyes widened. Could it be true?

The duke threw a sharp glance over his shoulder. "You don't seem that surprised."

Rudolph shrugged. "I suspected something of the sort. It explains much. Although your own knowledge is . . . unexpected."

He couldn't mean . . . She stared from one to the other, unease creeping up her spine.

The captain straightened. "I must also report that I disobeyed a command, Your Grace. The . . . warlock . . . invaded a neighboring territory in his pursuit of a wounded dragon, and I refused to follow his orders. I do not believe the Kin planned to attack us." He hesitated. "And I doubt you believed it, either."

The duke waved a dismissive hand, his eye glued to the green liquid. "Bah, what do you comprehend about matters of state? Leave me. I will deal with you when Shifton returns."

Lady Avila edged along the wall. Using her father's distraction, she slipped out after the captain.

Almar hurried to his chambers as fast as his rheumatic limbs allowed. His focus centered on the vial clutched to his chest, but Shifton's delayed return increased his anxiety.

Do I need him? Are further potions even necessary? No doubt this pure dragon's blood is much stronger than that diluted swill he provided me with.

The duke held up the small bottle, staring at its lazily shifting beauty. *It must work! Can I afford to wait for Shifton?*

He put it down . . . paced around the room . . . picked it up . . .

By the time he finally decided, the moons had set, and the morning sun peeked through the window. Almar removed the stopper, paused—offering himself one last chance to stop—then tossed the untreated liquid to the back of his throat and swallowed.

He waited.

Nothing happened.

The duke cursed his impetuousness. Perhaps the warlock's potions were necessary after all. Now, with the dragon's blood gone, he must hope Shifton returned with more.

He shattered the empty vial against the fireplace hearth and whirled around.

A stabbing pain shot through his guts. He folded over, clenching his stomach. He stretched out his arm, trying to reach the bellpull to call for help.

And paused.

His attention fixated on the back of his hand, where age spots receded like an ebb tide. The thin, wrinkled flesh firmed up. Touching his arms confirmed the muscles were growing stronger.

It worked!

49

One Day until Summer Solstice

Next morning, Nath cast a spell cloaking the settlement from sight with an illusion. Once again, the villagers remained in their homes as their shamans instructed.

Jenny seemed more subdued than usual, but he put it down to nerves. After all, today marked her first battle. Despite this, she insisted on staying with Marden. Nath welcomed her loyalty to the old man. With Marden's attention focused on her, he wouldn't be risking his life with an untested spell.

Marta kept Davy in the village with her as the others headed up the mountain.

As they'd agreed, Ganther hid the medallions in the small cave himself, refusing to allow anyone else to expose themselves to the cursed jewels.

Lauran lay tucked in a hollow with the younger shaman. The remaining Kin, also in dragon form, were concealed in dips and behind ridges, within listening distance of their baited trap.

Dram and Kellin monitored Shifton, updating Ganther on his progress. The warlock's soldiers had broken camp at dawn and were already on the march.

Around nooning, they all *sensed* the enemy's approach; the rod's magic sent out waves of nauseous energy.

Lauran hoped Nath didn't notice her quivering. Her short time as Shifton's prisoner had caused more trauma than she realized.

She forced herself to peek out and gave a low growl. *[He's wearing Ganther's pendant! The one I hid.]*

The warlock's voice rang out as he advanced, lifting his weapon high and moving toward the cave. "The jewel is nearby; my rod confirms it. The beast must be close!"

[CLOSER THAN YOU KNOW.] Lauran's roar resounded across the battlefield.

The soldiers cringed, and even the warlock held his head, stunned by her concussive *sending*, though she remembered to shield their human companions.

At this signal, dragons launched themselves into the sky on all sides, their massive forms casting ominous shadows over their adversaries. Flames erupted from their gaping jaws as they dived and swooped, raining fire upon the warlock's men.

Shifton threw up a defensive barrier, then retaliated with dark spells. He conjured shadowy spheres that hurtled through the air, making the dragons dodge and pull back.

As agreed, while Lauran and the others harried the

warlock, Nath raised his arms, chanting ancient words that summoned the spirits of nature.

Storm clouds gathered overhead, electrifying the atmosphere. Thunder boomed and lightning streaked across the sky, while torrents of rain and hail pummeled their enemies.

Shifton threw his hands up again, though when the whites of his eyes turned solid black, Lauran roared in shock.

He formed a shadowy barrier that absorbed the natural assault, then unleashed a torrent of necrotic energy at the dragons.

The golden dragon jerked aside as Nath countered with a summoning spell. An earthen wall of dirt and roots rose to block the strike. The ground shook with the impact of their magics meeting head-on, like stags doing battle.

Shifton couldn't help cringing as the mighty beasts roared overhead. His eyes narrowed as he considered the figure facing him, so puny in comparison to the animals attacking him. On the defensive, he fired incantations and spells, only to have them met with equal force.

His attire identified the young man as one of the Mountain People—a shaman, no doubt. Shifton hadn't anticipated this, but it didn't matter. The dark was stronger than the light.

Still, the dragonfire was distracting.

He waved the rod, but the flaming dragons flew on, oblivious to his commands. Driven closer to the cave by the searing heat, he snarled, "Engage the beasts, you fool."

Jareth, his new captain, glared but ordered his men

into defensive positions. "Aim for their wings. Their hides are sharding impenetrable."

Projectiles held the great Kin at bay, and the huge green lead dragon called a warning to the others, before falling back.

Refocusing his attention on the young shaman, the warlock sent his sinister energy bolts hissing through the air, only to be met by the shaman's glowing sigils that burst into radiant flames upon impact with Shifton's dark magic.

Shifton ground his teeth, his lip lifting. This was supposed to be his moment. The beast should have been alone, defenseless, easy prey.

Once more, the warlock assured himself of his victory. Yet a whisper in his mind asked what else he'd overlooked.

Jenny and Marden crouched nearby, studying the unfolding battle.

The dueling mages wove spells and incantations that clashed in dazzling displays of light and force that even a Common could see.

But soon, every spell Nath cast soared a bit slower than the last, as dark magic devoured white. The young shaman had a limited supply of power-charged crystals, and knowing this, Jenny watched him struggle. Her heart pounded, fast and loud, in her ears.

When he ran out, he would have to use his personal energy.

Yet the warlock's strength seemed insurmountable; what chance did they have of winning? She glanced at

Marden, recognizing the answer. Her anxiety increased. She really hoped his solution didn't become necessary.

Jenny saw Marden's eyes widen in alarm. "Get down!" he shouted, throwing himself in front of her, his hands casting a hurried shield spell.

The stray bolt of magic slammed into his barrier, and the force of the blow hurled them into the air. Her ears rang, and her vision blurred as she hit the ground.

"Marden!" He lay motionless a few feet away, his eyes closed. She scrambled to his side, shaking him with rising panic. "Please don't be dead. Wake up!"

She looked around in despair.

Shifton's gloating expression and Nath's bowed figure declared the warlock's victory inevitable.

Jenny stood amid the chaos, fear gnawing at her. Everything seemed to speed up yet move far too slowly. The stench of smoke . . . the tang of blood . . . She clasped her hands to stop their trembling. Why was she even here? What could she do?

She glanced at Marden's unconscious body, and it struck her.

No! I am no hero! I can't do this . . .

But who else was there? And what would happen to Davy if Shifton won? She inhaled a sob and raised her head.

Lauran! she thought as hard as she could at the golden dragon overhead.

[I'm a little . . . busy . . . here . . .]

I need to get to Nath. It's important.

Without hesitation, her friend called an order to the dragons. They renewed their attack, engaging Shifton's attention.

Jenny dodged through a barrage of spells, darting to the young shaman's side.

"Use me," she commanded.

He stared at her in confusion, sweat beading on his forehead. "What do you . . . ?"

"The spell needs a willing sacrifice; that's me."

Nath's eyes widened in horror as he understood. "No!" His wild gaze danced around the clearing. "Marden—"

"Wounded. Pretty seriously," she interrupted. "It has to be me. I'm young enough to survive, he said so himself." She crossed her fingers as she lied, hoping it was true.

Seeing him waver, she pressed on. "Do it now," she shouted over the cacophony of battle cries. "They can't keep Shifton distracted for long."

The shriek of an injured dragon punctuated her statement.

His shoulders slumped, and he gave a single sharp nod.

Jenny grabbed his arm. "But if I don't survive . . ." She faltered, then steeled herself. "Get Davy home. Promise me."

He nodded. "Eya, I promise."

"Then do it."

Nath chanted ancient words he feared might kill his young friend, his voice trembling with emotion. Tears blurred his vision as he whispered the incantation.

As the spell's energy built, he extended his fingers to the ground and pulled directly from that primordial source, amazed at how willingly the power leaped toward him—like a pup eager to play.

He ignored the noise and confusion, filling himself with more magic than he'd ever held before.

Then he reached out, and Jenny took his hand.

Her eyes flew wide, then filled with black. She trembled as grim energy coursed through her, and she became a conduit.

Nath gripped both her hands and completed the spell, amputating the warlock's dark sorcery and purifying it through Jenny's sanctified body for dispersal back into the ether.

Her head dropped backward, and a shadowy cloud burst from her mouth and staring eyes, followed by a blinding flash of light that devoured the darkness.

Nath turned his head, squinting to shield his vision.

It cut off as abruptly as it began.

Jenny met his gaze, then her eyes rolled up and she collapsed. He *felt* her heartbeat flutter, her breathing growing shallow, her life force dimming.

"NO!" Davy screamed, leaping out of hiding, startling the shaman, who staggered backward.

Marta came behind the boy, panting and trying to pull him toward safety. "I am sorry!" she wailed. "He snuck out to watch the battle. I tried to catch him . . ."

Jenny's struggling brother broke free and raced to her side.

Nath fell to his knees beside her unconscious body. Stifling sobs, he reached out, his hands glowing with healing energy, desperate to save her.

Davy cradled her head in his lap as the shaman began chanting once again.

50

Shifton stumbled back as the golden dragon swooped at him. Several flaming dragons followed her down, their fire turning the clearing into a hellscape. He swept a shield overhead, but it only covered those closest to him.

Tongues of flame caught the robes of a man outside his protection. His clothing burst into flames, and his screams unnerved the rest of the soldiers.

The warlock staggered, suffering a sudden weakness. The beast swung around for a return run, but Shifton was too disoriented to respond to the threat she posed. He swayed, losing concentration, and his shield collapsed, leaving him exposed.

Abandoning their burning companion to his doom, his men dropped their weapons and fled into the cave. He cursed their cowardice and his unexpected frailty as he lurched after them, deep into the dubious safety of the narrow cavern.

A searing jet of raging flames engulfed the entrance in

a blistering firestorm. The hungry blaze licked at the rocky walls, sending waves of intense heat rushing toward them.

His men shouted in terror, trapped in a fiery prison. They rushed deeper into the constricted space.

Shifton scrambled to erect a shield of dark magic . . . nothing happened.

He tried again. Still naught.

Panicked, he turned to his lesser-used personal sorcery. *I remain an Azure wizard, after all.* He savored the agony that shot through him at this assertion, welcoming every pain as he reclaimed his birthright. But the cries of those surrounding him recalled his attention to his peril.

How many years since I've relied on pure magic?

Dragonfire surged around him, singeing his hair and robes. His awkward spell deflected the flames at the last second. The fiery blast hit his shield, ricocheted to one side, and consumed his newly appointed captain, Jareth, before either could react. The engulfed man uttered a single scream, before his charred body fell at the warlock's feet.

The inferno abated, revealing an even larger green dragon outside, landing beside the gold. Fear clouded Shifton's thoughts. He pushed through his men, muttering incantations under his breath, but they jostled him, shoving him backward and breaking his concentration. He tripped over rocks, falling with a squawk.

Snarling, he sat up. He spotted his precious rod lying on the ground a short distance away. He scrambled toward it, but as he stared in dismay, the soldiers trampled it underfoot. The delicate carvings shattered, and he wailed in despair, *feeling* the power in the jewel around his neck fracture.

Desperation fueling him, Shifton turned and made complex gestures, erecting the strongest barrier he could using only his own magical resources. Yet the combined flames of the relentless dragons burned on. His defense held—for now—but the temperature within their obdurate tomb soared.

The stone walls groaned and cracked.

Large chunks of boulder fell, crashing down with deafening reverberations, crushing soldiers beneath their weight.

Frantic, Shifton tried to maintain a shield above him, but it flickered and failed as his focus wavered under the strain. *I am a wizard . . . and a warlock!* He clenched his fists, reaching for the power he'd once wielded so effortlessly. *I am invincible! I am—*

The collapsing cave swallowed his final defiant scream as he disappeared under a mountain of rubble and dust.

Avila sank onto her bed, pulling Pepper close. He licked her chin as she sat lost in thought. *Shifton is a warlock.* That revelation continued to shock her. *What scheme did he and my father concoct together?*

She stood, determined to confront Almar and demand answers, when the door to her suite burst open, smashing into the wall and startling her. Pepper yelped.

"Avila, I need your help." The man standing there spoke with the duke's imperious tone and bore a striking resemblance to her father. But he appeared no more than seventy, while the duke had turned ninety-five on his latest Name Day.

"Who are you?" She backed away. He wore the

clothes she'd last seen Almar wearing. What had this stranger done to him? Pepper barked, and she gathered the protective dog in her arms, shushing him.

"It's me, you stupid girl." The man scowled, waving impatient hands. "I drank the dragon's blood, but something went wrong. I'm growing younger, and it won't stop. You must send someone to find Shifton before I become too young."

Avila glared at him through narrowed eyes as she reached over and gave a specific sequence of tugs on the bellpull.

The madman ignored her, pacing up and down, raving about his youth and waving his arms in wild gestures.

Her hand flew to her mouth when his face rippled. He groaned and fell to the floor. Avila stared in disbelief. When he stood, he appeared five years younger.

Heavy footsteps pounded down the hallway to her door. Guards burst in, swords ready, answering her summons. She gestured toward the stranger, who glared at them in surprise.

"I don't care how he got in here. It's obvious he's insane. Take him to the Sisters of Mercy asylum. And send someone to check on my father. This lunatic is wearing Father's clothing."

"INSANE?" The man shrieked. "I'm not mad! Find Shifton. He'll explain everything." The guards lifted the protesting intruder until only his toes touched the floor. "Get your hands off me!"

Pepper growled at him as Avila stepped closer. "Calm yourself, sirrah." She held his gaze as she repeated her father's words back to him. "Allow the servants to care for you. Have a meal and leave important decision-making to those best equipped to deal with matters of state."

Dumbfounded, he stared at her, his mouth falling open and his eyes bulging.

Her sweet smile turned tender as she wondered if she'd ever seen Almar speechless before.

51

Any uninjured dragons joined Lauran and her father outside the cavern, their grim satisfaction reflected in the smoke and flames. They unleashed torrents of dragon-fire—lethal as lava—chests heaving and breath laboring with exertion.

The entrance collapsed inward with a resounding crash, sealing the warlock and his men inside their rocky grave.

Ganther flew close enough to rub his muzzle against Lauran's. *[It's over. He won't hurt anyone else ever again.]* They shifted to human form and went to check on Audra and Staton, both of whom had sustained injuries during the battle.

Staton's wounds, already half healed, didn't require the shaman's help, but Audra's wing, struck by Shifton's dark magic, refused to mend. Lauran frowned. Her eyes swept the area, searching for Nath. It wasn't like the young shaman to leave anyone to suffer.

She spied him kneeling beside a still body on the

ground. A mystical glow enveloped him as he rocked and chanted. Davy sat nearby, and Marta stood next to them, wringing her hands.

"Jenny!" Lauran's cry echoed through the smoky clearing.

The remaining Kin shifted to human form, donning the robes Callie handed out as they gathered around Nath, holding a silent vigil for their fallen friend.

The young shaman called upon the spirits of the forest, the mountains, and the sky to aid him. The radiance surrounding him intensified, but Jenny continued to lie there, pale and motionless.

Lauran and Ganther rested their hands on Nath's shoulders, reaching into the bone-deep memory of their ancient dragon ancestors and offering him their power. As the fervor of his chanting increased, his aura expanded to envelop all three of them.

They cried out in unison as they experienced the primal energy of draconic magic melding with Galahar's natural forces. The blaze of light extended to include Jenny, their combined strength reaching out to her fading life force.

With a final desperate effort, Nath recalled her from the spirit world.

Her eyes fluttered open, and she drew a shaky breath. He sagged back on his heels, shoulders drooping, sweat dripping from his face.

Davy threw his arms around his sister. "I thought I lost you!" He hugged her tight, his sobs mingling with the relieved murmurs rippling through those gathered.

Ganther clasped Nath's hand, pulling him to his feet and clapping him on the back. Nath staggered forward a step from the impact. Lauran joined them, sharing a tired but triumphant smile. Marta appeared, supporting Marden. He was alive, although he held his head and groaned.

Battered and worn, the friends shared a moment of peace, hearts lightened by their hard-won triumph.

Jenny watched from the sidelines as the Kin checked the clearing for fires, stomping them out. She wanted to help, but everyone insisted she stay seated.

She still found it difficult to imagine that she'd almost died. There hadn't been a bright light, but she remembered a sense of peace and welcoming that saddened her whenever she recalled leaving it—not that she wasn't glad to be alive!

As the second moon rose, the young shaman finished removing the dark matter from Audra's pinions. She bugled in relief as her wing healed, and moments later, she shifted into human form.

When Nath wandered over and dropped down beside Jenny, she noticed the bruised circles under his drooping eyes. She suspected he'd almost pushed himself too far in his efforts to save her. They were all exhausted, but the young shaman looked ready to fall over.

Ganther and the others joined them. They all sat in companionable silence for a while.

"Shall I check that silver chest for spell residue?" Nath asked eventually. "This was an untested combination of spells. We do not know what side effects there might be."

Jenny frowned in disapproval. He needed to rest, not take on another task.

The green man shook his head. "No need. I left it in the cave."

"What?" Lauran yelped. "Didn't you look inside?"

He gave her a puzzled frown. "No, why would I? Anyway, it was dark, except for a bit of glow moss. I set the chest down, facing away from me so I wouldn't get blasted when I opened the lid." His shoulders shifted uneasily. "I could still feel that creepy sensation, like fingers crawling through my skull, so I took off . . ."

Ganther stopped talking as Lauran began to chuckle, then laugh, pointing at her father. Jenny couldn't help smiling, though she wasn't sure what was so funny. It was just good to have something to smile about again.

"Oh, dear." Lauran's giggles subsided, only to burst out again at Ganther's growing annoyance. "I put all the jewels from your treasure in there for safe keeping." She pointed behind them at the collapsed mountainside. "Well, I guess they're safe enough now!"

Ganther began a stream of inventive cursing that had Davy staring in wide-eyed admiration, as the others joined in her laughter.

52

Summer Solstice

Jenny woke with a frisson of anticipation in the pit of her stomach. Today, she and Davy were going home—they hoped. She rolled over to wake him and found her stepbrother staring at her, his eyes bright with excitement.

"This has been fun," he said. "And I almost hate to leave. But I miss Mom and Dad. I'm ready to go back."

She reached over and squeezed his hand. "Me too."

They hurried to wash and dress. Before they left their room, Jenny bent down in front of the hearth and set out a curl of birch bark to act as a tray. On top, she placed a polished stone with a shallow dip in the middle, like a tiny bowl. Then she rummaged in her bag and pulled out a corked animal horn she'd begged from Marta the previous night. Pulling the cork, she dripped a dollop of honey into the stone's hollow.

"Thank you for the care you've taken of us," she

called softly. "This is not payment; it's a gift for your kindness."

Davy watched her with a half smile.

She grabbed his hand, and they raced toward the common room, where they came to an abrupt halt. People filled the chamber, overflowing into the hallway. Several of the women who'd befriended Jenny during the Gather rushed to greet her. Davy's new friends did the same. After bestowing hugs and best wishes on the bemused pair, everyone else departed.

"I made a special breakfast for your last day." Marta's cheerful tone sounded forced, and she kept wiping the corners of her eyes with her sleeve.

Jenny sniffled. "I'm sure the meal is wonderful." She rushed to help before they could embarrass themselves by bursting into tears.

"How many places shall we set?" Davy tilted his head to one side.

Marta grew still. "Polina left this morning to visit family," she said, her voice carefully neutral. "So we only need five." After an awkward pause, everyone began speaking at once. They laughed together, and the moment passed.

Jenny sent a silent wish for Polina's happiness and smiled at Nath, who appeared recovered from his previous day's exertions.

"One of the dragons should be here soon," he informed them. "We need not rush, though nothing is lost by arriving early." He paused. "We remain uncertain about what to expect in the Cavern of Whispers."

He turned to Marden. "I may not return before the second moon rises."

The older shaman patted his hand. "I have been doing this Solstice ceremony for centuries. I venture to say I can manage one more."

Jenny heard an undercurrent to their conversation, but it seemed private, and she didn't question them.

The crack of thunderous wings and the sound of voices raised in welcome told them their moment had arrived. They hurried outside to find Lauran and Davint in dragon form. Nath intended to accompany them, but they had to say goodbye to the others.

Jenny tried not to cry as she hugged Marta. "Here." She slipped the pastel wrap off her shoulders. "I can't take this home with me." She gulped. "I already have to figure out how I'm going to explain where we've been for a week without mentioning Galahar."

Marden, standing beside them, patted her shoulder. "I trust you will be successful. Yet to return a gift may offend the giver. Can you not find a hiding spot until you are able to account for its presence?"

Marta's hopeful expression made Jenny squirm.

"Well . . ." She scrunched up her face. "If I use a plastic bag . . ." She caught their puzzlement. "That's a kind of thin bladder—for protection, I suppose I could hide your present in my cave until I can pretend to go shopping and buy it."

"I would say such a claim is impossible in its current condition."

Jenny stared down at the fabric, which was covered in dirt and dragon blood, among other things. "Perhaps if I clean it?" She sounded dubious, even to herself.

Marden passed his hands down the length of the garment. When he finished, the wool glowed, as pristine as the day she'd received it.

"Oh!" She swung the ruana over her shoulders as Marta beamed at her. "Thanks. I hated leaving it!" She threw her arms around his neck and gave him a hug. As she pulled away, she planted a kiss on his cheek. The old man chuckled fondly as he patted her shoulder.

Davy waited with growing impatience for his chance to ride a dragon. He claimed the previous flights didn't count since the trips had been so short. He struggled to stand still long enough for everybody to say goodbye and wish them safe journeys.

Jenny swallowed a rebuke, though she rolled her eyes at his conduct. All too soon—with tears shed and everyone thanked and hugged—they were ready to go.

A full day's walk for a person was less than an hour's flight for a Kin. Before Davy could grow bored with flying—which he assured the golden dragon he never would—they arrived at the cavern.

The drake stretched out his foreleg, dipping his shoulder to allow Jenny and Nath to dismount, while her brother clambered down from the draikana as if descending from a tree.

Lauran blew hot breath on them, offering a draconic blessing. *[Be well, my friends. May our flights cross once more, in this realm or the next.]*

Davy rushed forward, wrapping his arms tight around her foreleg. "I'm gonna miss you most of all." He sniffled.

Jenny patted Lauran's scaled side. "It has been an honor knowing you."

[We could meet again. You never know!] Lauran gently bumped her muzzle against the young woman.

Davint nodded. *[We'll wait here, Shaman, to take you back.]*

Nath waved his thanks and led the others toward the entrance. They stopped for one last wave goodbye before ducking and entering.

The interior looked gloomy and dark after the afternoon sunshine outside. They paused, letting their eyes acclimate while Nath lit a torch. Jenny peered around, hoping the gateway would be waiting—but the first part of the cave remained empty.

"The original doorway was farther in." He led the way into the next chamber, where thick white mushrooms stood like silent warriors.

Davy seemed uncomfortable in the cavern and stayed close to Jenny's side. She didn't blame him. Creepy reverberations of their every step echoed back at them, as if sly footfalls followed them.

No sparkles beckoned from the inner room either.

Jenny grabbed the torch from the floor, using Nath's flame to light it. She raised the burning brand high, leaning to reveal a tunnel at the far end. She hurried over, recalling that that's where Nath had found her. Davy stayed right behind her, and the shaman followed.

They were met by nothing but bare rock and returned to the middle chamber.

She swallowed hard. "What if we missed the opening? Maybe it's already closed!"

"We are early yet." Nath's calm voice soothed her. "Time still remains. We must wait." He slid down, sitting with his back against a fungus-free section of wall opposite the side tunnel.

Her stepbrother scuttled over and joined him, but she stuck her torch in the ground and started pacing, muttering to herself as she waved her hands. "It's my fault we're in

Galahar in the first place. Davy never should have followed me."

"Jenny . . ."

She whirled, cutting Nath off. "You're not getting it. I love it here, and I'd stay if I could. But neither he nor I belong here. My mom barely survived losing Dad. If we don't go back—" Jenny's voice broke. "I need to get my brother home!"

As her final passionate words echoed through the cave, she saw sparks reflected on the wall above Nath's head.

She turned, gasping, as Davy scrambled to his feet and joined her. "Stepbrother, you mean?" he teased, staring wide-eyed at the tunnel's mouth.

Without taking her eyes off the sparkles, Jenny pulled him into a hug. "I said brother, and that's what I meant."

The sparking grew more focused and began swirling.

"See?" Nath's smile held a tinge of sadness. "I told you to be patient."

They stared, waiting eagerly, but the whirling pattern refused to grow larger. She started muttering again, marching around the tiny circle, hoping a different angle might be bigger. Nath and Davy exchanged worried glances.

Jenny seethed with frustration. *Oh, come on. We defeated the wicked witch. Now we get to go home.* She snorted. *Okay, not a wicked witch but an evil warlock. But you gotta admit, Shaman Marden is a real Great and Powerful Wizard—not a fake hiding behind a curtain.*

A wild idea teased at the edges of her mind, and her pacing slowed. *That's . . . No way . . . That would be too crazy . . .*

She whirled to face Nath. "How"—she flapped her

hands, searching for the right word—"sentient is the magic in Galahar?"

He frowned. "I am unsure what you mean."

She tsked impatiently. "I was transported here from another world. Then I referenced a line from my mom's favorite book soon after that. It's about a girl who also lands in a magical place."

"Hey, I did too!" Davy gawked at her.

Jenny nodded. "So, what if the power . . . the magic's essence,"—she shrugged—"whatever . . . considered it . . . well, a sort of blueprint?" She grew more enthusiastic as she explained. "Okay, Marta is Auntie M . . . an evil warlock who needed to be defeated instead of a wicked witch. Marden is a wonderful wizard . . ."

"Wow, that all fits." Davy snapped his fingers in excitement. "Nath showed tons of courage, same as the lion. Lauran's got a real ruby, not slippers. Except she doesn't need to get home. We do." He grinned at Jenny. "You're the same as the tinman, using your heart to accept Dad and I as your family . . ."

His sister began pacing, muttering to herself, while the bewildered shaman stared from one to the other. "Is this legit, or am I trying to force a connection? Courage, heart . . . okay, what about brains?"

"Oh yeah, what about the scarecrow?" Davy slumped back to the floor beside their friend. "The story isn't complete without the last character."

Jenny considered for a moment, then groaned. "OMG. That's ridiculous." The others looked up with matching hopeful expressions. "During our argument, I told Polina to smarten up and use her head for more than decoration."

Nath's eyebrows rose. "Eya! I did much the same afterward, and she said she would try."

"This is so cool!" Davy jumped up again, bubbling with delight. "Who am I? We have everybody we need, except . . ." His voice trailed off, and his face fell. "No way! I am *not* the dog!"

His indignation made Jenny laugh. "Well, you do follow me everywhere!"

She stopped pacing to hug him. "How about someone precious I love who reminds me I must get home?"

He quirked his mouth in a reluctant half grin. "I guess."

"I do not understand." Nath looked from one to the other. "What does this mean?"

She knelt beside him. "If I'm right, we've covered all the fundamentals from the original book, with minor modifications from the movie. Is that enough? What else should we do?"

He shrugged, spreading his hands. "I am unfamiliar with this tale, so your knowledge of the required elements would be stronger than mine."

Her brother started giggling, and Jenny lifted an inquiring eyebrow. "You know what Mom would say . . ." She just stared at him, so he hinted, "Click your heels . . ."

Jenny's mouth dropped open, then she laughed in disbelief. "Oh, no!"

Nath's puzzled expression only made them laugh harder.

"Why not?" Davy shrugged. "It can't hurt!"

She grabbed his hands, rolling her eyes. "I cannot believe I'm doing this. You better not tell anyone!"

Facing each other, they recited, "There's no place like home.

"There's no place like home!

"THERE'S NO PLACE LIKE HOME!"

They grew louder with each chant, until they shouted the last line in gleeful unison.

And with each repetition, the twirling portal expanded, until a whirling gateway stood there, enlarged enough to accommodate them.

They fell silent, hands dropping to their sides, as they stared at the hypnotizing display.

"I guess this is our final farewell." Nath's bleak voice broke the spell.

Jenny turned to find him standing behind her. She hesitated, at a loss for words to thank him and say goodbye. Impulsive as ever, she threw her arms around him and squeezed him hard. "You're like the big brother I always wanted. I'm going to miss you."

His return hug was warm. "Eya! And you are the little sister I never asked for."

They chuckled, then Nath reached over and gravely shook Davy's hand. The boy flung himself forward, clutching the shaman's waist in a fierce embrace.

Then Davy moved to Jenny's side.

Their hands gripped tight, they stepped together into the swirling light.

53

Jenny blundered into a stone wall, and her brother bumped into her from behind. The only illumination came from the whirling portal at their backs, already beginning to shrink. She pulled out her cell phone and turned on the flashlight.

"Wait! How do we know if we're home? I mean, in the correct world?" She heard the alarm in her voice and tried to calm herself, not wanting to upset Davy.

"Look! Here's your raincoat on the floor, right where you left it."

Jenny's face lit up. "Yes! We made it." Then she gasped, and her fingers flew to her mouth. "Oh no, how can we tell Nath we're safe? He'll be worried about us. I might be able to stick my head through . . ."

She started toward the shrinking sparkles, but Davy grabbed her arm. "Wait, Jenn! I have an idea."

With Davy's help, Jenny managed the narrow passage without injuring herself again. She breathed a relieved sigh when they reentered the main chamber a few minutes later. Then they peered outside, thrilled to discover the tide was out, leaving the sand exposed.

Jenny took a moment to wrap Marta's gift in her raincoat and placed it on a ledge as high as she could reach, promising herself she would return right away with a large ziplock bag.

She followed her brother, and they climbed down to the beach. The weather remained as gray and stormy as when they had left. *Doesn't the sun ever shine here?*

Teasing waves slapped at the shore, as if daring them to come and play. Gulls floating overhead called a welcome home.

She shook her head. "It all looks the same!"

Davy shrugged. "Maybe like Lucy through the wardrobe, time runs differently between the worlds. Best case, the portal returned us to when we went through."

He turned away, but Jenny touched his shoulder, and he looked back at her. "I want you to know that no matter what happens from now on, or how annoyed I get with you in the future,"—the boy snickered—"I'm glad you're my brother. Thank you for coming to Galahar to find me."

Davy blushed and ducked his head. "Like Dad says, family comes first."

"Well, let's go see ours!" Grabbing each other's hands, they raced down the beach to the cottage. They burst through the front door, laughing.

Jenny shouted, "Mom, we're home! Sorry we've been so long . . ." She stopped short as Carol came out of the kitchen. It wasn't the fact that her mother wore the same outfit she'd been wearing six days ago but rather the un-concerned expression on her face that cut Jenny's apology off.

The pair shared a relieved glance.

"You're not late." Mom's eyes widened as she saw them holding hands. "Actually, you're right on time. Dinner's almost ready."

"Great. Shall I set the table?"

"Wha—sure . . . thanks." Bemused, she stared at her daughter.

"I'll help," Davy offered.

Just then, his dad entered the room. He chuckled as the boy darted over and hugged him around the waist. "Whoa, tiger. What's that for?"

He grinned up at his father. "I felt like it!"

"Frank . . ." Jenny saw him brace himself and flushed at the cautious way he looked over at her. She recalled their last exchange before she left for Galahar, cleared her throat, and tried a smile. "If you and Mom want to go dancing in town after supper, I'll watch the—Davy."

Her startled stepfather glanced at her mother in surprise, as if asking, *What happened?* "Uh, yes, that would be nice. Thanks."

Her brother darted back to her side with a grin. She bumped her shoulder against his. "You wanna teach me that video game you spend so much time with?"

"*Realms of Destiny?*" His face lit up. "You're gonna love *RoD*. You get to choose your own avatar, and there's a cool dragon . . ."

Nath kept vigil as the swirling portal began contracting. He missed them already. *Magic always demands a price.* Soon, the opening grew too modest for a body to pass through. *We should have arranged some sort of signal . . .*

Before the last twinkles disappeared, a small object flew from the gateway. He caught it, laughing as he examined the minifig.

They were safe. He waited for a few minutes longer, holding his flickering torch, but the doorway to their realm stayed closed.

He joined the waiting dragons. "They are gone." Nath smiled. "But they reached their home." He held up the toy. "Davy sent me this."

Lauran gave him a gentle nudge with her muzzle. *[Are you going to miss her?]*

"Not in the manner you are suggesting." The shaman shook his head. "We became good friends, despite the difference in our ages." He shrugged and contradicted himself. "Besides, she is too young. She must understand herself better before she will be ready for a mate."

He frowned. "My master has handfasted three times. He outlived all of them—and a half dozen younglings as well—long before I became his apprentice. Marden claims love is worth the pain." Nath fell silent, unsure he agreed, then gave himself a shake. "Come, we have unfinished business."

As they flew over the village, he touched Marden's thoughts, but the old shaman declined to join them. *[My adventure quota is filled. Anyway, I consider this your Seven-Day Quest.]*

Back on the mountain, the remaining Kin returned to

human form to discuss their plan. By unspoken agreement, the dwindling members of their party were now
seated on the opposite side of the clearing with their backs
to the collapsed cave.

"Ganther's afraid Shifton may have left other magical
surprises behind, so he wants you to come with us," Lauran
announced. Her father glared at her.

Nath laughed but agreed. He intended to see this
thing through.

With two exceptions, the Kin paired up the same as
on their previous visit to Septain Territory, despite suspecting the duke had already discovered their secret.

Ganther now rode Dram since Zyre and Marissa had
not returned.

"And Lauran will ride me." Davint's firm voice
brooked no discussion. "She's spent enough time in
dragon form to do her quite a while." They prepared to
leave, and as he'd suggested, she mounted the big copper.

Remember to call him Ta'ran, Nath reminded himself.

He marveled that Shifton's three days trekking across
mountains and plains took only two hours as the dragon
flew.

54

Prioress Margon lifted her head at a sharp knocking. She set her quill aside with an imperceptible sigh, folded her hands on the desk in front of her, and pasted on a pleasant smile. "Enter."

Sister Greta poked her troubled face around the heavy wooden door. "'Tis sorry I am to be bothering you, Reverend Mother, but them servants caring for that poor soul Lady Avila sent over are fussing something awful."

The abbess raised her eyebrows.

The novice peeked back over her shoulder before whispering, "They say the room he's in be haunted."

"Nonsense." Margon pursed her lips. "Did you smell their breath? No doubt they've been drinking on duty again. I shall certainly speak with them about that . . ."

Her words trailed off as Greta gave a vigorous shake of her head. "No, mam, ain't nothing like that. I checked afore I bothered ye!"

She sighed. "Go on, then."

Encouraged, the sister crept around the door and

scuttled into the room with quick, restless steps, fingers fidgeting with her robe, until she stood before the wide oaken desk. Sunlight streamed in the narrow windows, catching the dust stirred by Greta's anxious movements.

The prioress made a note to speak with the servants, before lifting her eyebrows again, inviting further details.

"'Tis truth, he come in yesterday ranting as if he be a maniac. He were that uncontrollable, we locked him in a room by hisself so he don't hurt none of the others."

A slight frown creased Margon's brow, the most impatience she ever permitted herself to display.

But Sister Greta recognized the oblique hint. She hurried on with her story. "They been feeding him through the small wicket at the bottom of the gate to his cell since he arrived yesterday, and nary opened the door, despite his cries for help."

She looked around again, then leaned forward and lowered her voice, forcing the prioress to incline her head to listen. "But he stopped his shouting about midnight, and next thing, the warden claims a wee lad's crying and a-calling fer his mam."

The abbess raised her graceful arched eyebrows at Greta's vigorous nod. "'Tis true, Sister Piter says she hearkened on it moments ago. Swears a youngling's weeping. Now the servants believe he's possessed. Won't have nothing to do with him."

"Of all the sharding . . ." Prioress Margon caught herself. She rose from her desk, gathering her red robes with calculated dignity. "Must I do everything myself? The man is obviously insane and acting out his life's stages. Come along, we will open his cell ourselves. He may need restraints so he doesn't hurt himself."

55

Warned of the dragons' approach by sharp-eyed sentries, Lady Avila waited on the castle steps as the Kin landed in the wide courtyard, frightening the horses of the knights who met them.

She stood on the landing, holding the hand of a youngling of about five. Pepper sat quietly on her opposite side. The boy beside her fretted, and her glance down was fearful. Since the Prioress had summoned her early this morning, the youth had regressed three more times to his current age . . . and it seemed to be happening faster.

Avila had been relieved to hear of the Kin's approach and rushed to meet them. Now she searched behind them, dismayed not to see Shifton's thin, black-robed scarecrow figure there.

Their leader, Ganther, signaled the other riders to remain in place. They and their great beasts settled down to wait as he and a tall blonde Kin approached her.

Her expression didn't change when she noticed the Lowlander-sized young man accompanying them. But her cheeks reddened as they noticed the youngling and ex-changed surprised glances. She'd never mentioned having a son, and they no doubt wondered who the youngling's father was.

As they approached the top step, her visitors stopped, shocked, as the boy's face rippled. He contorted as if in pain, and she gathered him in her arms.

The smaller man leaped forward, but by the time he reached her, Avila held a boy of about three, whose clothes hung on him. Seeing a stranger's rapid approach startled the youngling, and he started crying, curling around to hide his eyes against her neck.

She gave a helpless shrug. "While I appreciate such a thing seems impossible, this is my father. He . . . he keeps *doing* this. We can't figure out how to stop it from hap-pening." Her gaze moved behind them. "Is Shifton with you?"

The man shook his head. "The warlock will not be returning. I am Nath, a shaman of the Anishinabe. Do you have any idea what magic he used?"

Avila accepted their knowledge of Shifton's disgrace. She took a step closer, away from her retainers, leaned forward, and whispered, "My father drank dragon blood."

He inhaled with a hiss. "A search for youth?" Nath's lip curled. "Does this explain the warlock's outrages, then?"

Before she could answer, the youngling in her arms convulsed. She slipped his robe off and used it to wrap the resulting one-year-old.

Nath frowned. "Drinking lifeblood may play a part, yet I am skeptical that alone would cause such a reaction." He laid gentle hands on the boy and closed his eyes for a moment as he sent his magic's intuition searching. "He must have taken something else that stayed in his system and interacted with the blood."

Avila hesitated, then shifted the youngling to pull a paper from her pocket. "I stole this from Shifton's workroom, but I don't understand what this potion does." She glanced down at the infant. "Or I didn't." She bit back a sob as he took the page. "To desire youth and strength so desperately . . ."

She blinked away tears, reaching her free arm out to Ganther. "I am so sorry for my father's misguided behavior. I hope his madness hurt none of your creatures." She smiled down at the patient dog sitting at her feet, watching her. "I understand how fond one gets of them."

The huge Kin stared at her outstretched hand but didn't take it. After an awkward moment, she used the excuse of cuddling the youngling to withdraw hers.

"You are not obligated to apologize for the wrongdoing of others." Nath glared at Ganther, who looked away. "No permanent damage has been done. Though not for lack of trying on Shifton's part." As he scanned the formula, the youngling seized again.

The shaman began muttering counterspells, pressing his hands against the boy's stomach and making him retch.

Avila hurriedly flipped him over, holding him at arm's length. A long rope of green vomit spewed from his mouth, filling the air with an unpleasant sourness. Several nearby courtiers drew back with disgusted expressions. Others turned away, lifting handkerchiefs to their faces to conceal their own nausea.

Nath continued chanting until the wailing youngling had ejected all the spell-slime.

Lady Avila cleaned his face with the clothes wrapped around him, rocking the exhausted infant until he fell asleep. His breath hitched as his sobs subsided. When several minutes had passed without the boy suffering another seizure, she looked up at the shaman, her eyes shiny with tears. "Thank you. We are in your debt."

She turned to Ganther again. "I cannot undo what my father has done, but I hope you will give us a second chance. I, for one, meant every word I said to your people." He stared at her without speaking. This time, she held his gaze, letting the moment stretch.

The statuesque blonde stepped forward and offered her hand. "I have discussed this with my dragon." She smiled at Avila's surprised expression. "You'll discover they're much more than pets. My name is Lauran. I'm Ganther's daughter, and I am delighted to meet you at last."

She waved at the courtyard, where the dragons waited. "The large copper is my companion, and you may call him Ta'ran. We would be pleased to function as ambassadors between our peoples."

"Another woman, how wonderful." Avila smiled in delight. "Too many of my father's diplomatic friends are stodgy, old men. We shall breathe fresh air into the politics of Galahar, won't we?"

She looked down at the baby in her arms. "However, my knowledge of raising dukes is limited." She brightened. "But my former nanny is certain to have heard of a suitable barren couple, someone eager for a son. Perhaps this time, he'll become a better man."

Ganther snorted, breaking his silence. "You're hoping nurture overcomes nature? I'll be interested in the results.

You just be sure they don't spoil him." His daughter gave him a reproving glare, but he appeared unrepentant.

"I will see the shaman home," the green Kin informed her. "Then I shall return to tell our Alpha what has transpired."

Lauran leaned closer to Lady Avila. Though she stood several steps lower, she still towered over the petite woman. "Would you happen to recall the name of the sculptor who created that gorgeous dolphin fountain in the square?" She glanced over at the copper dragon again, the sun reflecting off his scales emphasizing his sleek muscles. "I may have a commission I want to discuss with him . . ."

Avila handed the sleeping infant off to a waiting servant. "Actually . . ." She bit her lip. "I wonder if I might ask you all to stay. There is one more thing I hope you can help me with."

Lauran signaled Callie and Audra to join them.

Avila refused to explain, saying they needed to see for themselves. She led the way through the castle—selecting a route with ceilings spacious enough to accommodate her large guests—and up the wide staircase to Shifton's chambers.

Their startled murmurs of disgust at the state of the main room made Avila's cheeks redden again. "I understand Shifton declined to allow anyone in to clean—and it's quite obvious he never did so himself."

She hurried toward an ominous-looking black door standing open at the back of the chamber, and they followed in silence. Avila ignored the cut chain and thick bar that lay tossed on the floor from when she'd had them break in, searching for anything that might save her father.

She knew her grim face was making them wary, but it

couldn't be helped. Nothing could prepare them for what she had to show them.

Inside the room, masked servants surrounded a massive container, scooping water onto whatever languished within.

Avila instructed them to move aside.

56

A merman filled the generous tub, making it look small in comparison. Their party halted with exclamations of wonder mixed with disgust.

Dullness faded his once-vibrant scales, though Avila's people had been attempting to rehydrate him. He peered at them from under half-closed eyelids, pain and exhaustion clouding his gaze.

Rumors described the Mer as ugly, but Lauran didn't think that did justice to the reality. Stringy, greenish-black strands of hair; huge, watery, lashless eyes; and a slash of a mouth that drooped open to reveal pointed teeth with an extended snake of a tongue hanging to one side. The beautiful creatures depicted in story and song appeared quite hideous in person.

His upper body must have been beautifully muscular before his incarceration, but his long, almost eellike lower half ended in spiked tail fins, rather than the feathery angelfish caudal fins shown in paintings. Despite soaking up to his neck, his dried-out scales looked leathery, and his taut skin flaked and peeled. Fine cracks split his skin all over, and blood ran from the wounds, pinking the water.

There was a pronounced odor of rotten fish, which explained the servants' masks. Nath pushed forward, ignoring the smell. He paused, but when the wounded merman closed his eyes, Nath took that as permission and laid a hand on the creature's arm.

Lauran's skin tingled. She sensed him trying to heal the Mer's injuries, but there was too much damage.

In a voice tight with rage, the young shaman described the process of creating Mermaid's Tears to Lady Avila. He didn't explain their purpose, simply saying, "to aid in Shifton's spell."

Lauran took in the chains on the wall and the dried blood streaks. She realized Shifton had held the Mer captive on dry land for who knew how long, giving him sufficient liquid to keep him alive, but no more. Her breath caught in her throat.

To understand how Mers produced tears was one thing; witnessing the brutality firsthand horrified her.

"Can you help him?" Avila asked.

"Perhaps." The distracted shaman nodded. "I've stabilized him, but he needs salt water, eya. This fresh water will not do. Getting him home may benefit him the most."

Fortunately, the Mer breathed air as well as seawater through the gills on his neck. Lauran shuddered. *If he looks this bad after being revived, imagine how terrible his condition must have been when they found him.*

She turned to Avila. "It'll be faster if Ta'ran and I take him. Your people would require several days to make the journey to the coast." She nodded at the merman. "He wouldn't survive."

The servants shrank away from the huge women as she motioned Audra and Callie forward. The merman seemed past caring what happened to him. They lifted him out of the tub with surprising gentleness, while Avila bustled about, instructing her people to soak sheets in water to wrap around him, to keep him hydrated during the trip.

Minutes later, Davint met them at the castle entrance, his eyes whirling red with outrage. *[How unfortunate Shifton isn't still alive. We could kill him all over again.]*

Lauran gave a grim nod of agreement. She mounted, taking the Mer's body in front of her. His head lolled against her shoulder as he lost consciousness. His skin felt cold and clammy against hers, and she wished she knew if that was normal.

Nath climbed up behind her, reaching around and sliding his hand inside the cloth to touch the merman's scales, keeping the sheets wet with a spell. Lauran *sensed* him giving his strength to the Mer and hoped that would be enough.

The copper launched himself into the air, the others following in his wake.

Even for a dragon flying full out, the journey took several hours. Lauran only knew the merman still lived because Nath did not give up, though she *sensed* the shaman's energy levels dropping.

Affection and respect for the younger man filled her. He hadn't complained, although he must be exhausted after everything he'd done over the past few days.

The lowering sun made them squint as they flew westward. Lauran smelled the brine before she saw the sea, and the merman stirred against her, aware of the ocean even while unconscious. As they crossed the shoreline, she heard the breakers crashing against the rocks below the cliffs.

Davint didn't hesitate. Soaring out over the surf to deeper water, he held his wings steady, coasting closer to the surface. He tilted his body, adjusting his angle to minimize impact, and set down as light as a gull.

Waves surged up his sides, soaking their feet and legs and causing the dragon to rock up and down. Nath shifted back to give Lauran room, and she removed the sheets from the Mer. The stiff breeze blowing toward shore and the strong, briny smell of the ocean cleared the odor coming off his body.

Holding him under his arms, she slid the merman tail first into the water. His eyes flew open, and he gasped. He jerked from her grip and dived under.

She blinked. *What the . . . ?*

Lauran could have sworn his scales gleamed where the salt water touched them, and his skin seemed to heal as he swam. She flung an inquiring glance over her shoulder, but Nath appeared just as surprised.

A splash to starboard drew their attention.

The merman was back, and he wasn't alone.

[Thank you. Kinss iss friendss. We will not forget thiss kindnesss.]

Before they could respond, the Mer sank below the surface and disappeared.

Epilogue

One Year Later

Although the shamans expressed their objections, in the fullness of time, Avila delivered a chest filled with the warlock's notebooks and forbidden texts to the Citadel.

While she remained unaware of the Dragon Kins' shifting abilities, she understood that references to the power of dragon blood to extend life had led to her father's downfall. So her one concession was to allow the young shaman to review the material, removing every reference to dragons or Dragon Kin. She swore herself to secrecy and never shared the knowledge, especially not with her new court wizard.

The wizards took the shamans' word for the vileness of its contents and sealed the chest. However, they found themselves of two minds on how to proceed, so they held a convocation.

This great debate lasted all winter. Some favored destroying the material and, in so doing, barring its wicked knowledge from all further generations. Others argued the information might someday be needed—perhaps to fight off a greater evil.

The process took months, but one side eventually convinced—or wore down—the other. When the vote reached 75 percent majority in favor, they bespelled the chest with an additional enchantment. The "turn away" spell would ensure that all but the strongest wizards overlooked it.

Next, they covered it in solid chains, welded in place with heavy padlocks. And as a final safeguard, they placed the strongbox in the deepest, darkest portion of the Citadel, behind a two-inch thick door with four additional locks set with anti-tampering spells.

And there it sat, gathering dust, for over 112 years.

With another Summer Solstice upon him, Nath reflected over the events of the past year, as he had every season since assuming his duties. The village had grown accustomed to the change in leadership before Marden fell asleep and passed on to his next adventure.

Lauran and Davint had only stopped by once following his return from Duke Almar's castle. *Duchess Avila's castle,* Nath corrected himself. They had shared his grief at Marden's passing and revealed the news of their own handfasting.

The young shaman smiled, recalling Lauran's glee as she had regaled him with Marissa's successful pursuit of Ganther.

However, other tidings had trickled into the mountains from travelers. Rudolph had become Avila's consort and her wisest advisor, and they were expecting a youngling in the spring.

As Nath prepared for his first solo Summer Solstice ceremony, he smiled, remembering Lauran and the others and the joy of riding a dragon. Although he might never see Jenny and Davy again, he cherished fond memories of them. He hoped they recalled him the same way.

And whenever his herb gathering took him into the vicinity of the Cavern of Whispers, he could not resist checking for gateways. However, the grotto remained as gloomy as usual, with no sign that anyone besides himself ever went there. He assumed young men still completed the pilgrimage as a rite of passage, but he made no effort to confirm this.

With his supplies gathered, Nath headed to the special clearing used for these annual ceremonies. He prepared the ritual herbs by crushing them against a rounded rock mortar with a pestle he'd carved himself. He sat bare-chested inside a circle of blessed stones, preparing to calm his mind and body in meditation as he waited until the second moon rose.

Before he could begin, a crack of thunder sounded, wind buffeted the glade, and a familiar presence pressed against his senses. With an annoyed shout, Nath covered the herbs with his hand to prevent them from flying away.

The breeze stopped as abruptly as it had started. He glanced up, unsurprised to discover a huge green dragon in the middle of shifting into human form. The man towered over him, and Nath averted his gaze from his rather unfortunate line of sight, slipping his own tunic back on while Ganther dressed.

"Sorry to drop in on you unannounced." The large

Kin didn't sound repentant, but Nath was too pleased by his visit to complain. "You're hard to catch alone. Those sharding villagers are always around."

Being spied upon—yet missing something as enormous as a dragon doing the spying—left the shaman torn between annoyance and amazement. He settled for smiling and not saying anything. *It usually worked for Marden.*

Ganther shifted in his seat, looking uncomfortable. "I never gave you proper thanks for your help." Nath raised his eyebrows as the Kin looked away. "Lauran thanked you, but I am also in your debt. And I hate owing anyone."

He held his hand out and opened it palm up. Five jewels, in the magic colors of Galahar, twinkled in the fading daylight.

The shaman's eyes widened, and he reached out. He paused to glance up.

Ganther chuckled. "Don't worry, these are safe. I'm told shamans use crystals, and I figured you might like them."

Nath took the stones, turning them over with great respect. They had appeared small in Ganther's huge hand but filled Nath's palm. "I—I am speechless. They are beautiful, eya." Though reluctant, he tried to return them. "A gift is unnecessary. I was pleased to help the Kin."

Ganther held up his hands, refusing to accept the jewels. "You played a crucial role in defeating the warlock—who might have endangered all of Galahar given time. And you saved Lauran from a life of slavery. This is the least we owe you."

Gratified but embarrassed, Nath flushed and dropped his gaze. He fumbled for a change of topic. "How are the rest of the Wing? And of course, your lovely Marissa?"

"Oh, everyone is fine. I know Lauran's been to see you, so you know she and Davint are handfasted. Dram and the others send their regards." He gave a snort. "You never met Zyre, did you? Well, you're not missing much. Do you know, that old curmudgeon has taken himself off to live all alone. Has the draikanas all worried about him. They visit him regularly, like a sort of pilgrimage."

Ganther shrugged. "Been to see him a time or two myself. He can't even bother to take human form anymore. He might as well join the wild dragons and be done with it, but at least he's still talking to us!"

He shook his head, and his expression brightened. "My mate is well, and my daughter is waiting for her first eggs to hatch." Ganther snorted again. "Shards, the fuss those two females are making! You'd assume no one ever hatched an egg before." He winked. "Why, even I can do it!"

Nath laughed and tucked the crystals inside his robe with a nod of thanks. "Now I must hear that story. I do not need to begin my rituals until the second moon rises. Would you care to join me for a cup of kaffee?"

Ganther nodded, but he seemed distracted. "Did you ever notice that when wizards say 'shards,' or 'by the first shard,' they mean broken crystals? But when dragons use those same terms, they're referring to eggshells?"

"Let me remind you, I am a shaman, not a wizard." Nath pulled a pot from the hot coals and poured out two cups. "But that is interesting. I wonder which came into initial usage and which followed? Though I seldom interact with Lowlanders, I would be interested to discover if the convention has spread to the general population."

Ganther looked surprised. "I speculated on the same

thing." He held the small cup in his great fist. "I must admit, you have an unusually perceptive mind—for a non-Kin." He tossed the liquid back, disregarding the heat.

"Why, thank you, I was just thinking you yourself are remarkably intelligent—for a shifter."

They grinned at each other.

"More kaffee?"

"Wouldn't say no. But might you have a larger cup? This one's the size of a thimble. Now about that story. It involves Lauran's mother and those sharding Lowlanders . . ."

As the second moon began its journey, Ganther got to his feet, stretched, and shifted into dragon form. *[This was nice. I've enjoyed speaking with you. We should meet again.]*

Nath smiled. "That would please me as well."

The huge beast gave a decisive nod and launched into the air. The shaman followed his unusual friend's flight until he disappeared into the night sky. When the second moon finished rising, he took out the crystals, smiling as he replaced the colored stones at the center and four compass points of his circle with his new gems, before beginning the ritual.

He lifted his hands and began to chant:

> *Bring the essence of running water to ease our thirst.*
> *Add the warmth of flowing air to carry life to our crops.*
> *Give our harvest the sustaining strength of the quiet earth.*
> *Sacred Mishomis Ishkode, Grandfather Fire,*
> *Warm our homes and protect our people.*

*May the shining stars keep watch over us.
Let the gentle night fill our hearts with its peace.
Almighty spirit, pour healing on this blessed
land and make it fruitful,
as you guide Anishinabe through the coming
year.*

To Be Continued
in
Dragon Kin's Choice

Glossary

Algonquin Words / Spells Used by the Mountain People

Anishinabe—"the People"

Eya—interjection; "yes," "okay," "indeed," or an emphatic "right!"

Ishkode—fire

Kakandawin—the Gathering

Mahigan tribe—Wolf tribe

Makwag tribe—Bear tribe

millioke—the good land

Mishomis Ishkode—Grandfather Fire

Songiton—spell for throwing up a dome ("to strengthen against attack")

Waasaa—light

General Terms

far-reach—mental manipulation of the physical world (telekinesis)

kaffee—coffee

lumprig—tiny transparent creature that has a symbiotic relationship with mollusks

mind-speech—mental communication (telepathy)

mothal—nocturnal winged insect, attracted to light

nooning—noonday meal, lunch

shadow trade—black market

sharding—curse word, adjective form

shards—curse word, noun form

sirrah—sir

sqwabbit—prey animal found in the Dragon Spine Mountains

to Still / Stilling—to suppress the magic within a magic user

tahr—prey animal found in the Dragon Spine Mountains

Magic

Azure Wizard (blue)—strongest magic, associated with sapphire

Emerald Wizard (green)—second-strongest magic, associated with emerald

Citrine Wizard (yellow)—middle-strength magic, associated with yellow citrine

Amber Wizard (orange)—second-weakest magic, associated with amber

Crimson Wizard (rose red)—weakest magic, associated with ruby

Acknowledgments

Thank you so much for reading! I hope you enjoyed this introduction to Galahar as much as I enjoyed writing it. There are many more tales about the peoples of this mystical land to come. If you'd like to read the story Ganther told Nath while they drank their kaffee, visit my website (www.jo-gatenby-books.com) and join my readers club, and the story will be my gift to you.

Any author will tell you that writing a book is a solitary pursuit, but the journey to publication is very much a group effort. My family has been very supportive of me, especially my husband, Bill, who faithfully read sixteen versions! He is my biggest fan and harshest critic.

Thanks to my beta readers and my Jericho Writers alumni writing group—you know who you are. I couldn't have continued without all the wonderful feedback and encouragement, and I haven't forgotten my promise to give that little mermaid, Seraphina, her own story. I look forward to exploring the waters around the southwest coast.

And special thanks to my two wonderful editors. Tod Tinker, my developmental editor, pulled more out of my novel just when I thought it was done. Thanks to him, there's a little nugget waiting to unfold in the third book— but no spoilers!

Then my ever-so-patient copy editor, Charlene Templeman, who had to deal with my comma addiction. I'm in therapy and hope to make a full recovery.

Finally, an author is nothing without you, faithful reader. If you've enjoyed this story and want to read more of my work, I'd be grateful if you took a moment to add a review on Amazon, Goodreads, or wherever you share reviews.

If you'd like to discover more of my writing in various genres, you can also find links to free stories published in online magazines on my website.

About the Author

Thanks to her great-grandmother, Jo Gatenby is a status Algonquin of the Pikwakanagan First Nation in Canada. Jo writes whatever the voices shouting in her head tell her to. She has had more than twenty of her flash fiction and short story pieces published in online maga-zines, and she has self-published five children's picture books.